Adrian Mathews

VIENNA

V
VINTAGE

Published by Vintage 2000

2 4 6 8 10 9 7 5 3 1

Extract from *Meditations* by Marcus Aurelius, trans. Maxwell Staniforth (Penguin Classics, 1964) copyright © Maxwell Staniforth, 1964. Reproduced by permission of Penguin Books Ltd.

Extract from *The Bhagavad Gita*, trans. Juan Mascaró (Penguin Classics, 1962) copyright © Juan Mascaró, 1962. Reproduced by permission of Penguin Books Ltd.

First published in Great Britain by Jonathan Cape in 1999

Vintage

Random House, 20 Vauxhall Bridge Road, London SW1V 2SA

Random House Australia (Pty) Limited 20 Alfred Street, Milsons Point, Sydney New South Wales 2061, Australia

Random House New Zealand Limited 18 Poland Road, Glenfield, Auckland 10, New Zealand

Random House (Pty) Limited Endulini, 5A Jubilee Road, Parktown 2193, South Africa

The Random House Group Limited Reg. No. 954009

www.randomhouse.co.uk

A CIP catalogue record for this book is available from the British Library

ISBN 0 09 927357 8

Printed and bound in Great Britain by Cox & Wyman Limited, Reading, Berkshire

To Lizzie

ACKNOWLEDGEMENTS

The initial idea for this book first came to me during a conversation about genetics with Nick Toop, co-director of Cortex Controllers in Cambridge. So thanks to Nick, and to those who offered much-appreciated comments, suggestions and encouragement at different stages of composition: Bill Hamilton, Graham Woodroffe, Ian Smith, Gregory Mathews, Valerie Persinko and Marie. I am also indebted to the following authors and books, amongst many others: Bryan Clough and Paul Mungo, *Approaching Zero*; James Croft, *Corporate Cloak & Dagger*; Stephanie Jones, *The Biotechnologists*; Andrew Kimbrell, *The Human Body Shop*; Marek Kohn, *The Race Gallery*; Henry Leese, *Human Reproduction and* in vitro *Fertilisation*; Tom Wilkie, *Perilous Knowledge*. I am especially grateful to Colin Tudge, author of *The Engineer in the Garden*, for his invaluable suggested amendments. Thanks, lastly, to all at Jonathan Cape, in particular Dan Franklin and Charlotte Mendelson.

Immutable movement . . . is immoral movement *par excellence*. It is satisfied with itself, excludes the search for something else and repeats the same itinerary indefinitely. In short, from a moral point of view it is worse than the movement of walking backwards which at least takes you that way and has direction to it. . . . To turn in a circle is devoid of direction and goal; a man who turns round on the tip of his toes is self-satisfied, a creature of ridiculous and vulgar vanity. Moreover, dance is a feminine movement; more precisely, it is the movement of prostitution. It can be observed that the more a woman has the attitude of a prostitute, the more she loves dancing and the better she is at it.

One should also talk here about the 'national' character of the Austro-Bavarians, and more particularly the Viennese. Their taste for dance music is a fundamental element in this character. Circular movement suppresses liberty, making it submit to a law; the effect of repetition *ne varietur* is either ridiculous or disquieting. Now, morally speaking, the Viennese are fatalists in character ('leave things be, there's nothing we can do'); and fatalism, transposed into the intellectual domain, is indifferentism; hence the apathy and 'niceness' of the Viennese. The waltz is a radically fatalistic music; which is surely why it constitutes the musical expression that best suits the circle.

Otto Weininger
'Essay on Immutable Movements'

chapter one

poor old detmers . . .

Poor old Detmers . . .

At the *Wiener Tageszeitung*, we received the news story last week and the deputy editor holed it away on page four. I even saw his name on the Staatspolizei e-mail board but it didn't click. It's only when his wife phones and asks for me, Sharkey, that I make the connection. She wants to meet up; she wants to talk.

Poor old Detmers . . .

I mouth the words to myself as I put the phone down.

An area of low barometric pressure is crawling from the dark frontier of the Alps across the Danube basin and towards the Puszta, the broad Hungarian plain. It is 28 November 2026, a bitterly cold morning, and powdery theme-park snow is beginning to fall as I leave head office. Everyone is venturing out, bewildered. It hasn't snowed here for seven years, and we'd all assumed global warming had consigned the snow-flake to the history books. Yet for some reason this meteorological throwback is more horrific than joyous, another anarchic sign of the vicissitudes of the physical universe – intermittent resurgence, the reckless perversity of decaying laws.

My car is out of action so I wait for the tram, watching as the misty yellow eye of its single headlamp advances laterally through the gloom. I board and take my seat. Already the Baroque and Jugendstil skyline of the Ringstrasse is dusted with celestial icing-sugar. The two-tone tram whirrs and clatters past the Kunsthistorisches Museum, the Opera House and the Stadtpark; the driver has put up his leather door-screen against the cold, but to little effect. Vienna, in that perfunctory way of hers, has sighed and spread her legs to be shagged by the winter solstice.

Detmers . . .

I shiver, shut my eyes and pull the collar of my parka up around my chin, severing myself inwardly from the present moment as drastically as the passenger seated in front of me, blinkered with VR-Spex. I am taking myself back; back nearly three months; back to Schechat Airport where I met him.

I was sitting in Pier West when the PA system ping-ponged and a velvety, erogenous voice glided out over the airwaves: 'Will Mr Kaposi from Mars please go to the information desk.' Detmers was next to me on the injection-moulded seating and registered my surprise. He leaned over with a pally smile and enlightened me. 'The c-c-c-confectionary company,' he stammered with slight amusement, 'n-n-n-not the planet.'

There was something disarmingly familiar about Leo, though I couldn't then pin down what it was. He conformed to a type, a phenotype – I assumed – and it was one that was common enough in Austria, like generic supermarket packaging.

He was younger than myself, in his mid-twenties, a stocky, roly-poly man who would have been charged excess baggage had that baggage not formed part and parcel of his biological person, ballooning from neck, arms, pectorals and thighs. This human suet was buttoned into an open-neck Javanese batik shirt and Sta-Press trousers. In the breast pocket of the shirt was a C-series Bip-Bip Networker, the latest model of personal numerical assistant, powered by nanomechanical micro-reactors. Folded next to him on the seat was a light summer jacket with a limp carnation buttonhole. He was thinning with criminal prematurity on top but the hormone that had deserted his crown and temples had clearly had regrets, making ample amends in the regions of the forearms and eyebrows. The latter were a dense, ropey sisal that reared in mild surprise over baby-frank, pallid eyes. In short, his physical morphology was of the type one associates with joviality and the little ink-sketches of bacchic cherubs on the labels of Grüner Veltliner wine. As we got talking, however, I found myself mentally proof-reading the human galleys. The costive stammer, his off-colour complexion, the little anxious spasms in the muscles around the eyes and mouth – all were signalling a life-flow that was something less than smooth and strong. But what the hell? For a few brief minutes before boarding his company was not unwelcome.

We were both going to Hamburg for the annual Securicom colloquium on data protection. I was covering it for the paper. He had

2

professional interests that were never clearly divulged. The delta-wing Airbus was full so we sat apart but at lunch in the conference centre he collared me again and suggested an evening drink. I said 'yes' for the reasons that journalists do: curiosity, existentialism and a king-size nose for off-beat copy. But this time I was to be disappointed. Detmers was a melancholic – a doleful, maudlin bore. Yet he was also one of those inevitable people that life throws in one's path from time to time. I resigned myself flaccidly to his company. I'd bought the ticket – or so I reasoned with myself – and I might as well go along for the ride.

There was a foul Cambodian meal (his choice of hash house) followed by the four-hour spectacle of his kamikaze boozing at La Paloma, one of Hamburg's smoke-choked dockside dives.

Blurred swatches of his rambling monologue now come back to me: the death of his mother, his shaky marriage and an overdose of computa-babble. It crossed my mind that I'd saddled myself with a cyberpunk, an information barracuda. And, as he graduated to half-litre Krügels of Weizengold wheat beer, melancholy gave way to pie-eyed bonhomie on an exponential curve. By the end of the evening, the only thing holding him up was internal fermentation, the levitating carbon dioxide bubbles in his gut holding hands for Auld Lang Syne and buoying his invertebrate body into the seated position with miraculous gaseous counter-tension.

My own visual cortex was beginning to forget the basic principles of stereoscopy when he suddenly jack-in-the-boxed to his feet. It was one in the morning and I was surprised to learn that there were whorehouses on his agenda. I declined the invitation and we parted, but not before a statutory exchange of cards and a stuttering, overwrought profession of friendship. Those sisal eyebrows reared one last time above the pale baby-frank eyes as he left the bar, and through the bottle-glass window I saw him pitching and rolling, lit up like an ocean liner on the high seas of life. He waved disjointedly, struggled into a taxi and roared off God knows where. That old fairy godmother who gets drunks back to their hotel beds would, I felt sure, take care of him, but I was hugely, deeply relieved when he had gone.

Only now, of course, he has well and truly gone.

His name may not have sunk in at the time but it's been sitting quietly on the embossed visiting card in my wallet all along, undisturbed since that casual and unsatisfactory encounter. I take it out and look it over. 'Leo Detmers.' It's the name that appeared on the police bulletin board. His number came up, that's for certain. A hit-and-run at dead of night in the Prater Park. But what on earth was he doing there? It was too early in the year for snowdrops and if he was trawling for whores he'd have been better served outside the Westbahnhof.

Still – what can you say?

Poor old Detmers . . .

The tram pulls up in Löwengasse and, nostrils steaming, I walk briskly through the talcum-cloud of snow till I get to the Hundertwasser Haus apartment block. It's the address his wife has given me, the address that's on the card.

The building is one of Vienna's sights: an 80s folly, a crazy candy-castle of bubble-gum hues: blue, white and yellow flats, tree-topped balconies and onion-dome cupolas. A touch of the Grimms, a dash of Arabian Nights, and more than a hint of Klee and Mondrian. This is a far cry from Karl Marx-Hof, the Stalinian Red Vienna block in the North that is home to myself and two thousand other proles. This is easy street, the place they keep the bees. Here they use stock options for wallpaper, there are fat cats on the window-sills and golden geese roosting in the pantries. I look up at the wacky Disney façade and remember again the corpulent little man I met at the airport.

A case, if ever there was one, of square pegs, round holes.

Now, I think, for his other half. She's given me the entry-code so I tap it in, then I take the lift to the eighth floor.

Someone at the door

Time is not physics, but psychophysics; not representational, but expressionist. On one scale, it's each body's consciousness of its own rhythms of growth and decay. On another, it's the madhouse of interactivity, where rooms swell and diminish according to degree of presence or absence, perspectives betray, and it's emotion – not mathematical subdivision – that determines the dimensions of life.

Five hours with Leo Detmers flew into oblivion.

Petra is another matter.

From the landing, I hear her voice: 'Hold on. There's someone at the door.' Then a lengthy fumbling of door-chains and firing of electronic bolts before she opens up. The reason for the delay is clear at a glance. There's a Bip-Bip wedged awkwardly between her left ear and shoulder, a tall drink in one hand and a VA remote in the other. She winks by way of greeting and proffers a wrist the way car mechanics do when their hands are black with axle-grease. I shake it between thumb and forefinger and she beckons me in. Meanwhile, the third party on line (acoustic only) is getting an earful.

'Don't use those words with me, Gisa,' she's saying. 'How d'you expect me to know what a debenture is? Can't you get Markus to come and sort it out?' She gestures quickly with the drink for me to sit down and a fluorescent ice-ball makes a break for it, flying over the salt-frosted rim of the glass and skating across the parquet till it butts the skirting. There's a long pause while she listens intently. 'Well tell him to come back from Costa Rica!' she moans. 'I'll give you the Asprey choker, and he can have one of those portfolio things – anything. But someone's got to look into that stuff before they come snooping round here again.'

She prowls across the room, throws the voice-zapper on to a pile of Tibetan cushions and stands peremptorily by a large plate-glass sliding window that looks on to a terrace. There are a few potted conifers outside and, high above, the gleaming ogee pinnacle of the building. The pearl-grey morning snowlight washes across her with a sudden pallor.

This specimen has presence. She's class, but high maintenance. Life arranges itself obediently around women of her sort, like iron filings round a magnet. There's a natural grace and authority in her move-ments that make her seem older than her years. Like her husband, I guess, she must be in her mid-twenties and, eerily, I feel an echo of him in her movements, her attitudes. The head is broad-boned and very Austrian in its no-nonsense beauty, dominated by startling pale eyes and accentuated, circumflex eyebrows that give her a discriminating, snazzy air. Her nose is small and slightly upturned, ending in an inverted triangle of cartilage that peters away to an insolent peak in the flange between the nostrils. The sharp tapering has the effect of pulling the attention down to the fleshy, glossed lips which she stretches and pouts into tense grimaces, as if doing a facial workout, while she attends to the voice on the line. She turns slightly away from me and shifts from foot to foot every now and then and this makes her prominent, well-rounded buttocks change position. One goes up, then the other comes down. I feel juvenile staring at this rearguard phenomenon, but I can't help myself. It's fascinating, like watching lift-indicators at the Intercontinental Hotel.

Thick, black, pillowy hair falls in a sumptuous mane to her shoulders, and whenever a strand loses its hold and swings down across her left eye, she brushes it impatiently away and poses an elegant hand on her bosom, with a hint of photogenic affectation, as if weary of life and operatically breathless. Miss Weltschmerz, 2026. She wears seamed tights, a Lycra button-fly skirt and, over the top, a laminated cotton housecoat printed with giant, garish Van Gogh sunflowers which bulges enormously in the middle.

The bulge, by my reckoning, has roughly a month to go.

Petra swallows eagerly from the glass, coughs and speaks again. Her manner is suddenly dry and brittle, the voice diminished. 'Yes, Gisa. Yesterday. It was a simple service. At the Wotruba Kirche . . . Uh-huh – yes. The Zentralfriedhof.' There's a pause during which I can just make out the remote tintinnabulation of a woman's voice before she answers. 'I know. Thank you. But you know how things are. They've been here already. No, quite. It's not exactly my idea of fun either.'

My gaze drifts across the rangey and eclectic apartment. On one wall hangs a grotesque de Kooning, a slapdash female figure with cavernous, horrorshow eyes, writhing in plastic frenzy. Below this, and to the right, a Garouste & Bonetti leopard-print chaise longue, draped with Burmese cashmere throws. There's an upright piano against the wall. A glass coffee table is piled high with scrapbooks, bound piles of sketches, smooth beach pebbles and sun-blanched gnarls of driftwood, along with various auto-defence weapons, among them an Oleoresin Capsicum red-hot-chilli aggressor spray. Beyond this array of heterodox items is a bead curtain and a dining-room, equipped with Saarinen tulip chairs. There are plants everywhere, wired across to each other on loop-circuits with party lights and jacked into the fibrophonic walls.

To my left, opposite the de Kooning, a Biedermeier chair and a dog-basket have been pushed up beside the fireplace above which a ram skull, nailed to the wall, leers unpleasantly with its curly horns and vacant eye-holes over a wall-window Plasmavision TV, let in flush with the wall-facing. The screen is on but soundless, and she was evidently surfing the Net when I arrived. A list of bucket-shop flights to various destinations, quoted in US dollars and Euros, scrolls over an animated VR background of dreamy reefs and archipelagoes in wide, unsullied, virtual seas.

I notice a copy of the *Wiener Tageszeitung* tucked like a lining into the dog-basket. It's open at 'Sharkey's Day', my own regular column for the day before yesterday, and it's stained a urinous yellow. She and the absent hound have evidently found it absorbing reading.

She finishes her call, snaps the Bip-Bip shut with a gesture like a card-sharp, and smiles apologetically. 'Sorry,' she explains, 'Sympathetic friends. Let me fix you a drink. What'll you have?'

'What's your poison?'

'Tequila Sunrise. It's a stand-in for the real thing.' She raises her eyes wittily towards the wintry view.

'Thanks, but I don't think my bloodstream's up to it at ten in the morning.'

'Some coffee, then. A Mokka?'

I nod my agreement and she smiles winningly before turning on her heels and heading for the kitchen. Her smile lingers around for a few seconds to keep me company before making its excuses and following her through the bead curtain. A moment later and the lights on the Venetian glass chandelier in the centre of the room plunge suddenly into darkness.

'Wave your arms around,' comes a disembodied instruction from the kitchen. 'The sensor's overtuned. If you don't move the system thinks there's no one in the room.'

all about leo

We talk about Leo, all about Leo. And as we talk the snow falls thicker and faster outside, encrusting the conifers in their terracotta pots and scooping up bewitched little vortices of flakes when the fingers of a trick wind find their way into the dip of the terrace. There's silence all around. The drifting falls seem to be bricking us in, centimetre by centimetre, filling the angular corners of the windows with their unique algorithmic geometries, muting and padding the roofs. Petra pours some volatile fluid into the hearth and cracks a match, and the hospitable catarrhing and hissing of homemade paper fire-logs and sundry combustible tinder fills the room. It's as if the spritely poltergeist of Leo himself is stuttering incoherently, gesticulating for attention in the flames. 'How on earth,' I want to whisper to him, 'did a schnook like you end up with *her*? And why the backstreet whores?' I try to picture them together, Leo and Petra, as man and wife in this outrageously chic apartment, but even the human imagination has its tensile limits. The idle speculation is going to have to wait. For the time being, there's just one square peg and too many round holes.

It had been a carrycot romance.

Their mothers met at the kindergarten in the Hofburg quarter to which they brought their respective children and struck up a friendship. Petra can't remember a time when they didn't know each other. Before they married, there'd never been another man in her life. As teenagers, they went to Glo-Bal Tekno nights at the Nachtwerk Club and even backpacked to New York City until the scale of the troubles there got bad and President Buchan brought it under military rule, a no-go area for tourists. They married at eighteen, in the same church where Leo's funeral was held.

Leo, she informs me, had been hooked up to the InfoNex server since his early teens and worked as a lone-eagle broker in commodities and precious metals from his telematic office in their own apartment. In three years he'd amassed a small fortune through judicious and timely dealing. But a year ago now things had started to go wrong . . . not financially, she assures me. It was Leo. His mother had died and he'd started to get depressed. The ever-ready schnapps bottle and other mental winders and benders had allayed the distress. He'd promoted himself recklessly through the whole hierarchy of designer drugs – Stargum, G-Whiz tabs, Dreamboats, Ultrajoys, Nose Candy and Psycho-Cola – never happy unless turbo-charging his system. Petra had been considering leaving him when he was killed. 'Now look at me,' she says in mock self-pity, emptying a solitary drop from her second tequila on to the nap of a Persian silk rug, 'an old soak. All alone in the world.' She pats her pregnant belly and scowls.

She's about to light a Cannaboid when she jumps violently. The lighter flips out of her grasp and her hand shakes involuntarily. Something has detonated in the distance and a soft orange glow appears over the rooftops, shuddering like lightning against the low undercarriage of the winter sky. We stand up and walk to the terrace window. The falling snow picks up the orange light and diffuses it into a soft aureole, a dandelion puffball.

'What is it?' she asks, wincing.

'Another fire-bomb, I guess. The Festung Europa people must be partying again.'

'I thought the Staatspolizei had broken them.'

'They got Werckel and a couple of his stooges, but the FE are organised bastards. They work in hermetic cells. You think the cops have killed it but they've just cut the worm in two. In any case, teenage jackboot wannabes are never in short supply.'

Black smoke piles from the fire till it fuses with the aerial blanket of cloud and from somewhere towards the Donaukanal a siren is fast approaching, whooping like a war-crazed Cheyenne.

Her hand is steadier now and she lights the Ultralite industry-standard reefer and passes me a Juju too. Like children, experimentally, we sit down on our knees and puff in front of the comforting hearth. The blaze is the living symbol of a safer era, responding to a strange atavism in the blood. In the few moments of silence that ensue I realise I've been talking to her in the manner of a chequebook journalist with his reinforced toe-cap in the door. It suddenly occurs to me that things are quite the other way round. The simplest question of all is as yet unanswered. It's with something like embarrassment in my voice that I put it to her: 'Why me? Sorry – but why did you want to see me?'

She quizzes me with her eyes. It's the look of a jeweller, staring into the guts of a new and unfamiliar chronometer.

'You're Sharkey, aren't you?' she answers at length. Genuine doubt and surprise are vying for ascendancy in her voice. 'You're his *friend*.'

She says it so simply – 'his *friend*' – that my brain pinks for a moment on the uphill grind.

'You do know,' I say, 'that he and I only met once? Some three months ago, in Hamburg? We had a few drinks together, that was all.'

'I realise that, but –' (she sucks thoughtfully on the hollow roach, squeezing it flat with her lips, still with that interrogative stare) 'since you met he never stopped talking about you. I was pleased. You see, he never had any real friends as far as I know. Men friends, I mean. He always liked your column, you know. And your politics.'

'What politics?'

'Don't ask me. That's what Leo said. All I'm saying is he was really happy to meet you and – you know – *hit it off* like that. And –'

I see that she's struggling to express something. 'What is it?' I coax.

'Well, he told me. You see, he knew he was going to die. He didn't say it in so many words, but I could tell.'

'It was an accident,' I say, but she doesn't want to hear.

'He took out life insurance three months ago. Before, he wouldn't even have dreamt of it. He wanted me to be okay. And he told me, just a few days before he died – he told me that if anything should happen, I should contact you.'

I swallow hard. 'In my capacity as a journalist, you mean?'

'In your capacity as his *friend*.' She looks at me beseechingly now, begging me to understand. It's one of those looks that, by design or not, reads like a promissory note. 'Just agree,' it says, 'just trust me, and I will respect you forever.' It's one of those looks that anyone with a normal instinct for self-preservation avoids like the basilisk's eye.

'He said he told you things,' she goes on hesitantly. 'When you were together in Hamburg. Important things. Things it would be important to know about if anything happened to him.'

I feel intensely ill-at-ease, despite the warm brain-buzz of cannabis.

I look away, finally, from her imploring eyes to get my bearings but I'm out of luck, for my gaze alights on Leo in vivid Holocolor. There the miserable sod is, on a Werkstätte sideboard, posing in a mosaic photo-frame in happier days. He has a full head of dark hair and is holding up a starfish between thumb and forefinger. He grimaces with spoof pop-eyed terror at it, like a creature out of a Tex Avery cartoon. But the hologram triggers nothing other than the vague recollection of his dypso beer-guzzling and droning voice at the Paloma. That evening – twelve weeks ago – is a virtual lacuna, a page torn from life's calendar and tossed into the office-shredder of time.

'Your husband said nothing of the slightest importance to me,' I conclude flatly, pulling myself together.

She doesn't speak but stares at me with bleak disappointment. There's something unmanning in that stare.

I glance at the snapshot again and a tiny recollection stirs. It's just a little thing, but I can't help smiling. 'Well he did say *one* thing that I recall,' I correct myself. 'Just before he left. He was drinking beers – a *lot* of beers. And he said: "I shouldn't be drinking this with what I've got".'

Petra crumples her brow curiously.

'Well naturally – I thought he was ill. So I said: "What have you got?" "Two Euros," he answered and he fished them out of his pocket and put them on the table. Just like that!'

She laughs with dry-throated merriment, then coughs hard.

'It was his way of telling me I was paying for the evening,' I explain, raising my eyebrows helplessly.

She looks up with wifely fondness and clears the phlegm-frog from her throat. 'That was Leo. He was cheeky. He had a sense of humour.'

Then she runs her finger over the salted rim of the glass and licks its tip with a slick salamandrine flicker of the tongue.

did you love him?

'Why did you ring me?' I ask suddenly. In the absence of sodium pentathol, it's an old journalist's trick for basic lie-detection. Stimulus-Response. Gunfire questions get surefire answers, like psychologists' association tests.

'Leo said I should.' Her voice is simple and childlike. 'He said I should ring you if I was in trouble.'

'And you *are* in trouble?'

She nods reluctantly and screws the wedding ring round the articulation on her finger like a nut on a bolt.

'What kind of trouble exactly?'

'I don't know. I can't be sure what shape it'll take. But it's coming. It's on its way, that's for sure. The claims adjustors are in with the Polizei. And they've both been hassling me.'

'Over the life insurance?'

'Yes.'

'It's their job to hassle. I wouldn't worry. And besides, I've never heard of suicide being disguised as a hit-and-run.'

'Not suicide, perhaps,' she replies with scrupulous hesitation, 'but murder.'

'You didn't murder him,' I state simply. Against my will, the slightest hint of a rising interrogative intonation crimps the tail-end of the statement.

'No,' she replies, unfazed. She sighs and looks wanly at his mugshot on the sideboard. 'But somebody did.'

I raise my eyebrows. 'What makes you think that? Accidents happen, you know. All it takes is a drunk driver who does a runner. Do you have any idea what they get for manslaughter these days?'

'He was murdered, Mr Sharkey,' she answers flatly and firmly. She stands up, shakes back her thick dark hair and runs the palms of her hands over her full womb as if trying to take the measure of the situation. 'Something happened to my husband. Don't ask me what. About a year ago. It wasn't just his mother dying, you know. There was something else going on. He changed. Overnight, almost. One day he was a happy man, the next he wasn't. He stopped confiding in me, you see. It was as simple as that.'

'Did you love him?' I ask.

She stares me straight in the eye. 'Yes,' she replies.

I swallow the last of the Mokka and the silt of the grounds sticks like river-mud between my teeth. Something about this affair is beginning to unnerve me. I have a sudden, malevolent desire to curdle the milk of human kindness.

'Tell this to the Polizei,' I say. 'It's their job, not mine.'

'I don't trust them, and neither did Leo. They're in with the spin-doctors and the racketeers. Now they've got me in their line of fire.'

'Who exactly is looking into this?' I ask. 'From the Vienna police, I mean.'

'His name's Uscinski. He's been over here, asking questions.'

It's a name I recognise. I've crossed his path before. He's a medium-sized cheese in the BKA – Bundeskriminalamt, the federal criminal investigation agency. A Chefinspektor FGr. 6, I believe. He is, as far as I know, upfront, but I doubt if there are many charm-school rosettes in his office. 'And what does he say?'

'He doesn't say anything. He just – you know – investigates.' There's a note of throwaway contempt in her voice. 'They're treating it as suspicious, at any rate. But as far as they're concerned the suspicion points at me. I just *know* there's some kind of tie-in with the insurers. I can feel it in my bones. They ask the same kind of goddam questions.'

'You may be right,' I concede. 'Put yourself in their shoes. It's a motive. But if you didn't murder him, you've got nothing to worry about. And if you didn't murder him and you think he was murdered, then who did it? And why? I presume you've asked yourself that.'

She turns to the mantelpiece above which the ram-crested Plasmavision screen has reverted to the Net Menu-Bar and a Travel-Forum Screen-Saver. It displays a Smiley Planet Earth Emoticon with sunglasses clutching a suitcase plastered with 1930s tourist stickers for places like Alexandria and Port Said. Beside it is the face of a grey-haired woman in her sixties, the interactive butler-icon of her Agent Program. It's a friendly, soothing face – intelligent, too – that conjures up motherly images of family gatherings, kitchen aprons and grisly crucifixions nailed over ancient bedsteads. Kinder, Küche und Kirche. She smiles and nods her head, blinking occasionally. I'm thinking that she looks dimly familiar when I have to remind myself that 'she' is hardly the word. The image is an infographic camouflage dreamt up somewhere out there in the Metaverse and clothing a chunk of software with a human personality and a name. A servant program, semi-autonomous, familiar with Petra's likes and dislikes, the little patterns of her daily life, but no more than a ream of binary digits for all that. Below the benign physiognomy of the agent, on the tiled chimney-piece, is a small Chinese jar from which Petra extracts a key.

'Come with me,' she says, 'I want to show you something.'

We go down a short corridor to a double-locked door which she keys open. She grasps a couple of times in the dark for the light-cord and eventually finds it, tugging it on and waiting for the nerve-jarring warm-up flashes on the overhead flo-ring to desist.

'Hmmm. Retro,' I say.

'Leo refused to wire his cubby-hole into the domotic system, apart from the external Telekom link. He was never one for servomechanics, anyway. Liked doing things his way.'

It's a small broom-cupboard of a room dominated by an early green fluorescent protein computer, the kind where the silicon's replaced by jellyfish molecules. The GFP's cabled across to modem, phone and a battery of other homemade gizmos stacked up on cheap japanned warehouse shelving. A desk-calculator sits in front of the VDU with a bog-roll of figures coiling out of it and trailing across the floor. The wall is smothered with Post-its and, when he ran out of these, Leo evidently took to writing directly on the plaster like a tagger – names, numbers, indecipherable scrawls. In the centre, in frantic blue felt-tip letters, is what looks like a mathematical formula: SS15698–B/157 +

ES27372–B/231 = ???????. The writing slopes down madly and ends in a mass of haywire question marks. Above this inscription a number of press-ads for live 3D Networker chat-lines – the vanilla suburbs of WorldsChat and AlphaWorld – have been taped up. The shelving is stacked with telephone and alphanumeric Bip-Bip directories, dialling-code handbooks, sheaves of perforated print-out, lists of Telnet and Gopher sites and rn commands, a stack of Mormon publications from Salt Lake City, Utah, and a software handbook entitled GeneDraw. Five LCD travel-clocks, each with a different time, have been taped to the wall and labelled 'New York', 'London', 'Paris', 'Vienna' and 'Hong Kong' respectively.

'Leo's office,' she murmurs, looking around her blankly. 'Don't ask me what went on in here. He never let me in. When he was at work, I had to E him from the living-room to get a response.'

'Why are you showing me this?' I ask.

'Leo made a lot of money, Mr Sharkey. I told you: he was a broker. He had one flesh-and-blood friend – a recent acquaintance – and that was you. At least you were the only person, to my knowledge, that he felt friendship towards. He had no flesh-and-blood enemies. He never met anyone. But, if you ask me, people who make that kind of money do have enemies. Somewhere.' She looks at me significantly and raps her knuckles on the plastic box of the GFP. 'In here, perhaps,' she adds, 'in hyperspace – if not out there . . . if not in that solid-state world of ours.'

I sit on Leo's swivel-chair and look at the tomb-grey flip-up screen of the GFP computer. Through the fur of dust that sticks to its static I see nothing but my own ghostly features looking back. Sharkey; 30; 1m. 90; 78 kg; shoe size 43; collar 40 cm. Short dark hair with left parting. A fresh, enquiring, brazen face, with the kind of ears that people love to box. A face with olive-shaped eyes, one of those 'hard' mouths with no upper lip and that news-hungry, freckly, truffling nose, straight as an Innsbruck ski-jump. Sharkey – monger of news, purveyor of mindless tittle-tattle. I swear to God: if I weren't such a shit, I'd hate myself.

The screen's non-tactile and despite the mike there's no response to voice-commands, so I feel round at the back of the console for the manual switch and click it on. The hard disk flywheels into action and the computer boots up, a string of machine-code digits scrolling at subliminal speed across the now-live darkness of the screen. Then suddenly a little red cartoon door appears in the middle and a ghoul-show jingle strikes up. The door creaks open, sound effects and all, and a huge bug-eyed hairy Yeti jumps forward and runs towards the front of the screen. 'Ho! Ho! Ho!' it guffaws, 'Not so quick, Buster! I'm the Cookie Monster, and I want a Cookie!' The monster's chin drops with a crash like a cash-till and a big pink tongue comes lolloping out with, at its centre, a blinking cursor waiting for the log-in. 'C'mon! C'mon!' it wheedles in hillbilly English, 'Gimme! Gimme! Gimme!'

'Take me there,' I say, turning to Petra.

'Where?'

'The Prater Park. Where he was killed. I want you to tell me how it happened.'

'It's very simple,' she says. 'He was walking the dog.'

'Aw shucks!' – the voice of the Cookie Monster, complaining as I put the computer through shutdown.

'What dog?' I ask after a mental double-take, 'I haven't seen one.'

'Argos. The dog's called Argos. Come on, I'll introduce you. He's been a very bad boy and I'm not too pleased with him. I've locked him up in the loo.'

walking the dog

'Nice name, Argos,' I comment as we approach the makeshift slammer. 'Isn't that what Odysseus called his?'

'Uh-huh. Take care, though. He's a bit – you know – nippy with strangers.'

I've always prided myself on my instant rapport with dogs. At the Heurigen wine-cellar my mother runs in Perchtoldsdorf, we had a succession of big, musclebound mutts: a mastiff, then a pinscher, then a bulldog. I'd walk them in the southwestern part of the Vienna Woods in my teens. When they jumped up they might knock me over, but it was all in play. So when Petra releases Argos I feel confident of my PR skills. He's a stumpy-legged Jack Russell – small-fry. He stands there moping up at me, a new biped in his doggy existence, and his tail hangs limply between his legs. He has a martyred expression that reminds me of Savonarola at the stake, a VR image on a 'Famous Saints' CD we studied at the Akademisches Gymnasium. I lower my hand to administer a compassionate pat and in a flash the little fucker's got me, sinking his fangs into the meaty pad to the side of the right palm, below the little finger. I yelp in pain and I swear that he smiles, a flicker of canine Schadenfreude playing on his rubbery pink lips.

Petra murmurs 'I told you so' and leads me into the bathroom, shaking her head. 'You're not sero-wotsit, are you?' she enquires in passing as she fishes a first-aid kit out of the medicine cupboard and looks with distaste at the two vampiric holes, pissing blood, that man's best friend has just punctured in my flesh.

'No,' I reply, 'just rabid. Will that do?'

When she's patched me up, she glares disapprovingly at the dog before turning to me. 'You've nothing to worry about now. He calms down once he's tasted blood.'

'That's comforting to know.'

'I guess we'd better take him too. He hasn't been out since that last night with Leo. Do you have a car?'

'Not at the moment.'

'Me neither. The Polizei impounded Leo's Alfa for forensic tests. We'll take the bike, if that's all right with you.'

In the Wintergarten below the Hundertwasser Haus, Petra Detmers keeps a collector's wildcat under lock and chain. It's a 1960 Panther 100 Springer, single cylinder, 598cc, over half a century old. Incongruously, a twee little wicker bike-bag has been wired to the front, and this is the crow's nest from which Argos surveys the macadam horizons like Ishmael the pilot. Petra togs up in a black fur-collared leather overcoat and, what with her belly, only just manages to hitch her leg over and rest her mass against the handlebars. I sit pillion as she fires the bike with an electric starter, revs up and rides the short distance to the Prater over the freshly sea-salted roads.

We pass the Ferris wheel and the serpentine rollercoaster in the Volksprater funfair, a black out-of-season twist of defunct Meccano against the frost-grey sky. Then, towering over both, the sky-high column of the Hellevator, a terrifying free-fall vertical joyride for those citizens whose sensory palates are so jaded that only a near-death experience will jarr them momentarily into a semblance of life. They drop like stones on chairs that run down the column, their fall broken by electro-magnets seven metres from the ground. The experience might be more meaningful if, halfway down, there was a power-cut.

I cling to Petra's distended waistline, above the impressive ballast of her arse, as we roar on. The scenery changes to the dark woods along the Hauptallee with its skeletal rows of leafless chestnuts, the branches freighted with snow like solid toplighting. Then the bridge over the Heustadelwasser lake. She pulls in, eventually, by the Lusthaus pavilion, a restaurant and former hunting-lodge, where the Haup-tallee, Aspernallee and other assorted spokes converge at the axis of a roundabout. Opposite is another restaurant, the rustic Altes Jägerhaus.

When she switches off the ignition, the quiet's unearthly. The little octagonal pavilion is closed and there's no traffic. Only brooding trees and, a little further to the south-east, the slumbering grandstand of the Freudenau racetrack.

Duck-down snow tumbles out of the sky. The steaming bike's motor reminds me of a horse's flanks in the chill air. And the dog, like overwound clockwork, leaps from his basket and tears off into a copse of trees, in hot pursuit of a lone grey squirrel.

Petra pulls her helmet and gloves off and looks around to get her bearings. Her breath comes in warm, vaporous gasps. Then she crosses the road to the far side of the Aspernallee. In the black leather coat she looks like an Obersturmbannführer, but this hard little negative thought evaporates when she turns. She's wiping back tears from her eyes. She gasps, gives a down-mouthed anti-smile and gets a grip on herself. 'His car was here,' she says, pointing to the roadside, 'and he was hit there.' She indicates a point on the opposite side of the road. 'I came the day after, but there was nothing left. The minute anything like this happens the hygiene department moves in with high-pressure hoses.' She nods towards the restaurant. 'Gore on the road. It's bad for custom.'

'You said he was walking the dog. Did he always come out by car?'

'Yes. What I ask myself is what he was doing *out* of the car . . .'

'He may have been stretching his legs too.'

'Oh no, not Leo,' she says, shaking her head categorically. 'If you'd known him better, you'd understand. Leo was the laziest bastard alive. You see, Mr Sharkey, he had a system. He clipped one of those old-fashioned electronic pagers to Argos's collar – the kind doctors used to use in hospitals. Then he'd kick Argos out of the car. After ten minutes, when he reckoned the dog had done enough running and rooting around, he rang up the pager on his Networker. He'd got him trained. He'd come straight back to the car when he heard the bleep, jump in at the open door, and home they'd come. He was crazy about gadgets, Leo was.' She subsides into an inward state, musing on Leo's technophilia.

'This was the night of Friday-to-Saturday. 20 November. Eight days ago.'

'That's right.'

And on Friday 4 September Leo and I were in Hamburg. It's hard to fathom. We assume, when people pass out of our field of vision, that their lives persist invisibly elsewhere, chugging determinedly along on their own personal tramlines. This is not always a trustworthy assumption. I contemplate the point in space where the fat man's existence was so abruptly extinguished. In some countries they put plaques up at the quasi-mystical sites where notable individuals cash in their chips: writers, painters, resistance fighters. Here, there isn't much one can do. Carve his name on a tree? I imagine his disconsolate spirit knocking at the doors of disbanded bars and brothels in celestial cyberspace. In a vague gesture to placate it, I place two twigs crosswise on the kerb. I instantly feel stupid but Petra puts me at my ease.

'Thank you,' she says, 'Leo would have appreciated that. He was a very religious man, in his way.'

'Were there any witnesses?'

'It was past midnight. Quarter past, or thereabouts. The Altes Jägerhaus was closed. The boss at the Lusthaus was counting up the day's takings. He heard the impact, but he saw nothing. He found the body. Leo had died instantly. And he called the cops.'

She shades her eyes and peers into the woods to the left then inserts two fingers into her mouth and lets rip a piercing wolf-whistle. There's no response.

'That fucking dog,' she mutters.

'He only responds to the pager?' I hazard.

'Right.'

'And where's the pager?' I experience a shiver of discomfort as I ask the question and she looks at me curiously, picking up the odd, quavering frequency on the air.

'Dunno. When the Polizei brought him back he wasn't wearing it. It must've dropped off round here somewhere.'

I purse my lips tightly, summoning up my powers of mimicry, and begin: '*peep–peep, peep–peep, peep–peep* . . .'

'What are you doing?' Petra laughs in surprise.

'I'm paging Argos.'

'It wasn't like that!' she remonstrates. 'It was more of a: *ping–ping! ping–ping! ping–ping!* . . .'

We both *ping* simultaneously to boost up the volume and before long the dog comes snuffling into sight, leaving a zigzag track of clover-shaped pawprints behind him in the fresh meringue of snow.

'Bravo!' says Petra, 'Here he comes. Our only eye-witness.'

A wood-pigeon flaps into flight from a branch high overhead and the dog yaps reflexively at it before ambling over to join us.

'You think whoever hit him was biding their time, is that it?' I ask. 'Somewhere along this stretch of road?'

'Yes. Leo was a night owl. He'd come here with Argos every couple of nights, at about the same hour. It was routine.'

'But you have no evidence for your suspicions whatsoever.'

She crouches down and rubs some snow and leafmould off Argos's rump. 'I have my intuition,' she replies.

A sudden blast of icy wind funnels at rocket-speed down the Aspernallee and flips open my loosely fastened parka, inflating the arms and torso like a beach mattress. The temperature seems to plummet five degrees in a second. It feels like another body is trying to get into my clothes with me, a poltergeist. I quickly do up the internal zipper and expel the invading air. This place is beginning to give me the creeps, a bad case of the heebie-jeebies. The blind little shuttered pavilion. The glowering, speechless trees. And the multiple paths centring on the roundabout. Stemmerallee, Schwarzenstockallee, and so on. I try to picture it all from a wood-pigeon's perspective, cocking its pea-brained head and looking down from the uppermost bough with its glassy little eye. A man, a woman, a dog and a motorbike, planted forlornly in the centre of a straggling snow-encrusted spider's web of roads and paths.

'I'm not a policeman and I'm not a private dick,' I say to Petra, 'and I'm not even a crime reporter. Never have been, really. You know my column. It's gossip, social chitchat, junk news. Nor, I hasten to add, am I a friend of your Leo's.' She looks stung but I continue coldly. 'For me, he was just a guy in a bar, right? A very drunk guy, if you want to know the truth, and a fucking pain in the arse.'

'He told you something,' she interrupts pleadingly. 'I know he told you something. Something important.'

I hold up my hands to brake her flow.

'Maybe. Maybe it'll come back. I'll do my best, but I can't promise anything.'

'If it's money . . .,' she begins.

I tick her off with a wagging finger. 'I'm cursed with chronic curiosity. It's job-conditioning. I'm prepared to go along with this up to a point. Just far enough to see if there are any grounds for your suspicions.'

Her expression's humble, *laissez-faire*.

'What are we today – Friday?' I stall.

'Saturday.'

'Next week, then – if I can arrange it – I'm going to come round again to look over that office of Leo's. I'm not exactly a road-hog on the information superhighway. More of a hedgehog, actually. But I haven't been flattened yet.'

Remembering Leo's fate, I regret the metaphor, but there's no going back on it now. 'Do you agree?' I ask.

She nods.

'Which reminds me. What did the Polizei say to you?'

'They said they'd be back. They said I should stay put, that I didn't have the right to leave Vienna.'

I sense her resistance and recall the flight-info scrolling on the TV when I arrived.

'Do as they tell you. In the meantime, I'm going to make some other enquiries.'

'What sort?'

'Never you mind.' Now it's my turn to play my cards close to my chest. I don't tell Leo's wife, but something on the far side of the roundabout beside the pavilion has caught my eye and roused my meddlesome nature. It's just a street-lamp, an everyday street-lamp, but perched high up on top of the street-lamp there's a little friend. Not a wood-pigeon, but one step better.

She lifts Argos into the basket and turns to start the Panther, but when I don't budge she realises I'm not going to join her. 'Let me at least give you a lift. You must be frozen.'

'Strangely enough, I'm okay after that blasted gust. Adapting and surviving. I guess it did something to my thermostat. So don't worry. I'll do without that lift. I really think I'd prefer to walk.'

I turn my back on her and set off at a good pace.

'Where are you going?' she calls after me, her curiosity gingering up into words.

I wander a little further down the long white track of the Belvedereallee and turn, cupping my hands into a megaphone to make myself heard above the fartings and throat-clearings of the motorbike.

'I'm going to see a man about a dog!' I yell. Then, as an afterthought, I wave goodbye. Nice and cheery, like, because I feel sorry for her. And because it's so bloody perishing cold.

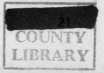

chapter two

the stone-cold eye

As you turn the street corner, the beefy appearance of the new Polizei headquarters in the Fleischmarkt is about as reassuring as a shotgun muzzling between the omoplates. If Adolf Loos came up with 'buildings without eyebrows', this is the next step into unembellished barbarism: 'buildings without eyes', a further cleansing, another nail in the worm-eaten coffin of baroque Habsburg grandeur. It is a windowless hulk, a chrysolite, a huge polyhedron stuck at every angle with jagged shards of mirror-glass that fling back the reflection of the city's startled face in a myriad smashed and disfigured forms. Das österreichische Antlitz. As if to render the nightmare in glorious Technicolor, at production stage each shard was dipped into a cocktail of photo- and thermo-sensitive chromatic chemicals. Now brutal, fractured images burn and flare in an op-art frenzy of hues – gold, ultramarine, violet, primrose, puce – dissolving and enhancing as the intensity of daylight changes and the stone-cold eye of the sun climbs and ducks and dives behind multiple veils of wintry cloud.

Over a cavernous doorway, the horizontally-striped Federal Republic flag – red-white-red, the Babenburg colours – shivers and undulates. It spawns miniature clones of itself in the identically-striped collar chevrons of the officers who pass beneath like dung-beetles, a ceaseless ebb and flow of uniforms and black-peaked caps, shoulders braided with the gold insignia of rank.

Across the road, an *ad hoc* crowd of Hungarians, Romanians and Bulgarians with chalk-white faces huddles under a makeshift banner and cardboard placards. They're protesting against this morning's firebomb.

I spot Ernst Ashmeyer, a colleague from the *Tageszeitung*. He's checking the VA on the handcorder docked to his Bip-Bip.

'Thule Omega or Festung Europa?' I ask in passing.

'Probably Festung. A guest-workers' hostel. Five dead. There were Fylfots and Kruckenkrenz crosses on the graffiti. Might as well be Mickey Mouse for all that means these days.'

Festung Europa, the right-wing Fortress Europe Movement, has got a firm toehold in Austria and just about everywhere within the last decade. It's possible that a handful of their sympathisers have their infant-blue eyes on us right now, peering down from the crystalline chunk of one-way mirror-glass on the pavement opposite. I stare back adamantly at the invisible seraphim, finger the amulet in my pocket (a bent ten-groschen coin, fifty years old, that I found in my toilet cistern at Karl Marx-Hof) and cross the narrow road.

The pleasure-dome's shared by a number of state bureaux and a big multidirectional signpost stands just inside the entrance: Bundeskriminalamt; Schutzpolizei; Vollzugspolizei; Bundesnachrichtendienst; Bereitschaftspolizei; Bundesgrenzschutz; Militärische Abschirmdienst; Europol; Bahnpolizei; Sturmpolizei, and so on. Here, big cops have little cops upon their backs to bite 'em. Much as I dread it, I take the high-tech lift to the 20th floor, an eight-second ascent. I emerge with ears popping and gorge rising. It's a nasty case of the bends, and there's not a decompression chamber in sight.

A pencil, a pad, a Bip-Bip and an overtalkative cop are standard equipment for any self-respecting paparazzo. The first three items are in the pockets of my winter jacket. The fourth is in office 204 and answers to the name of Walter Reik.

The information revolution did not arrive too soon for Reik. He's an agoraphobic, allergy-ridden individual who, even though forty per cent of city-centre transport has gone electric, lives in terror of ozone depletion, lead poisoning, carbon monoxide, diesel aromatics, CFCs, methane, nitrous oxide – you name it. The sad thing is he's right, though the damage has already been done. He's known to change the air-conditioning filter in his office once a day at his own expense. In obedience to this mania, he's become increasingly deskbound until even a walk to the latrines involves a physical effort of pentathlonic proportions. By now, I'm thinking, he probably has one of those colostomy bags strapped to his inner thigh.

Perhaps to compensate for this entropic tendency to inertia in his external existence, his digestive tract has scarcely known a second's rest in half a century of life. Reik is a scavenging, muck-sucking little pig.

Leberknödelsuppe, Eierspeise scrambled omelette, Wiener Schnitzel, Gefüllte Paprika – he shovels the stuff in, day and night, like a blast-furnace stoker. There's never a moment when his snout is not in the trough. And the logistics of his working life have had to adapt to this one, ineluctable fact – an all-consuming edacious process. Two local eateries, Weiber's Wirtshaus and Schimanskzky's, are on-call round the clock. His office is stuffed with napkins, plastic cutlery and bottled potations. And, since voice-activated data-processing is out of the question, given that the recognition software is not used to coping with words filtered through gobfuls of boiled potatoes, he's developed a curiously dainty technique of operating the keyboard with his little fingers while holding top-heavy forks and spoons between thumbs and middle fingers at the same time.

In defiance of all reasonable expectations, he's a remarkably healthy-looking, eupeptic fifty-something, with bright, sparky eyes under hooded lids and cheeks like prime silverside, though when his heart gives out it will go up like a percussion mine. At such a time, he could probably be processed into excellent *pâté de foie gras*. He has a nap of back-combed, grease-impacted jet black hair, and there's something of the quick, finickity delicacy of the lemur – definitely lemuroid rather than porcine, on close inspection – in the efficient, businesslike movements with which his hands flick constantly between the pointed muzzle of his lips and whatever provender happens to be set before him.

Yet the blood-rich odour of pork, beef and lamb that hangs like chip-fat in his office is enough to turn anyone's stomach, and turn everyone's stomach it does – even those of his colleagues who spend their days putting the leftovers of terrorist attacks into polythene bags. This suits Reik down to the ground. It means he's left alone. And the fewer the physical interruptions the happier a man he is. Promotion, kudos and peer-approval mean not a lot to him. He's the Garbo of the force. Few of the Vienna officers have set eyes on him. He's a name to them, an MBX at the end of a fibre-optic cable, a noumenal synapse in the data-flow, an all-seeing deity through whose hooded retina the entire panoply of Staatspolizei activities seems to pass. I too have to set a time-limit on my privileged access to his company in the interests of personal hygiene and my own fragile digestive system. But, say what you will – Walter Reik is a useful little lemur to know.

I knock and enter, and surprise surprise . . . he's tackling a platter of Bauernschmaus, a selection of hams, frankfurters, smoked and roast pork cutlets with juniper-flavoured sauerkraut, dumplings and gherkins. I shake the greasy, redundant little finger on the fork-wielding hand.

'What d'you want, Sharkey?' he manages between surly mouthfuls. Speech and mastication are mutually antagonistic. Investment in one means downtime in the other. He shunts a roulade of Mohnstrudel towards me and I amiably shunt it back. No complicity . . . he doesn't like this.

'Leo Detmers,' I say, in the brusque telegraphese I know he works with. 'A week back. Hit-and-run in the Prater. Uscinski's department. Do you know where they're at?'

Reik pulls a face. He hates questions. When he swallows his Adam's apple bobs like a massive flotation buoy that warns of heavy seas.

'ZKD, the insurers, are pushing for action,' he growls, wiping his mouth on the back of his hirsute hand. 'They think it stinks like pigshit. Especially the wife, the rose in the manure.'

'He took out the policy in August.'

'Uh-huh,' Reik nods. 'But that's not all. When they got him to the clinic, he was carrying a Harvest Contract card.'

'An organ donor card, you mean?'

'No – Harvest Contract. Never heard of it?' He grins gruesomely. 'It's all the rage. It permits organ, blood and tissue sales.'

'I thought that kind of deal was illegal.'

'Not since the Court of Human Rights' protocol collapsed. A case of semantics and niceties. They couldn't get away from the fact that body parts are commodities. And commodities can change hands, at a price. We're looking into a scheme to give prisoners reduced sentences if they agree to Harvest Contracts.'

'So who benefits?'

'Payment in full to the next of kin.'

'The wife, in Detmers' case?'

'Yup.'

Reik is about to lay into the sauerkraut again when I stay his hand. 'That can't be worth much,' I say. 'Not compared to the policy.'

'You wanna bet?' he challenges.

'I thought they just grew organs these days.'

'Sure, but it's slow and expensive. Besides, demand still outstrips supply. Harlem Sunsets are always popular.'

'Harlem Sunsets?'

'Car splats. If it's a clean death, you're talking 270,000 Euros for every major organ. Think about it. Okay – you've got liver, kidneys, heart and lungs. But the list doesn't stop there. They can use the lot. Corneas, inner ears, jaw bone, heart pericardium, pancreas, stomach, bones, hip joints, ligaments, cartilages, bone marrow. On top of that you've got over two square metres of skin for burn victims, plus a hundred thousand kilometres of blood vessels. They reckon one card-carrier can end up in over fifty people. But this Detmers character was lugging around the bonus-prize.'

'How do you mean?'

'He had a very high concentration of antibodies for hepatitis B in his blood. They take the plasma and fractionate it. They break it down into antibodies, antihaemophilic concentrates and albumin. A little cloning and you've got vaccines and diagnostics – marketable stuff. On top of that, a guy who dies nice and quick like he did with minimum body damage – he's perfect. It's like stripping down vintage cars for spare parts. HBPs, you know – Human Body Parts.'

I happen to meet his gaze and there's something unsavoury in it. This list of human offal seems to be whetting his appetite again.

'I went to see her,' I say, mulling things over.

'Who?'

'The wife. Your prime suspect. She never mentioned the card.'

'It's just possible he hadn't told her and she never had the gumption to rifle his wallet,' says Reik sceptically. 'But she'll know soon enough when they've tissue-typed him and cashed him in. Generally the durable stuff has a fixed tag and the major organs are auctioned off on the Net to the highest bidder within a week. The clinics keep ten per cent as a handling fee.'

'Which clinic was it?' I ask.

He scratches his chin with the meat-moist points of the fork. 'Donaufeld, I think. Just out beyond UNO-City.' Something resembling the tender emotions traverse Reik's well-fed visage. 'Did you know him, this Detmers character?'

'We'd met,' I reply. But Petra's words – 'you're his *friend*' – are reverbing like a shocked reproach in some remote cerebral echo-chamber.

Reik returns to his mental calculations, a lump of schinken in his cheek. 'A high-premium policy,' he says, 'payable over his widow's lifetime. She's a young woman, so that's quite a tidy sum. Add to that the organ harvest and you've got some nice little murder-motives paddling around in the sharkpond.'

'Sure. She reckons he was murdered too,' I confide. 'But by third party or parties unknown. He was some kind of futures broker. It's not impossible he trod on somebody else's corns.'

'Nothing's impossible,' concedes Reik. He has somehow managed, I realise, to sustain the foregoing interchange while polishing off the remains of the Bauernschmaus and is now merrily harpooning a slice of marbelised chocolate Guglhupf and airlifting it to his spacious buccal cavity.

Compulsively watchable as Reik is, I suddenly recollect the Prater Park, and the street-lamp by the pavilion.

traffic monitor no/e.8:g.3

'There was a Lepers night-camera on the street-lamp at the inter-section where he bought it. I guess Uscinski's looked into that already.'

'Coordinates,' snaps Reik, waving his knife at a Vienna streetmap on the wall. I point to the roundabout and read the little fluorescent identification-tag on the map: 'traffic monitor NO/e.8:g.3'.

Reik's hard at work at the keyboard. 'Date and time?'

'Morning of November 21, just past midnight.'

A window opens on the Plasmavision wallscreen and an aerial, nocturnal view of the Lusthaus roundabout, freeze-framed at 00.10.32, glows in starry pixels on the desktop. I half expect to see Petra and Argos standing there, as they were this morning, but the road is deserted. The scene bears the macabre hallmarks of infra-red surveillance, that queasy, psychotropic off-kiltering of the colour spectrum.

Reik looks at the last consultation-time in the corner of the screen. 'You're right. Uscinski's seen this,' he remarks, 'and he may have copied it. From the traffic cop's point of view this is a low-security area, so they use economy takes. One every two seconds and fractalised. Shall I fast-forward?'

The images pulse rapidly forward then suddenly Reik brings his finger down on the joystick button and stops them. He shifts them back a few seconds in time. It's 00.12.40. The camera's pointing in such a way that we can see one side of the roundabout and the left-hand side of the Aspernallee but not the other. We're looking away from the Lusthaus, and something has slipped into sight. It's just the front bonnet of a car, left of frame. A slight mismatch with the previous lacunary image on the extreme left indicates the nearside door has been opened.

Reik places an eyeglass icon over the bodywork of the car and clicks. The spectrographic analysis indicates red.

'BMW Z10 roadster, probably the A-range. Came out about eight years ago.'

'How can you tell?' I'm genuinely impressed. The image is crude and partial, to say the least.

'The shape of the wing mirror,' he answers. 'A rhomboid. They went for a round design after this.'

We saccade carefully forward, but all's quiet. The BMW remains *in situ*. No sign of action. Then at 00.16.08 the door shuts and the vehicle takes off.

'Some acceleration,' says Reik. 'When did your man get it?'

'Right there,' I reply, pointing at the screen. It's 00.16.10 and just off-screen Detmers is meeting his maker. 'His killer's in the BMW.'

'And him? What was Detmers in?'

'An Alfa of some sort. Not sure. According to his widow, you people impounded it. He's definitely off-camera, though. His car was found over to the right. He was on the pavement opposite. He was walking the dog.'

Reik licks his lips. 'So at 00.16 he gets out of his car and wanders across the road. Cue hit-and-run. Think he'd have seen the BMW lying in wait?'

'No. It's on the roundabout, and the copse of trees behind curves round, providing cover. The BMW obviously thought of that. Could we recap?'

It's one of those rare occasions when Reik's mental curiosity overrides the slavering roar of hunger from the food-annihilation plant that he calls his gut. 'Uscinski will have to know about our little chat,' he warns.

'Of course. But as you say, he's been here too. At the last count he had a regulation pair of eyes. If he's really done the business, he may even have tread-marks filed and be out looking for cross-matches.'

Reik shrugs non-committally.

'Do you reckon this will take some of the heat off the wife?' I ask, trying my luck.

'Shouldn't think so.'

This is a known factor in doing business with Reik, his rhada-manthine justice and inflexibility. He'll tell you anything you need to know, but so he will with everyone. He's as anarchically free with information as the Net. But he'll never make a decision or put in a word for you. It's one of the endearing things about him, his data-transparency. You know where you are. You know how things stand.

At his invitation, I take over the joystick and go back to 00.15.00, then forward up to 00.15.20. Something caught my eye in this sequence earlier and now I know what it is. I experience a little wave of self-satisfaction, like someone who's just found the answer to the last clue in a 3D cryptic holocrossword. As a deliberate tease, I look at Reik pointedly and inject a healthy dose of mystification into my voice. 'Well, well, well,' I say, 'what d'you think of that, then?'

'Again!' he insists, looking worried, and I run through the ten screens once more. He's put on his little half-moon glasses and his hooded eyes are whizzing around all over the place. He's trying to spot something out of the ordinary. It's a nice feeling to have one over on Reik for once. He shakes his head forlornly, then turns sour. 'You're not wasting police time, are you, Sharkey?'

I freeze-frame on the opening image and point with a pencil at a tiny white crescent shape projecting at ten o'clock above the car bonnet, beside the open door. In the next frame it's still there, but its angle has shifted to 2 o'clock – then 10, then 2, then 10, then 2, and so on for a further four screens.

Reik harrumphs. In an unprecedented gesture, he sweeps crockery, cutlery, gristle and crumbs to one side of the work-surface in front of him with an impatient movement of the forearm. 'A pennant?' he hazards. 'Some kind of fancy aerial?' I can see that he's hating this. 'Whatever it is, it's swinging in the wind.'

'No wind. Look at the trees in the background. Not a whiff of wind to swing in.'

Again he makes a noise in his throat like a disgruntled lion. 'We'll try the CYC,' he says, shunting a scalable frame over the crescent shape.

'What's that when it's at home?' I ask.

'You don't get these at home. It's strictly cop-shop. It can analyse anything, based on millions of codified contexts.'

The frame shimmies into place and starts thinking. After a few seconds a voice announces: 'Based on available data, the item selected appears to be a metronome or a windscreen-wiper.'

Reik thumps his forehead with the flat of his hand and delivers a well-turned curse.

'Great stuff.'

'Okay,' he capitulates. 'Spit it out.'

'That's the tail of Argos,' I reply, getting to my feet and preparing to leave. I raise the forefinger of my right hand in the air and wag it from ten to two o'clock. 'See?'

He stares in frustrated ignorance at me.

'When Odysseus, the mythical king of Ithaca, returns home from his voyage to Troy after twenty years of absence, his dog Argos is the only one to recognise him. The dog's too old and knackered to move. So he just lies there, wagging his tail. Then he conks out. The emotion's too much for him.'

Reik's stare decomposes suddenly into anger. 'Don't piss with me, Sharkey. You're referring to the Detmers' dog, right?'

'Right. The only problem is that whoever's in that car, it isn't Detmers, because Detmers is over to the right twiddling his thumbs and waiting to get killed. It isn't Odysseus either, come to that. And in my experience, strangers don't get the waggly-tail treatment from Argos. Strangers get a different kind of welcome altogether.' I peel back the plaster on my hand to reveal the rivet-holes of Argos's dentition.

Reik toggles between two of the tail images for that crude early-animation effect, then looks at the hand wound, then back to the screen. And suddenly his prehensile lemuroid chops crease up into a smile, the jaw cracks into a grin, and the grin explodes into a schoolboy laugh, spraying the wallscreen with dewdrops of phlegm. 'Get out of here, Sharkey!' he wheezes genially, slapping me on the arse. 'I'm an old man! What is it you want from me, eh? You want me to *die* laughing?'

Svetlana

I cut across the Danube canal by the Marienbrücke and make my way on foot to a garage in the district bordering the Augarten Park to pick up the car.

It's good to get out of Reik's office, that gloomy vestibule of his long intestine. Though to be fair that little electric car of mine is no bed of roses either. It's a Puch Gringolet, the colour of catsick. It looks and stinks like a squirrel-cage and sounds like a sewing-machine. And, in common with other townbuggies, it has the advantage of getting you from A to B, though venture any further into the alphabet and you're asking for trouble. A week ago it was vandalised and the combined cost of panel-beating, windscreen replacement and graffiti-overspray suggests a put-up job. I imagine armies of yobs clambering into their beds in the wee hours after nocturnal sprees of destruction. They emerge from the toast-warm sheets at dawn to slip into mechanics' overalls and set off for their state-of-the-art workshops where they calmly reap the profits of their mayhem with zippered, smiling lips.

When your name's Sharkey the good thing about little whimsies like this is that they're more than the passing clouds of brain-weather. They're bread and butter. I make a mental note to write this one up for Monday. 'Sharkey's Day.' 2,000 words of daily Vienna, five days a week, courtesy of little old me – Joe Soap, Jedermann, *l'homme moyen sensuel* . . . Easy money, the envious might say.

But right this moment, it's good to drive again. It makes me feel vaguely human. And the Luddites have missed my music cache. In a fit of pre-natal nostalgia, I stick on Iggy Pop's 'Nightclubbing', clucking and neck-dancing along to the madly infectious beat. Ever mindful of technological precautions, however, I tune in the Cooperative Guidance System to take my mind off the road. Inside, I'm rolling back to a stabler, happier world. Far, far away from the stark machine-efficiency and supertransience of the present day.

Meanwhile, the winter evening's spreading its pinions and the snow under foot and tyre no longer scurries, blows and lisps away. It's grey, gritty, cowardly and sloppy, keeping up the bluff of crumpy structural firmness but smashing to mush and water under the slightest rolling pressure. In the trees, however, something of the diabolism of this season persists against the anthracite hue of the sky and the evening's automatic mosaic of electric signals and illuminations. In the trees, the snow still glitters maliciously like teetering diamonds, just out of reach, thrown up there by passing billionaires to taunt the one-legged beggars, midget lepers and children with amputated arms who populate the paranoid scenarios of their dreams.

But what's worst about this hour of the day is the rear-lit 3D street-posters. You never spot them till they're right on top of you, then Bango! – some leering grocer is shoving ketchup in your face, or a ten-ton weight, demonstrating the virtues of Maxiglu, is hanging over your horripilating skull. At least in the car there's a little body-armour against it all.

I'm driving North now, home to Karl Marx-Hof, when I get stuck in rush-hour traffic behind a Gräf Steyr hopper-bus.

It's that hour of the day when just about everyone wears the same expression. A look of hacked-off weltschmerz which marks out the faces of those who've done an honest day's work.

The sky is all Sturm und Drang – very Viennese, in fact – though out to the West it starts getting Secessionist in its cultural leanings. I'm struck (buzzing down the window for a closer look) by an uncanny resemblance to Oskar Kokoschka's celebrated painting, 'Die Windsbraut'. Just to encourage me, the clouds do a little pas de deux and adopt for an instant the precise form of Kokoschka's two translucent lovers whose bark of anguished love is carried away on a wild tempest of Indigo, flecks of fire like Bengal lights, Payne's Gray, and that Brown Madder that's as sticky and coagulate as butcher's blood. I'm marvelling at nature's capacity to imitate art when at the precise point where the woman's head reposes on the man's shoulder in the canvas, the sky opens up like a wound and a shaft of dying Indian-Yellow sunlight slants across the sky, past the crenellated, turreted roof of the Gothic Rossauer barracks, and into the fogged windows of the Gräf Steyr bus, picking out – the anointing sword of God – one pure face from amongst the assorted bats, buzzards and jackals that are shipping themselves home.

Svetlana.

For the moment I just look at her, haloed in light through the condensed halitosis of humanity. She's around twenty and the daughter of my upstairs neighbour, Marta. Her face is a sunstruck planet, aureoled with the fur trimming of her hood. A little blonde spitcurl drops across her forehead above those Slav eyes, blue as swimming-pools. At that age, most physiognomies are out to lunch these days. The lights are off, the shutters are down. It's the modern world that's doing it. Compare the snapshots across three generations and there you have it. The long, slow pull-out of the armies of the mind, the neurone-spangled banner of the United States of Consciousness marching relentlessly over the horizon. But Svetlana's different. There's something about her that seizes you by the hair. She's already her history, hers and the history of her race. Under that simulacrum of young adulthood, there are runes chiselled into the warm white bones.

The car's bang up beside the bus now so I honk the horn. It makes me laugh when she jumps and that bovine look of passengers on public transport is blown away by a flash of human recognition. She gives a minimal wave, crooking her fingers in unison a couple of times, and alights at the next stop to join me in the car.

'Hi, Sharkey,' she says, clapping the door behind her. 'How goes?'

'Okay, thanks. You? Been to Uni?' (Svetlana studies electronics at the Technische Universität.)

'Not today. Just seeing friends, chilling out. Reading. Stuff like that.'

She has a slim print volume of Stefan Schweig's *Amok* in her mittened hands.

'You got the car back, then?' she says, suddenly noticing that she's sitting in it. 'I hope the mouse family hasn't moved out.'

'Ha ha, very funny . . . How's Mum? I haven't seen you for a fortnight, have I?'

Svetlana grabs a chamois and gives her side-window a swipe.

'She's all right,' she says, a hairline leak in her conviction. 'She was worried, though. She thought it was 'cos of us they did your car.'

'Crap. It was just kids.'

'She said they sprayed something about her on the bonnet.'

'They spray that kind of anti-foreigner thing everywhere. They don't even know what it means.'

This seems to pacify her and she smiles confidently across. It's kitsch, but I can't look at her without screening out the surroundings. I see a peasant girl, that blonde spitcurl, tending goats in a bright meadow, high in the Carpathian mountains where her mother's family comes from. A Slovakian Heidi. The father was an Austrian doctor who stuck the marriage for three years before breezing. Possibly because of racist taunts from his patients.

Marta, the mother, is one of the Fates – Atropos, to be precise. She spends her days stamping the word 'DECEASED' on patients' dossiers in the bowels of the Allgemeines Krankenhaus, the Vienna General Hospital. She is forty-three and came to Austria as an illegal immigrant in her teens, some years after Slovakia became an independent republic. Her marriage to the old doctor for whom she'd worked may not have lasted, but at least it gave her paper legitimacy. Unlike her daughter, who has sprouted under the abundance of food in Austria, Marta is short and squarely-built. But she too walks in the aura of that other land, a smell of hay, a softer music to the language and a gaze that's levelled higher, as if carrying with it the elevated, circumscribed perspectives of the Tatra and Carpathian mountains.

The traffic frees up at last, and the last leg, up Heiligenstädterstrasse, is nice and easy. Then before you know it, it's Karl Ehn's Workers' Paradise. The big fat peach-and-salmon fortress of Karl Marx-Hof, with its 1,200 metres of façade and 1,600 apartments. The Austro-Fascists had tried to smash it with their artillery way back in 1934, but there it stands in all its ideological pomp and glory, home to the neue Menschen of the Socialist future, the People's Palace. The back of the block has been covered with genetically engineered Virginia creeper that produces crops of beans and strawberries. But at the front there are spindly Martian effigies sculpted over bunker arches, tiny sun-shy workers' windows and – shooting up from the red turrets – the rods of bellicose steel flag-poles that skewer the clouds like kebabs, the naked standards of a disbanded legion. There it stands, the phalanx of a dead utopia. Home sweet home . . .

'Mum misses the Scrabble,' says Svetlana, as we pull up on to the concrete forecourt. 'Will you be seeing more of us now?'

I look around and take the precaution of backing into a streetlamped corner of the parkade, though owing to bureaucratic oversight or indifference there are no surveillance cameras around here.

'How about tomorrow? I really ought to get some work done in the morning, but perhaps we could go for a stroll after lunch. Will you see what she says?'

'Sure.' She wavers a moment. There's something else on her mind. 'Um, Sharkey – what's this?'

I lift up the object cradled in the palm of her hand. It's a little key-chain, with a hologram of what looks like an insect's head, with long antennae, two spherical eyes on stalks and a long, tapering proboscis. I've no idea where it comes from. Perhaps the mechanic left it behind.

'Where'd you find this?'

'Here, on the dashboard. What is it?'

'It's yours,' I say, and suddenly – I can't think why – the whole damn Detmers affair is flogging through my mind again. I look up, confused, but Svetlana's off, so I call after her. 'And tell Marta, will you – tell her I want to speak to her!'

'Urgent?' she queries, twirling the key-ring on its chain from her forefinger.

'Not really. I just want to talk.'

She stands there for a couple of heart-beats, beautiful and smiling. And – as the key-ring catches the last anger of the setting sun – the hologram iridesces into sudden, laser-bright rainbows, stabbing the eyes, like sunlight flaring on petrol in the puddles of a rainwashed town.

let the dead man talk

This is Marta's idea.

It's late Sunday and here we are in the Wiener Rathauskeller, of all places – Marta, Svetlana and I. I don't want to drink this damn beer, this Styrian Eggenberger Urbock, on a Sunday afternoon, but I'm doing it all the same. It's something to do with memory, Marta is telling me. A Proustian triumph over time.

This afternoon, the three of us went to the Museum of Austrian Baroque in the Lower Belvedere, the former state apartments of Prince Eugene. We visited the Hall of Mirrors and the Hall of Grotesques, full of Jonas Drentwett's paintings of fantastic, hybrid creatures from folklore and myth – hippogriffs, centaurs, chimeras, and sinister gold-crowned women with swans' necks, dragons' wings and talons, and the lower bodies of dogs. Then out into the palace gardens, where a fresh fall of snow overnight had encrusted the hedge gardens and alleys and statues. It sat like stiff white saddles on the backs of the lion-bodied, human-headed Sphinxes, with their breasts like giant door-bells and their Cobra headgear and their lazy, sightless eyes.

'Shut your eyes, Sharkey,' says Marta. 'Relax.'

I like her Slovak accent and her broken German, but the situation's making me self-conscious. There are only a half-dozen other people here and I can sense that waiter leaning against the door-jamb like a street-lout. He adjusts his dinky bow-tie and raises his eyebrows superciliously.

'Forget we are here. I want that you float now. Let your memories go back to Hamburg. Remember the little fellow who was with you.'

I'm beginning to wish I'd never mentioned Leo. Why is it that all East Europeans leap at the opportunity to practise a little amateur mesmerism, Tarot reading, pendulum prognosis or table-tapping? It's as if the real world of mesons, neutrons and quarks leaves something to be desired. I told Marta about Leo, our meeting and his death. I told her about Petra's certainty that Leo had confided his secrets to me. Now here she is in her new role, midwife to my memory. An hour ago I took a Mnemosyne, a memory-enhancing drug with mildly hallucinogenic side-effects that's normally prescribed for people with Alzheimer's. I must imagine that the Rathauskeller is the Paloma in Hamburg, Marta tells me. I must cast my prosaic mind adrift and allow the memories to arise like dolphins from their subliminal depths.

I must let the dead man talk.

I'm going to give up soon, because this is beyond me. 'We must recreate the circumstances,' says Marta. But the big cellar room of the Rathauskeller, carapaced like a Nissen hut, is nothing like the Paloma. And Marta and Svetlana are staring at me like punters watching a steeplechase. They want results. And that air they are playing, over the stereo, Strauss's 'Vienna Blood' waltz, swells graciously and twirls. It's like a sunlit curtain billowing at an open window, the sudden exaltation of a rush of memory, the steady throb of a great central artery. Stärkt Wiener Blut den Mut?: 'Does Vienna blood strengthen one's courage?' The music is Vienna itself. It's so hauntingly beautiful that I couldn't write a shopping list under such circumstances, let alone engage in astral projection. What's more, I'm cheating, but Marta can't tell. I'm screwing my eyes shut but they're just a tiny bit open – two sneaky little slits. Enough to see the big receding perspective of tables with their dunce-cap napkins. Enough to see the three rows of chandeliers, like UFOs in formation flight. Enough to take in the musty tunnel of the restaurant, impregnated with the pungent odour of malt and hops, travelling back to a vanishing point it never reaches because the whole thing stops abruptly at the flat half-moon of the far wall, like a bricked-off tunnel.

I open my eyes and give them the white-flag look.

'It's no good. I'm here with you, not there with him.'

Marta bites the end of her thumb and assesses the situation. 'We must start with what you do know. What do you remember that he did tell you?'

'This man was drunk, Marta, very drunk, and he had a bloody awful stutter. Added to which, I'd had a snoot-full myself. I remember he was telling me about his mother – or maybe it was his father – or his wife ... See? It's gone.'

Marta cranes back, waves a finger in the air and orders two more Seidls of beer.

'What are you trying to do to me? I've got to work tomorrow. So have you.'

Nevertheless, we dip our noses in the creamy froth, and it's then that Svetlana pulls that stunt of hers again. She has the key-ring with her, the one I gave her, and she's spinning it round like a propeller on her finger. It fascinates me. I reach out and grab it off her.

On the plastic thong is the hologram I glimpsed yesterday and it still looks like some magnified insect's head with antennae, eyes on stalks and a sharp, hollow proboscis. Strangely, it also makes me think of the 'Hostile Forces' section of Klimt's 'Beethoven Frieze' in the Secession building. But now I see that there are numbers and symbols on either side of the insect head. I feel as if I ought to know what it is, but I don't, so I hold it up so they both can see.

'Put me out of my misery,' I say. 'What is this. It's some kind of insect's head, right?' I point out the eyes and feelers.

Marta and Svetlana look at each other, surprised, and laugh. It's mother-and-daughter laughter, contrapuntal, a tone apart in pitch.

'What did they taught you at school in Austria?' asks Marta, grinning. 'These men, they know nothing!' she adds with a wink to

Svetlana. 'You make me laugh, Sharkey. Look. Not feelers. See? They are – how do you say?'

'Fallopian tubes?' said Svetlana.

'Right. And those eyes, they are ovaries. This is no insect! It is – what d'you say? – the cervix, the neck of the womb.'

I look again and clap a hand against my right cheek. Sure enough, the logo is a simplified diagram of the uterus, and the little symbols on either side are the sex symbols (the male arrow at one o'clock, the female cross at six) and beneath each, for a reason which escapes me, is the number twenty-three.

Marta flips the thong over and I read the address on the back. It's a key-ring advertising a private maternity clinic in the Mariahilf district of western Vienna.

And it is at this precise instant in time that something terrifying happens to my mind. It is not a dolphin but a whale, a great killer whale, that looms up through the waters of the unconscious and suddenly breaks the surface, its huge cetacean form wheeling up through the air in slow motion, blotting out the oceanic light. It is indescribable. And all at once I am a crazy man, white as a ghost, tapping madly at the little diagram on the key-ring. 'This is it!' I say. Marta and Svetlana are staring at me in alarm. 'This is it! Leo – the guy in Hamburg – when we were in the bar – this is what he drew! He drew it on a paper serviette. I remember, now. That son of a bitch was giving me a sex lesson!'

Nothing – not even 'Vienna Blood' – will stop me now. I shut my eyes, good and proper, and out of the inner darkness he comes. That fat little face, those baby-frank eyes, those sisal eyebrows.

'At last!' says Leo. 'What took you so long?'

'I had a block. I forgot.'

'How c-c-c-ould you! I told you it was important. This thing, it has changed my life. I'm not asking you to sympathise. I'm telling you because you're okay, I like you. And you're a journalist. You people look into these things. You'll get a prize for this one, believe me. You'll thank your lucky stars you met Leo Detmers!'

He burps with a force that surprises even him, opens his eyes wide like a goldfish and covers his mouth prudishly with his hand. A devilish little hiccup that sounds like corks being pulled out of bottles has got him in its grip.

'Oh no! Not now!' I find myself saying. I bring up my hand and smack him viciously across the face. He's flabbergasted and stares at me in disbelief. His cheek is burning like a brazier.

'I'm sorry,' I say, 'but I had to. I need you to concentrate. You must tell me again. I want to help, really I do.'

the principle of the thing

'You've g-g-g-got to understand the principle. It's the principle of the thing you've got to understand,' he's saying as he sketches the female genitalia on the napkin. 'You think there's only one way of doing it, right?' He makes a doughnut with the fingers of one hand and pokes the forefinger of the other hand in and out. There's a beery grin on his fat features and the double-glazing fitters are getting to work on his eyes. 'Sex, right? That's the traditional way. But there's more than one way now, see? Times have changed. You've got to stick in there with the Zeitgeist. There are sixteen ways of doing it now. They've reinvented sex. There's g-g-g-gamete intrafallopian transfer, there's zygote interfallopian transfer, there's tubal embryo transfer, partial zona d-dissection, microsurgical epididymal sperm aspiration . . . You – you do it one way, right? But *they* can do it any way they like!'

'*They*? Who are *they*?'

'The b-b-b-buggers in the clinics. This is what I've been telling you!' He pauses to lower the Hoover nozzle of his lips into the Krügel of beer and aspirate the head of froth that rears like a pastry crust out of the glass. Then he rocks back in his chair and opens his arms in an expansive gesture.

'Put yourself in my position. Father dead, right? And mother dying . . . I go to see her, and she's sitting up in b-bed. She's suddenly realised. She's realised there isn't much time. And she's got this thing on her mind, this thing she wants to tell me. She brings her head up close to mine and she says "Oh, Leo! Oh, Leo! I should've told you! All of these years, and I should've told you!" "Told me what?" I say. "About your father," she says. "What about my father?" I say. "He isn't," she says. "Isn't what?" I say. "He isn't your father!"' Leo snaps his fingers and grimaces wildly. 'Would you c-c-credit it? My father's *not* my father!'

I look blankly at him, trying to make sense of his ramblings. 'So who is?' I say. 'Who is your father?'

'The donor! Don't you see? Jesus! My mother was getting on in years when they had me. And my father – maybe there was a problem. Low sperm-count, that kind of thing. Okay, they can supercharge sperm by manipulating FPPs in the fluid – that's fertilisation-promoting p-peptides. But that d-d-doesn't always work. I know about all that kinda stuff now. Then again, if it wasn't low sperm-count maybe it was w-w-worse – Huntington's disease, or D-duchenne's muscular dystrophy. You know – they didn't want him to pass it on. Anyway, they went for IVF, *in vitro* fertilisation.'

'It's not uncommon.'

'No, of course not. It's common, I know. But somehow, for whatever reason, they didn't tell my father. He *thought* he was my father, see? He contributed the sperm for the IVF, but they didn't use his. And they didn't *tell* him.'

'Sounds unethical to me.'

'Me too. But what can you do? They've both passed on now. Nobody can prove it. Anyway, it must have been my mother who held back the information, mustn't it?'

'Your father's feelings were spared. Is that necessarily a bad thing?'

Leo waves the matter away pettishly with the plump fly-swatter of his hand. 'No. Not a bad thing. But what about me? How do you think I feel when she tells me this?'

'I imagine you're curious to know who your genetic father is.'

'Right!' he exclaims, banging his fist emphatically on the table. 'But they won't tell you, will they? It's in their f-f-fucking records, but they won't tell you. An adopted child has the right to know at a certain age, but not an IVF baby. It's confidential. Sperm donors are anonymous. Maybe these guys – the donors, I mean – maybe they don't want to be found out a quarter of a century on. See what I mean?'

I see what he means.

He winces slightly and reflects self-pityingly on his internal pain. With a ballpoint he's scoring over and over the diagram of the uterus until the tip nearly cuts through the paper. Then he brings his nose down to the paper and looks from it to the tip of the ballpoint. It's a pen he borrowed from me.

'What colour is this?' he says. 'It's not black. Is it red? Or green?'

'I don't know,' I confess, without giving the matter much thought. Pretty soon his mind ratchets back into gear.

'I don't like b-b-bureaucrats, Sharkey. Know what I mean? I don't like those guys with their r-red tape. And I'm pretty nifty, you know –' He drops the pen and waggles his fingers about, typing on an imaginary keyboard. 'I know my way around these systems.'

'From home, you mean?'

'Sure. From home. From anywhere. So, naturally, I decide to get round them. The f-f-fucking bureaucrats, see? I decide to nip in the back door.'

'You hacked into their records?'

He nods and gives a little conspiratorial wink. 'With a little help, yeah. That's what I did.'

'And you found out who your real father was?'

'No. They have codes. No names. Just codes. I found the code for the donor. The thing is,' he adds, looking nervously around, whispering now, 'I found out something else. Something they didn't want me to know.'

I wait while he guzzles his wheat beer. He smacks his lips and when he eructates again it's loud enough to offend the sensibilities of a number of hardened barflies in the vicinity.

'What did you find out?' I'm prompting hard, but he yaws and tacks in the mental wind. I sense a sizeable periphrasis approaching in the narration.

'It's the principle,' he mutters. 'It's the principle of the thing you've got to understand. Look,' he says, glancing up at me. He's grabbed another napkin and is drawing what looks like a petri dish with tadpoles of sperm wiggling around in it on one side and the eggs biding their time on the other. 'It's like cookery, really. They get the spermatazoa, right? But they have to get rid of the plasma. So a bit of dilution, then centrifugation. Thirty minutes in a culture of albumin and blood serum, then they rake off the little fellas and stock 'em in liquid azote. M-m-m-meanwhile, back at the ranch, someone's got to look after the eggs, haven't they? They use hormones to produce three or four oocytes, gather them up by coelioscopy, then incubate for four hours at thirty-seven degrees C. That's Oocyte I. It has forty-six chromosomes. Follow?'

My eye is cornered on my watch, but I nod nevertheless.

'Then the female egg, with twenty-three chromosomes, is produced from the primary oocyte by meiosis. Something like that, anyway. But the thing is, this is the m-m-m-moment they've been waiting for, see?'

'Who?'

'Who d'you think? The clinic buggers. Who d'you *think* I'm talking about?' His voice is plaintive, reproachful, but he quickly recovers and returns to his recipe. 'Anyway, in goes the sperm with *its* twenty-three chromosomes – still thirty-seven degrees – for six to twenty-four hours in a CO_2 incubator. Twenty-three chromosomes on each side – sperm and egg – and Bang! – together they come. A new human being!'

'I remember something of the sort from biology lessons,' I say. He's losing me and I can feel an all-engulfing yawn coming on.

'So what you've g-g-got now,' he continues tirelessly, 'is embryos! With me? The clinic buggers have done their job. That's when we come back here,' he says, jabbing the uterus with his pen. 'When the embryos are up to four or eight cells, they stick two or three back in. Either that or they freeze them . . . you know, for later use. They use a catheter, and put them here – into the – through the cervix and into the uterus.'

'Sweet mystery of life!' I murmur, elevating my eyebrows. The chaff and grain are posing a separation problem.

'Yes!' he says, nodding his head eagerly. 'It's child's-play. They do it all the time – with animals . . . with p-p-people . . .'

'So what's new?'

Leo knocks off half the Krügel in one massive gulp. When he opens his mouth again, his speech is beginning to diffract. Grammar, syntax and lexis are losing their battle against the copious dose of monatomic ethanol that's piping round his tubes.

'W-w-what I'm t-trying to t-tell you, Sharkey . . .'

He raises a finger to jab me in the chest, but I lean back as a precautionary measure and the finger lands in the ashtray.

'W-what I'm saying is . . . think of all the time . . . the time those b-b-buggers have got the sperm and the egg. Or the embryo, if you prefer. They can d-do what they like, can't they?'

He's rocking now like a ship's cat and trying to keep me in focus.

'That's w-what I'm saying . . . I got the codes off their f-f-fucking computer. I told you, d-didn't I? So okay, there was this d-donor. But the f-f-fucking egg was d-donated too! See? You . . . see what I m-mean?'

I look him over quizzically. He's tried my patience to the limit, but this time – second time round – I'm *listening*. I wasn't the first time, but this time, I'm keeping up – grabbing at his arguments on the wing, an infant snatching at hot-house butterflies with its bare hands.

'Okay,' he burbles, 'my father's not my father. But, f-f-fuck me, my f-f-fucking mother isn't my f-f-fucking mother either, see? Not even *she* knew that, d-d-did she?'

That first time, in Hamburg, I'd abandoned him by now. But this time, my second Mnemosyne chance, I push him further. I use my memorial privileges to the full.

'Surrogate motherhood,' I deduce, 'without consent?'

'Exactly!' He bangs his fist drunkenly on the table again and the ashtray jumps into the air, throwing its contents around into the sticky puddles of beer and attracting a cautionary glare from a bouncer-waiter. 'Changeling,' he murmurs bitterly, as an afterthought.

'I'm sorry?'

'That's their n-name for it. Changeling. For what they were d-doing.'

'Why?' I say. 'Why should anyone do that? You weren't claimed by your genetic parents subsequently. It doesn't make any sense. There's no logic in it.'

'But listen to me! L-listen! You think *that's* bad luck! There's w-w-worse . . . ! I'll show you, Sh-Sharkey. I'll show you on their computer. You wouldn't b-b-b-believe what those f-fucking clinic buggers get up to . . . Oh yeah, they have fancy w-words for it. Changeling. Safe. Winnow. Fancy words, Sharkey. But it's d-double-talk. You've g-got to ask yourself, what's behind the words. You've got to g-go . . . behind . . .'

Then suddenly the seance is over. The mental lights dim ghoulishly and his voice distorts into a horrific Donald Duck mockery of itself, a deep-sea diver on helium.

The roulette wheel of time tires and clacks to a halt.

It is too late.

From the Wiener Rathauskeller, from the living world, Strauss's 'Morning Paper Waltz' is drowning him out. His panic-stricken face has turned livid. His head rises like a hummingbird into mid-air. There's darkness all around, falling in swathes. Darkness like air that has become too heavy, too heavy to breathe. And with a noise like thrashing wings his sad, rattled features hurtle away from me and diminish in scale at a rate of knots until the head is a plum, a pea, a pin-prick, a scintilla of sickish light – and then nothing. Just a stuttering echo and the nauseating airborne memory of his sweet, beer-swamped breath. The merest afterwhiff of a close encounter.

I open my eyes and Marta and Svetlana are watching me with deep concentration. I feel suddenly cold and I bring the palms of my hands up to my cheeks to warm myself.

'Christ!' I say, with a tremor in my voice. 'Where was I?'

They say nothing but in their canny way they seem to know. They know that recollection is selective, ego-driven, but memory is indis-criminate. By instinct – with hints and prompts and dark suggestions – we follow it back, unforking its divagations, nearing the strong stem, till we reach the first utterance, the first term of its rhetorical development, the hidden radicle. I look down, and that little sigil of a uterine hologram is still glittering in my palm. There's something otherworldly about it, like a chunk of radioactive meteorite, a souvenir from space.

'Where *did* this come from?' I ask, hardly expecting an answer. 'Do either of you know?'

'Oh, Sharkey! *I* gave it to you,' says Marta. 'Dr Büchner, one of the visiting surgeons, gave it to me at the hospital.'

I return the key-ring to Svetlana and wipe the stinging pearls of sweat from my eyes.

'Are you sure you don't need it?' she asks in all earnestness.

'No thanks. Not now. I did need it, Svetlana, but it's served its purpose. I don't need it any more.'

chapter three

a very naughty boy

'Your husband,' I'm saying to Petra, 'was waltzing from the waist down.'

'It's what they say about the Viennese, isn't it?'

'Right. Stiff as a ramrod from the waist up, a picture of honesty and rectitude. Then down below, all the fancy footwork. Formality and exuberance, licence and constraint. In this city, we've been doing it for centuries. The guy who gets me is Felix Salten. Everyone knows he wrote *Bambi*. But who knows he also wrote *Josephine Mutenbacher* or *The Story of a Vienna Whore*? Do you know it?'

She shakes her head.

'It's a kind of female "autobiography" – sheer pornography. There's a moment in the film when Bambi turns round and says "Mother, what is vulgarity?" Well Salten sure as hell knew the answer to that question. Anyway, you get the drift. Round here, the right hand never knows what the left hand's doing.'

'Has Leo been a naughty boy?'

I'm sitting in Leo's office, in front of his lit-up GFP computer. Petra has just brought a tray of Pharisäer coffee in, chased by noggins of rum. She's sitting cross-legged on a Traditional Pod bean bag in the corner. Argos is on her lap, cocking his furry ears. He's pissed off because Nature has put human language just outside his reach. It's not fair. He can get the sounds, but the semantics elude him.

'He's been a *very* naughty boy. But it may not have been his fault.'

'How do you mean?'

'I believe it's customary to blame criminality on the extra "Y" chromosome.'

This afternoon, I've had the run of Leo's office and it's been quite a turn-up for the books. Appeasing the Cookie Monster was the first post, but the log-in – 'Odysseus' – was a piece of cake. Argos came in useful there. And for an hour now I've been skipping through Leo's files, a veritable black museum of moral turpitude to rival the Kriminalmuseum in Grosse Sperlgasse on the North bank of the Danube.

'I think you should tell me what he's done.'

I'm keeping my eye on Petra. I want to know if she's for real.

'See those numbers?' I say, pointing to column after column of digits on the screen. 'That's nothing to do with stockbroking. Those are access device encryptions. Mostly credit card numbers and telephone authorisation codes. Leo was a hacker. He traded in numbers. Maybe he got them from other hackers through bulletin boards or voice mailboxes, maybe he cracked into credit agency computers. But in my opinion those card numbers are all live.'

'Meaning?'

'They haven't been cancelled. They still have credit on them. MasterCard. Visa. American Express. Digicash. I figured as much when I saw these.' I indicate the ads for Undernet subscription chat-lines on the wall. 'A classic turn for petty criminals. When you get a new card number, the simplest way to find out if it's live is to swipe the number into the chat-line access gate. If it's accepted, you know you're in business. I did a feature on this trade in the *Wiener Tageszeitung* last year. It's possible to use the numbers to buy old-fashioned money orders and have them made payable to yourself, perhaps under a false identity. But that's risky. You need a dead-letter box. It's also small-time. You've seen these?'

I hold up a little black leather-bound notebook with ruled pages and a diary I found in Leo's drawer. If Petra's in on Leo's scam she's doing a good job of hiding it.

'I've seen them. Leo carried them round with him everywhere.'

'Hackers can never be sure if they're under surveillance or not. A raid can come any time. So they have to be prepared. This machine here,' I say, tapping a black box of tricks on the desktop with the pad of a forefinger, 'is degaussing equipment. A magnetic wiper for data-clips. It can spell the difference between ten years in jail and a non-trial. But Leo needed a hard-copy of his important numbers. That's what this little notebook is.'

I flip through the pages till I come to the one I want.

'What he's got here is connection numbers for TCP/IP networks, the type used by commercial carriers like Telenet and Sprint. They're numbers used for EFT – Electronic Fund Transfer between banks. As far as I can make out, Leo got hold of the address-codes of the BCE bank in France in this system. He found his way into the DECNET, a digital system linking computers. I'm assuming he was familiar with Triple MD5, the global algorithm standard that's used for data encryption and authentication. Next, he pinpointed one terminal whose job was to transfer funds and had a recce round its insides. Look.'

I click on a dollar icon on the screen and another sheaf of numbers and letters springs up.

'Leo created a capture file. His own computer was decanting the control sequences that were used by the French bank. Do you follow?'

She gives a so-so gesture with her hand.

'When they transfer funds, bank computers talk to each other to check each other out. They use a protocol called R. U. Sirius. The sending bank makes the transfer, then the destination bank repeats the transaction details and sends a Transaction Completed message together with its Federal Reserve or European Banking Consortium ID. Okay?'

I turn my attention to a plastic wallet file I was flipping through earlier.

'Exhibit B, here. Know what this is?'

She shakes her head, flinching at the wormwood taste of it all.

'Your husband had six bank accounts under six different identities. This one here, a numbered account at the Ernste Bank in Vienna, was opened a year ago. The others are in banks in the Czech Republic, Hungary, Italy, Switzerland and Germany and they were opened shortly after. One Austrian and five foreign accounts. Right? Now Leo turns his attention to the BCE computer that controls the EFT transfers. There's a neat little diagram here to show how it works.'

I hold the notebook open for her at Leo's organigram.

'We have dates here, and everything. On 8 May, Leo found an unused Telenet terminal and collected the BCE bank's transmissions on it. He returned the correct acknowledgements and IDs, so the BCE bank computer was happy. When he'd collected enough in a kind of limbo account, he turned off data-forwarding on the target computer and ordered the EFT machine to syphon the funds off into the Ernste Bank account. As far as Ernste Bank is concerned, it looks like a normal transmission because it comes through their own EFT computer. Next step.'

I hold up a little wad of counterfoils, neatly pinned together.

'Leo e-mails five withdrawal forms for 225,000 Euros to Ernste Bank, instructing them to send that sum to each of the foreign banks.'

'Why 225,000?'

Argos has given up on us and is resting his sleeping head on her knee.

'Easy. Because above that sum the authorities have to be notified. It's no longer considered a routine transfer. That's 1,125,000 Euros in one day, right? Well, according to his records Leo kept this up for four days, transferring a total of 4,500,000 Euros. Did Leo travel for business, Petra?'

'From time to time. Once a month he'd go for a day or two. Then at other times he'd be gone about a fortnight.'

'And how often? How often did he disappear for a fortnight?'

'Once a year. Sometimes twice.'

'When did he begin this travelling?'

'Three years ago, roughly.'

'Then we can be pretty sure that Leo's been screwing the banks for three years. The last one was BCE, but there were almost certainly others before that. Each time he must have opened a new Austrian or Swiss account and five new foreign accounts. I doubt very much whether he'd use the same six banks twice over. It's too risky. But take a look at the addresses of his five false-name accounts from the BCE job.'

I lay out the cards of the banks on the floor. Mühldorf in Germany. Znojmo in the Czech Republic. Sopron in Hungary. Brunico in Italy. Arosa in Switzerland.

'They're all on or near the border,' she says after a moment's perusal.

'Precisely. So when Leo disappeared for a fortnight this is what he was up to. Remember, each time he pulls this heist off he has 900,000 Euros in each bank. In-person withdrawals of over 150,000 attract attention. So what does he do? He gets in his car and drives from bank to bank, withdrawing just over 125,000 Euros from each – sometimes cash, but mostly digicash using swipe-cards. It's all down here in his little black book, though no mention, strangely, in his diary. Can I hang on to this?' I hold up the black notebook. She nods. 'He visits every bank in two days, then does the same tour the next two days, and so on for a fortnight. The Tour of Austria, seven times in a fortnight. That's about five hundred kilometres a day.'

'He was always shagged out after his business trips.'

'You surprise me. Mind you, he only had to do it once or twice a year, didn't he? For the big money, I mean. He evidently kept a trickle of cash coming in from the stolen credit card numbers too. Just for rainy days.'

'Jesus!' whispers Petra.

'Well, we live in an enterprise culture. All things told, he was quite an entrepreneur, your husband . . .'

It's all coming home to Petra now. She brings up her hands and clutches her dark hair as if she's going to tear it out in clumps. In the Encyclopaedia Universalis of Facial Expressions, hers is the one that goes by the name of Sheer Terror. I don't think I've ever seen anyone look so frightened, and suddenly – by Psychical Fear Transfer, no doubt – she's downloading her angst on to me. A frisson of panic climbs my back and the nape of the neck, then dances its macabre little Totentanz on my scalp with razor-tipped tap-shoes.

'What the fuck do we do now?' Her voice is small, bereft of its usual assurance. I'm not sure I like the plural pronoun but I let it pass.

'That's a very good question. I guess we could start by drinking this rum.'

'Your coffee's cold.'

'I drink too much of the stuff anyway. My birthday's a national holiday in Brazil. By the way, Petra . . .'

'Yes?'

'Just one more thing. Who or what is "Zak"?'

'I've no idea. Why?'

'It's in Leo's diary. Just about the only thing in his diary, in fact. Starting around February. Once a month or so he scribbles in a time and the word "Zak". It looks like a rendezvous of sorts. The Zaks get more frequent round September and October.'

She shrugs her shoulders and brings her hand up to her mouth, crenellating her thumb-nail with her front teeth.

There's something else I've spotted amongst Leo's incriminating papers but given Petra's state I decide to keep it under my hat. It's the bill for the meal we had together in the Cambodian restaurant in Hamburg, a meal I paid for. On the back of the bill, Leo has furtively scribbled a number which strikes me as rather familiar. It's a number I've seen around somewhere before, and this is hardly surprising. When it occurs to me where I've come across it, it only takes a second to check. It's the number embossed, *basso rilievo*, on my own Iridium MasterCard.

'Thanks, Leo,' I hiss between gritted teeth. 'Thanks a bunch.'

I can feel the weight of his little hobgoblin ectoplasm squatting on my shoulder and it whispers back beerily into my ear.

'Oh come on, Sharkey! Don't take it like that! After all, what are bosom friends for?'

taking the air

All at once Leo's hot little high-tech broom cupboard gets to me and I suggest we take some air. We go down the corridor and step out on to the terrace garden, overlooking the Kegelgasse. Eight floors down there's an argument going on between a cop and a tramp who'd been trying to bed down in the antique red English telephone-box outside the building. The tramp's chucking litter into an incinerator-bin and warming his hands when the gas jets trip in. From time to time he turns round to spit or bark insults. The café-owner comes out from under his awning and offers his perspective on the kiosk-occupation. There's a lot of gesticulating. It's not clear whose side he's on.

Petra's dressed lightly in one of those bell-tent cheesecloth frocks for mothers-to-be, tastefully rimmed with Juju burns. But she picks up a baggy cardigan on the way through and holds it round her. There's no snow today but the temperature's hovering around zero and amongst the potted conifers and empty terracotta vases on the terrace I spot a free-standing silver Deutz champagne bucket, loaded with ice-balls and a jeroboam on stand-by. It looks out of place. At the moment there doesn't seem much to celebrate.

I sit down on a white plastic sun-lounge and bring my knees up, hugging them to my chest. The sky's a crisp, untroubled manganese blue and all around us the frost-sharp rooftops of Vienna huddle together in cold storage. The air up here travels through you like a dose of salts. It takes your breath away.

'Sharkey,' she says, then hesitates. 'Is it Sharkey, or Mr Sharkey, or what?'

'Sharkey will do. I did have another name but I shelved it.'

'What shall we do, Sharkey? Should I ring the Polizei? Should I give Uscinski a call?'

'I don't know,' I say, in all honesty. 'I'd leave it a bit. We should try and get a bit further on our own. Uscinski's said to be a stickler for formalities. The minute we draw him in he's likely to block us out.'

'Out of what?'

'Exactly. We don't know yet. But tell me, Petra, just one thing – you knew nothing, right?'

'When we married, Leo worked for Creditanstalt as a broker. It wasn't his chosen career. In fact, he'd always wanted to be a pilot, but they wouldn't have him. Then three years ago he went freelance. He talked financial markets from time to time – CAC 40s, FTSEs, DAXes, GZ share indexes, Hang Seng, keeping up with the Dow Joneses, that sort of thing. But I never knew he was embezzling. We have a joint account and every month it's topped up, regular as clockwork, with our allowances. I didn't have any worries. I didn't ask any questions.'

'And what about you? What do you do?'

She seems surprised by the question.

'Me? Oh – things. I go shopping.'

'Shopping?'

'Yes,' she says, smiling with pride and some self-consciousness.

'Well, there are noble antecedents, I suppose. Julius Caesar, for one.'

'I'm sorry.'

'Oh, nothing. It's just a bumper sticker I saw. "I came, I saw, I did a little shopping."'

'I buy up second-hand books, posters, magazines – anything I can get my hands on. Then I bring them home and chop them up. I do collages. I'm following evening classes at the Academy of Fine Arts. I'm influenced by Duchamp, Arp and Picabia.'

'Oh.'

'I'll show you some time. I also do kind of solid collages. I get old boxes and trays from the Kunst und Antikmarkt and fill them up with things that look nice together. Bits of religious statue, old keys, maybe some sepia postcards stuck in the background. Then I hang them on the wall, the originals that is. If anyone wants to buy, I have stereolithographic copies made up in polymers.'

'Nice.'

'I call them Time Capsules. I'm supposed to be exhibiting at a place in Kärntner Strasse next year. Leo set it up for me. And, as you can see,' she adds, indicating the plants in the living-room, 'I wire up plants and trees to chlorophyll-active light and sound sensors so that the spiritual bodies of the dead beings that have been absorbed through the roots can send us signals or sing through the synthesisers.'

I nod broad-mindedly.

'And I play piano,' she adds, smiling.

Suddenly a white stork arises with a great commotion of wings from behind the gold ogee dome above and tacks out towards the Prater Park, trailing its long legs behind it.

'What's he doing?' she asks. 'It's unusual to see them in winter, and it's rare to see them here. They're common round the River March.' Her voice catches emotionally at the oddity of the sighting.

I'm about to make a cheap riposte that's not unrelated to Petra's condition when a sharp recollection of my decent upbringing gets the better of me. I turn, instead, to other pending matters.

'Know anyone who drives a red BMW Z10 A-range?'

'No,' she answers, raising her already-raised eyebrows – from Decorated to Perpendicular Gothic arches – at the *non sequitur*.

'Did you know Leo carried something called a Harvest Contract card?'

'A what?'

'A card that authorises use of his body parts in return for payment to next of kin.'

'I've never heard of such a thing.'

'You'll hear of it again soon enough. Leo left himself to science on that condition. I take it they let you see his body after the accident?' I add, mentally covering other eventualities.

'I saw him all right,' she replies. Her voice is sad and cold. 'I saw him in the Donaufeld Clinic. Eine schöne Leiche, a beautiful corpse.'

She intercepts my questioning look.

'He was dead,' she confirms with some irritation, 'if that's what you're trying to get me to say.' She pouts a little, turns away and then pinches her cheeks against the cold, colouring them up like the cheeks on dolls. She does this with little finger-pecking motions as if plucking banjo-strings, pizzicato.

A thought crosses my mind. 'He never used a soul catcher, did he? Before he died?'

'A what?'

'A kind of questionaire-based personality download. You know the thing. 3D bodyscan for a physical image, voice storage, then keying in memories, behaviour patterns, likes and dislikes. A ghost Leo in the machine. A lot of people do that these days. It's not real immortality, of course. Just an illusion of being around after death, to console those left behind. A lot of widows and widowers have soul-catcher agent programs.'

'You've seen my agent program. It's a woman. Leo didn't go in for that afterlife stuff. Anyway, I suppose we're closer to knowing who did it,' she says after a while.

'Did what?'

'Killed him. If he was ripping all these people off, one of them must've had enough of it.'

'I doubt it. On the contrary, Leo seems to have got away with everything. Look at it logically, anyway. He had two kinds of victim. Private individuals and their credit cards, for one. Now these people wouldn't lose out. The credit agencies all insist on insurance these days, so the card holders never pay for theft. As for the agencies, they actually budget for a wide margin of losses through fraud. And in either case, who's going to kill someone for embezzlement from corporate funds? If someone nicked your credit card would you hire a hit-man to get him?'

She huffs, taking the question as a slight to her intelligence.

'By the way,' I say, to make amends, 'I do have some news for you. I remembered.'

'What? What did you remember?'

'I remembered some of what Leo was telling me in Hamburg. The stuff that was supposed to be so important.'

Now she's interested. She comes over and sits on the edge of my sun-lounge. She crosses her long goose-pimpled legs and hooks her left foot behind the right ankle. She's tense with curiosity. She looks into my eyes with unblinking expectation.

'Leo didn't tell me anything about what we've just discovered,' I begin. 'It was another matter that was preying on his mind. All evening long, in Hamburg, he was bending my ears back with a lecture on *in vitro* fertilisation.'

'Oh God!' exclaims Petra, puffing her cheeks and collapsing them. An exasperated aerosol of vapour jets into the icy air.

'You know something about this?'

'I know *something* about it, yes. What did he tell you?'

'He told me that on her death-bed his mother revealed that his father was not his father. They used DI, donor insemination. I gather his father never knew this, though apparently they did tell the mother. It's not uncommon. Eighty-five per cent of DI couples don't tell their children.'

'That's right. It cut him up badly when he found out. Leo loved genealogy. He was an only child. That may have had something to do with it. Over the years, he'd drawn up a family tree of the Detmers clan, and t   Wärndorfer clan on his mother's side. When he found out his g etic father was an anonymous donor, it scuppered all his fancy di rams. He was devastated. It seemed to split him up. Between his mi d feelings for his dead adoptive father and his curiosity about the o er one. Who knows, perhaps the other guy was still alive.'

'   rhaps. Did he contact the clinic where he was conceived?'

' es. That's what he told me. They checked on their files and   ified the mother's story. From what he was saying, they were very elpful there. For medical reasons they hadn't been able to use the sperm of Detmers senior, and the mother had agreed to donor sperm. Leo told me the clinic people must have assumed she would tell her husband, and then she never did. See?'

'That figures.'

'But of course when it came to identifying the donor for Leo, they couldn't. They were bound to confidentiality. It's the law, apparently. After all, the donors need protection. They might find themselves, years hence, being sued for non-fulfilment of paternal obligations by their own offspring.'

'Or they might enter into litigation themselves with the nominal parents, if they have regrets and decide to assert their genetic parenthood.'

'Quite. It's logical, in a way, the anonymity thing. But at the same time I knew how Leo felt. As far as he was concerned, his father was out there somewhere. He got manic about it. Sometimes we'd just be sitting in a café and he'd see a guy in his forties or fifties nearby. He'd grow convinced there was a family resemblance. But there wasn't much he could do. You can hardly go up to a complete stranger and say "Excuse me, but did you by any chance jerk yourself off into a specimen bottle at the Hofburg Maternity Clinic twenty-five years ago?".'

'So what did Leo do?'

'Nothing. He dropped the thing.'

There's a pause that's almost long enough to merit the epithet 'awkward'.

'How do you know?' I ask.

'He told me. He said that was that. There was nothing more he could do. He was a practical man, and he was just going to get back to business and leave the matter there.'

This time we're out of the awkward pause category. It's more of a communications breakdown, in fact, and it's long enough for Petra to look around fearfully. She senses we're heading for radio-silence.

'Was he lying?' she asks suddenly.

'I'm afraid so. You told me last time we met that Leo stopped taking you into his confidence. Things started getting difficult between you. Did this coincide with the time he was contacting the Clinic?'

'More or less,' she admits, puckering her brow as she back-somersaults through time. 'What exactly did he tell you?'

'I think you've got to bear in mind Leo's psychology. Leo was a hacker, right? A data traveller, if you prefer. People like that don't take kindly to coming up against bureaucratic brick walls. Almost by definition, hackers thrive on freedom of information and if they don't get what they want by legal means they resort to sabotage and stealth. And if you think about it, this one doesn't really represent much of a challenge, does it? I mean, a man who can wander at will through high-security international banking systems isn't going to have much difficulty consulting the computer files of a low-tech maternity clinic, is he?'

'Is that what he told you? He accessed the Hofburg clinic's files?'

'Yes. He didn't find the name of his genetic father, but he found a code relating to the sperm donation. He also discovered that the eggs that were used for the *in vitro* fertilisation were not his mother's. They came from a female donor. According to him, nobody had known this.

Not even his mother. Except of course now she *wasn't* his mother. She was just an incubator. He found out, in effect, that he had no genetic relation whatsoever with the people he called father and mother.'

Petra gives a long diminuendo whistle.

'Leo, Leo, Leo . . .' she murmurs disbelievingly. 'Why didn't you tell me?' Then she looks up at me sharply. 'But why? Why should the clinic carry on like that – so secretively?'

'That's what Leo wanted to know. But it's not certain they did. They were simply acting within the law. If his father never knew about the sperm-donation that could've been at the mother's instigation as we said. She may well have known about the egg donation too and decided not to reveal it. Her death-bed confession, to put it another way, was a half-truth. She couldn't bear to tell him she was not his mother.'

'What else did he tell you? Is that the lot?'

'That's all I recall. Oh yeah – Changeling, Safe and Winnow. Do those words mean anything to you?'

She shakes her head.

'I reckon there was more, but he never delivered. He was lit up to the gills. And what bothers me is there's nothing in his office. He's left enough paper evidence of his bank deals in that black notebook to clock up several life-sentences in the Sin Bin. But there's not a trace of his investigations into the Hofburg Clinic. In fact he seems to have covered his tracks. A packet of pages has been torn out of the back of the notebook. There's no way of telling, but that could've been it. Nothing on the hard disk. Nothing on any of the data-clips.'

'If there was more,' says Petra slowly, 'the only place he could've got that information was the Hofburg archives.'

'That's right.'

'So if we want to know what Leo knew, we have to go there too,' she states blandly.

'Right again. But how? When I did my feature on data-crime, a hacker put me through the paces. They use what are called War-Diallers to get access codes. They're electronic boxes that run through hundreds of multi-digit calling permutations until they hit on the right access code. Leo's got one in there,' I add, thumbing back in the direction of his office. 'But don't ask me how to use it.'

Petra stands up and extracts a Juju from the pack in her cardigan pocket. She's smiling in an odd sardonic way to herself.

'Have I inadvertently said something amusing?' I ask.

'Uh? Oh no – not you! I'm thinking of Leo, something he used to say. "Petra," he'd say, "there's no point in being devious in life. If you want to know something, just go straight to the person who knows it and ask. Puff yourself up, put a bit of authority into your voice, and ask your question. You should never underestimate the essential helpfulness of the human species."'

'Not bad for a maxim.' For the first time today I'm getting the feeling that Petra and I are homing in syntonically on the same wavelength.

'He had a name for it. He called it "social engineering".' She grins with malice aforethought, then looks at the tube of Indian hemp in her hand as if someone else had put it there, scrunches it up and throws it aside.

'I like the sound of that too,' I say, watching her. 'Shall we give it a spin?'

social engineering

We go back indoors, sliding the plate-glass window behind us.

'From the living-room or Leo's office?' asks Petra.

'The office. It looks better. We'll need some things. Got any blue overalls?'

'Sure. I use them for painting.'

'Get them. And a pair of headphones, a telephone handset. Oh, and a screwdriver. That should do the trick.'

She comes back with the gear and I slip into the overalls, drape the headphones round my neck and rough up my hair. Something's missing – identification. I pick up a telephone unit and I'm in luck. On the base there's a big round Telekom sticker with prominent logo, a pass certificate in fact. I peel it off and transfer it carefully to my lapel.

'How do I look?'

'You look the part.'

In Leo's office, I train the miniature camera on top of the screen upon myself and do a spot-check. It's quite convincing. The tools, electronic gimcracks, wires and stuff in the background. And me there centre-screen, clutching a phone and screwdriver. I warn Petra to keep out of shot. We do a find on the Hofburg Clinic and the computer calls up their exchange.

'Hofburg Maternity Clinic, can I help you?' says the girl. It's a lukewarm blonde. She's plucking hairs off her forearm with electric depilatory tweezers.

'I'd like to speak to your data manager, please.'

She glances up listlessly at my image on her screen, then taps me through. A large matronly woman with bobbed hair and a masculine voice appears. She's obviously a formidable creature. She makes me think of battleships with names like *Doughty*, *Stalwart*, *Dauntless* and *Invincible*.

'Yes?' she queries gruffly, thrusting her nose towards the camera.

'Hello, this is Josef at Telekom.' I'm trying hard with the accent. I speak the way I think people think telephone engineers speak. 'We're fixing the lines in your district. Have you been having problems with your computers?'

There's a moment's hesitation, then a wavelet of relief travels over her hard features. 'Oh, yes. Yes – we have.'

'I thought so. We'll be needing to check the line, in that case. Can you start up your system and run me through it? What's the dial-up?'

'It's 678 666 543.'

'And the log-in or password?'

Now I'm pushing my luck. I see her baulk, remembering whatever book of rules she's swallowed and preparing to regurgitate it and throw it at me. She's just limbering up mentally, her lips parting for the sally, when I beat her to it.

'Oh look, it doesn't matter. I don't really need it. I'll just stay on for a few minutes and check the connections. If you like, I'll buzz you back when I'm through and let you know where we are. What's your name, love?'

'Elsa – Elsa Moser.' She's smiling vaguely. Perhaps it's not every day that a man asks her name. At any rate, she's becalmed. The wind knocked clean out of her sails.

'Thank you, Elsa.'

The smile broadens and the cheek pixels darken up a couple of tones.

'That's all right, Josef,' she parries. 'Sit tight. I'll put on the system. You've noted the dial-up?'

'I have. See you soon.'

The screen fizzes over, traversed by a couple of lightning-bolts of static. Then a big full-colour logo comes up. To my surprise it's the same uterine emblem that appeared on the key-ring. In a moment it has gone to be replaced by a menu and winking log-in.

Petra breaks her silence. She pushes the black cascading hair out of her eyes. She laughs through her nose.

'Thank you, Elsa!' she mimics. 'You've got a nerve! Did you see her blush! And what would you have done if she'd said there was nothing wrong with the computers?'

'I don't know. It was a gamble, but not such a big one. These days there's always something wrong with any system.'

Petra nips into the corridor and fetches a wicker stool for herself. I get rid of the clobber – the headphones, phone and screwdriver – and clear the decks. Looking at the screen, we both realise just how far we've got.

'No log-in, though!' she notices. 'What now?'

'I admit it's not very promising. We can try a bit of imaginative war-dialling – thinking up possibilities relating to obstetrics.'

'Words like Nativity, or Childbirth, or Gooseberry-Bush?'

I key the first one in, but a few gloomy chords from Gounod's *Faust* chime up along with an error-message:

THIS LOG-IN IS INCORRECT.
YOU MAY MAKE TWO FURTHER ATTEMPTS.
IF, ON THE THIRD ATTEMPT, THE LOG-IN IS INCORRECT,
DATA-PATROL SECURITY SYSTEMS WILL BE ALERTED.

'Shit,' says Petra.

'Two goes. Well, there is one possibility. These small-business systems generally have what they call a de-bug port. When the computer's delivered it has a default log-in. In seven out of ten cases the people receiving the system never change it. It's useful for computer engineers. A kind of deliberate back-door to facilitate testing.'

'Fine, but what's the default log-in?'

'There are five or six common ones. "Test" for example.'

I type the word in and the error-message leaps up again. One go left.

'Write the others on a piece of paper,' says Petra.

I jot them down and she picks up a pen and circles it over the list with her eyes closed. She jabs it down suddenly on one of the log-ins.

' "Sysmaint",' she says. 'Meaning?'

'Systems Maintenance.'

I type it in, press Enter, and for one hollow, heart-thwopping second the screen blanks out. Then in next to no time there's a VR Welcome Mat up there and we're moving through a swish hospital corridor with doors on either side. 'When you get the service you require, please say Knock-Knock!' says a disembodied speech-generator on the Agent Program.

I knock-knock at 'IVF' and we pass into the electronic ecosystem, a little waiting-room with an aspidistra, some homely copies of *Profil* and *Kurier* on the coffee-table and a mini-skirted cartoon nurse with blimps for tits rises with vamp-like animation to greet us. She ushers us around, presenting a number of other doors, and I rap at 'Records'.

'What was his mother's name, her Christian name?'

'Gertrud.'

Under Search-by-Name, I call her up from a quarter of a century ago. The data-sheet scrolls out neatly on to the screen and my eye travels across it, arriving, ultimately, at the ineffable moment of Leo Detmers' birth. We knock out a hard copy from the print-slot at the base of the screen.

Hofburg Maternity Clinic, 112 Löwelstrasse
Fertilisation / Embryology Dept.

Assisted Conception Program

Patient: DETMERS Gertrud, née Wärndorfer
Place of Birth: Vienna
Date of Birth: 05.03.62
Entry date: 02.07.2001 / file transfer from Donaufeld:
                  no previous pregnancies/terminations

Spouse: DETMERS Hermann
Place of Birth: Vienna
Date of Birth: 06.04.55

Haematology: sample taken, 02.07.2001
Blood count: leucocytes (by mm^3) 4,200; red corpuscles (by mm^3) 4,150,000; haemoglobin (g/100ml) 12.50; hematocrite (%) 37.00; average count volume (in u3) 89; TCMH (picog) 30.12; CCMH (%) 33.78.
Leucocyte formula: polynuclear neutrophiles (%) 47; polynuclear eosinophiles (%) 3; polynuclear basophiles (%) 3; lymphocytes (%) 34; monocytes (%) 16.
Blood platelets: 193,000 per mm^3.
Speed of sedimentation: first hour (mm) 35; second hour (mm) 74.
Immunological Tests: rubella serodiagnosis, 105 UK/mL; toxoplasmosis serodiagnosis: immunoglobin G, 50 UI/mL; immunoglobin M, 0; serology of HIV1 & HIV2 infections: search negative.

Salpingitis: slight trace infection. Under surveillance.

Hünnertest: evidence of asthenospermia & oligospermia – confirmed.

Ovulation Cycle: periodic irregularity, type DF307

History – Consultant: Emil Fischer

05.09.2001	IVF Consent – Dual Donor (Primogen recommendation, after gen-diagnostic on spermatazoa/ oocyte & DNA-sampling of couple): SS15698-B/157 ES27372-B/231
06.10.2001	4 embryo culture, SS15698/ES27372
07.10.2001	Primogen: genetic diagnosis, histology & DNA-typing
11.10.2001	2-embryo transfer (2 frozen, LN Bank 543) *double pregnancy selectively reduced to one (potassium cyanide – administered EF) No complications – but foetal haemoglobin recognition reveals G6PD deficiency
10.07.2002	b. Leo Detmers, 2.5 kg, male; Jettmar Ward, Hofburg
12.08.2002	File Transfer Request granted: Reprotech, Donaufeld#

Attn. Security Clearance Red

There's no doubt about it. Here's the source of Leo's troubles. I glance at the wall of his office where the formula SS15698-B/157 + ES27372-B/231 = ??????? has been scrawled. Scrawled with such mad energy, I might add, that you don't need diplomas in graphology to diagnose Leo's state of mind.

'What do you think?' I ask. 'Any good at interpreting this?'

'I've been through most of these tests myself recently,' she says, stroking her swollen belly unconsciously. 'It seems to bear out what Leo said. Both Gertrud and Hermann had problems that might have made conception difficult. If there were any risks of inherited disorders – Tay-Sachs disease, sickle-cell anaemia, cystic fibrosis, that sort of thing – then there's no sign of them here.'

'Can't they stimulate sperm and egg production in cases of poor fertility?'

'For the man, yes, I think so. Leo told me about it. They manipulate something called FPPs in the semen.'

'Yeah, Leo told me that too.'

'As for the woman, they use hormones. Pergonal and Metradin. So I've been told. They get the Pergonal from the piss of menopausal Italian nuns. Would you believe it? But you'd have to get a doctor to look this over if you wanted to know whether the problem lay there. On the other hand, maybe there isn't enough information.'

'It seems to me that the decision for egg and sperm donors to be used was taken outside the Hofburg Maternity. Any idea what Primogen is?'

'No.'

'You're not having yours through the Hofburg Maternity, are you?' I ask. It's crossing my mind that Petra might be taking this badly.

'No. Mariahilf. The other side of town. I was born at the Hofburg, though.'

I speed-read the file again.

'What's all this about Security Clearance Red at the bottom? It seems that in August 2002 her file was transferred. To a place called Reprotech in Burgenland.'

Petra shrugs.

'Poor old Leo,' she says, half to herself.

'Don't look at it that way.'

'I can't help it. I mean, using a sperm donor's a kind of technological adultery, isn't it? But when the egg is donored as well it's turning so-called parents into living orphanages.'

'Leo was lucky to be alive, as we all are, Petra. Admittedly it was a doctor at Hofburg who decided which bit of semen should go with which egg. Not Mother Nature, elective affinities, or whatever. There was a degree of calculation in it. But in terms of modern eugenics that should've made him a healthier individual.'

Petra looks at me with ill-concealed surprise. It's as if soap bubbles are coming out of my mouth rather than words. 'He was a boozehound and a druggie. Those are supposed to be genetically acquired characteristics, aren't they? If they'd been doing the job conscienti-ously they'd have snipped that bit out of the germline.'

'Well, we don't know what the results of the DNA diagnostic were, do we? They're not on this file. Apparently that was done by a party called Primogen. But if you notice, the pregnancy was selectively reduced. Leo was lucky there too. He could've been the embryo that was killed off.'

Again Petra gives me a look that feels like a pit-stop IQ-check. 'That's not what I call lucky,' she says drily. 'If the other embryo had survived and not Leo, then we'd be saying how lucky the other person was. Or two other people might be saying how lucky they were. That's not luck. That's just the labyrinth of chance.'

She's right and I admit as much by my stand-corrected silence. Argos noses open the door and spots me. Somewhere in his tiny brain he ticks me off the list of reluctant volunteers he's phlebotomised and turns his attention to Petra, licking the skin-salt from the cracks between her fingers.

'He's hungry,' she says. 'I'll just go and feed him.'

She's gone. I sit staring vacuously at Gertrud Detmers' file for several minutes. I'm having trouble coordinating my thoughts. The more I look at the medicalese, the more I sense that something is wrong. It's a gut-reaction. My knowledge of biology stops at Hochschule and there's nothing in the file, as such, to merit appre-hension. Yet there's something Petra said just a few seconds ago. What was it now? 'I was born at the Hofburg.' I quickly page Petra on the living-room Plasmascreen and she appears in front of me, looking up from Argos's gnawed and lived-in dog-basket.

'You said you were born at the Hofburg Clinic, Petra. While I'm here, I might as well look you up too. What was your mother's name?'

'Alma Olbrich . . . Oh stop it, Argos! Wait till I've emptied the can, you dumb mutt!'

I key back to the archives, call up Alma Olbrich and print. Petra, I see, was born a year after Leo. Another only child, though the mother had had one pregnancy termination in the year 2000. To my layman's eye, there are no abnormalities in the tests run on her parents, Alma and Werner, yet here they are, in IVF. My professional curiosity bristles. Then suddenly it catches my eye. Even before I have time to assimilate the information I feel in my bones what it is, and Leo's words in the Paloma come back to me, his drunken, slurred, stammered exclamation: 'But listen to me! L-listen! You think *that*'s bad luck! There's w-w-worse . . . !' He was right, there's no doubt about that – and he'd made this connection too. All at once I'm in a flat spin. I clench my fists tight to stabilise my nerves as I read through the deadly little snippet of text again:

07.10.2002 IVF Consent – Dual Donor (Primogen recommendation)
        SS15698–B/157 // ES27372-B/231. LN Bank 543. Frozen embryo
        culture
        SS15698/ES27372.

It's hardly necessary, but I check and double-check the numbers against Gertrud Detmers' records. My eyes zigzag back and forth. My brain whirls. Then I flop heavily against the sprung back of Leo's swivel-chair. I'm in a cold sweat.

SS15698/ES27372

The code burns itself on to my retina like a cattle-brand.

Under my wrists, set into the work-desk, there's a half-opened drawer and I happen to look in it again. Beside a stay-fresh polythene wallet of blue Whizz-Bang pills and a Five-seveN pistol with a round of loose ammo and shoulder-holster, I spot Leo's false passports. They're snapped together with a rubber band, and I take them out, one by one. I flick them open between trembling fingers. In the Czech passport he's wearing a little Far West string-tie with a buffalo thong and a gormless smile. In the Italian passport, a bow tie and one raised eyebrow, for all the world like the novelist Robert Musil. In the Swiss, he's open-necked and tweedy. Despite the corpulence, he's sucking his cheeks in and making a passable impression of gaunt asceticism, the Ludwig Wittgenstein look: 'Whereof one cannot speak, thereof one must be silent'. I throw them down in despair and they fan out mathematically across the work-desk.

Whatever you think of him, he was quite a guy, our Leo – the late, departed Leo. And if anyone deserves a place in the *Who's Who* of international malefactors, it's him. The Man of 1,001 Faces. Flamboyant dypsomaniac. Furtive pill-popper. Highwayman on the information freeway, a master of defalcations. Armchair bank-robber and murder victim. And to top it all, I'm thinking – staring at the two print-outs till I nearly go boss-eyed – he went and married his own sister.

SS15698/ES27372

Same sperm. Same egg. Same embryo culture.

All part of life's rich pattern, eh Leo?

Suddenly, I'm getting that stop-the-world-I-wanna-throw-up feeling.

The screen starts frying over again then briskly clarifies into Petra draped across the leopard-print *chaise-longue* in the living-room. She's turned on the sound-and-light boxes wired to her rubber plants and they're all singing their vegetable hearts out like baby Stockhausens in the background. Meanwhile, she conducts the random cacophony with her lacquered index fingers. Argos squats on her portable tumulus and licks her nose appreciatively.

'Well?' she says. She dodges his tongue and looks up at me seriously. 'What's up, Doc?'

chapter four

ill tidings

I call up Elsa Moser again for propriety's sake and give her computer system a clean bill of health before slipping out of the denim overalls and back into character. Then I make my way slowly down the corridor to the living-room to break the bizarre ill tidings. The elderly President Schwarzenegger's right-angled jaw fills the wallscreen. He's pronouncing sententiously on the extremist independence movement in Italy's Alto Adige province that wants to be reunified with the South Tirol. And when he's finished, there's a yellow-peril bulletin. For the third year running, the Chinese GDP has outgunned the US, the European Confederation and the ruined fragments of the CIS. This is followed by more paper tigers, more great leaps backward. Plus, of course, the week's big story. The Sozialistische Partei and the Volkspartei getting their teeth into the militant neo-fascists affiliated to the World Union of National Socialists, and vice-versa.

Petra has sensed that trouble's in the air. The plants have been unplugged, the dog has ducked for cover in his basket and she's sitting on the *chaise-longue* like the schoolgirl she once must have been, waiting outside the Direktorin's study. Her knees are knocked together. Her heels are clumsily splayed. She nibbles the parma-violet nail varnish with her front teeth. I hand over the two print-outs of the medical records and leave her to compute. It's not a happy moment. I stand with my back to her at the terrace window, watching an Apache AH–68 helicopter hovering in a stationary trance like a dragonfly over a brooding lily pond. When I turn back her eyes are bright and wet and her lower lip is moving as if in prayer. There's something iconic in her posture, like a Pietà, that moves me physically and emotionally towards her. I sit beside her and rest one limp arm round her shoulders. With my free hand I pile back the thick tumbling hair from her forehead unthinkingly. Her pale northern eyes are downcast. But, riding the bad weather, the dark bows of her eyebrows overarch her misery, ciphers for sustaining powers of mind. Then all at once they too subside. She speaks in a small, choked whisper. 'Leo was my brother?'

I nod.

She wants to speak, but can't. Her vulnerable gaze questions me telepathically.

'I don't know. I don't know how this could've happened. I've heard of near-misses in the States, where children from the same donor-sperm have nearly married in small towns. What's incredible here is that Leo was not a half-brother. He was your brother, period.'

In her confusion she's trying to make sense of this. She's not alone.

'Never, never, never did my mother say anything about IVF, Sharkey. That's what gets me. She never said anything about IVF. I swear to God. I was brought up without subterfuge in the clear and simple knowledge that my parents *were* my parents. I suppose they could've had IVF without donors of any sort, couldn't they?'

'Quite possible. Especially at the turn of the millennium. That's when pollution and other factors were beginning to affect fertility rates seriously.'

'But they didn't even mention that. I can't believe they've been hiding this from me all these years.'

'And then we'd be assuming that your parents donated egg *and* sperm to Leo's parents.' I shake my head. 'Crazy. It doesn't add up. Where are they now?'

'In Graz. Dad retired early from Siemens-Nixdorf and they're both in a Longevity Centre.'

'You've got to see them. At least call them. You've got to speak to them about this.'

She bites her lower lip hard, leaving two white indents. Her silence stands in for assent.

For my own part, I'm astonished at the lack of superficial resemblance between Petra and Leo, and I tell her so. 'You look more like *her* than him,' I say, pointing to the computagraphic agent on the wallscreen.

'It's true. But come to think of it, we had little things in common, Leo and I. We had moles in the same place. And we both had ear-lobes that attach to the jowl low down. They don't curve up, like most people's do.'

I remember the little shared behavioural characteristics I spotted when I first met Petra which reminded me of Leo, those analogies I read as the mimeticism of couples. They are now taking on a distinctly genetic colouring.

'But what about within your own family? There couldn't have been any physical resemblance between yourself and either of your parents.'

'Well, we're all tall and dark. Not unusual in Austria. Mum used to say I was the spitting image of her grandfather. A throwback. But maybe that was just wishful thinking.'

'It seems to me,' I say after some reflection, 'there are two things to sort out here. First, you must speak to your mother. You must find out if she knows what happened in that clinic in 2002. Was she aware of what was going on or not? If she wasn't, then something very irregular was afoot. If she was, you've got to make her speak. Even if it means raking up the past. Even if it means opening old wounds. Then there's another question. You and Leo were both conceived from the same embryo culture. In your case, and perhaps in his, from frozen embryos several months or even years old. Later in life, you met and married. Now was this accident, or was there some purpose – some design – in it?'

There's physical pain in her eyes. She twists one fist into the palm of the other hand, cup and ball fashion, in a determined, grinding motion.

'It must've been accident, Sharkey. I told you. Our mothers met at the Hofburg nursery school. It's part of the same foundation as the clinic where we were both born. The coincidence isn't as wild as all that. If anything, there's a kind of blind logic to it. Alternatively, perhaps my parents were doing his parents some kind of weird favour. But as you say, that's crazy. As far as I know they weren't even acquainted earlier, when we were conceived.'

She looks out of the window at the Vienna skyline and when she speaks it's as if she's addressing the rooftops.

'Do you suppose . . . do you suppose there's something that draws brother and sister together, Sharkey? Some instinctive, filial thing that we mistook for love. For marital love?'

'I'm sure that you loved him, Petra.'

'So am I. But what *kind* of love? Was it the wrong kind?'

'You're taking us back to Apartment 6, Berggasse 19. Back to Freud's couch, Petra. We know that there's such a thing as the incest taboo. And taboos operate when the thing being forbidden *is* extremely attractive. The question is, can the family attraction be felt at an instinctive, intuitive level? Between two people, like yourself and Leo, who don't realise they're brother and sister. Perhaps it can. After all, there was an especially strong attraction between you two. In myth, at any rate, Jocasta and Oedipus were deeply attracted to each other before they found out they were mother and son.'

'And what happened then?' she asks. 'What did they do when they found out?'

It's a good question, but now is perhaps not the moment to answer it. I guard my tongue, but discretion has never been my strong point. My attention's fixed again on Petra's full womb. Before I can help myself I've spoken out of turn. 'You're carrying his child,' I say. I say it as much to myself as to her, but this hardly matters. She has heard. I hate myself, suddenly, for the pointed accuracy of the observation, the unspoken deduction it leaves in its wake. But no sooner does this happen than I'm baffled again. Petra's expression clears. Her eyes are limpid. And when she speaks it's with lapidary weight and clarity.

'It's not his. It's not Leo's.'

I sit back on the *chaise-longue* and stare at her.

'Don't you see? Leo found out a year ago what we've found out today. That's precisely when things stopped between us. Physically, I mean. He went to his whores. I knew about that. And last March, I was so full of hate, of spite towards him, that I let myself go. I had a fling.'

'An affair?'

'A fling. Not an affair. One night.'

'Who with?'

'A guy. I don't even know his name. He sold U-bahn tickets from one of those Tabak-Trafik kiosks. I used to talk to him on the way to the Academy. I've never seen him since. I changed my route.' She pauses and brings out a scrunched up handkerchief from her pocket, inadvertently knocking the packet of Cannaboids on to the floor where it tips open, spilling on to the parquet. 'I was angry with Leo. I didn't know why. I didn't know why he no longer wanted me. Why he became hard. I couldn't have known, could I? I couldn't have known what he knew. I wanted to hurt him like he'd hurt me. It worked. When Leo found out I was pregnant it really got to him. And now – God, Sharkey, I feel like shit now. Leo did love me really, didn't he?

He was protecting me from what he knew.'

'I guess he was. I guess that was what he was doing. It's what a brother would do, isn't it?'

'A fling. And now this – a child! It's dreadful. Do you think I'm very bad?' There's a brutal honesty to the question. She's not fishing for sympathy.

'No, I don't. All things considered, I think adultery was probably the most conventional aspect of your marriage with Leo.'

A thought occurs to me – a presentiment, a warning.

'Have you told them at the Mariahilf Clinic? Have you told them that Leo's not the father?'

'No. I couldn't bring myself to do it.'

'Don't.'

'Why not?'

'Just don't, Petra. You're in a lot of trouble. This fling, as you call it – it could have bad consequences for you. The Polizei have you under suspicion. The insurance company are looking for any excuse not to pay up. So just keep this to yourself. Don't tell them a thing. You need that money. For you and your child. When's it due, by the way?'

'What? When's what due?' she asks innocently, confusing subjects.

'The child, Petra.'

'Three weeks or so.'

'Then believe me – you must look after yourself. Don't let them know a thing.'

There are tears trapped in her eyelashes like raindrops on a spider's web. She wipes herself roughly with the handkerchief then reaches out and holds me tight by the hand. Her eyes are full of trust. She firms up her lower lip into the recovery of a smile. The gesture – the look – print themselves indelibly on my emotions, a moral and sentimental commitment that bypasses the precautionary checks of rationality.

'You're right, Sharkey. Thank you. I don't know what to say.'

'Don't say a thing. You've said enough. There are too many damn questions flying around as it is.'

'Yes,' she replies, 'like "Who killed Leo?"'

'Like "Who killed Leo?",' I repeat with some deliberation. 'And "Why?".'

between the lies

The job of a newspaper, to paraphrase someone or other, is to say 'Vice-Chancellor Bahr is Dead' to people who never knew Vice-Chancellor Bahr was alive. It's a device that can't tell the difference between a bicycle accident and the collapse of a civilisation. But people continue to read between the lies on the age-old principle that, if nothing else, believing what you read in the papers makes them – and life – more interesting. And what is the journalist's role in all this? To stroke platitudes till they purr like epigrams. To plagiarise like mad. To curry favour. To stay in work, whatever the cost. That, at least, is how it sometimes seems to me on my numerous off-days and days off. Ours, however, is a profession that lies in wait and, from time to time, brilliantly justifies its existence. Yes, that's what we keep telling ourselves . . .

I joined the *Wiener Tageszeitung* ten years ago as a stringer. It's one of the two or three more liberal papers in Austria, though the proprietor – the German press baron, Heinrich Möll – has been known to let his personal right-wing opinions get the better of him. As an inveterate smoker of Cuban half-coronas, though, he unconsciously subsidises the world's last *pochette* of Marxist-Leninist beatitude. It's said that, in his monthly meetings with the editor, whenever he manipulates a cigar-cutter in the form of the French guillotine and simultaneously mentions a journalist from his stable by name, the juxtaposition of name and gesture does not go unnoticed.

The editor, Alfred Dehmel, is a Triton among the minnows. He's a laconic fifty-year-old with a large, ugly head and rangy body. His gangling limbs and loose articulations are those of an unwieldy school-boy, trapped in a perpetual hormone explosion of adolescence. It's the kind of body on which clothes will always look like drapes and dust-covers, worn for concealment rather than style. He has what people call an Extraordinary Brain. Ferocious in logic. Commodious in memory. Infallible in hunches. And grotesquely downsized in the emotion department.

The paper operates from a functional high-rise block in the 5th Bezirk. My office is on the 39th floor.

I started 'Sharkey's Day', my daily column, half a dozen years ago. Now – apart from the occasional feature – it's my sole money-spinner, syndicated in abridged form to weeklies in Linz and Salzburg. On most days I write up at home and e-mail before midday for the next morning's issue, often drawing on a pool of pre-drafted all-purpose material, tightly shoehorned behind a topical leader. I break up my 2,000 words into four or five soundbites, each in a different typeface, and strike a range of registers: informed tittle-tattle, the earnest apostrophe, the vitriolic vignette, the strange-but-true human anecdote, and so on. Anything pompous and power-seeking is fair game. In my mind's eye, 'Sharkey's Day' is like one of those little volcanic atolls that pokes its head out of the sea in the Caribbean. It's utterly arid and infertile until birds start landing and shitting on it, and then – wonder of wonders – as the weeks and months go by, exotic flora begins to flourish from the impacted guano.

The column appears on the top of page four, accompanied by an ink portrait of its author that makes him look like an investigative sleuth of the first water. There he is, complete with pencil stub behind the ear and semi-translucent sun-visor, *à la* Citizen Kane, an accoutrement he has never possessed and never desired to possess. None the less, there must be some passing resemblance. I'm regularly spotted in the street and harangued for my forked and scurrilous tongue. The Viennese are human haystacks, stuffed into shirts, and I'm the guy who puts the needles in the haystacks. There it is, a little prick, niggling away at each of them every time they move. How they'd love to find it and bend it in two. Even Dehmel only tolerates me on the vague principle that the paper should have one airheaded jackass to cock a satirical snook at the bourgeois moguls of orthodox taste. Put another way, if Vienna's the oyster, I'm the lemon. At the *Zeitung*, I'm a tiny concession to frivolity and radicalism in a world of monumental gravity. Rumour has it, however, that the arm-rests of Dehmel's swivel-throne conceal miniaturised smart Scud-D missile launchers. And it hasn't escaped my attention that, during our Wednesday editorial meetings, those deadly little rests often point at me. So far he hasn't fired, but maybe he's just waiting for Karoshi to get the better of me, that fashionable Japanese malady of death through overwork.

Come Wednesdays, we meet in Dehmel's pentagonal war-office on the 25th floor. It's decked out with posters and memorable front pages in clip-frames. In pride of place is a huge mural depicting a vulture tearing voraciously at a lump of carrion in the shape of our dear homeland. The vulture bears a striking resemblance to the long-since-ex-President, Dr Kurt Waldheim. Hanging on a noose strung up to the ceiling rose is the Archduchess Barbie doll. It's modelled on Sissy, the wife of Emperor Franz Josef, and togged out in white silk dress and tiara, produced in the good old 90s in collaboration with Archduke Markus von Habsburg-Lothringen and the American toy company Mattel. She's hand-in-hand with a homemade Klaus Barbie doll and together they flourish a miniature bottle of vintage antifreeze wine. Cast around in odd corners of the room are other such two-edged reminders of the glory that was Austria. Dehmel takes a mischievous delight in the national 'Leichte Begeisterungsfähigeit', our infinite capacity for self-deception. His *tour de force* is the vocal message that keeps you on hold when you phone in to the paper. It's the message of peace that, somewhere out in space, is still being broadcast by the American spacecraft Voyager One, for the benefit of any extra-terrestrials who happen to tune in. It was recorded by the then Secretary-General of the United Nations – dear old Kurt Waldheim again, Austria's favourite ex-Nazi. It's a pity, says Dehmel, that the Salonikan Jews who finished their days in Auschwitz are not around to hear it.

Once everyone has arrived, about twenty in number, Dehmel slopes lankily in, closely followed by his fetching, Junoesque secretary. The night editor dubs her Dangerous Curves. She's good for Dehmel's self-esteem. With her in tow, he feels like 007.

Dehmel has a stiff neck. In order to pan around the assembly he swings his knees from left to right in the swivel-throne. To add to his charms, he looks as if he were born without a mouth and, noticing the oversight, an obstetrician had promptly set things to right with a brisk slash of a carpenter's knife. When the slit eventually opens, the voice that emanates is astonishing. It's everything a man could wish his voice to be. Rich. Charming. Mellifluous. Witty. It's the one thing he has to be vain about and, in consequence, he has no video-port on his Bip-Bip. Women burn for him, just for the voice. It's also a voice that delivers the goods, CIF, from cerebral warehouse to recipient lug-hole. No damage, leakage or loss. When Lutine Bells ring, it's rarely his fault.

'As you're all aware,' he begins, 'in a month's time we're starting a Friday colour supplement which will also be available to News-Web subscribers. Ernst, here, is running the show, and we want a strong first issue. He and I have decided on the line-up, more or less. The first number will be a stock-take of some of the flashpoints in the modern world. We're getting the guys from the CSCE Conflict Prevention Centre in Vienna to steer us around. Islamic fundamentalism's for a later number. For the moment, we want pieces on the border conflicts in Belarus and the Ukraine, the Macedonian independence problem, and the Moldovan movement for reunion with Romania. We'll also be looking at Hungarian minority problems in Transylvania and ethnic disputes in Armenia and Azerbaijan. I believe you're taking on those last subjects, Markus?'

Markus – shock-haired, eyebrows like swallows' nests – puckers his lips and nods gravely.

'Make sure you get something on the Armenian Secret Army for the Liberation of Armenia. You know they have cells in Austria, and it'd be a real coup if we could find someone to speak on their behalf. I want the whole thing to take a long hard look at the European Confederation too. We're twenty-seven members now, and the cracks are showing. On a more domestic issue, Peter, you're doing the Dollfuss article, I think? For those of you who're not up-to-date on this one, we want to put it direct to Chancellor Flöge why nowhere in Austria is there a monument or square in honour of the Austro-fascist leader Engelbert Dollfuss, the only Austrian politician who gave his life defying the Nazis in the failed Nazi putsch of '34.'

'You mean the little geezer who teamed up with Mussolini? The one they called Millimetternich because he was so short,' interrupts Lederer, a young rock journalist in glasses with diamond-studded frames. They allegedly once belonged to a now-forgotten rock star called Elton. 'Don't you think that's a bit *vieux jeu*?'

'No, I don't,' snaps Dehmel. 'Take a trip out to the Mauthausen camp some day, Lederer. Austria had a Jewish population of 200,000 in 1938. Today it's just a handful, no more than 5,000. As Simon Wiesenthal pointed out, Austria was only eight per cent of Hitler's Reich but Austrian Nazis were responsible for fifty per cent of the murders of Jews. Hitler, Eichmann, Kaltenbrunner, Globocnik, Amon Goeth – Austrians, to a man.

'And incidentally, that brings me on to Festung Europa and their successor-in-waiting, Neues Östmark. We're hanging fire here. As you all know, the Polizei got Festung's top dog Werckel not long ago and it looks as if the charges are going to stick. Which means he'll be going away on holiday for a while. It also means that Festung could soon be old hat, meaning mass defections to Neues Östmark. We're keeping this one on the back-burner to see what happens, but if any of you have leads, follow them up and keep Rudolf Dreiser informed. I want him to build a profile on this. What else is there?'

He spins brusquely towards Dangerous Curves, forcing her to take avoiding action. She's been caught this way once too often. One scratch from the footplate of the swivel-throne and there go those Wolford stockings – laddered again.

'Environment,' she says, holding the vocal minute-taker to her lips.

'Oh yes. I want someone to go to Copsa Mica in Romania. Someone with strong lungs. This is an old one but it's still hot. Lead, cadmium and sulphur dioxide fallout over 180,000 hectares. No one's got anywhere nearer clearing it up. We'll take a look at Bohemia and Upper Silesia too. We've got info coming from AFP on the chemical-plant fire in Zambia. On the home front, we're still up against photochemical smog in Vienna and Salzburg. More than the con-vection towers can cope with. And nitrate and phosphate pollution in the Danube. At the last count the Biochemical Oxygen Demand level was eight milligrammes per litre. Again, we want reactions from Flöge. We also want to know where the hell this snow comes from, don't we?'

There's a concerted nodding of heads.

'What is this? Another Ice Age? Just when my melanoma and cataracts were getting along nicely. Berta – get on to the Met people, plus that Chaos theorist at the University if he hasn't fractalised into one of his own Mandelstam blots. Any *good* news, Alma?'

He swings round recklessly towards the secretary. There's a flash of irritation in her eyes, but her voice is level.

'New Year's Concert with the Vienna Philharmonic. *Die Fledermaus* at the State Opera. Mid-January Mozart week in Salzburg.'

'Well yes, of course. The usual New Year merry-go-round. Spice it up a bit, will you Kraus? This is tourist-page stuff, but stick it all under one leader. That Lippizaner stallion at the Spanish Riding School who failed the dope test, okay? See if there was any money dancing on him.'

Dehmel consults the Bip-Bip Networker on the arm-rest, then spins that death-dealing part of his furniture towards me.

'Sharkey – that story of yours about the guy from the Atomic Research Authority. According to you, he was driving drunk down the Landstrasse Gürtel at two in the morning. A cop stopped him and asked him to identify himself. He looked in the rear-view mirror and said "That's me".'

There's a hyena chorus of sniggering paparazzi.

'Is it true?' he asks.

'It's on good authority.'

'What does that mean?'

'A woman I know. A radio-operator with the traffic police. She picked it up off the air.'

'Well get better authority in future, will you? We've had a complaint from the ARA. You had the decency not to name him, but they all knew who he was over there. It seems he's a quondam director of a nuclear power plant in Belorussia. This is not the kind of story that makes the atomic boys look good. You know me, I don't care about that. But I do care if they sue. This also applies to your piece on the garage mechanics. We've had two unions blanket-bombing the mailbox. Be nice to me, Sharkey. Please.'

'Sure. Sorry folks.'

'I think it's Musil who says that in youth the urge to shine is stronger than the urge to see by the light one has. I'd like you to remember these words.'

'I'll do my best. In fact, to take up your point about getting the info right, I'm working on something and I need a researcher for a day or two. Can we spare one?'

'Have you finished with Beate, Peter? Well in that case, take her, Sharkey. Legit' purposes only.'

The meeting closes. Dangerous Curves signs off into her gadget and leaps aside as the footplate slices round like a rotating knife. I go down a floor and see Beate Kaminer.

Beate's the soulful type, around twenty-six. She lives off bags of cashew nuts, aspartam-rich spearmint gum and Herkner Mineralwasser. It's the only water she'll drink. The other brands, she claims, are calorific. She's pale and beautiful in a wasted, waif-like way. She has an ironical drawl that makes me think of Dorothy Parker, though I've no idea what the doyenne of the Algonquin's Vicious Circle sounded like. It's a drawl that makes commonplaces come out burnished and brassy. She's also a damn good researcher, the paper's best. I give her three names on a slip of paper: 'Hofburg Maternity Clinic – Primogen – Reprotech.'

'Find out what you can, will you Beate?'

'What do you want exactly? Can we get a bit more specific?'

'Anything legal. Company structure, how they're related, finance. Try Kompass online, McCarthy Information, Who Owns Whom, Dunsprint, *FT* Mergers & Acquisitions, Austrian Company Index, Exstat. You know the databases I mean. Get me names, addresses, auditors, SEC code, financial history, company activities – the lot.'

'Hofburg Maternity . . .' she muses, pulling a stringy hammock of gum out of her mouth between thumb and forefinger. 'Is this a midwife-mixed-the-babies story?'

'Not this time. Oh, there was one other thing – the name of someone who knows their way round biotech issues. The best in the business, while you're at it. If possible, someone we've dealt with before.'

'Whatever you say.' She removes the gum and wraps it in the little rectangle of foil, then wanders off down the corridor, whistling lazily to herself.

It's a good ten minutes before I realise what she was whistling. A jazz number that goes 'Is you is, or is you ain't, my baby?' Marilyn Moore, if I'm not mistaken. But that's Beate. She drops little mind-bombs as she passes, each tailed with a slow cordite fuse.

residential complex xi

I'm stuck in the office all day, editing down last week's columns to one for syndication, liaising with Jürgen the cartoonist and vaguely wishing I'd been a pastry-cook on the grounds that Sachertorte is a damn fine anti-depressant. So by the time I get out and into the Puch Gringolet, night has fallen with a leaden thump and it turns out I've only got one headlamp. Even that would raise a scornful laugh from the average Wienerwald glow-worm. After counting the remaining points on my driver's licence, I take it slowly round the Ringstrasse. A spot of Mahler's *Des Knaben Wunderhorn* in my ears helps steady the nerves and keep the mind focused on the great eternities.

On Währingerstrasse the shops are open late. They cast a golden light outwards, resplendent with the ritzy highlights of their chic wares, the cornucopia of their lavish window displays. All at once, behind me, there's the phut-phut of a dirty exhaust and Petra burns past on the Panther with Argos in the basket. His ears are buckled back in the slipstream like the leather flaps of an aviator's helmet. The bike pulls in at a branch of Zum Schwarzen Kameel, the wine and food store, but I decide not to stop. There's a Polizei wagon on my tail and I don't want to look like I'm volunteering to be hauled in. Just as I'm thinking this, though, the strip of fairy-lights on the roof twinkles on and the siren kicks into action. The van pulls out, rocking its suspension sideways. Then it skews off into the distance on the wrong side of the road. It's not long before another cop-bucket joins it. Then another, and another. And soon I cease to be paranoid about my cyclopean headlamp. They're in one hell of a hurry, and some of the vans are marked Gendarmerieeinsatzkommando: Cobra Unit – the anti-terrorist squad.

And now a funny thing happens. There's a dizzy rush of adrenaline to my head. I'd wonder what was going on if the symptoms weren't depressingly familiar. Professional deformation. My presshound blood is up. With a weary sigh I step on the pedal and try to hold my distance behind the Wild West posse of strobing lights and wailing sirens. They roar and ululate down the bank of the Danube canal, then sharp right and across the river into the working-class suburb of Floridsdorf.

At the outer limit of the Wasserpark, against the bombazine darkness of the night, a stick of brutally flashing light waves with sudden aggression in front of my windscreen. I pull up hard. The brakes lock and the car squeals to a halt. It's a traffic cop with a lumino-kinetic night stick. There are tubular steel barriers everywhere and fluorescent incident tape has been hastily festooned across the road. Beyond him I see wire-grilled personnel carriers, water-cannon and massed troops in visored helmets, flak jackets and full riot-gear in the middle distance.

'Where are you heading?' asks the cop suspiciously.

'Home – to Donaufeld,' I lie. I'm not sure whether to flash the presscard. It could do more harm than good.

'You'll have to double back and go over the Brigittenauer bridge. This area's cordoned off.'

'Why? What's going on?'

'Just some kids. High spirits. We'll soon be out of here. Oh, and Sir

– one other thing . . .'

'Yes?'

'Get that headlamp fixed.'

I double back but, once out of the vivarium-blue wash of the street-lamps, I kill the lights and bump up over the kerb. The Gringolet rolls to a standstill under a tree and I slip back to the scene of the action on foot, under cover of darkness. There's a boating lake here, I remember, and it looms up beside me. A shimmering black expanse of water. It's just visible over to the right, under the thin shadow of the Donauturm viewing tower, a hypodermic against the sky. Then, on the far bank of the lake, a recreation ground and a bland stretch of wasteland. That's where most of the vehicles seem to be massed. Here, on the cold turf, the snow has held its crystalline grip. It crunches and squeaks underfoot like polystyrene as I skirt the bank of the water.

The riot boys are ranged up with their backs to me. Big starburst arc-lights sweep across an isolated building over three hundred metres away. It's a block I've been to before. I wrote up its inauguration three years ago. An Ausländerwohnheim. A rough-and-ready dormitory for foreign workers, mostly Slovenes, Hungarians, Bosnian Muslims and Croats. They're not asylum seekers, as such. Just young men and women allowed over on fixed-term contracts to do dirty work that no native Austrian feels inclined to do. Here, from the six-storey Residential Complex XI, most of the workers are bussed out to Friedensreich Hundertwasser's plasma incineration plant at Spittelau. The plant's a devil's kitchen of hellfire and brimstone. A nightmare megapolis where thousands of tons of domestic waste are burned twenty-four hours a day in various processing units under the 100-metre-high golden globe of a central enamel-tiled control tower. The dross and débris of Vienna, combusted into the black banderole of an eternally smoking flame.

One of the Robocops turns around. He spots me and breaks away from the rank and file. I watch as he draws an Air Taser from his belt of weaponry. Air Tasers are nasty things. They're compressed air cylinders that launch two wired probes towards their target. The probes attach themselves like plant-burrs to clothing and discharge a tiny T-wave electric pulse that jams brain messages and scrambles the neuromuscular system. Result: total breakdown of co-ordination. I'm a talkative fellow. I like to have a chance to explain myself before being reduced to a gibbering wreck. So I raise my hands and shout 'Press!' He won't put the Taser away until he's had a good look at my pass, though. He checks the mugshot with the considerably paler realworld version he sees before him. Under the helmet and reflective visor there's not much one can see of him other than a jaw like a pit-bull terrier which opens to reveal broken and badly-capped teeth. A cemetery of vandalised headstones.

'Over there,' he says, indicating a white vortex of light beyond a paramilitary vehicle. 'Your people are over there. They're interviewing Reinhardt, the Interior Minister.'

'Thanks. What's the problem, exactly?'

'Kein Problem, kein Problem. Just a bunch of neos.'

'What?'

'Skins and neo-Nazis. A few kids who've had too much to drink. They always take it out on the Pollacken and Fidschis. Citizens' Initiative. That's what they call it.'

As he speaks, the sound of breaking glass reaches our ears. That, and a medley of cries. 'Fuck off, Muslim dogs!' 'Foreigners Out!' 'Heil Hitler!' Incongruously, there's a mobile Worstelstande, a sausage-stall, doing brisk business behind the riot trucks. A number of Polizei are queuing up for einmal Heisse Wurst mit Senf, hot sausage with mustard. I approach the food-stall and, from its side, observe the spectacle. The Workers' Complex is surrounded by a milling throng of skinheads. A hundred and fifty, at a guess. They're in regulation collarless black flight jackets and stonewashed jeans. One swings a three-quarter size white baseball bat around his head like a mace. From a high, roaring bonfire, a few pyros lift blazing firebrands. The more exotic louts masquerade as caped crusaders, wrapped in huge Third Reich flags. The capes are attached at the neck and flow behind with folksy romanticism when the stiff night breeze rises to the occasion. From time to time there's an abortive attempt to remember the words of the 'Horst Wessel Lied'. When it breaks up, the group's unanimity splinters into insults, yelps, pogo-jumps and a frenzy of saluting and sloganeering.

'It's amazing, isn't it?' says one riot-cop in the queue. 'The one thing that sells really well in the sports shops in Vienna is baseball bats. But no one plays fucking baseball! Well they don't, do they?!'

I move away from the hungry laughter that follows and towards the outside-broadcast TV crew. Reinhardt's getting a quick primp and preen from the cosmetics girl, a pom-pom of blusher in her hand. Sitting cross-legged behind him on the bonnet of an armoured personnel carrier is Uscinski in full Polizei regalia. He's wearing dress uniform, with chevrons at the collar, double helpings of gold braid on the epaulettes and a smart piece of headgear from which a Networker eye-piece hinges down above a pea-sized mike. He's eyeballing something off the viewfinder and firing rapid instructions into the mike. 'Z-Squad, pincer round by the Old Danube and the railway line. Low profile. This is blue alert, so don't get panicky. Nothing's happened yet. I want Cobra Unit and a Press Focus Group to cover the Floridsdorfer Aupark exits. Arm up for rubber bullets and gas. No maverick action please. No heroics. Await further orders. Your playtime will come.' Beside him, leaning nonchalantly on the radiator, is another cop. It's a man in his mid-twenties with, on his shoulder, the insignia of the Bundesgrenzschutz. The BGS is Federal police, responsible to the interior minister. Their task is to control the Republic's external borders. There's something swannily effeminate about this character. He's tall and feckless in appearance. Bony, drawing-room features and an imperturbable, sardonic smile. His hands are long and tapering. And, while he idles, he winds an elastic band round a couple of fingers with an adroit little motion. When he raises the fingers, the elastic magically jumps on to the two adjoining fingers. It's a party trick which he's got off pat. A trick-turned-tic, performed for nobody's benefit and which even he doesn't bother to observe. Uscinski, meanwhile, is still reading data off his head-up display. He pauses then rattles instructions into his mike. Suddenly the ear-phone on his digital helmet screeches electronically. With a strangled 'Shit!' he knocks his headgear off and I glimpse the mass of Tetra digital circuitry under the rim.

'What's up?' says Reinhardt, centring the knot of his Kettner tie.

'The little fuckers are jamming our frequencies,' curses Uscinski. 'Excuse the language, Minister.' Without the helmet, he looks a tad less grand. He has cropped ginger hair, a red puffy face and a king-size misshapen hooter that looks like it was bashed into being by some half-blind three-year-old retard out of Play-Doh. Beside him, Reinhardt's a matinée idol. Soft, photogenic skin, like good-quality maroquinerie. Those *éminence grise* eyes, that white patrician hair. And a high, domed forehead, the cupola of a mental observatory, that hints suavely at the capaciousness and breadth of his ministerial thoughts.

lights, action

A workhorse shoulder-camera nuzzles in. A technician in the background checks the connections on the dish. Lights, action. The interviewer speaks to camera then turns to Reinhardt.

'Could you tell us what's happening, Minister?'

Reinhardt coughs lightly into his clenched fist. 'Well, as you can see for yourself, the foreigners' Residential Complex is under siege.'

'By neo-fascists?'

'Um, yes – radical nationalists of some description.'

'Festung Europa?'

'Do we have any information, Chefinspektor?' says Reinhardt, turning to Uscinski.

'Neos,' says Uscinski briefly. 'Opposed to foreignisation. We don't know what their affiliations are exactly, but we will do by this evening when they're cooling their heels in the cells.'

Reinhardt smiles serenely.

'Are they armed?' asks the interviewer.

'I'm informed they have baseball bats, knuckle-dusters, gas pistols, switchblades and something fancy called Ninja Stars. An unpleasant variation on the Frisbee, apparently.'

'No fire-arms?'

'Not that we know.'

'And what action's being taken?'

'We don't as yet know whether there are any Gastarbeiter in the Complex. We're waiting for news from the Spitellau incinerator where they work to see how many are on shift. Once we've got an idea how many are being besieged the Cobra Unit will work out which gameplan to follow.'

'Couldn't you move in now? The situation seems serious.'

We all instinctively turn to look in the distance. A firebrand is thrown in through a ground-floor window. At the top-floor there's some movement. Silhouettes edge against the brickwork. People looking down. A hand waves in a lie-low gesture. A dark shape, a piece of furniture perhaps, is shunted across a room.

'Only material damage so far, I believe,' says Reinhardt. Uscinski nods in confirmation. 'When we go, it'll be brisk and clean. We don't want to provoke a pitched street battle.'

'This is the tenth such bombing this year, Minister. The consensus of opinion is that Festung Europa and possibly Neues Östmark high-command these attacks. The ultra-right seems to be going from strength to strength in France, Germany, Italy, the United States and many of the former communist states. Do you see them ever achieving executive political power?'

Reinhardt eases gently into his well-rehearsed discourse. 'I think we should get things into perspective. What we're seeing is nothing new. Ethnic tension has been rife for over a century, since the dismantlement of the German, Habsburg, Russian and Ottoman empires. A lot of those misguided hot-heads over there are actually expressing real frustrations that we on the conservative right feel too. They want discipline, security, full employment. They're actually sick of drugs, the sex industry, crime and over-liberal immigration policies. Their belief in nationhood – in descent, language, customs, history – these are things we want to encourage. Since the Tokyo earthquake and the world recession that ensued, we know that economic health depends on building strength from within, rather than relying on foreign investment. But a homogeneous ethnic nation-state is not achieved by attacking foreigners who're here with legitimate papers. Nothing's solved by this kind of Ausländerfeindlichkeit.' He uses the more acceptable, bureaucratic word for 'racism'. 'We need Lebensraum, and we need more restrictive citizenship laws. Most of us are agreed on that. But within the context of a free-market democracy. Through negotiation and debate in the Federal Assembly, not random acts of mindless violence.'

'So the political ultra-nationalists have no future in your opinion?'

'No. They can't have. Not in their present form. For the simple reason that the ultra-right doesn't serve business interests. Nationalist ideologies are based on ethnicity, notions of mystical destiny and Volksgemeinschaft. They're opposed to capitalism as a Jewish-inspired system with a technology and profit culture that clashes with nationalist ethics. In terms of modern market economics, these idealists are antagonistic to denationalisation because it sells off state property to private – and often foreign – investors. It undermines the centralised, *dirigiste* and ethnically purified state they desire. At least in the European Confederation, free movement of peoples and information and liberal privatisation policies are the way forward. At the same time, our democratic parties have to define the limits to multi-ethnicity. I, personally, am not opposed to the idea of an ancestry pass, or something along those lines. We also need to channel the national pride of those young people out there into constructive, wealth-creating projects.'

'The so-called neos,' says the interviewer, 'are mostly pan-German nationalists who want to restore to Germany what they call the "lost territories" – Alsace-Lorraine in France, the former Sudetenland in the Czech Republic, former East Prussia, Western Poland – and Austria, of course. The unification of the two Germanies was just a first step for them. Does that kind of pan-Germanism have any real political voice?'

Reinhardt raises his chin demagogically and is about to respond when the smash of glass and liquid flares of light from the direction of the Workers' Residence draw all eyes away from him, including the demogorgon eye of the camera.

'Shit! Now the damn foreigners are chucking Mollies!' shouts Uscinski. He catches a loudhailer that's tossed to him by the driver of the armoured car. 'Get in there – Victor, Delta, Foxtrot – all front units. At the double! Dog crews first!' His voice sears with exceptional clarity through the clean, frictionless medium of the sub-zero air.

The firebrand that was thrown in at ground-level caught in one room only, but it flushed the residents up to the top of the building. The signs are they were prepared for this attack. A salvo of Molotovs hails down from the top windows. They smash on to the concrete forecourt among the neo rabble. One of the Nazi capes flashes into flame. Its wearer struggles with the knot at his neck. He runs amok through the darkness, trailing fire like a comet. Now the others are baying for blood. They pile into the Residence and take to the stairs. Only one breakaway group seem to have their wits about them. They've seen the dog-handlers approaching over the stretch of waste-ground. They've seen the jog-trotting wall of riot-police. They run to the side of the Complex, wanting out.

The scene has resolved into four strata of illuminations. The deep night sky girdled with the pale lights of the Milky Way. The garish building, underlit with ground-fires and flooded with arc-lights. The serried balls of the police helmets, reflecting fires like black marbles and bouncing inwards towards a common destination. And lastly the POLIZEI logo on a yellow day-glo strip on the back of each cop's flak jacket.

Events take a nasty turn.

On the top storey, there's an almighty fracas. The skins have broken in. The dog-handlers are inside the building too. They race up the stairs, but too late. The thugs have got their sacrificial victim. They've doused him in fuel. The man is torched and thrown flailing out of the sixth-floor window. We look on with passive voyeuristic horror. Nobody believes this is happening. 'Defenestration!' Uscinski barks into his microphone. 'Get the paramedics in there, quick!' The Interior Minister checks anxiously around him. He brings a handkerchief up to his forehead, then ducks and weaves back through the pack of journalists towards his chauffeured limousine. I notice that Uscinski's gameplan is less than foolproof.

Uscinski has indeed covered two flanks. His men are moving in with a pincer movement. But between the closing nippers of the pincer there's a blindspot down towards Floridsdorfer Hauptstrasse and the breakaway group of neos notices this too. In the semi-darkness, darker still from the pupil-contracting arc-lights, they tear off towards the loophole. In ten minutes they'll have dispersed into the gridiron of residential streets in Neujedlersdorf. I take to my heels, sprint back to the car and fire the starter. I keep the single headbeam off, however, switching instead to infra-red headlamps for night navigation.

The world's in a spin, but I follow my nose, careening through a web of alleys in the Floridsdorfer Aupark. Then suddenly I'm on Prager Strasse. I blaze through a stop-light and wheel round to Am Spitz. Am Spitz is a triangular junction. It will – I reckon – be their first point of dispersal. By the time I arrive, though, most of them have scarpered. I stamp on the brake and wipe my brow. There's the reek of hot rubber in the car from my threadbare tyres. I don't even know what I'm doing. Obeying an instinct to pursue, I guess. But to what end? Reportage? The transcendent truth of the eye-witness account? Turning life into words, that must be it. The unquestioned alchemical mandate of the gentlemen of the press.

In the gloom of the darkened shop fronts I spot one limping figure projected up from the infra-red equipment on to the reflective inner surface of the windscreen. I move off again in the Gringolet and cruise along the sidewalk till I draw even with him. Strangely, he doesn't make a run, but he doesn't like the attention either. The side-window winds down. 'Can we talk?' I say, hoping that speech recognition counts among his life-skills. I begin to regret my informal overture when I notice that, like an escaped monster in a horror film, he's trailing a length of heavy chain. The chain comes up and flops with a loud menacing clunk on to the car hood. For a moment we're staring stupidly at each other, neither of us knowing what to do or say.

He's a slight individual, no older than nineteen, with a stringy adolescent body – stringy but strong-fibred, vulcanised by the fires of mob ideology. He wears lacerated jeans and a black bomber jacket with 'Kansas City Stars' emblazoned down one side of it and a grinning death's-head daubed on the other. The neat skull is shaved close, of course, ridged with the seams of parietal, frontal and occipital bones, yet I'm suddenly struck by the face. This is not the Cro-Magnon throwback I'd half-expected. There's native intelligence in the dark glister of the eyes as he throws a sharp strategic look back down the street. It is only a question of time before the cops arrive in force. He knows that. And so do I.

'I'm from the *Wiener Tageszeitung*,' I say. 'I just want to talk. I want to find out about you and the others. So we can tell people what it is you want.'

He twitches, hesitates, then all at once his face shudders with dreary pain. He hunches up and vomits over the front fender of the car. The chain drops from his hand and into the gutter.

'That wasn't me, back there,' he bleats, spitting sick from his lips. 'I didn't kill the guy.'

'Get in,' I say. 'Now.' There's nothing in sight behind us but distant sirens are filling the air, wails of lamentation.

He crawls in and we gun off down the empty thoroughfare.

'Where to?' I ask. It seems a stupid question. For a moment I feel like a taxi-driver on the Hades ring-road.

'The Leopoldau Station.'

It's a three-kilometre trip, and all the time I'm wondering whether I'm being the responsible citizen I've always taken myself for. On the one hand I'm aiding and abetting an accomplice to murder. On the other, this is solid gold copy with a human face and form.

'Can we go somewhere to talk?'

In the rearview, I see him wiping a vivid streak of blood off his forehead and on to the back of his wrist.

'I do appreciate,' I concede in a low voice, 'that now is perhaps not the moment.'

Silence.

We're approaching Leopoldau through Schererstrasse and my stomach turns too, strangely enough, at the thought that I may lose him. He may not look much, but he's the stuff that red-hot scoops are made of.

'Okay,' I say. 'Just tell me where. Tell me where I can find you.'

'You're serious,' he says, half surprised. A slender tendril of sputum hangs from his lower lip.

'Yes.'

We pull up at the station and he looks around ith the qui vive of a sniper before swinging round and levering him if out of the car.

'The Bronxx Jugendklub,' he says.

He's about to hobble off when I call after him and he turns.

'Just a minute! What's your name?'

'Moos,' he says, breathing the word like a spell. 'Ask for Moos. The Bronxx Jugendklub. Remember.' A train rumbles into the station. He turns with a slight tripping motion, is if dribbling a ball, and vanishes into the shadows.

The Gringolet's hood was ravined by the force of the blow but it gets me home to Karl Marx-Hof. I see that the lights are on in Marta's flat and I drop in on her and Svetlana. They've been watching the evening's events in serial news-flashes in Plasmavision, and they're none too calm. But the sight of me chases their fears for a while. 'God!' says Svetlana. 'What's happened to you?'

I make my way down the hall to a mirror to share in the spectacle. My eyes are dilated, I'm groomed like a firework and sweat is pouring down my face despite the permafrost outside. I stay an hour, and they clean me up and attempt to bring my heart-beat down from its tachycardic peak with Stolichnaya-spiked camomile tea – a new tipple for me. When they reckon I've rejoined the human race they accompany me across to my flat. I pick up the post from under the door on the way, dropping it on my bedside table and sheepishly bid them goodnight.

It's nearly one now, but I'm unable to sleep.

Stark images rush up towards me and pass through my body like neutrinos or devilish incorporeal things. A blazing man passes slowly through the darkness behind my eyelids, a falling star, his eyes sparkling like rhinestones. A baseball bat twirls in mid-air like a majorette's baton. The face of Moos hovers over me with nauseous, uncomprehending eyes.

Just recently I downloaded Marcus Aurelius's *Meditations* into my digibook because somebody told me he wrote it in Vienna. In a half-hearted attempt to escape these visions, the whirligig of my thoughts, I switch on my lava lamp and thumb the book open at random. My eye falls immediately upon the following:

> *In a brief while now you will be ashes or bare bones; a name, or perhaps not even a name – though even a name is no more than empty sound and reiteration. All that men set their hearts on in this life is vanity, corruption, and trash; men are like scuffling puppies, or quarrelsome children who are all smiles one moment and in tears the next.*

There's something about this Stoicism that deepens my alarm. I flip over the page and try another apothegm, hoping against hope for some consoling utterance.

> *Look beneath the surface: never let a thing's intrinsic quality or worth escape you.*

I place the book face down beside me on the counterpane, spine arched archly. Then I turn to my e-mail print-outs, for another, less specious kind of reassurance. The hard facts and cold print that chronicle the unfolding journey of my life. It's bills, all bills. But one of them, a quarterly statement from Mastercard, reminds me urgently of something – that ticket for the Cambodian meal on which Leo wrote down my card number. Now, I'm thinking, for the moment of truth. My eye bumps hastily down the ladder of figures and does an emergency brake at one oddity. 1,011.97 Euros. It's been used to pay for an international money order.

The solution to this little mystery lies amongst my snailmail. There's a video postcard from the treasurer of an orphanage in Port-au-Prince, Haiti, with a ten-second animation of children playing in a school yard. Accompanying it is a personal letter thanking me for my donation to his institution but hinting somewhat reproachfully at the smallness of the sum. 1,011.97 Euros, to be precise. Why, Leo, why? Why not '1,000' or '1,100'? Did those years at Creditanstalt, those years as a furtive embezzler, put you off nice, round, simple figures?

1,011.97 Euros.

I repeat the sum out loud to myself till I'm sick of the sound of it.

I chuck the mail on to the floor and I'm about to close the book and hit the sack when my eye catches the page and Marcus Aurelius speaks to me again across nearly two millennia.

Look beneath the surface: never let a thing's intrinsic quality or worth escape you.

I stare into the molten haemoglobin of the lamp then pull the pillow down over my head. I may not be tired but I'm in no mood for metaphysics either. Don't ask me why. It's annoying and probably more than my shallow little brain can cope with. My apologies to Marcus Aurelius, but right now there are some things I'd rather not think about.

chapter five

squalus

Spring has come, and it's morning. A perfect morning, more beautiful than any I have known.

I stand on a bluff outcrop of rock, beside a stream, overlooking a woodland lake from the slight prominence. I shut my eyes for an instant. I stretch back my shoulders and breathe. The air's indescribable. It's so fresh it's almost alive. It falls coolly from the misty bluish undershadows of the woods into the brimming bowl of earth. The soft hills, for their part, swathe up and round. They circle and elevate, grabbing the soul by its hand and drawing it up into a lilac-blue icily tinctured heaven. The scents of beech, spruce and Scots pine mingle with the cool, dry wind. Sounds, tiny living sounds, emanate from invisible realms. The strenuous warbling of a songbird. The soft and ponderous clunk of cow-bells. The bumbling drone of a distant buzz-saw. They reach my mind in intermittent waves, and then are flushed away. A turn in the breeze or the restless gushing of the stream usher them elsewhere.

I know this place so well. I've been here many times.

Here, there's no past and no future. Only a present moment that's all light and the living pulse of life. There is only this moment. And this one, single moment holds everything in its grasp. Nothing escapes. It holds me, the hills, the weed-wraithed silence of the lake. It holds the trim little village, neat as a pin, sitting complacently on the far bank of the waters under a pleated backcloth of woodland. It holds the timber clock-tower of that church, with its painted onion dome. Is this Pressbaum? The Wienerwaldsee? It's somewhere near Perchtoldsdorf, the meridian of another life re-visited. It's the Vienna woods, configured anew. A bright heartland of eternal recurrence.

This moment holds even the lazy metallic gong of the church bell – a bell in a glass cloche – as it chimes the hour, for each discrete 'Dong!'

finds no egress, but flies like the wind round the sloping banks of the lake to return upon itself, and upon its successor, which too returns upon itself, till each toll is swallowed again by the vibrant foundried mouth that uttered it. After midday it will tire of its narcissism and return to a single stroke, but each hour it will fall in love with itself again.

And this stream . . .

Where do the swift waters come from? I don't know. I've not found their source, which antecedes mine, though behind me, in the rocks, they must issue from a secret gash in the tectonic plates, a split in the strata of geological time where they well up from inhuman caves of ice. I kneel and splash the water into my face. It's as pure and cold and transparent as this singular moment. Over there, ahead of me, the stream burbles on. But all at once its filaments pull apart. Its currents draw off in silver-backed skeins or river-eels that plait and braid and knot their separate ways round moss-furred rocks, then meet, inosculate, binding into a stronger flow that spits with sudden, fizzing fury, and disappears. I rush over to the edge and look down on a cascade. It stands upright, a column of watery smoke or smoking water, white and luminous and beautiful in the narrow, dark brown gorge that thirstily swallows its light. The spray rises like reverse dew. It atomises upon my face, my neck, my bare arms. It softens the dry effrontery of the morning sun.

To the right is an irregular track. It slopes down away from the waterfall through a copse of oak and hornbeam. The incline is so great and hampered with boulders that I'm on my hands and feet, crawling down backwards. But soon the track levels out under the leaf-jostled sun. And the copse is no more than that – a copse. Its shade is shortlived. It breaks open into a wide, hummocky meadow, a meadow of bright, young grass, that sings with flowers. Aster, flax, poppy, pink, gentian, primulas.

At last I can run, and when I run I'm like the Föhn wind. I'm a featherweight paper kite, fresh from its shop-wrapper, waltzing, tumbling, bowling, through the empty spaces of eternity. The meadow glissades and carries me with it, rolling and shouting. Down, down, down – rolling through dried-up cow-pats and mole-hills and daffodil bells – till the world stops, though my vision is still spinning, beside the sleeping lake. I lie on my back, panting for breath. Then I turn my head. The waters of this greenwood lake are the very face of peace on earth. They're a deep, quiescent blue, fringed with the dark heave of bladderwort and duckweed near the shore. And in this blue liquid eye, the hills, woodland, village, church and sky study themselves in silence, glassy and spellbound.

Not another human soul is in sight. I ease back my head in the fragrant meadow-grass. Up above, at a tremendous altitude, a golden eagle turns in slow, stratospheric orbits. It rides the wind on great, outstretched wings, mastering itself and all that lies below, this *mappa mundi*, forest, lake and me. I too stretch out my arms as I lie on my back in the grass and, for this unique and unrepeatable moment, the eagle will find in me his spellbound other, polarised below as the mountains, woodland, village, church and sky are polarised in the iris-blue eye of the lake.

The eagle planes dreamily back to his eyrie. I gather my strength, propping myself up on my elbows. I've stuck a dandelion behind my ear, and my fingertips are stained black where I picked it. Over to my left is a short stone jetty with steps leading down to a boat. It's a rowboat, freshly painted in a livery of blue and yellow. It's moored with a single rope to a wooden capstan on the jetty. Stencilled in black on the prow of the boat is the silhouette of a leaping fish, and beneath this a word – SQUALUS – the boat's christened name. I stand up. I brush the seat of my pants and walk down to the jetty for a closer look. Inside the rowboat there's an embroidered cushion on the wooden transom-seat. The yellow-tipped oars are propped up in their iron rowlocks. They're raised in a V, drip-drying in the sun.

It's like the little wooden Egyptian boats in the Kunsthistorisches Museum, the solar boats that transported the immortal *ka*, the individual's cosmic double, through the waters of eternity. It's my boat. Of that I'm sure. It's waiting for me. So I lift the hoop of rope off the capstan and tug. I pull the vessel heavily through the water till it bumps up against a pair of rubber tyres flanking the stone flight of steps. I jump in and raise my arms for balance as the boat rocks, absorbing the shock of my arrival. Then I dislodge the ends of the oars and bring their spade-like blades down into the water. They slice in with delicious ease. And when I pull on them, a force, a resistance, extends through my arms, across my chest, drawing the boat and me out from the shore and into the still lagoon. Again the oars fall with a plop into the water. Again I pull. And gradually the inertia with which we started is overcome. The energy of my will, my arms, has travelled into the very atoms of the boat, spiriting it over the silence. And the fantail of our wake opens behind us, widening and dissipating, but constantly renewed.

In the centre of the lake I cease my efforts and pull the oars in. The boat drifts for a while. It loses momentum then gradually stops. Now its only movement is an infinitesimal pitching whenever I shift my balance lightly. I'm dead centre of nature's bowl. And from here the hills don't 'sit' on the meniscus of the water. I sense, on the contrary, their invisible dive, where loamy fingers of primeval tree-root tunnel, mesh and cup in watertight communion. Perhaps this was once the crater of a volcano where not water but glowering magma hissed and spat from rim to rim. Perhaps it was smashed out by a meteorite or scooped and buffed into being by the slow creaking progress of a glacier. But today the only sound is the odd tail-flip of a curious grayling or tench, venturing out of its medium. The only disturbance, a ripple of concentric rings – a belated target on the departed scaly visitor, an idle afterthought.

I feel in this still moment the transmission of my life into that of the world. There's no boundary between my stillness and that of the mountain, the water or the doe who dips her head to drink quietly on the southern shore against the sombre army of tree-trunks then stares pensively into the distance. I'm eidelweiss. I'm a boulder, crowned with crustaceous lichens. I'm a blue hare, pricking my ears up in the sun. I'm an infant and a decrepit old man. Here, as the fish's ripples diffuse, the rings of causation converge. Something will be made or broken. There's new life here. Or new transition into death.

Over to the North, there's a saw-mill. A man appears momentarily from the darkness of the wood. He raises his arms together above his head and dives with a great bellyflopping clap into the lake. He disappears from sight for several seconds, then his head breaks the surface a few metres forward of his point of entry. I watch him disconnectedly, his lungeing butterfly stroke, his strenuous dog-crawl. He's like some kind of seal, rolling and propelling his old, blubbery body through the lake. After a while, he stops and treads water. He gasps and smiles. I dip my fingers into the lake and pull them out quickly, as if out of flame. The water's intensely cold, unnaturally cold even. My fingers are like marble, blue and hypothermic. I look with new wonder at the old man and ask myself how he can take it. Yet there he is, splashing and grinning. He dunks his head under and spouts water from his lips. His skin is old and tanned like good saddler's leather. What remains of his hair is wetted back on his large, happy head. I feel sure that he hasn't even noticed me, though after the next dip he bobs up and he sees the boat and waves breezily in my direction.

I resent this recognition. I don't know why exactly. Perhaps he has encroached upon my solitude, making it social – kindred. Nevertheless I raise my hand in a stiff salute.

He's encouraged. With slow, loping strokes he pushes out towards the centre, closing gradually on the boat. His feet smack up behind him, kicking sparky spindrifts into the air. He arrives, in due course, to port. And his body upturns and he treads water again. There's great warmth and humanity in his elderly face. It's a warmth that oversteps the boundaries of metaphor and reminds me again of the intense frigidity of the water in which he's swimming.

'Hello!' he calls, cheerily.

'Hello!'

'Do I know you?'

'No. I don't think so,' I reply.

'I think I do.'

I stir myself, and slide over to the rim of the boat, resting my folded arms on the wooden edge.

'Isn't it cold in there?'

'It is. It's unbearable.'

'Then how – I mean, how can you stay there? How can you swim?'

He looks worried for a moment and casts his gaze to left and to right, then behind him. It's as if he's suddenly becoming aware of his predicament and assessing his distance from dry land.

'I can't,' he says at length. 'I can't stand it. I'm frozen to the bone. That's the problem.'

I stare at him incredulously. 'Then why? Why did you come out swimming?'

'Well you have to, don't you?' He laughs, though an expression of panic, or alarm, traverses his face.

'Why? Why do you *have* to?'

Again he laughs, though the fear's now audible in his voice. 'To say

"Hello", for one thing – and, for another . . . well, you know what they say, don't you? "You either swim or drown!"'

I look at him coolly. I sit in my boat and I look at him. The coldness that was in my fingertips has spread up my arm and into my chest, chilling over the internal organs.

'And which are *you* doing?' I ask.

By now all trace of good cheer has fled his features. He coughs and looks embarrassed. 'I think I'm drowning,' he says, with exemplary candour. 'But unless I'm mistaken, that isn't a problem because you're here.'

'How do you mean?'

His head vanishes for a moment beneath the surface of the lake then with a flapping commotion of hands he brings himself up again. He spits and shakes the water-drops off his head like an old dog.

'I mean,' he says, 'that I'm not obliged to turn round and swim to the shore. I have only to reach out my hand and you will pull me up and into your boat.'

Despite my anger at his presence, there's something touching and touchingly familiar about him that moves me unexpectedly. I try to shake the coldness out of me. I try to get to the heart of his predicament.

'Is that what you want me to do?'

'Yes!' he says. I notice that those are not drops of lake-water coursing down his cheeks. He's crying. He's frustrated with me. He's trying to make me understand. 'That *is* what I want you to do! Help me. Help me – please!'

He reaches a hand out of the icy water. I hold on to the fingertips lightly, like a manicurist.

'You have to put an effort into this,' he pleads. 'If you don't make an effort, I'm going to go down. I don't think I have the strength to bring myself up again. I want you to understand, to feel with me, how very very cold it is here. Do you understand that? Can you understand? It's exceedingly cold. Colder than anyone can imagine.'

I reassert my grip on his fingertips. I slide my hand down till it's level with his wrist. But something has happened. His forearm slithers smoothly out of my grasp. For a split-second his face and mine are all that exists. We're no more than a metre apart. There's chagrin in his eyes. There's a profound sadness in his voice.

'You've let me down,' he says. 'You were my only hope.' And – with that – swiftly, silently, he slips away. The waters close over him. There's a spiralling flume of silver air-bubbles as his lungs expire. And the falling shroud-shadow of a face.

In a moment there's nothing. I happen to glance across at the forest. From the shadows, three motionless wild beasts observe me. Only the bright points of their eyes are visible, that and the vague outline of their forms. I look down at the water again, then close my eyes. There's only the last warmth of the man's wrist, his arms. It fades like memory from the chill tips of my fingers. And there's a deep pain, a terrible ache within. Who was this man? Did I know him? Who was he? And why did I let him go? More than anything, now, I want him to come back. I want him to come back and forgive me. I want him to grasp my hand so that I can grip him firmly and pull, drawing him up into life.

The grasp tightens. A voice penetrates the inner darkness.

'Sharkey!'

I open my eyes with sudden relief.

Beate Kaminer, the *Wiener Tageszeitung* researcher, is standing over me. She's clutching at my hand.

'Sharkey!'

'God!' I exclaim. 'Where did he go?'

'Who?' She looks down with some concern, sitting in the office, slumped in my chair.

'Nobody,' I say. I'm shaken to the core but my nerves tighten bureaucratically. I pull myself together. 'I must've dropped off. It was a dream.'

'The sweet variety, I hope.'

'I don't know about that,' I say, half to myself. 'But it was real. More real than real. I'm in no hurry to go through it again.'

'Recurrent?'

'I don't know. Familiar, rather than recurrent. I can't make head or tail of it.'

'Tell me about it.'

At a certain point in their lives, all Viennese get to sounding like head doctors. Beate has just touched base.

'Not today. Another time, maybe. You tell me. You tell me what you've got for me.'

Beate's in a tight satin A-line skirt and white cotton cable-knit bustier. She has shoulder-length blonde hair. On a chain round her neck she wears an elaborate gold filigree crucifix, antique, studded with tiny gems. The ensemble suits her fine. It brings out that dissipated Jugendstil pallor of the convent girl, brought up in strict seclusion by the Little Sisters of Providence. She perches on the edge of my desk and riffles through a sheaf of notes. I watch her carefully. She's a curious fusion of lethargy and intensity, a malnourished waif by Egon Schiele where all the sensuality has fled to the eyes. The skin on her high forehead and the underside of her forearms is translucent and marbled with blue capillary veins. She's at home wandering through this anaemic realm of paper, white, well-laundered shirts, glimmering screens and indirect cornice lighting. Direct sunshine would blind and wither her. Even her breath is indoor breath, the soft respiration of air-conditioning.

She finishes her paper-shuffling and, looking up, catches my gaze. It's thrown back, wrapped and beribboned with a slightly condescending office smile. 'There you are,' she says, banging the A4 sheets square on the desk-top. She drops them in a neat block in front of me. 'Mission accomplished.'

'Thanks.'

She gives a token bow.

'Talk me through it, Beate, will you? I'm not a great one for reading. It's those lines of words going from left to right, then back again.'

'I know, I know. Typewriter neck, it's called.'

'Yeah. I start make pinging noises when I get to the right-hand margin.'

'A night on the tiles, was it Sharkey? Okay,' she punctuates firmly, signalling business. 'But let's make it snappy. Hofburg Maternity Clinic. Primogen. Reprotech. Those are the names you gave me, right?'

'Right.'

'Well, basically they're all the same thing. We're talking about a biotech multinational with several subsidiaries. It started life in 1989 in the US before migrating to Europe and chiefly Austria. Big business. Where do you want me to start?'

'Start in 1989.'

'Okay. 1989's a good year to start. It's when a lot of bio-tech start-ups were being put together in the States with seed cash from venture capital funds. One of them was and is called Biomass. Founded by an American of Austrian parentage called Peter Diessl. Born 1962. His parents were scientists who emigrated from Vienna to the States after the Second World War. Diessl had a distinguished academic career. Cornell University, then the Cold Spring Harbour Laboratory on Long Island. He was twenty-seven when he started Biomass and he certainly knew what he was doing. He had a very simple philosophy, which was, at the outset, to keep things simple and deal in bulk. The McDonald's of the scientific establishment. They were one of the first get-rich-quick bio-companies because they moved into fermentation technology fast. That's the trick to scaling up novel products into commercially viable volumes.'

'What kind of products?'

'Mostly diagnostics and reagents, but also growth hormones and human insulin. Mass-market stuff. They were very good at installing the basic technologies as they came along – recombinant DNA, biochemical reactors, mass cell-cultures, that sort of thing. They took off because they ignored the orphan drug problems. If costs were high, or if a particular illness only afflicted a small percentage of the population, their pharmaceutical division kept well clear. With me so far?'

'Sure.'

'Diessl put together a very good show. He was Chief Executive. His Head of R&D was a woman called Elsa Lubitsch, an old Cornell buddy. She also had a big stake in company equity. Chief Financial Officer Purkiss – also good – multinational connections. Plus a solid core team of scientists, lab assistants and licensing experts. There's a full list of the original personnel here. It was blue-chip, with all the right Ivy League connections and old school ties. Within five years they had public liquidity, a low burn-rate and a good pipeline of new proprietary branded products. They made over a hundred patent applications. By the early 90s, things were in full swing. Product royalties pouring in, a $350 million preferred stock offering and additional public offerings, a non-US convertible debenture and limited R&D partnerships. Purkiss originally operated the financial side of things through offshore trust funds in the Cayman Islands, but around 1994 they shifted all transactions to Liechtenstein. And for a very good reason.'

'They were coming to Austria.'

'Right. But by this time they'd begun to diversify. With serious genetic engineering on the horizon, Diessl could see that bio-tech was going to be bigger than even he had imagined. So he wanted a finger in every pie. It was only by supporting a critical mass of new technologies that he could keep the field open. The crucial thing was the Human Genome Project. What did they call it, now?'

'HUGO.'

'Right. That started in '88 and finished in 2005, when the entire human germline, as we know, was fully mapped. Diessl reckoned that HUGO would determine the future. Consequently Biomass was one of the many worldwide laboratories involved in cracking the codes of the human gene. Until it was completed, broad diversification was the best policy.' She hesitates a moment and catches my eye. 'Of course, all this intelligence is public domain. I haven't been phone-tapping and disguising microdots as beauty spots.'

'You disappoint me, Beate. But tell me, which fields was this Diessl guy working in?'

'Food – ag-bio. Disease elimination. Effluent treatment . . . they made great strides in biodegradability. Pharmaceuticals too. There was also some hush-hush cross-work with the military. And, of course, reproduction technology.'

'Hence, Reprotech.'

'Yes, but hold your horses. I'm coming to that. In the early '90s, Diessl and Lubitsch decided to set up in a big way in Europe. They centred their activities in Austria because – as I said – that's where Diessl's family came from. Lubitsch's too, as it happens. I'm not sure, but there's some evidence that Biomass fell foul of the Biomedical Ethics Review Board and various lobbies in the US and wanted more latitude. Who didn't in those days? One of their main opponents was a former Cornell classmate, Hannah Delbrück. Europe was perfect, then as now. The diversity of nations and interests meant that legal constraints on bio-technology were confused, slow in coming about and tangled in circumlocution and problems of interpretation when they did become law. So – lots of loopholes, which was just the ticket.

It gave them time and legal grey-space for manoeuvre. Ethics have always been the worst commercial enemy of bio-tech.'

'What happened to Biomass in the States?'

'It's still going, but on relatively non-controversial projects, chiefly agro-alimentary. They produce insect-repellant plants, less stringy celery and olives with a bit of tomato growing in the middle, new colours for flowers, decaffeinated coffee beans, enhanced ice-crystals for artificial snow. What else?' She glances at the papers. 'Plants re-engineered with antifreeze genes from flounders to help them grow at lower temperatures. Fluorescent genes from fireflies inserted into tobacco plants.'

'To help smokers find their butts in the dark, presumably.'

'I guess so. The list goes on. All those little things that make life worth living. Know what I mean? It's so respectable now that it even receives government funding. Basically, the low-profile technology was left over there and the hot stuff came over here.'

'By "hot stuff" you mean "human"?'

'Yes. Particularly pharmaceuticals, healthcare and reproduction technology, a pretty new science at that stage.'

'Sensitive areas. Precisely where the bio-medical ethics people in the US were most likely to pounce.'

'Right. And also the areas where the most money is – at least since the completion of the Human Genome Project. Twelve per cent of Austria's GDP now goes on healthcare, if that gives you some idea. You've also got to have the patents, and Reprotech has. Over 500 at the last count. Anyway, Diessl bought out an Austrian bio-tech start-up called Transwitch in the year 2000, sacked all the old staff and restructured the plant and management. In 1998 he'd set up Primogen in Europe. It's basically a consortium of maternities, IVF clinics, general clinics and genetic engineering labs. Three clinics in the Vienna area – Mariahilf, Donaufeld and Hofburg. Five or six others elsewhere in Austria. And a dozen others elsewhere, mostly in France and Germany. In the same year, 1998, Biowares came into being to head up pharmaceuticals and pesticides. They also act as distributors for Biomass-USA products in Europe. Crop-sprays and water purification systems are two of the growth industries there. The other outhouse is Reprotech. What am I saying?' She double-checks her notes. 'In fact it's the umbrella organisation that covers

Primogen and Biowares. It's basically an R&D boutique, but it's also where the movers and shakers and licensing lawyers operate. They have to keep themselves up there on the cutting edge, fight off rivals and make sure the products are subject to industrially mandated criteria.'

'What are they worth?'

'The whole show? US and Europe?' She glances down at her figures on the top-sheet. 'A share rate of $600, as of today, and stock value in excess of $420 billion. How does that grab you for a rainy day?'

'Dandy.'

'It's a lot of money for what's really a small, high-intensity operation. They have a core staff of 2,000 in Europe, with 1,400 square metres of laboratory and 3,200 square metres of pilot production facility for Biowares products.'

'And Diessl, is he still at the helm?'

'He is, yes. His R&D woman, Elsa Lubitsch, died in a car accident in Orange County in December 1997. Diessl runs the European show and Purkiss is his CEO in the States. He was on the initial bench of scientists in 1989 – a close associate of Diessl's, also with his own stake in Biomass equity. After Lubitsch died, Diessl wanted to return to Austria. That's why he took over the Transwitch assets here and upgraded and streamlined them. In their company literature he says he's sticking to the line Lubitsch defined: keeping bio-technology on parallel tracks, as a manufacturing industry and as an enabling science, run by what he calls a "small commando team of well-networked individuals". A continuous feedback loop between research and production. Very market-driven.'

'So Diessl fronts Reprotech. What about Primogen and Biowares?'

'Diessl again. You'll find all the names and mugshots in there. I've added the stats of a bio-tech specialist. Oddly enough, it's Hannah Delbrück, the woman who took a stand against them. She's back in Austria too. A VIP. Fronts the European Bioethics Convention. And she's a world expert on patent law. As for the Reprotech gang, some came over with the start-up stable from Biomass and others were headhunted here. But I haven't gone so far as to memorise the company telephone directories yet.'

'Nevertheless, you've done very well.'

'Do I get a medal?'

'We'll see. For the time being, you get to sign the Sharkey Pledge of Official Secrecy.'

Beate wises up, nodding her head as if totting up some mental arithmetic. 'I thought so,' she says, flaring her nostrils and speaking in her low, knowing drawl. 'I spent a good seven or eight hours of company time collating this. If this is some private scam, you'd better let me know now.'

I stab at the tilt-lever on my office chair and lean forward. 'It's private for now,' I concede, 'but getting good enough to go public.'

'What's that supposed to mean?'

'Feature stuff. Investigative.'

'That's not your line of country.'

'You forget my computer-crime story.'

'I remember the lawsuit.'

'It wasn't finalised. We settled out of court.'

'Sure, but you nearly got the elbow. Dehmel was furious. And now you're dragging me in.'

'Now and then we have to run risks in this game.'

'Jesus. Are you on some kind of medication?' She stands up, winces and rubs her left leg. 'Shit. It's gone to sleep.'

'You know what Marcus Aurelius says, don't you?' I persist.

'Marcus who?'

'The Roman emperor. He says you should exchange your fear of having to end your life some day for a fear of failing even to begin it on nature's true principles. Something like that, anyway.'

She stares down at me pityingly. 'I guess you're right, Sharkey. After all, what are all the things we attach importance to? A job. A livelihood. Food. A roof over one's head. Baubles, right? Not worth the brine to pickle a herring.'

'Ultimately, that's right. To thine own self be true, Beate. Provided you can look yourself in the face in the bathroom mirror and say "I've lived in accordance with my nature. I've done what I was destined to do." – nobody can fault you.'

She nods compassionately. 'And if the bathroom mirror's at the pawnbroker? Where do you look at yourself then?'

'In a puddle,' I say. 'Or a lake.' And suddenly a brief scrap of my dream revisits me, an old man's face sinking away from mine beneath the waters. It freezes me up for an instant.

102

'Seriously,' she's saying, 'let's just don't do this again, huh? Or if we do, clear it properly with Dehmel first.'

'But you'll bear with me?'

'Do I have a choice?'

'It's good, I promise you. At least, I think it is. And we'll split the laurels, Beate. Onwards and ever upwards.'

'You keep the glory, Sharkey. I'll just stick to my job. What's this all about, anyway?'

I look out of the window at the sprawling circuit-boards and living-machines of city streets and buildings. And out there – over the rooftops, within the double hoops of the Ringstrasse and the Gürtel ring-road – is the tree-bordered grid of grey marble slabs that is the Zentralfriedhof. That's where Leo is, somewhere over there, languishing in his pinewood kimono in the company of Beethoven, Schubert, Brahms and the whole Strauss family. He is, at least, not in the Cemetery of the Nameless Ones, where corpses found floating in the Danube are deposited each year. The distant plot of land fills me with a dreary melancholy.

'It's about a man who died,' I say.

hackers' happy hour

It's only late morning, but when Beate goes I feel even duller and more lumpish than usual. It's one of those lackadaisical, locationless days. Rudolf Meister of Current Affairs drops in for a chinwag then sets about stringing a tangled mess of fairy-lights round the office Christmas tree. I watch him tackle the task. You can tell a lot about a man's mind-set from the way he takes on a Chinese puzzle of this sort. Then a little later the old enemy on the wall tells me it's time I set about cooking up another column. President Schwarzenegger has stamped on plans for a festival of his films in Salzburg. It's worth a rib-dig, so under the sub-title 'PreS.O.S.' I review the darker moments of the celluloid career of our *primus inter pares*. Then a couple of neat little stop-gaps courtesy of Reuters. One's on the vogue for toad wine in Phnom Penh and the Cambodian government's discovery that the bevvy contains dimenthyltryptamine and bufotenine, psycho-active drugs. The other concerns the rising tide of cricket hooliganism in the

UK. When that's done, there are 600 words left to account for.

I rack my brains and stare out, as is my custom, at the 160-floor Uropia tower to the west of Meidling in the slim hope that it'll inspire a tall story or two. Then my gaze slips to the press calendar in the corner of the wallscreen. Today's date, December 21, is pulsating in a bold, happy-go-lucky typeface. 2027 is creeping up on us. Only ten days of the old year remain. I pull the bendy Cobra flex of the mike up out of the desk and improvise a little competition: bottles of bubbly for the most off-beat New Year's resolutions. This will have the provident advantage of padding out another column just post-Christmas. Finally, a word of warning about seasonal gormandising and a plug for a foodie manual written by a friend who's a vitamin counsellor, nutriceutical scientist and health impresario.

My vocal utterances trip into print on the screen above me. A quick word-count, then today's encyclical is piped down the line to the subs. I swallow the dregs of the camomile tea and pick through the fruits of Beate's research into Reprotech.

I made one three-way tie-in while Beate was talking me through her donkey-work and my scan through the paperwork confirms it. Hofburg where Petra and Leo were born, Donaufeld where Leo's body was carved up for organs and Mariahilf where Petra is scheduled to give birth – all came, and come, under the aegis of Primogen and, ultimately, Reprotech. But there's hardly anything sinister about this. Whatever healthcare plan their parents bought into at their children's birth, the likelihood was that the private contract was with Reprotech and subsidiary medical facilities. I register that Reprotech and Biowares are based solidly outside Rust in the federal district of Burgenland. Primogen have further clinics in Graz, Salzburg, Innsbruck and Linz.

On impulse, I call up Petra. She's playing piano, beautifully. Behind her, in the living-room, is a large glass tank with an underwater nativity scene. Mary and Joseph are repainted Nintendo robots and a few live angelfish circle the crib, evidently standing in for the asses and oxen. There's a sunken shipwreck, a lump of coral, and the oxygenator has been fed into the plastic Jesus's head and bead-strings of bubbles waver out of his facial orifices. One of Petra's homemade Time Capsules, I deduce, a briny Bethlehem. Argos is flat out on the carpet. His Sartrean eyes roll up philosophically to the Superscreen when I come through. I get some feedback on how I shape up from her point of view from the videocam looking-glass on the screen. A trifle liverish and plump round the cheeks it seems to me. I discreetly tone up the complexion and morph down the jowls on the Cosmeticon control-bar. Then I lean in to camera. 'What is that you're playing, Petra?'

'Oh, hi Sharkey! It's Schubert. One of the late sonatas. Number 20 in A major, the *andantino* bit. Such sad music. An infinite sadness.'

'You're a very talented woman.'

She laughs. 'Oh, it's not me. It's Afanassiev. My teacher in Paris. You're sharing the screen with him.'

'Not *the* Afanassiev? He must be as old as the hills.'

'Older.'

'You're wearing haptic finger sheaths, then?'

'Sure. With activators. He's the one who's playing. Just putting me through my paces. You're interrupting my weekly piano lesson.'

'I can call back . . .'

'No, no. We can talk. He's zoomed on my hands. He can't hear us chatting. But I'll have to keep playing.'

'I was just wondering. Have you heard anything from Uscinski or the insurers?'

'Yes. Good news, at last. The cops have been over the place. You've got Leo's notebook, haven't you? Well, I stashed away all the other incriminating stuff – the gun and the drugs and that. Since they left, I've put it back. They seemed satisfied the place was clean.'

'Did you see Uscinski?'

'I did. With the CCTV surveillance evidence, he accepts it's no regular hit-and-run. But they're deadlocked for the moment. The good news is that, what with the Polizei taking my word for things now, ZKD have accepted the claim and they're going to pay up in full. I also got the Harvest Contract payment.' She tenses and, instead of relaxing into her teacher's remote guidance, hits a bum note with her little finger then winces at the mild electro-shock she gets from the haptic sheath. She looks up guiltily. 'Of course, that doesn't bring Leo back, does it?'

'True, but there's always the thought that he's keeping other people alive.'

'Yes, there is that.' She concentrates, frowning, on her hands again, doubtful about this posthumous merit.

'Petra –'

'Yes?'

'I've been thinking. That connection between Leo and you. We should pursue it, shouldn't we?'

She looks up silently.

'For one thing, it's a flagrant case of malpractice. You could sue. But what's more important is there may be some link with Leo's death. Remember, it was Reprotech he was blathering on about when he met me.'

She bites her lower lip and nods her agreement grudgingly.

'At the moment we've just got the two IVF print-outs to go on. We need more. Remember the okay for dual donors was given by Primogen? Well, they're one step up in the business hierarchy from Hofburg. They must be on a closed architecture system with dedicated file-sharing.'

'You want to try your luck again?' she asks, raising one topiarised eyebrow.

'Yes. Is it convenient?'

'Sure. Come on over a little later. We'll have a Hackers' Happy Hour.'

The music stops and she regains control of her hands. She exercises the fingers by making grabbing motions in the air. I can see the sheaths now, and the fine wire connections. All at once the piano maestro is back online. She squeals as her own right hand tweaks her nose and slaps her lightly on the cheek.

'Time for the Scherzo, I think,' she says, smiling. '*Allegro vivace.*'

I tug on the flo-ring and Leo's office comes to life, complete with face-lift. There's a woman's touch to it now, Petra's touch. Most of the paperwork has been junked and the wall graffiti emulsioned over. There are little doilies, of all things, on the worktop and a potted Venus flytrap next to one of her Time Capsules with a lewd garden gnome centre-stage. Petra herself is tinkering with the subaquatic nativity scene in the next room. She's stuffing lead-shot into a slit in the plastic Jesus to stop him floating away from his crib. I've got the Telekom engineer outfit on, just in case anyone should come online, but I'm banking on the cheat mode. I'm banking on accessing Primogen through Hofburg. Basic network-weaving: jumping from low-security to high-security networks like a trapeze artiste.

I dial-up Hofburg and finger in the 'Sysmaint' password. So far so good. I'm back in the VR waiting-room and the top-heavy usherette in the nurse's uniform is beckoning me through again. Down the corridor we go. 'General Obstetrics.' 'Paediatrics.' 'Termination.' 'Sterility.' 'IVF.' 'Cardiology.' 'Diagnostics.' 'Feto-Maternal Blood Incompatibility.' 'Surgery.' 'Endocrinology.' 'Premature Birth.' 'Neuro-Muscular Illness.' 'Neo-Natal Haemobiology.' 'Post-Natal.' I'm getting edgy. We don't seem any warmer. And the dead-end of the corridor is fast approaching. Then suddenly there's 'Administration' and I blurt 'knock-knock!' on impulse. The nurse smiles toothsomely. The virtual door swings open. Another corridor. Another perspective of services. The VR sways from left to right, lingering on the doorplates. 'Personnel.' 'Registrar.' 'Warehouse.' 'Primogen.' As we freeze-frame on the last I knock-knock! again. The door opens. The cybernurse precedes me. She adopts a Jayne Mansfield pose, pouts and indicates a wall-sign with a lazy forefinger:

WELCOME TO PRIMOGEN:
MANAGEMENT AND RECORDS
access reserved for staff with sysman status
Are you a sysman?
YES   NO

Pushing my luck, I click on 'Yes'. I'm getting a floating, swampy feeling. The focus is going in my eyes. The muscles in my stomach tighten up into a hard, pessimistic unit. I try to keep my thoughts centre-on, but somewhere in Binary World my fate is being sealed. On screen, a little gold bell appears and it rings charmingly. It rings with the same chirpy two-tone as a Networker. I'm attempting to work this one out when I hear the same ring coming through the open door. It's coming from Petra's Bip-Bip in the living-room. How on earth can that be? The Bip-Bip must be on the same circuit as the GFP. I hear Petra drop what she's doing. She shifts her bulk over to the *chaise-longue* to answer it. At the same time, a message flashes up on the screen:

SORRY TO KEEP YOU WAITING
YOUR LINE IS BEING VERIFIED
PLEASE RESPOND AND KEY IN YOUR
SECURITY CODE UPON CONNECTION

I rip out the plug on the GFP, kick back the chair and stumble towards the living-room. 'Don't answer it!' I yell. But it's too late. I can hear the plastic clunk as the Bip-Bip lifts off its cradle. I can hear Petra's voice: 'Hello? Petra here . . . Petra Detmers. Hello?' As I get into the living-room I grab her hand and slam it down. I slam it down, Networker and all, on to the base-unit. So hard it cracks.

'Shit!' yelps Petra. 'What's got into you?'

My heart is batting away like a mad thing and I squat down on the floor to gather my wits.

'Fuck and double fuck!'

'What is it?' she asks, aghast.

'I've just done something stupid, Petra. That call . . . There was no voice on the line, right?'

'Right. Just a clicking noise.'

'That was Primogen checking on my credentials. I may have pulled the plug on them in time. If not, they'll know they've got a hacker. And they'll have a trace on this line. It was really stupid of me. I shouldn't have gone for the short-cut. I should have got your LEN code.'

'My what?'

'Each telephone has a line equipment number. If you hack into it, you can reroute calls through exchange switches and satellites. You can go from Vienna to Moscow, Moscow to Beijing, Beijing to San Francisco, and San Francisco back to Vienna again. It's the oldest trick in the book. The phone-phreaks used to do that over half a century ago. It's time-consuming, but the thing is, if you reroute, they can't do a back-trace. Ensign systems – the redial security systems – can't weave through the exchanges. Instead, I've now made you a sitting duck.'

'For what?'

'Litigation, for a start. There are laws against computer misuse and data-crime.'

She looks glum then picks up on my despondency, decides to make the best of a bad deal.

'Never mind,' she says. 'I hope you were quick enough, that's all. If they do trace the line, there's no concrete evidence, is there? Nothing solid to go on.'

'I guess that's true.'

'Still, it's a shame. Leo obviously did better than us, except –'

'That's a big "except", Petra. I'd rather we weren't made an exception of in the same way, no? Let's just put our trust in the old adage: *the second mouse gets the cheese*. I might even adopt it as my personal motto. A purpure escutcheon, with yellow mice rampant or trippant or something. What d'you reckon?'

positive symbiosis

I get up and give Petra a hand to pull her tonnage off the *chaise-longue*. She puffs a bit and cranes her neck back. She pushes the flats of her hands on her lower back.

'I don't wish pregnancy on to you, Sharkey. Women are beasts of burden. You know they have those acrylic gestation-tank wombs for premature babies? Well I reckon they should do all births that way. Huge hothouses full of the tanks – like salmon-farms. Artificial amniotic fluid. The mother's heart-beat pumping out of a PA system. And after nine months the doc comes round, fishes the kid out and delivers the goods. It'd spell an end to stretchlines, and birth trauma too. A new era of perfectly adjusted, standardised human products. You're not married, are you?'

I shake my head.

'Girlfriend?'

'Not in Vienna. I have a cyber-date in Providence, USA. We meet up and talk on line. It's good for my English and good for her German.'

'I see,' says Petra, nodding her head ironically, 'Interactive conversation classes. Full-immersion social intercourse.'

'It's not what you think.'

'No robo-doll?'

'I don't even have a body-suit. No tactile bodynet. No haptic effectors. She's my soul-sister. It's a meeting of minds.'

'And good-looking with it?'

'Sure. Who isn't these days?'

'So you see her avatar, but you've no idea how morphed she is. It's the old, old story.'

'She hasn't got extra limbs or an extensible chameleon tongue, if that's what you mean. Nothing obvious like that. She looks genuine to me.'

'Sure, as genuine as anyone can be in an age of mass individualisation, right? I'd watch it, Sharkey. She could be an undesirable alien. She could even be a *he*. Or worse. A smart chimp in some high-tech zoo.'

'I don't date outside my own species, Petra. Anyway, it's just cyber. It's metaphysical. Our two hearts beat as one. It's a question of wavelength and pulse frequency.'

'I'm having a party on Christmas Eve,' says Petra, changing the subject without preamble. 'I'd like you to come. It's costume. Some gallery friends and old acquaintances.'

I hesitate a moment and think of Leo. The thought must be strong because she reads me like a book.

'I know it's soon,' she says, weighing her words. 'But that's why I want to do it. Not to forget Leo, but to be with him. He liked parties. I want to feel that he's here with us too.'

There's a moment's silence between us. Not for the first time, I feel Leo's presence palpably in the flat. I look around me. Odd, ectopic items protrude on my consciousness, items that do not sit easily with Petra's moneyed dissidence, her well-heeled Bohemianism. A modest framed diploma. A statuette of an Olympic discus thrower. A pewter-lidded stein with 'Beck-Bier' embossed on the side and plastic foam bubbling over the rim, clearly a bar-top advertising prop. Even the movement sensors in the room-corners to economise on juice are signed 'Leo', a practical, male intervention. We're so still, indeed, that the lights begin to dim and Petra raises a hand and wiggles her fingers to reassure them of our continued existence.

'You will come,' she says. It's a statement, not a question. 'The problem is, I don't know what to wear myself. Just look at me! I've thought of Orson Welles or the Michelin Man.'

'Come as Mary,' I say, looking at the figurines in her aquarium. 'Come as the Virgin Mary.'

She laughs drily and hugs her belly. 'What are you saying? That this is the Virgin Birth?'

'Why not? You might be the first authenticated human case. Never heard of parthenogenesis? A single cell is shocked into parthenogenic fertilisation. You get it in many fish, some lizards, and even domesticated turkeys. Dandelions too, come to that. Nonsexual reproduction. It's the basis of cloning.'

'Human cloning's illegal, Sharkey.'

'Lab-cloning, yes. But we all know it happens. In Hong Kong, for example. They call them Chinamen, the Hong Kong clones.'

'Okay,' she says. 'The Virgin Mary. Perhaps it's not such a bad idea. But on one condition.'

'Namely?'

'That you'll come as Joseph.'

We laugh and shake hands on it.

'I'll rig up a couple of outfits for us, so turn up early. Before eight, anyway. How does that sound?'

'Fine, Petra. That sounds just fine.'

She switches register all of a sudden and reaches out to hold my hand. 'I do appreciate it, you know. I appreciate what you're doing for me. Helping me out, and that.'

'Don't think I'm all heart. Let's just call this positive symbiosis.'

She withdraws her hand, crosses her arms and angles a cognisant smile in my direction. 'I know, I know. Wavelength and pulse frequency. You're a journalist, right? And women who marry their own brothers are good copy. Newsworthy. Especially when the brother in question gets wasted in the Prater.'

'Petra – if you really want to help me out you have to tell me everything you know. For example, did you do as I said and contact your parents in Graz?'

'I did. I phoned through to the Longevity Centre. I told Mum I was thinking of having the child at Hofburg too. I asked her what it was like. She had no complaints. Anyway, I asked her if she'd ever thought of IVF and she was really surprised by the question. She and my father had been in perfect health. There'd been no need. She had the usual fertility tests, and when I was conceived Hofburg ran DNA tests on the embryo to check for defective genes. All run of the mill. I didn't push the matter. I knew she was telling the truth.'

I run my fingers over the stubble on my chin. 'You know what this means, don't you?'

'I think so.' Her voice is breathy and nervous. 'Someone's got something to hide.'

'Looks like it. Remember, this was before foetal blood cells could be sampled directly from the mother's circulation. My guess is that your mother may have *thought* they were karyotyping the embryo. In fact they were implanting another embryo entirely. It was IVF, but she believed it was a biopsy or something like that.'

'The same thought crossed my mind,' Petra admits. 'I quizzed her about the pregnancy. She told me she was on Pergonal and also had to use an inhaler. At the time of conception a catheter was introduced. She's not the type to bother doctors with questions. But that's it – isn't it? It was IVF. Technically speaking, all the signs are there.'

I nod slowly. 'As you say, someone's got something to hide. And you know where they've hidden it?'

She doesn't move but waits, in mental suspension, for my conclusion. I tap her lightly on the sternum with my forefinger.

'In you. In every cell of your body. Someone's little secret is encoded into your DNA.'

I sense that she's deduced as much but hasn't formulated it into words. The news seems to ice her up even harder.

'I want you to do something,' I say. 'An independent DNA test, through the Allgemeines Krankenhaus. I've got a Slovak friend, Marta, who works there. I'll speak to her. I'll set everything up. All you'll have to do is ring her and do as she says.'

Now she looks warier than ever.

'Nobody's going to vivisect you,' I add hastily. 'You just spit in a cup. Your saliva contains cells from the inside of your mouth. That's enough for them to go on.'

This is some consolation, but she's still looking at me coldly, critically.

'There's one thing I don't get,' she says. 'Just what was it you were hoping to find out about Leo from Primogen's files?'

'Primogen did a DNA-test on Leo at embryonic stage. Plus chorionic villus sampling on the foetal tissue. I wanted to get the results of that test so we could get an expert to match them up with your own DNA fingerprinting. It would be clear, neutral proof that you're siblings. Now it seems that the only alternative is exhumation, if anything's left of him after the Harvest Contract.'

Petra lightens up and looks surprised. 'You don't need to go to those lengths,' she says almost gaily. 'Remember, not so long ago Leo took out the life insurance. The DNA-test was *de rigueur*. ZKD will have the results. Perhaps they'd give them to me, if I asked nicely.'

I give her suggestion some serious thought, but once bitten, twice shy. I'm wary now of naïve optimism, not least my own.

'People are not so nice these days, you know. However, if ZKD have the test results the chances are the Staatspolizei have them too, what with the enquiry into Leo's death. Petra – another call? May I?'

'Be my guest.'

I trip back to the office and call up Reik. It feels more sanitary confronting him on a screen than in person, but as soon as his image pops up and resolves out of simple fractals I realise he's got one of his black dog moods hanging over him. He's wearing thick braces and one of the epaulettes on his shirt has come unbuttoned and is hanging sloppily off the left shoulder. He runs his fat fingers through the black, larded hair. He raises his lemuroid nose disdainfully.

'Oh, it's you,' he mutters. 'Calling from her place, I see.'

'How d'you know?'

'Uscinski spoke to me from there. I recognise the décor. What d'you want now?'

'I want your help, Walter.'

I think it's the first time I've ever used his Christian name. I'm not so sure, now, it was a good idea. 'Ingratiating,' is what he's thinking. I can feel him bristling all the way down the fibre-optic cable.

'The Staatspolizei has a Press Office. Remember that. And you might like to remind Dehmel too.'

'This isn't for the *Tageszeitung*.'

'No, I thought not.' He twists his head to relieve a neck-crick then stares back with receptive suspicion. 'I suppose you're still chasing the ghost of Leo Detmers.'

'Kind of, yes.'

'Well, I've got nothing new. Uscinski's of the same mind as you. He thinks the circumstances are cause for concern. But if Detmers was killed, we're no nearer getting his killer.'

'I know. Petra told me – his wife. What I wanted to ask is something else. You've been working on this with ZKD, right? What I want to know is, do you have access to their files?'

'We do, yes,' he murmurs, wheeling his chair up to the screen, snouting things out. 'What's that to you?'

'When Detmers took out his policy they DNA-ed him. What I want is the result of that test. I think it might tell us something.'

For a moment Reik drops his guard and looks genuinely interested but he quickly checks himself. 'How did you know there was an irregularity?' he asks in a low, cautious monotone.

Now it's my turn to falter. 'I didn't say there was an irregularity. Why? Is there?'

Suddenly one of the elastic bands that holds his composure together snaps. 'Goddam!' he shouts, and thumps his fist on the table. It feels like he's going to get up and climb through the screen to thrash me. 'Why should I tell *you* anything? What do you lot give us in return? It's just give, give, give. Never any decent trade-offs.'

'I'm not *you lot*. And anyway, maybe there is something I can give you. For one thing, you're at a dead-end on the Detmers affair, and maybe I'm not. For another, maybe I'm finding out things about neos – about Festung Europa and Neues Östmark, for example – and maybe you're not.'

'That's a lot of maybes.'

I tend to agree, but I don't let on. My brief freemasonry with Moos was hardly propitious. But Reik, I assure myself, is not to know that. My stab at bluffing is hitting home. I can sense him thawing. I can feel him reaching for compromise. He cracks a little and sniggers nasally in a way that strikes me as slightly insane.

'Okay, Sharkey, okay. I'll tell you what I know. And you'll return the compliment. Are we dealing?'

'We are.'

'But it won't get you anywhere. ZKD couldn't make any sense of it, and neither could we. Your man, Detmers – there was something ambiguous about his test. These insurance fellows, they look out for genetic anomalies linked to life-threatening hereditary defects and illnesses. For obvious reasons – to set the premium or reject the client. They run a standard gamut of diagnostics. According to their tests, Detmers was almost clean as a whistle. Only one minor thing. G6PD deficiency. They were bound by their codes of practice to open a policy with him.'

'So what's abnormal?'

'You know about the Human Genome Project, of course?'

'Naturally.'

'Well according to ZKD's medics Joe Public thinks we've got the human genome tabbed, but we haven't. There are parts of the genome that are switched off most of the time. We don't know how they're switched off, or why, or what organises the whole thing. In fact, their guy told me that most human DNA seems to have no function at all.'

Reik looks around vaguely, as if hoping to find the words he wants on top of a filing cabinet or flying through the air. 'It's like – it's like fragments of text . . . of nonsense text. That's the way they put it. Nobody knows what the fuck they mean. Anyway, you've heard of transwitch technology?'

'No, I haven't,' I confess.

'It's what the genetics people use to turn off certain genes themselves. Genes that would be switched on under normal circumstances. They've applied it to plants for ages. You can get a particular flower colour by turning off certain genes in the flower. With sweetcorn, they can turn off the gene that turns sugar to starch once it's picked. It keeps it sweeter longer. That's just an example.'

'An example of transwitch.'

'Right. ZKD's medic reckoned your Detmers had been transwitched too.'

'To keep him sweeter?'

'Don't ask me. There's somatic gene therapy when they get in on the adult cells, then there's germline therapy where the work's done on the fertilised egg. The guy I spoke to reckoned he'd been germlined. He said the advantage of germline therapy is that whatever they do is passed on to the children.'

'Detmers didn't have any children.'

'I know that.'

He's beginning to lose me. I try to pin him down. 'Let's get this clear. You're saying he was transwitched at embryonic stage?'

'Not me. ZKD. That's what they say.'

'Yes, of course. But if certain genes were turned off in his genome, which ones – and why?'

'That's what they can't figure out. I've got a copy of their report here.' He flags the paper in his hand. 'Their labs say it's all to do with preferential associations between HLAA and HLAB genes. They've tied it down to the HLA system.' He glances down at the sheet. 'Human Leucocyte Antigens. Certain of these associations have been shut down on your guy Detmers, but they haven't got the foggiest what the reason may have been. All they said was that it was clever stuff for the early days of the millennium. That's when he was born, of course. But their lab people are basically robots. They trot through the same tests, day in, day out. Anything unfamiliar's beyond them. There are over 10,000 known single-gene defects which are potentially fatal. Their charter obliges them to check only for these. Sickle cell anaemia, Tay-Sachs disease, cystic fibrosis and thalassaemia, that kind of thing. If the tests are positive, the policy application is turned down or the premium pitched high.'

'That's legal, is it?'

'Sure. It's legal, efficient and happening. And not just in insurance. Starting last September, the Wienerberg Gymnasium accepts pre-natal applications for school places, provided they get a bona fide genetic profile of the foetus. Anyway, at ZKD they'd followed their own protocols. They saw no reason to refer the matter to other geneticists. After all, pure science isn't their thing. Insurance policies are. They're just a bunch of high-tech barrow boys.'

'Could you buffer that over to me – the diagnosis?'

'I shouldn't, you know.' He hesitates and does so, feeding the diagnosis and a gel electrophoresis transparency into his print-slot. Hard copies promptly emerge from mine. 'Have you got multi-tasking on?'

'Yes. Why?'

'I'll download the ACGT encryption. But, whatever you do with this, keep my name out of it.'

It occurs to me that our entire conversation has taken place without refuelling.

'Is everything all right?' I ask, *à propos de rien*.

'How d'you mean?'

'With you. Personally. You're looking . . . different.'

Reik comes over sheepish all of a sudden. 'I guess so. I'm on a diet.'

'Oh. Any particular reason?'

'The wife,' he offers, by way of explanation. It comes as a surprise that such a creature exists. I'd had Reik down as an anchorite, bricked into his hermetically sealed *sanctus sanctorum* with only the occult cabbala of constabulary metaphysics for meditation.

'Oh well, good luck to you then.'

'Thanks. And Sharkey, just one thing –'

'Yes?'

'I'll be waiting to hear from you.'

He taps his nose – hugger-mugger – sticks his thumbs under his braces and twangs them out. Then he signs off with a charming little wink. He's been good to me, I can't deny that. I feel I owe him. I almost want to call him back and spill the beans on Petra and Leo, but for the moment that will have to be my bird in hand. And besides, I've just thought of a little gift that's worth a few more brownie points in his valuable esteem. I call through to my vitamin counsellor friend at his health-food shop in Kruger Strasse. 'Put together a slap-up brunch for delivery tomorrow, will you Theodor? For Walter Reik, office 204, Staatspolizei Headquarters, Fleischmarkt. No Eggo Waffles, Buddha Burgers or Pop-Tarts. Low-calorie – everything low-calorie.'

'Consider it done, Sharkey. Acidophilus with blue-green algae, antioxidant enzyme nutrition, liquid chlorophyll, citricidal, basic synergistic multiple and fructo-digosaccharides. How's that?'

'Fine.'

'Anything for the card?'

'*Keep this up and you'll be hanging from a charm bracelet.* How about that? Let's hope the man has a sense of humour.'

chapter six

a funny old world

By Christmas Eve, Vienna has lost confidence in its textbook winter and shamefacedly returns to modern times. There's 15° of balminess, easily singlet weather, and (as ever in these greenhouse days) biological havoc reigns. Crocuses are peeping out in the Prater. The birds are busting their guts with song. And lovers are necking in the Esterházy Park. Conned, one and all, by their circadian clocks into believing that spring is here to stay. This makes the Santas outside the Haas Haus shopping centre, the troikas and reindeer in the shop-windows and the carillons of Yuletide bells piped into the pedestrian precincts seem a trifle odd. It's like Christmas in Australia or some geek copycat planet where, try as they might, they can't get things quite right, a Dadaist slippage between the place and the event. The effect on the human metabolism is something akin to jetlag. It gets you reaching for the Melatonin.

I was brought up above a Heurigen wine-cellar in Perchtoldsdorf and absorbed, throughout my childhood, the jovial Teutonic euphoria that ruled there. As a result, I've had a lifelong aversion to festivity. I distrust parties. I dislike the forced sense of communal gusto. It evaporates into nothing more permanent than singing ears and a stinking migraine when the sun whacks into the reddened eyeball on the morrow. But on this occasion I've decided to put a bold face on things. I've decided to camouflage my latent misanthropy for a few, insignificant hours. It's Christmas, after all. And it's Petra's party. I want her to have a good time.

When I arrive, just after eight, she's wearing her Madonna costume. It's a full-length Marian blue cassock with a simple linen scarf over the head. And floating above her is a brilliant halo. It's one of those plastic tubes with luminous chemicals inside. The tube is turned round on itself and held aloft by a perpendicular wire which rises discreetly up the back of the neck and round the rear of the skull. This wire, in turn, is attached to a stabilising structure, also in wire, that stretches across the upper back and sits under the shoulders of the garment, stitched into the shoulder pads. The outfit she's prepared for me is identical except that the cassock is brown, like a friar's habit. I'm not too sure if Joseph was a bona fide saint, but it doesn't seem to matter. In fact, I'm amazed at how quickly I get used to the halo. It's as if we were made for each other.

She's laid on a buffet of petits fours, cocktail sausages and other finger-food, and the fridge is chockful of Deutz champagne. By nine, the other guests start arriving. There's a sweet little Marie Antoinette who props herself up on a shepherdess's crook, flounced with white and blue ribbons, a string of oyster fruit round her neck. Then someone in a rubber pig's mask with top hat, hunting jacket, jodhpurs and riding crop. As the hour advances, the flood of masked humanity swells. It's Noah's Ark, recast by Luis Buñuel with single members of each species. A gorilla with a monocle and a malacca cane. A neutron bomb of a woman clad entirely in a black rubber second skin, with eye- and nose-holes and a YKK zip for a mouth. A man rigged up like a bipedal book, his duck-white suit, shirt, tie and shoes overprinted with slogans and uplifting quotations from world literature. A lean, stooping figure in a Pluto outfit. A vamp clad entirely in a microbiological spider-silk dress, soft to the touch but tougher than steel, spun from the cultured excretions of the orb-web spider. There's a lovely, pale adolescent girl in a porcupiney Vasari costume of glowing fibre-optics who illuminates everyone she passes with a swaying, cornfield light. When she smiles even her teeth are studded with micro-fairybulbs which trip on and off in series as if chasing each other around the scimitar perimeter of her lips. Argos is in costume too, with a blue bandanna, a fake Parakeet wired on to a collar and a black pirate's eyepatch. The eyepatch, I'm pleased to see, is driving him mad. It gives him a neurotic tendency to walk in circles.

As the evening progresses, the music elides from the quiet lift-ambiance stuff you can talk through to New Barbarian and Hoodlum. There's nothing for it but to bop till you drop. In the dining-room, Petra's cleared a space for the cybernaut teamsters. There are four of them now, with VR-Spex and haptic body-suits. They wander around each other like fidgety blind people. They jump, turn and squeeze virtual rays and lead out of their airy firearms and into whatever infographic decor feeds through their heads. From the Plasmavision screen, which she's wired up as a monitor for curious non-participants, it transpires that they're killing *us*. Using OverLap Scramblers, the VR-Spex have turned the party-goers into death-dealing mutant cephalopods in the gamesters' optic nerves. I look away just as my tentacular alter ego is dispatched with a laser whip.

I'm a wayward librating communications satellite in this crowd. I get into unstable geo-stationary orbit on a few conversations, but they're not my set. Jons, Petra's gallery-man – the one in the literate suit – gives Petra's aquarium nativity a once-over while holding forth on his latest show of loans from the Boston Museum of Bad Art. I duck out of the fray by bending down to read his turn-up – 'Ein unnütz Leben ist ein früher Tod', 'a useless life is an early death'. Then I spin round on the ball of my heel and re-emerge next to the teenager with the Las Vegas teeth. All goes well till she asks whether I'm an architect. When I say 'No', she cuts me dead and walks away.

'I should have warned you about Helena,' Petra says. 'She only goes for architects.'

'Any particular school? Cyber-Baronial, Haute Geek, Techno-Nouveau, Living Brick, Intelligent Systems?'

'She's not too fussy. It helps, though, if you look like Adolph Loos and get on well with active materials. I've left some pheromone spray in the bathroom if you need it, by the way. You never know, chemistry may work where compatibility fails.'

It's nearing midnight.

Petra takes me out on to the balcony and we crack open the champagne in the ice-bucket and chink glasses. It's not my first glass of the evening and I'm experiencing that nicely swimmy, happy buzz as we look out over the soft glow of the urban skyline. The huge zigzags of glazed tiles on the roof of the Stephansdom Cathedral confuse the vision like op-art in the air. From behind the roof, bright against the winter night, a cluster of Suntower, Sunflower and Sundisk orbiting solar power stations twinkles by like the dying glitter of fireworks. They're traversed by a silver wheel that rises gracefully through the starry darkness. We watch the Marriott Space Hotel in its slow orbit, an AMROC polybutadiene-powered Spacecab circling its central docking-station.

'Wouldn't you like to be up there?' I say. 'Planet Earth below, and sixteen sunsets a day.'

'Mmmm. I'd love it. You know, nearly all the clients are supposed to be couples who want to try sex in space. You're more or less normal weight on the outer rim of the wheel. But the real honeymoon suite is at the hub, where it's nearly zero.'

'Microgravity's the word.'

'Yeah. But can you imagine it? Weightless sex?' She sniggers and brings a hand up to her mouth. 'I mean, it must be dead slow and really frustrating – floating apart all the time! Not to mention the mess.'

'Well give them a year or so and the Moon Hilton will be ready. They're building it in a vast lava-cave on the Sea of Storms. Sex in one-sixth gravity should be better than weightlessness. They're incorporating a maternity for moon-births. And unlike the Marriott, when you get sick of procreation you can nip outside for a round of golf.'

Petra digs me in the elbows and giggles. Then she notices that our haloes are failing and she wants to change the tubes. I slip a refill under the crocodile grips on her wire infrastructure and she does the same for me. As she brings her arms round my head to do the finishing adjustments she suddenly drops her hands on to my shoulders, shuts her eyes and kisses me full on the mouth. It's a warm kiss and a wet kiss, and very sexy too. No intro. No formalities. Just smack on the lips. It's also a surprise, a nice surprise, and I stand there for a moment, bringing my hands up around her sides. I'm sensing the opening movement of a symphony of neuro-hormones somewhere in the vicinity of my pituitary gland. When she pulls away our haloes get tangled together. There's a little head-manoeuvring, like battling deer with locked antlers, before we free ourselves and part. She laughs, and so do I. We both feel flushed, emboldened and embarrassed, an inner tug-o'-war going on between shyness and impulsiveness. A phantom Leo stares at us in horrified surprise. For a second, those endocrine glands hold their fire.

'Don't worry,' I say, 'It's the champagne.'

'It isn't,' she replies. 'It's the LP9s.'

'The what?'

'I thought they were Leo's G-Whiz tabs. I popped a couple around ten to gear myself up. When I looked at the pack again they were Love Philtre No. 9s. Fuck it. I guess Leo shovelled them down before going to his whores.'

'Shit. How d'you feel?'

'Fine. Just – you know . . .' She's slightly cross-eyed and wears a woozy, promiscuous grin.

The Stephansdom clock strikes midnight and the party goes wild inside. Streamers stream and plastic trumpets trumpet. Then someone puts on the CD of a Hoodlum band called Happy Feet knocking out 'Silent Night'. It's a great, stomping headbanger of a rendition and the volume is full-blast. Petra groans and loses balance slightly. I sit her on the sun-lounge. She seems to be in pain. Her eyes are shut tight and her mouth is tense. Meanwhile, at streetlevel on the Kegelgasse the traffic is steaming in gridlock, but two motorbike patrolmen, war-lights bluing, have woven through and ridden up on to the kerb. I peer over from the terrace. The two helmeted officers are trotting GI-style into the Hundertwasser Haus on Petra's staircase.

'Do you get on with the neighbours?'

'No,' she replies with a faint groan. 'They're party-poopers.'

'So you didn't invite them . . .'

'Of course not.'

'I think they're about to let you know you didn't. We've got company. Cops.'

'Oh hell. See to it, will you Sharkey?'

I nip indoors, turn down the volume and quickly explain about the police before returning to the terrace. Petra's lying full out on the sun-lounge now. Her halo's blazing and she grips her belly tightly. Her eyes are screwed up. When she speaks her facial muscles are bunched lumpily with tension.

'It's coming.'

'What? What's coming?'

'Three guesses,' she mutters through clenched teeth.

I look round, panic-stricken. 'Well hold on! Don't move!' The advice seems redundant, like asking a beached walrus to stop bodypopping.

'Get on to the Mariahilf Clinic,' says Petra. 'They've got to send an ambulance.'

'No, not the Mariahilf. The General. You've got to go to the General.'

'Everything's arranged with the Mariahilf. A water birth, dolphins attendant. That's what I ordered.'

'They're part of the same operation as the Hofburg. Trust me, Petra. I'll get you to the General.'

'Whatever.'

Every few seconds a contraction grips her and she moans balefully.

At the front door the cops have arrived. The pig in the hunting outfit is explaining about the noise. I butt in and prioritise the situation with Petra. The cops are both greenhorns and they look at each other with wide-eyed disbelief before getting on to the Allgemeines Krankenhaus on their Bip-Bips. The exchange is brief and strained.

'It's no good,' says one of the officers. 'The traffic's snarled up.'

'So what do we do?'

'They can get an air ambulance. We'll have to clear the Löwengasse-Kegelgasse intersection for a pad.'

We agree on this and the arrangement's made. The cops go down to block off the crossroads. The gallery-owner and I flatten out the sun-bed and kick in the tubular aluminium legs, turning it into a make-do stretcher. How we were planning to get her into the lift is anyone's guess. Petra tells us to stop fussing and stands up. The pig and I support her under the arms like members of a press-gang and frog-march her to the lift, then down and into the street.

The cops, true to their word, have held up traffic in all directions and a dazzling star is suspended over us. It closes in, a white, raking beam of light and the sound of scything rotor-blades lowering out of the firmament. A party's going on in the Kalke Village café downstairs and a couple of hundred people have scrambled out on to the terrace to join in the fun. I thank the pig and tell him I can manage. And, as the helicopter lands, the mini-hurricane of its downdraught blowing the party hats off the café's merry-makers, Petra and I waddle forward to meet the paramedics.

'Jesus Christ! It's the Second Coming!' The cry comes from a drunk with a red plastic nose who's fallen to his knees. All at once the full visual impact of the scene we're creating begins to sink in. Here we are, Joseph and a visibly pregnant Mary, with two spanking new haloes, off to maternity by helicopter on Christmas morning. In a spatter of camera-flashes we clamber on board. The drooping blades whop slowly at first before rising as they pick up speed till they're nothing but a translucent roar of motion above. And with a gentle pitching motion the craft lifts, bobs, noses left, then suddenly tilts upwards and soars into the higher reaches of the night. I cling on to my safety belt in mild terror and look down at the impromptu substitutes for shepherds and oriental Magi. I've noticed at least three palm-top Handicams trained on our antics. The queasy feeling that we've just passed muster for breakfast news on Christmas Day hits my stomach and puts the Deutz champagne that's sloshing around there through a second fermentation. I am haunted, for a moment, by a mental premonition of Dehmel lining up the arm-rests on his throne and firing those fabled Scud-D missiles at me with a fevered cry of 'Banzai!'

Petra leans across and smiles faintly. 'Okay?'

'I guess so. You?'

'Couldn't be better.'

'It's one damn thing after another, isn't it?'

'It certainly is, Sharkey.' She clenches herself against another pang of pain, another thrust of the infant battering-ram at the uterine cervix door. 'You have to admit, it's a funny old world.'

how's it going?

Vienna General Hospital, Bezirk 9.

It's one o'clock on Christmas morning. Petra's contractions grew less frequent when airborne. Now she's slumped in a wheelchair beside me, sipping a Marie Brizard miniature and waiting for registration. The haloes are gone, but we're still togged up in sackcloth mufti like extras from a Cecil B. de Mille blockbuster. Here, in Outpatients, nobody bats an eyelid. And as we look round, we soon realise why. Here, we pass for Mr and Mrs Normal.

The room is a Kubrick space station, a big oblong of easy-wipe surfaces, injection-moulded seating and that merciless halogenated light that's a foretaste of solar explosion. There are pot-plants everywhere, the extra-planetary kind that grow out of tubs of hydroponic chemical nutrient, their roots scrambling for purchase on thousands of tiny brown plastic balls. And draped around, in various states of presentability, is a bumper crop of Christmas Eve casualties. Champagne cork injuries and extreme pixilation predominate. But broken limbs, whiplashed necks and bungled suicides do not go unrepresented. The ethery stench of antiseptic does what it can to sanitise the scene, but that's as much as an Airwick in an abattoir.

I stand up to read the posters on the walls. 'Did you possess one of the following cellphones between 1998 and 2013? If so, you were exposed to unsheathed e-m radiation. Make an appointment for a brain-scan now.' There are posters for Creutzfeldt-Jakob clinics, posters featuring syringe-crucified heroin addicts, posters on all the latest T-cell lymphocytotrophic viruses. Tracheal candidiasis, extrapulmonary cryptococcosis, disseminated coccidioidomycosis, immunoblastic lymphoma, progressive multifocal leucoencephalopathy. I look around for a poster warning against posters. The place is an angstfactory, scrupulously designed to induce mortal terror. I pocket a plastic beaker from the drinks machine and return to my seat.

'How's it going?' I ask.

Petra's on a volatile haemal cocktail of LP9s, Deutz bubbly and Brizard. There's a long string to her kite, but the kite in question is nose-diving aerobatically. She looks nervous. She's sweating. She wraps her arms protectively around her distended belly.

'More contractions. Not so strong. I'm beginning to regret this, Sharkey.'

She casts me an anxious look, but the anxiety addles into virulence. 'Damn men! Why do they get off so lightly?'

'They don't always, you know. In Vienna, okay, things are not so bad. But suppose you're a man and you're born a Papuan in New Guinea. There's a circumcision rite I read about that's – well – demanding, to say the least. You start by fasting, then breaking the fast by eating nettles cooked in bamboo with pork fat. The throat swells up and two days later sharp pegs are hammered into your nostrils. Little slivers of flesh are cut off your dick which is then beaten with the bamboo handle of a circumcision knife. Finally, what's left of your sex organs are given a bloody great rub-down with salt and nettles. Childbearing, by comparison, is a game of Snap with a tortoise.'

'Fuck,' says Petra appreciatively. 'You certainly know how to put a lady at her ease.'

I take her hand and hold it between mine. She looks away and sighs. We're doing some deep-breathing exercises together when the Tannoy strikes up: 'Mrs Detmers to Registration.'

The nurse is an efficient woman in her forties. She has slightly chromed hair tucked neatly up under a white cap and a Bip-Bip dedicated to records. She's an example to us all, emanating health, starch-bright cleanliness and an attentive, compassionate manner that – to my surprise – seems fresh and authentic, despite the relentless march-past of human misery to which she must bear witness. She takes Petra's pulse and runs the palms of her hands over the high protuberance. These neat, economic movements of the professional carer have a special beauty about them, a formal elegance. I feel I could watch her forever. She returns behind her desk, but when Petra speaks she's strangely unresponsive. She taps her left ear with the palm of her hand.

'I'm sorry. Did you say something?' She taps again. I realise she's partially deaf, trying to activate a defective sonic implant. Her extreme attentiveness is, perhaps, a consequence of this handicap. Petra has made the same deduction. She sharpens the outline of her words the way one does with the elderly.

'I said that it's going to be my first – my first baby, you know.'

'Your first! How lovely – how lovely for you,' The nurse's voice is soft and dreamy. Her smile lingers on her lips for an unconscionable time. At last she recollects herself and presses a key on her Networker. 'You're not registered with ante-natal,' she remarks, glancing at the small screen.

'No,' says Petra, swallowing a hiccup, 'I'm registered at Mariahilf.'

'Then why didn't you go there?' She poses the question with gentle reproachfulness. It's as if she's been personally hurt by an inexplicable breach in medical etiquette. 'You know you should've done, don't you? You shouldn't have come here.'

Petra glances irritably in my direction. 'I went into contractions. We had to get a move on. I told the paramedics to take me here because it's closer.'

'It would've taken you another five minutes to Mariahilf. They have a heli-pad too.'

'I didn't realise.'

She taps her left ear again, like a swimmer trying to expel water. 'How strong is it?'

'I beg your pardon?'

'Your urge to push. How strong is it?'

'It was strong on the way here. But it's less regular now. Every twenty minutes perhaps.'

The nurse looks at her abstractedly. Her hand is bent back and she runs a fingernail around the embroidered edge of the collar to her uniform. 'We'll have to transfer you,' she says after a while. 'After all, there doesn't seem to be any hurry now, does there?'

'She'll stay here,' I chip in. 'That's what we've decided.'

'Are you the father?'

'A friend. She'll stay here because we like it. There's a nice atmosphere. Professional. It inspires confidence.'

The wan, compassionate smile flickers on the nurse's lips again. But this time there's a little quaver, a ripple of unease around the kohl-dark eyebrows.

'Frau Detmers has paid up on the Mariahilf plan. We're State here. At Mariahilf, she'll get the attention, a room of her own, good meals. It's *better*. And anyway,' she adds, a hammer-blow of hard reason knocking the argument home, 'you've paid for it, haven't you?'

'Sure,' says Petra, 'but I also pay my social security. And as he says, I like it here. I guess it was a mistake to come, but now I'd like to stay. I don't want to be moved again.'

The nurse nods understandingly. 'That's your right, of course, as an Austrian citizen. But this is an irregular situation. You see, your ante-natal records aren't here. They're at the Mariahilf. There may be information the obstetrician requires. Important information.'

'Couldn't you get them transferred?'

She peels back her lips and taps the manicured fingernail against her front teeth thoughtfully. 'Wait here. I'll see what I can do.'

'Christ!' hisses Petra, when the nurse has gone.

'Listen,' I reply, urging her attention. I realise Petra is going to be taken from me shortly and there's unfinished business on the counter. 'I told you before. The Mariahilf's the same operation as the Hofburg and Donaufeld. Reprotech. That's the name of the organisation. Somewhere along the line they're responsible for the surrogacy of your parents and Leo's. They may also have something to do with you marrying your brother. On top of that, we know Leo was looking into Reprotech – that he was on to something heavy – when he got himself killed. You do what you like, but I think that's a good enough reason for steering clear of Mariahilf, don't you?'

With a curt nod she concedes the point then rummages round under the folds of her hair-cloth. She fishes out an infra-key and hands it over to me. 'I asked the guy who was dressed as a pig to shut up the flat after the party. But the thing is I don't know how long they're going to keep me here.'

'Assuming they *are* going to keep you here.'

'Well, yes. But Sharkey – could you look in on the flat? Tomorrow, I mean. When you've got time. Please. Someone's got to feed Argos.'

'Sure.' I look behind me at the nurse hunched over a large terminal in a glass-paned office at the far side of Outpatients.

Petra follows my eye-line then glances at me for answers.

'I reckon she's on to the Mariahilf for your records. What tests did you do in ante-natal?'

'Standard. Anaemia, syphilis, AIDS, rubella. All negative. Then blood grouping, blood pressure and urine for pre-eclampsia.'

'And most recently?'

'CTG and Ultrasound. They check the heart and look out for breech presentation.'

'And everything was clean?'

'Absolutely.'

I suddenly recall my last conversation with Reik. 'No diagnostic tests? Genetic diagnosis, I mean.'

She shrugs uncertainly. 'If they did, they didn't tell me.'

'And you wouldn't have known. They get the foetal information straight out of a standard blood test.'

Time is short. The nurse is rounding off her enquiries.

'I told you about Reik, Petra? Walter Reik of the Staatspolizei? He's been on to ZKD concerning Leo's DNA. As you know, there was no problem as far as the payout was concerned. But they did pick something up in the fingerprinting. Something that happened before Leo was born.'

'What?'

'That's just it. They don't know. Somehow – when Leo was a foetus, or maybe just a fertilised egg – his genetic germline was interfered with. They call it transwitch technology. But they're not sure and they don't know what was done to him. We haven't got that far.'

'Why are you telling me this?'

'Because he was your husband, for one. Not to mention your brother. For two, because if someone tampered with Leo's germline then chances are it was Hofburg, right? The same people who implanted Mrs Detmers with someone else's fertilised egg.'

Petra shivers perceptibly. I lower my voice and grip her arm, holding her attention.

'What I'm saying is: stay here. Have nothing to do with Mariahilf.'

She screws her eyes shut and nods. There's a hard concentration in her now. The message has sunk home.

'If you leave things to me, I'll see what progress I can make. In the meantime, you've got to get used to being a mother.'

In the glass-paned office, the nurse straightens up. She heads for the door. I remember the plastic cup and bring it out from a pocket under my cassock.

'Spit into this.'

'Why?'

'I told you. We have to be sure you and Leo are brother and sister. We need to compare DNA. My neighbour Marta works here. I'll get her to run a diagnostic on this. She'll come and see you tomorrow. Which reminds me, can I get you anything, Petra?'

'Get me a ticket to that Space Hotel. I'm tired of this blasted planet. I'd like to be up there looking down on you, for a change.'

The nurse is back. She watches bemused as Petra summons her saliva and gobs into the cup.

'Morning sickness,' I explain with a friendly smile. Her curiosity flickers as she watches me fold the lips of the beaker inwards. I raise my cassock and pop the receptacle into my jacket pocket, taking care to maintain it in an upright position.

'Well?' says Petra to the nurse.

'You can stay, Mrs Detmers. Don't worry. We're having your file transferred. And we're getting a bed ready for you on the third floor, Ward 37. If your friend would like to go home, he can ring in tomorrow and see how things are going.'

'I'll stay.'

'No. Go home, Sharkey. Ring tomorrow if you like, but don't worry about me. I'll be all right. Worse things happen at – where is it now?'

'At sea, I think.'

'Right. Worse things happen at sea.'

I squeeze her by the hand once more and plant a kiss on her forehead. She smells individual. Her skin has the soft, warm smell of a boiled egg.

Before leaving, I slip down to the basement and ask to see Marta in

Records. I knew she'd be working nights over the Christmas period. She's surprised to see me, but I quickly fill her in on Petra and pass her the plastic beaker. I have two requests: a copy of Petra's Mariahilf file, when it comes through; a DNA fingerprint from Petra's saliva. The procedure's fast, she explains, but the bureaucracy will take time. They don't dish out minisatellite RFLP patterns with Brussels sprouts and mashed potatoes in the staff canteen. However, there's a technician in the lab who's one of Marta's buddies. She'll see what she can do. As I'm talking, a sudden wave of fatigue engulfs me. I catch a glimpse of myself in a mirror: hollow-eyed, haggard and rapidly flagging, a valetudinarian ghoul in an Edvard Munch picture.

'There are taxis outside,' says Marta in her lazy Slav accent. 'Go home. You worry me, you know, Sharkey. You overdo it. No sport, either. You need to relax.'

'I guess you're right. But this is important. I've got a feeling about it.'

'Important! What's that important, Sharkey? Nothing! Read your Bible. Consider those little lilies in the field – how does it go?'

'"They toil not, neither do they spin."'

'That's the one.'

'Okay, Marta, but they can't play canasta, roll a joint or mix a Manhattan either. If you ask me, the lilies of the field are not the perfect role-models.'

She gives me a despairing look and I take the air.

A brilliant swollen moon presides over the Alsergrund District and the stars tremble coldly through the darkness. Unbidden, one of Marcus Aurelius's meditations comes to mind: *Survey the circling stars, as though yourself were in mid-course with them. Often picture the changing and rechanging dance of the elements. Visions of this kind purge away the dross of our earth-bound life.* I glance up at the third floor of the hospital and spare a thought for the poor little mite who's soon to issue, uncomprehending, from his amniotic dream into this universal ball-park of ours. The poor little upshot of Petra's brief congress with a randy U-bahn ticket vendor. An Immaculate Conception indeed. It's a kind of destiny, I guess. No better, no worse, than another. A new life, with a new past to purge away.

thanks, argos

On the empty, sun-swamped Judenplatz, a coltish morning breeze has locked itself into mad dancing vortices around the statue of Ephraim Lessing, striding forth in his great trench coat. A Styrofoam hamburger carton tumbles and frolics fitfully in front of the pedestal. Long fluorescent paper streamers from last night's celebrations wind, curl and tangle impossibly about the effigy's neck and wrists, tugging away in the wind as if the German playwright were free-falling through eternity. The square seems dispossessed, relinquished. The second-hand shops on its perimeter are closed, as are the old Great Jordan house and the Teddybären Museum. And the sky is an unmarred, primary blue, pristine as the mind of an amnesiac. Only a Maxivision billboard outside the monumental Bohemian Court Chancery performs its functions in the confident assumption of an audience: Gans down quilts, Rasper & Söhne porcelain, Maglev train-trips to the Park of Sensations – the silent ads churn on regardless, but I turn my back on them.

Peace . . .

The ephemeral peace of a voiceless world.

Only the slack dragging clop of hooves as a fiaker appears from Wipplinger Strasse, two blonde tourists in the rear of the black open carriage. The bowler-hatted, bewhiskered coachman gently skims and flicks his whip across the broad rumps of the two horses. The fiaker passes the former Jewish hospital and the headquarters of the Viennese Tailors' Organisation and disappears from sight. The clatter of hooves, the trundle of wheels, dwindle ever so slowly, with leisurely, mind-stilling power. It's a world gone wrong, postcard-perfect, focused with that mushy insouciance where things lose their edge and hardness and echo with the numbed inner-ear acoustics of lost worlds, recollected only in dreams.

But after the long, drowsy, morning-after morning it's good to take the air in town this Christmas Day, when scarcely anyone is about. I make my way down the narrow Kurrentgasse, with its little bars and restaurants, its serene Baroque façades. The Grimm bakery is open and I buy a Salzstangerl sandwich of smoked fish and a bottle of still water. It's Friday, but there is a most dominical doziness in the air. The four days ahead are free. My next deadline at the *Tageszeitung* is on Wednesday 30. Even Petra's predicament takes two steps back and ceases to clamour for attention. It's one of those days when nothing much seems to matter. The mind lies fallow and the city reasserts its stoniness, the sculpted density and geometry of its longsuffering historical presence. The hands on my watch move too quickly, or so it seems to me. There is another scale beneath their tetchy urgency, the slow aeonian calibrations of geological time.

The car is parked beside the Collalto Palace on the big enclosed square of the Am Hof. And beside the Palace, under the old iron inn-sign of the Urbanihaus, an old man is scraping away at a violin. He could be two hundred years old, for all I know, this bedraggled creature of the past. He's a freakish throwback to the Vienna of Beethoven and Schubert, the Vienna of Franz Grillparzer's eccentric plays and tales. He performs without music, a discordant free fantasia of cracked and off-pitch tunes beneath which, at times, I fancy I hear the lineaments of ancient Yiddish airs. There's something frenzied in his pantonal sawing. He plays in the gypsy manner, holding the fiddle now high in the air, now down, crouching over, as if playing into a well. But at odd moments the pandemonium ceases and he draws the bow out with excruciating slowness across one pure protracted note. And this peculiar, almost neurotic, improvisation evidently delights him, for his eyelids are pressed shut with sweet intensity. A huge, self-satisfied smile passes across his face like sunlight fanning through clouds on to a landscape of rain-torn hills and valleys. I flip a couple of Euros into the open fiddle-case at his feet and he opens his eyes, happily startled. He nods and breaks off his playing, removing the violin from beneath his chin. 'Du hast es dir selbst zuzuschreiben,' he says with formal courtesy – 'You have yourself to thank for it.'

'How do you mean?'

'Nobody here,' he says, waving a hand to indicate the largely deserted Am Hof. 'Just you. Just you and me. Until you came, there was no music. It's in your ears, not mine. I'm tone-deaf,' he adds, sticking a finger that is little more than misshapen bone into his right ear and jiggling it about, grinning. 'I'm unspoilt. No learning. No scales. You should try it.'

'Try what?'

'Impromptu. Extempore. You live by the rules, you die by the rules. Me – I don't live by them. Don't even bloody know them. Neither should you. Try it.'

'Thanks for the advice.' I raise a hand in farewell, smile uncertainly and make for the car.

'Try it!' he calls after me eagerly, pressing the message home.

I wave again in acknowledgement and walk round the car, passing one of the huge oyster-grey ducts of the city's air-conditioning system. It emerges from the cobbles like the horn of a wind-up gramophone. My lungs suddenly fill with its wonderful, processed gas, filtered and cleansed of all death-dealing micro-particles and slightly aromatised, I detect. The fragrance suggests daisy-studded pastures, freshly mown hay and just a *soupçon* of cow-dung, a little authentic olfactory detailing to appease the anti-sentimentalists. It's so long since I've been back to the real country that my suspicions are aroused. Did air ever *really* smell like this? There comes a point – and I've long exceeded it – where ersatz becomes the norm, the new benchmark, displacing Mother Nature. For the lucky few who can still remember Her.

I fumble in my pocket for the car-keys. Petra's key and key-ring come out tangled in my own and I shake them free, recalling her request of the previous night. Of course. The dog. Argos is not a beast of solitude. He'll be fast tiring of his purdah. But even now I have a qualm, a misgiving, as I hold that infra-key. It's attached by a loose-linked chain to the fossil-grey whorl of a tiny ammonite. Between my fingers, the key lights up – flashing through its encoding sequence – and, as it does so, the ancient fiddler brings his bow down on to the strings with such belligerence, such diabolic energy, that a *frisson* passes through me, a tremor of somatic fear, as if he had inadvertently struck one of the secret frequencies of the human body and sent it jarring out of control.

I gulp a last lungful of pastoral make-believe, nearly hyperventilate and climb into the car.

The breeze-rucked silver vector of the Donaukanal races beside the road. A Sea-Wing ferry scuds like a missile across its surface and miraculously leap-frogs the new glass bridge, its S-shaped ailerons flipping up and over, and soon I'm there again – Hundertwasser Haus, on the corner of Löwengasse and Kegelgasse, in all its polychromatic 80s glory.

I tap in the entrance code, take the lift to the top floor and point the rapidly chittering light of the electronic key at Petra's door which buzzes in recognition. It shoots back its electronic bolts and swings open. The fake candles on the Lobmeyr chandelier flame up, illuminating the scene. In the hallway, there's a demure marble-topped Napoleon III side-table with gold, fluted legs and, just above, a framed lithograph of a Moorish villa, all stucco, slatted shutters and crabby olive trees. A couple of Petra's dioramic time-boxes project from the walls. I stare into their meaningless topsy-turveydom. The first is a funfair scene, dominated by a miniature carousel on which lifelike model horses ride painted wooden humans. The second offers a convincing perspective down the cabin of an aircraft, each seat occupied by a headless and armless electric blue Venus statue, à la Yves Klein.

Art?

It is, at least, more aesthetic than the rest of the débris here. On the hall-table and floor there are scattered reminders of the party – half-eaten cocktail sausages, a ransacked chest-of-drawers chocolate box from Altmann & Kühne and a Musselinglas wine goblet lying on its side. But further down the hall I'm surprised to see that the door to Leo's office is ajar. I peer in. All is much the same since Petra's spring-cleaning. I'm just about to close up when something – a barely discernible negligence – catches my eye. The top drawer beneath the work-station has been pushed shut clumsily. One corner sticks out further than the other. I tap the drawer-knob sideways till it glides smoothly on its rollers and pull it out. Everything seems to be in place: the passports, Whizz-Bang tabs, Five-seveN pistol in its shoulder-holster, loose ammunition. But one thing is missing. Through the overlay of memory, I can *see* its absence. It is Leo's diary which (as I recall) registered nothing of significance apart from his mysterious 'Zak' days. His notebook I pocketed, but not the diary. Perhaps the police snapped it up when they searched the flat. Why that, though, and not the other junk? It makes no sense. Unless they know something I don't. My bewilderment is goose-pimpled with apprehension. I have a sudden urge to slip the holster on, complete with 5.7mm Belgian bean-shooter and 2-gramme bullets, sliding their brassy shanks into the serried leather slots, and that is what I do, buttoning my ample jacket to conceal its presence. This bit of hardware and I are acquainted from military service days. It's matched with the P90 submachinegun, has low recoil, a muzzle velocity of 650 metres per second and can penetrate 48 layers of laminated Kevlar armour at 200 metres. Handy, if your peace of mind is just a fraction below par.

Leo, the console cowboy . . .

I cast a final sweeping glance around his wirehead 'office', his personal service station on the global Infobahn. Then I pull the door to, shaking my head. Argos, I recollect, is why I'm here, so where is the mutt? Ahead of me the living-room is in curtained darkness. I'm just about to enter it when, somewhere behind, a frantic scratching starts up. I double back to the kitchen and open the door. With a triumphant bark, the dog emerges and springs into the air. He's out of luck. Twice shy, I've raised my arms on high, well out of range of his steely dentition. But I've cruelly misjudged his humour. The poor little bugger's been locked in so long that he pogos up and down on those stumpy Jack Russell legs. He's desperate to reveal his gratitude, craving some serious emotional bonding. Eventually, he settles for embracing my shins and licking my knees pathetically. I squirm out of his hold and shake him off with impatience. I notice – as I do so – that some kind soul has at least left bowls of food and water for him in the kitchen. And now – remembering, I guess, his canine oath of fealty – he heads off perkily down the corridor in search of Petra.

And it is precisely here that it ends. It is here that the world falls apart. It does so with the gruelling slowness, the hallucinatory clarity of ultra-slow playback, heading – frame by frame – for that paradigm shift into oblivion.

I see it all so clearly as it happens, the content of those last few seconds. I see it in bright and manifest detail. And I'm utterly helpless. Time, at this instant, is inexorably unidirectional. No act, no decision, can deviate it from its goal. And so I watch – powerless – as Argos trots expectantly towards the black rectangle of the living-room door-frame, black as doom itself. I know what's going to happen. It's no big deal. It has happened before. The light's going to come on, that's all. The motion sensors will pick him up and the light will come on.

But what a light . . .

I'm flying backwards through the air. I watch amazed as my legs rise off the floor. Beneath me, the Napoleon III table splinters to matchwood. There's a rush of wind – terrible, scorching wind. It funnels cyclonically down the hallway. A peal of bursting glass. Then dust. Then static. Then music.

Yes, music.

Dazed, a searing pain in my side, my breath clogged with a poison odour I don't recognise – it isn't that patented stench of Semtex, present at nearly every Festung bombing I can remember – I can hear it, this music, though it sounds a world away. My ear-drums are singing with tinnitus, but I can hear it notwithstanding, exuding from the cellular, fibro-phonic walls. It's the 'Rondo Burleske' from Mahler's Ninth Symphony in D Major. In my distraction, I fancy I can see the orchestra. And the ancient creature from the Am Hof, the centuries-old fiddler, he's here too. In dickie front, velvet cummerbund and neat bow tie, here he is, playing first violin. 'Try it,' he whispers intently, fixing me with his antediluvian eyes.

There's blood in my hair, but it's not my blood. I'm lying here flat on my back. And for some reason my vision's double and the corridor's thick with plaster-dust and smoke and there's an odd backdraught because the apartment door has gasped open behind me, but above my head I can see it all the same. It's a bit of Argos, hanging from the Lobmeyr chandelier. It's hard to say which bit, because there are probably quite a few of them right now, dispersed around the place. A leg, perhaps, or the tail. It doesn't make much odds really. The flat's full of atomised dog. And slowly, as I lie here on my back, I realise that it could have been me hanging up there and dribbling down the wallpaper, this time-travelling entity I call 'me'. And then, as I go on lying on my back, I realise that it *should* have been Petra. So thanks, Argos – thanks for the noble sacrifice. Thanks from both of us. You've laid down your life for two friends. And whatever Happy Hunting Ground you're discovering in the deathly shock of this moment, may Leo be there with you. As I close my eyes to shut out the pain in my hip I can see you leaping into his arms, you or your otherworldy *animus*. 'Argos!' he laughs, 'What on earth brings you here, old friend?' You lick his beaming face, your chipper white tail wagging like mad, reassuringly attached to your spiritual body. Down on Earth, let's face it, you're something of a mess. Down here you've had your day. But up there, beyond the Lobmeyr chandelier, you're all in one piece. Up there, let's hope, dog does not eat dog and perhaps – just perhaps – old dogs and new tricks go together fine.

And lastly, old boy, of one thing you may rest assured. Whoever did this is right at the top of my Shit-List, and there they're going to stay.

Whoever did this is going to have to pay.

This is what I'm thinking when another presence looms forbiddingly over me. I stare up from my unconventional resting place. Whoever it is, they're standing behind my head, so I see them upside-down and with alarming foreshortening. It is, however, neither a horseman of the Apocalypse nor the Grim Reaper in person. It's simply Uscinski. The red puffy face, ginger hair and unaesthetic nose, shaped like a Siamese mutant strawberry. He's in civvies, but for a service jacket draped over his shoulders, and he's standing there calmly with his hands on his hips, gazing down at me.

'I know you,' he says after a while. His voice is dry and unemphatic, divested of emotion. 'You're the hack. The one from the *Tageszeitung*.'

I try to answer but only a primal groan escapes my lips.

A drop of blood splatters on to his left shoe and he looks up. He looks up at the chandelier, hung with dog-meat. Then that jaded police gaze wanders round the flat, taking it all in. There's smoke and dust everywhere, and it catches nastily at the back of the throat. Not a stick of furniture's intact. And even now there's the occasional distant burst of vitreous tinkling as a large shard of glass, somewhere out of sight, slumps out of its hairline balance in a picture-frame or window and explodes into smithereens. Uscinski brings a big, spatulate hand up, clad in a leather glove, and scratches the short ginger hairs on the back of his neck, looking down at me again.

'Good party?' he asks.

the right hands

He prods me with his foot. No yelps of pain. Ossature intact, he concludes. So he sticks his gloved hands under my armpits and levers me upright. With the help of another officer, he supports me as I limp my way to the lift. I can't say how long I was lying there. Nor do I know if I was conscious all the time. But the BKA have had time to get a helium blimp into position overhead. It's a Skyship 600, stationary at about 2,000 metres and no doubt packed with thermal imaging and surveillance equipment. I look up and mouth 'Cheese' feebly. Whoever's manning it, using Computerised Face Recognition, can scan a crowd at the rate of twenty faces per second and match the images against a database of millions of photos. Technology's one thing we journalists know all about. Alternatively, they could count my grey hairs, if they got their kicks that way. Today I wouldn't recommend it. It'd be like painting the Golden Gate Bridge. By the time they finished they'd have to start all over again.

My head's still ringing with the final held organ-chord of the explosion and my vision's dust-choked and blurred, but I'm vaguely aware of activity at street-level. There are people, civilians and emergency personnel, milling everywhere. Someone from the *Tageszeitung* with a shoulder-camera recognises me, though my sight's blurred and I can't quite put a name to her. And there's the white crunch of pulverised glass under our shoes as we walk. The blast has popped out plenty of windows in the vicinity. We make for an incident van that's been driven up on to the Kegelgasse sidewalk. A hydraulic door hisses open on one side.

Inside, it's furnished with blue-grey leatherette benches and laminated tables bolted solidly to the floor. The far end is roof-high with communication gizmos. The operator, a uniformed hour-glass back with ponytail, doesn't even look round when we enter. She's watching *The Sound of Music* in Optivision. It's that political bit where the officers rip up the Nazi flag. Uscinski calls in a paramedic to check me over. A small head wound: I can feel the tacky dark blood clotting in my hair. A bruised hip. Possible right ear-drum damage: to be kept under observation. He passes a hand-held scanner over my head to check for internal haemorrhaging. 'Just dazed,' he says. 'You're a survivor.' But I wish I could be so sure. The dark, cool interior of the van's like a celestial ante-chamber and there's something in Uscinski's anodyne manner that suggests an otherworldly auditor tallying the profit and the loss, the dismal balance-sheets and ledgers of the years. He's calling me into account. He sits me at a table with embedded mikes and screen and produces a flask, pouring a black crude-oil coffee that kicks my brain into gear. Slowly, attentively, he takes my brief deposition. I scroll the text-conversion through when we've finished and endorse with a thumb-print on a sensor-pad.

Apart from the night when I saw him at the residential complex, I've crossed Uscinski's path once before, years back, at a BKA press briefing session. I know him better through reputation: a redneck, a martinet and a tinpot shogun. That's what everyone says. Right now, none of these epithets seems quite fair. Disregarding his neutral manner, there's something homespun and well-worn about him, a fifty-something Santa-like *embonpoint*. He sits there in his handknit jumper graced with leaping white elks and bunny rabbits under a brightly buttoned and braided uniform jacket. A family man, on Christmas Day. He has milky-blue eyes and pale lashes. The flesh of his face is comfortably oversized, a baggy XL to the L of his skull, sagging hangdog-style at jowls and dewlap and rising to the culminating glory of that unsightly proboscis. At the same time, he has about him an unflappable, icy sureness, a rocksteady sangfroid which goes with certain dirty jobs. It's a monumental poise, born of dehumanised serenity, an aura. I sense it as we go over the details of the Detmers saga, as I try to figure out where he's at. But this is not so easy. Men like Uscinski are impregnable. They have wives at home who don't ask questions, and the first question they don't ask is 'Had a nice day?' I try my luck and pitch things at peer-level.

'Walter told me you'd seen the CCTV frames, the ones with the car that got Leo Detmers.'

'Walter?'

'Walter Reik.'

He nods, and for once my namedropping has scored. He's impressed. He also sharpens up, getting on the ball. He can't quite tell how deep the Walter-Sharkey confidences go. From an inner pocket he pulls out a little pair of round-framed glasses. He pokes them into place on his rubicund nose. In these easy eye-op days, specs are a retro fashion accessory. Except, perhaps, with the police. Reik, I recall, is another eye-glass fogey. They suit Uscinski not at all. He's a grizzly bear with intellectual pretensions. But they're his way of saying he's got me in his sights. He's not going to miss a trick.

'No progress,' he grunts in reluctant response. 'Red BMW Z10, A-Range – as you know. They're not common, but then they're not uncommon either. Used to be a popular company car a few years back because of the cut-in petrol engine. Could be anyone.'

Behind us the Rodgers & Hammerstein theme merges into a Findus jingle for frozen ostrich steaks, then an ad for Soap-on-a-Rope. Uscinski looks round, distracted. There's irritation in his eyes, but he keeps it under control. 'Could you leave us, Jana?' The ponytail switches off the TV and sidles past us with an apologetic smile. The door sighs shut behind her.

We're on our own now in the polarised blue-black light that filters through the tinted one-way windows of the van, creating an illusion of twilight. Uscinski leans forward on his elbows. He tugs with thumb and forefinger at the lobe of his right ear. When he speaks, it's with his habitual cool. He seems satisfied not to have manifested his irritation. It belonged to an inferior division in the corporate pyramid of his emotions, just a little outside his chain of command.

'You knew nobody at this party, apart from the wife. Is that right?'

'Right.'

'But the bomb. It must've been one of them, mustn't it? One of the guests.'

'I don't know about "must". It seems likely. You'd have to ask Petra – Frau Detmers, that is. I guess she knows who she invited. Unless you want to put out warrants for Pluto, Marie Antoinette, Frankenstein and company. It was fancy dress, as I told you. But that bomb wasn't meant for me. It had Frau Detmers' name on it. Whoever killed her husband has obviously got it in for her.'

Uscinski stretches his arms in an accommodating fashion over the top of the leatherette bench and nods encouragingly. He waits for me to continue. I recall, meanwhile, my bungled attempt to access Primogen: the false claim for sysman status; the line-check by Primogen security; and Petra picking up the phone. My blundering and her innocent gaffe may be behind today's firework display. Since when, though, did hacking carry the death sentence? Chances are, Uscinski knows nothing of Leo's crimes and misdemeanours. Nothing, moreover, of his telematic clamberings into his own family tree.

'I was thinking . . .' I say, picking at another thread.

'Yes?'

'She's in Ward 37 of the Allgemeines Krankenhaus. When they – whoever "they" are – realise they didn't get her here, they'll be after her there.'

'I can arrange short-term protection. But not when she comes out. We have statutory responsibilities. Bodyguarding's not one of them. The best thing you people can do is tell us what you know.'

'Frau Detmers told you what she knows. And Walter's kept you informed of my involvement. There's not a lot to it. I spent an evening with the husband in Hamburg on September 4 – social. When he got killed, the wife phoned me. Okay, I want to help her. But I'm also, as you pointed out earlier, a "hack". If there's a story in this affair, I'm not afraid to chase it.'

'It's your neck,' he shrugs. 'But you tell me one thing. Why were you asking after his DNA profile?'

'I heard there were anomalies. I reckoned ZKD were going to default on the insurance payment on the grounds that Leo's genetic risk-grouping was inaccurate – that he'd made a false declaration.'

'Under normal circumstances, that would be because he didn't declare a predisposition to a fatal medical condition, and the DNA screening had failed to highlight it too. That doesn't seem applicable.'

'Sure – unless one can be genetically predisposed to becoming a murder victim. Unlikely, though come to think of it I know a few people who'd fit that bill. All the same, while ZKD's position was unstated, it seemed to make sense to get in there first, while the DNA probe was still accessible, I mean. As it turned out, they paid up. End of story.'

He's pulling at that ear-lobe again, wondering whether to believe me. Call it visceral if you like, but I'm taking no chances with Uscinski. I'm pretty sure he knows nothing of Leo's computer-crime, and I want to keep things that way, for Petra's sake. But just what *does* he know?

He leans forward and rests his ginger-stubbled chin on the heel of his hand. Under the glinting discs of his spectacles, that nose looks alarming, like some horribly vesicular penis, blighted with herpes simplex. Meanwhile, he appears to be tuning in telepathically to my thoughts of a moment ago.

'We're nowhere in this investigation,' he says in a low confiding voice, fixing me with those lactic eyes. 'We've drawn blank after blank after blank. And now this,' he adds, waving a hand despondently in the general direction of the bombed-out flat. 'That woman's a bad risk. We'll see what Forensic says, and I'll send someone over to the Allgemeines Krankenhaus to get her line. And a list of the party-goers – as you said.'

'Can you leave it a while? She's having a kid. She's got enough on her mind.'

'A couple of days, maybe. No more. But evidently she's in danger, right? We may not be able to move fast enough. If there's anything that you're withholding . . . anything you think you should tell me . . .'

I shake my head slowly and he lightens up with a subtle smile, leaning a fraction closer, man-to-man.

'You like her, don't you – the wife?'

'We get on.'

'But you *like* her.'

'I wouldn't want her to come to any harm. Do you have kids?'

'You know that once she's out of hospital she'll have to fend for herself.'

'Great.'

'That's life. People get killed, kids get orphaned. It happens every day. Somewhere else, generally, but it happens all the same. But I don't need to tell you that,' he adds with a faint smile, recalling my own close shave. 'There's no cure for it. The only preventative medicine is good information. Good information in the right hands.' He splays open his large, spatulate palms and the smile broadens. 'If it's a story you're after, okay. Journalism and policing are not incompatible. But good life expectancy depends on informed policing. Ruhe und Ordung. Remember that, my friend.'

I spit into my palms and rub them together, wiping the plaster dust away.

'And pass the message on to Buczak, while you're at it,' he adds, easing himself up off the leatherette bench.

'Who?' It's a name I've never heard before, but there's something partially familiar about it.

'Buczak, Nathan Buczak.'

All at once, a logic-gate somewhere in my subconscious opens and the connection snaps into place. Of course: 'Zak'. The name in Leo's diary. An abbreviation, I guess, a familiar diminutive.

'I don't know any Nathan Buczak,' I confess.

'You're kidding me!' He slaps me on the back with theatrical *bonhomie*. The slap sends shock-waves that end with a pang in my hip. 'Buczak – the American. We found his number in Detmers' diary. And in the memory of his car-phone. We've finished with the Alfa, by the way. Here are the keys. Perhaps you can give them to the wife.'

'You were saying – about Buczak . . .?'

'We interviewed him when Leo got killed. Americans! – all out to lunch, of course. But this guy, he was complicated with it. You know the kind. If he swallowed a nail, he'd shit a screw.'

'Who is he?'

He pulls on his kepi, then presses a button and the hydraulic door of the Incident Van swishes open. My eyeballs ache in the white shock of sunlight.

'Apart from *you*,' says Uscinski after a moment's hesitation, 'I guess he was Detmers' only friend.'

He brushes the last of the bomb-dust off my jacket shoulder, a solicitous wife coping with hubbie's dandruff, then turns to look at me, gauging my reaction.

A coach pulls up at the traffic-lights at the corner of Löwengasse and heavenly song emanates from its open windows. It's the Vienna Boys Choir, all ninety-six of them, on their way to the Palais Augarten: blue-eyed, blond-haired youths, the Austrian eagle branded on the left breast of their sailor suits and their caps marked 'Wiener Sängerknaben'. They're practising Mozart's *Laudate Dominum*.

'Ah,' says Uscinski, 'will you listen to that? No Herr Singers and Bronfmans there, my friend. True Austrians. Just Das gold'ne Wiener Herz . . .'

His unprepossessing features suffuse with a beatific smile and he puts an arm round my shoulder, tapping his leather-gloved fingers rhythmically on my upper arm. I look at him, sideways-on. Under the glossy black peak of the kepi, his little round glasses blaze like double-suns in the stark brilliance of vertical midday light.

chapter seven

the nitinol tree

Yesterday I bought Petra a present.

It's a little sculpted tree, a Bonsai, cast in Accelerated Nitinol, a new biomimetic alloy of nickel and titanium with fast formal memory. As microscopic changes in temperature occur during the day, the Nitinol tree changes form, wilting one moment, burgeoning the next. I fancied it then, but this morning I was reading my medical dictionary and it got to me. I started taking it personally.

In the nineteenth century, the German psychiatrist Griesinger likened the human ego to a tree, buffeted and abused by the gales of external phenomena and changes of mood from within. Each such tree is prey to deterioration, exogenous and endogenous. To survive, it needs to be robust and flexible. Its roots must grasp the loam. Its boughs must bend with the storm. But every fresh assault of adverse circumstance weakens it. Some withstand, weak though they are. Others succumb and break. Then, at the turn of the century, Kraepelin described the relatively robust, flexible trees as 'manic depressive' and the damaged trees as victims of 'dementia praecox'. This formulation pleases me, perversely, assuming 'manic depression' as the norm. Today I'm beginning to doubt my strength and flexibility even to this enfeebled point. It's crazy. I'm lucky as hell to be alive. But it was not exhilaration I felt when I woke this morning. It was not freedom. It was not even the excruciating pain in my hip, bruised from my fall, and the ache in the tympanum. Or not only these. No – it was something else, something metaphysical and probably very Austrian. I felt nailed to this place, this city and this moment as surely as a hawk moth is stuck with a pin in the tomb of the lepidopterist's drawer. I felt like the undead. Like my pyjamas were made of lead chain-mail. I felt like a paralytic.

Post-traumatic stress it may be, but personally I blame Marcus Aurelius. Him, Zeno, Seneca, Epictetus – the lot of them. I've had it up to here with Stoicism, and I've hidden those *Meditations* under my Gel-O-Morph mattress. They get you down in the end. Who needs to be constantly reminded that life is nasty, brutish and short? What we want is rays of hope, bowls of cherries, straws to catch at, rose-coloured spectacles and lights at the end of tunnels. We want nil desperandum, cards up our sleeves and chickens agogo to count before they're hatched. What we want is lies. I'm thinking of wiping the digital ink from my electronic book and downloading something else. I'm thinking of giving Epicurus a go, or maybe Boethius – *The Consolation of Philosophy*.

'Consolation': that sounds more like it.

Laugh and the world laughs with you. Cry and you cry alone. For laughter triggers Immunoglobin A and happy-hormone cytokines which ward off diseases, from colds to cancers. Misanthropes, on the other hand, are stuffed full of bad old cortisones that don't put up a fight.

However, fine words and scientific wisdom are not the only cure for depression and existential angst. We each have a mental cookbook of favourite folk-remedies and this morning I tried the best of them. A steaming Badedas bubble bath with aromatic ginseng oils. A large bowl of protein frosted Korn Klones and a glass of mango juice. Clean Calvin Klein underwear. A white shirt and Hugo Boss jacket, both crisp from the cleaner's and pungent with perchloric. Then a blast of Handel's 'Hallelujah' in the Gringolet as I drove down the Währinger Gürtel to visit Petra. And amazingly it worked. By the time I got to the Allgemeines Krankenhaus, I'd relapsed into a calm, rational state of uncomplicated manic depression, with not a cytokine in sight. Nice and normal, in other words. The way we like things to be.

'Now you see me – ,' says Petra as I enter her shared room in Ward 37, '– now you don't!'

She brings her hand down on a bedside button and we vanish into instant darkness. She does it again, and the sun trips in.

'How d'you do that?'

'Liquid crystals,' she giggles. 'The windows are coated with liquid crystals. Pass a current through them and they line up, blocking the view.'

'Fun.'

I glance out the window at the ugly tower of the Narrenturm, a former lunatic asylum that's now the Federal Museum of Pathological Anatomy, then look around me and nod at the other woman in the room. She's so pregnant she's fit to explode. She's sitting on the edge of her bed with a boy of about six, helping him through a picture book. The room has nursery wallpaper, pastel blue and primrose yellow, depicting crooked houses, shock-haired rag-dolls, shoe-box cars and smiley boss-eyed suns. It's naïve, but not child-naïve. It's the way naïve adults think children they think are naïve think. It's the stuff that nurseries are papered with in horror films.

Petra's in a white frill-necked night-dress and terry-towel bed-jacket, propped up in bed on a big L-shaped orthopaedic pillow. She looks pale but happy, slightly extra-planetary. Her dark bushy hair hasn't seen a comb for some time. I like the slope of her neck, the fall of her shoulders.

'So how *are* you? I phoned the hospital and they told me. How was it?'

'Fine!' She nods her head and smiles back in reflex. It's a pouty, rather prissy 'W' of a smile. Her speech is a little slurred. 'Fine! Didn't feel a thing. They gave me oxytocin on a drip. It's a hormone, to strengthen contractions. Then an epidural. Then this great stuff called pethidine. It's like trampolining in your head, Sharkey.' She leans forward and whispers mischievously. 'That was twenty-four hours ago and I still haven't hit the ground.'

'A natural birth, then. Shame about the dolphins, though.'

The little boy from across the room wanders over, timidity contending with earnest intention in his face. He's got a colouring book in one hand and a polychrome Pentel photon-pen in the other. 'Frau Detmers – can I . . . can I draw you a picture?' he asks with courteous Germanic formality. It's not necessary to meet the father to know what he's like. A model gentleman, but humourless – perhaps a bore. The child unconsciously spoofs his hesitations and tics.

'Oh please, Wolfgang! I'd love that.'

'What? What shall I draw you?'

'I don't know . . . let me think. A fish! Why don't you draw me a fish?'

The boy smiles compliantly and toddles back to his mother who probably instigated the mission.

'Oh, by the way, I got you this. I thought flowers or grapes – you know, it's banal.'

She opens the wrapper and stands the Bonsai on the bedside table.

'It's made of Nitinol. It's kind of alive. I thought it was – well, your sort of thing.'

'Beautiful,' she says, kissing two fingers and placing them on my cheek, and we watch as the outermost metal leaves and branches flex back ever so slightly, as if stroked by the breath of heaven.

I hear a cough behind the door of the room. There's a cop stationed outside, Uscinski's man. He checked my credentials on the way in, but Petra knows nothing of him. The flat. The blast. The fate of Argos. These little contretemps are not to trouble her yet. For, after all, every cloud has a silver lining, and this one's no exception. I peer over the bed and check round the room. The silver lining's nowhere in sight.

'Petra –'

'Yes?'

'Wasn't there – ?'

'What? Wasn't there *what*, Sharkey?'

'A baby – a baby boy?'

She seems startled by the question, then recalls herself. 'Yes, of course! Of course there was!'

'Well where is he? Where's your son?'

She looks around her, as if she's mislaid something: a Q-tip, or a nail-file.

'Shit,' she murmurs. 'They took him away, didn't they?'

'I don't know. Did they? I've just got here, remember.'

'Yes, they took him away. There was a problem, but they said not to worry. It wouldn't be long. He had to be somewhere germ-free. They wanted to do tests.'

'How long ago was this?'

She frets her eyebrows and stretches her sensuous lips into caricature dumb-dame grimaces. It's as if I'd posed some high-falutin' heuristic maths problem for which no algorithm exists.

'One hour? Two?' I suggest. 'More?'

'Maybe more. Perhaps a little more,' she says with shaky confidence. In her present state, chronometry is not her forte. She blanches slightly, hitting that point I've seen junkies hit. It's the point at which the absolute reliability of sensory data flips into its opposite – a morass of doubt and bafflement. It's like watching a lifebuoy sink.

'Would you like me to find out? Would you like me to ask someone?'

She nods nervously.

'What's his name, at least?'

'Whose name?'

'The child. Your son.'

'Scheisse! I hadn't got round to that. Don't hassle me Sharkey, will you?' She looks agitated, burdened with self-reproach.

'Did Marta call on you?'

'Yes – yes, she did.' Her mood loosens up fleetingly. 'She's very nice. I like her. She asked me to give you this.' It's a manila envelope, and I check the contents: Petra's DNA electrophoresis, a two-dimensional pattern of strips like old-fashioned bar-codes on a large transparency, plus a data-clip, no doubt harbouring the ACGT read-out. I look deeper into the envelope, but there are no medical records from the Mariahilf. She must have drawn a blank there.

'Keep yourself busy while I'm gone,' I say, handing her back the envelope and a pen from my inside pocket. 'I want you to write down the names of all the people you invited to your party. Okay? On the back of the envelope. Together with the way they were dressed, so I remember them.'

'Whatever for?'

'Tell you later.'

I make my way out into the hospital corridor.

The cop's sitting on a stool to one side of the door, a quarter of the way through a crossword in the *Wien Aktuell*. He looks up as I appear. He's early twenties, the Schutzpolizei insignia on his upper arm and his kepi pushed back on his forehead as he scratches an eyebrow with the plastic cap of his Bic. He could be a provincial postman trying to decipher an address. He looks wrong in uniform, at any rate, and this is partly his age. The authority that serge and braid and metal confers lies just outside his scope. His shoes are over-buffed and half a size too big for him. There's still a bloom on his cheek, no irony in the eyes and the fractional delay of uncertainty in his movements. His only redeeming blemish is a nasty scar on the upper lip. It may be no duelling scar, acquired in some student brawl in a disreputable Salzburg estaminet, but it'll have to do. The flap on his holster hangs open, adrift from its press-stud. I can't tell whether he's teed up and operational or just downright slovenly.

'You know she's in danger, don't you?' I indicate the closed door.

'You know about the bomb?'

'Natürlich. I've got a list of authorised visitors here, for her and the other woman. We wanted to move her to a Privatzimmer, a single, but she didn't want it. Said she'd be lonely. Still – anyone who's not on my list doesn't get in.'

I put my hands in my pockets and gaze down the long, strip-lit corridor, painted two-tone yellow and blue. It's pretty deserted just now, with only a porter humping bin-bags past a fire extinguisher and down a service-stair. Above our heads, one of the neons is flickering with the irregular buzz of a bad connection, a bee in a jam-jar.

'I believe they came for her child. The nurses, or the doctor. Were you on duty then?'

'Uh-huh. Around 9.30.'

I check my watch: 12.43.

'Where did they go?'

He points down the corridor but spots my dissatisfaction. 'I don't know *exactly*. They said just for a few tests. They said they'd be back later.'

There's a pause. I'm weighing up whether to risk offence. 'You recognised these people?'

'Of course. I check all ID. Even hospital staff. Uscinski's orders.'

'Okay, thanks. I'm sorry. But it's best to be sure. And by the way – Gefahrenpunkt.'

'What?'

'3 Down. Gefahrenpunkt. It fits with Dunkelheit. 2 Across.'

He looks down, surprised, at his paper. 'Ach, ja. Herrlich! Vielen Dank.'

the belly of the machine

They cure phobics by giving them homeopathic doses of the things they're scared of: sunlight, water, flight. And gradually they become aware of the irrationality of their fear. Walking down this hospital corridor should be doing the same for me. It should be, but it isn't. For as long as I can remember there looms in the hurricane-eye of my nightmares the Great Archetype of all Hospitals. It's a macrocosmic machine, modelled on the human anatomy itself. The iron lungs of its air-conditioning. The brick and plaster ventricles of its passages and conduits and lifts. Its administrative cortex and the discrete cells of its rooms and wards and theatres. I hate its science, its arrogance, its irrefutability. I hate the way the great iconic moments of life – birth, parenthood, death – must come here to be overseen and rubber-stamped by officialdom, to the crushing aseptic warren of this nightmare. It is the State itself, swallowing us whole. Alpha to omega. Womb to tomb. And so, when I die it will not be on a ventilator, with a plasma drip over my head, or with someone slamming electrodes on to my chest. It will be in a silent field, with tall grass waving. The ravens and ants will pick my bones. The sun will scorch me to dust. And the single cloud that saw me expire will weep to earth as rain. That's what I tell myself, but without a gramme of conviction. I will die in this, or another, labyrinth of two-tone corridors, yellow and blue, in a strip-lit box of gadgetry, the reek of Mercurobutol in my nose.

There's no getting away from it. We're all in the belly of the machine.

At the end of the corridor there's a coin-op snack vendor and a small recreation-area for visitors' children. The area's equipped with a book section, a see-saw and a climbing-frame made of primary-coloured plastic tubes, with balls at each node. It's almost molecular, a helical waltz of 3D modelling. The corridor forks left and right. I stop to look at a circuit-diagram of the hospital on the wall. Post-Natal is right, unless I'm mistaken, and as I take this route my senses confirm this. There's the milky, peachy, talcum smell of infant-care products everywhere. That, and the occasional cough or bawl of factory-perfect lungs.

A nurse comes out of a side-room. She's spiralling the peel off an orange with a penknife and looks me up and down. I walk past her confidently, with a know-where-you're-going bravura. It's supposed to work like 'Open Sesame' in faceless Megaplexes, forestalling suspicion and verbal challenges. Her attention reverts to the knife, skeltering around the upper hemisphere of the fruit.

Further down, the corridor broadens into a wider reception area. There's a black leather clic-clac and, in one corner, a human-size polymer reproduction of the Venus of Willendorf. The Venus is a late Stone Age limestone fertility figure with a blob for a head, great sagging mammaries and a massive belly, propped up on short, knock-kneed legs. Beneath it is a little brass plate with the words 'Make sure your waist-to-hip ratio is a cool 0.7'. To one side, on the wall, a gold-framed print of Pieter de Hooch's painting of a woman with a child at her breast, the original of which I've seen in the Kunsthistorisches Museum, and a dog-eared poster of a statuette of Isis breastfeeding Horus.

On my left, a door paned in frosted glass leads into a small vestibule. It's open, a matter of ten centimetres, no more. And to the right of the door there's a large window, the size of a Plasmavision screen. On the other side, there are babies everywhere: dozens of prototype heads like tomatoes, and aimlessly gesticulating arms and legs. There are long aluminium tables with oval indents. In each indent, wound like warm bread in a white towel, another incipient human gurgles, dozes or wails. Incipient actuaries, plumbers, waitresses, interior decorators and, why not, U-bahn ticket vendors.

A nurse is showing one befuddled specimen with bluish wrinkled skin and a misshapen cranium to an astonished couple through the giant window. The tiniest creatures are in incubators like supermarket bubble-packs, with rubber gloves moulded to apertures in the sides and sheaves of wires and tubes extruding to banks of monitoring equipment on castored steel shelving. There's weighing gear, measuring gear, scanning gear. No sooner has a larva been dropped, it seems, than it's callipered, probed, gauged, mapped and timed, to establish each differential from the norm, each calibrated deviation. Each kid has a rubber name-tag round the left foot and I have a sudden urge to find Petra's on my own.

Four or five figures with skull-caps, blue tunics and white fibre-foam face-masks are hunched over one hi-tech cot at the far end of the battery-farm. As I stand there wondering what to do, I become aware of a man's voice behind the slightly open frost-paned glass. It's a medic – I can just spot the blurred clinical blue of his theatre-gown. He's standing in the little curtained vestibule talking into a Bip-Bip. There's something about his tone, its quietness, that makes me want to hang around.

'Sure, sure,' he's saying, 'Sure I'm surprised. As surprised as you are. But there are some things that can be anticipated, aren't there? You could've interviewed the damn woman – checked her out. She may have lied, but you'd have sensed that and run a CVS.'

He pauses as a harsh stream of back-chat breaks from the ear-piece.

'Because if we'd known,' he answers frigidly, 'we'd have germlined the embryo at blastocyst stage, as usual. This may be a one-off, but it complicates the pool. It weakens the core pool, that's the point. What? Sure, sure . . . that's easy to say, but how were we to know it wasn't his? He probably didn't know himself. She wouldn't have told him, would she?'

Another pause. Another fine-pitched flow of words.

'Great, Gerhardt. Grand idea. Haven't you heard of the anti-slavery amendment? The most I can do is keep them in a bit longer and speak to her. I might glean something. Then if you think she's a security risk, you can deal with it. What? Yes – I know. I'm doing the paperwork. The kid will have to be re-grouped. Down-graded to the B-pool. By the way, did you know that Primogen have closed access to parts of this file?'

There are brisk footsteps advancing down the corridor round the corner. I shift away from the door and into the reception area. I pick up a babycare magazine from one of the leather armchairs.

It's a male nurse and his eyes flick down to my chest. It's an automatism. He's checking my visitor's badge. I thought I was kosher, but evidently the colour-coding has cabalistic undertones of which I'm unaware. He takes me firmly by the elbow.

'You shouldn't be here, sir. I'm sorry. This zone is restricted. May I ask your business?'

'Sure. I've come from Frau Detmers' room, Ward 307. She's pretty anxious. She had a kid yesterday and it was taken away for tests this morning. She hasn't seen it since.'

He's aware of the case and the edge of alarm abates from his voice. His grip on my elbow permutates into a squeeze of professional reassurance.

'Are you the father?'

'No. A friend.'

'Well please, go back to Frau Detmers. Tell her not to worry. The birth wasn't without complications. There was a little postpartum haemorrhaging and foetal distress. The child had a slow heart-beat and there was some passage of bowel contents in utero. It happens, from time to time. Everything seemed all right after the birth, but we wanted to bring him in for another CTG today. Just to be on the safe side.'

'Just a CTG – that's all?'

'That's all. He's got a good ticker. Nothing to worry about. If you'd like to go back to Frau Detmers' room we'll bring the little devil along in a minute.'

I glance through the window and a middle-aged medic is raising his gown and clipping a Bip-Bip to his belt. He looks up and back at me. There's an air of thoughtfulness, of disengagement, in his eyes. He's short in stature with skin that looks as if it's been scrubbed clean too hard. It's soft as a marshmallow with a fretwork of tiny broken veins on the cheeks. His person is pretty-perfect, manicured and groomed to a T. Even his silky white eyebrows seem to have been brushed up cosmetically, forming two snail horns at their upper extremities. He picks up a clipboard with fluttering notes and graphs. He looks at me again – this time with more engagement. I thank the nurse and head back to Petra.

'Here you are.' She hands me the manila envelope. 'That's all I could remember.'

I glance down at the list of party-goers.

'Ever heard of someone called Buczak? Nathan Buczak?' I ask. The name's not on the list.

'No. Should I have?'

'Just wondering.'

'Why, Sharkey? Why all these questions? Are you going to tell me?'

'Soon, Petra, soon.'

'You're such a tease – you really are.' I'm sitting on the edge of the bed, but she pushes me further away, feigning peevishness. Then remembering something she beckons me back and I shift up closer. 'Look!' she whispers. 'Will you look at this?'

It's a drawing of a large orange square. We both glance across at the boy and his mother. We grin foolishly when they turn and meet our eyes.

'I asked him to draw a fish!' she whispers when they turn away. 'You know. You were here. But what do you make of this?'

I peruse the sketch for a few seconds and it suddenly speaks for itself.

'I think,' I say, drawing out the suspense for all it's worth, 'that you're a charming and unique woman, utterly innocent of the ways of the world.'

'What the fuck are you talking about?'

'You've obviously never set foot in a MacDonald's.'

'No. I think you're right,' she says, after a moment's reflection. 'So what?'

'If you had, you'd understand what that is. An irreproachable representation of a MacDonald's Fishburger. Dear little Wolfgang's never seen a fish in his life.'

There are footfalls in the corridor. The door opens. It's the vein-cheeked medic. He's all smiles and out of his clinical gown now, ushering a smart blonde nurse into the room. She cradles a child in her arms and, after a last performance of Eskimo nose-rubbing, she gently transfers the bundle to Petra's care. The tiny creature has fine dark hair. It looks wizened and aged, screwing up its wrinkled face-muscles and working its miniature arms and fists.

'Frau Detmers!' says the medic, folding his arms. 'How are you today?'

'Fine. Er – Sharkey, this is Dr Büchner. He did – you know, the birth.'

The arms unfold and we shake hands. The flesh on his palm is dry and yielding, slightly cold to the touch.

'I seem to recognise you,' he says. His gaze becomes intent. A few millimetres behind those antenna-browed eyes he's attempting to pick a cross-match for my features from an invisible data-stream of physiognomies. 'No, it's not the face. The name. Of course. The *Wiener Tageszeitung*. Am I right?'

I nod and he smiles complacently, content with his mental functioning.

'I like your pieces. They are – what? "Blunt," "scabrous" I suppose. I like that. There are too many stylists in Vienna, don't you think? Uncut gems have a more *earthy* appeal than their smooth-faceted, hand-fashioned cousins. A pleasure to meet you.'

He bows his head, with quick, ironical courtesy.

'And you, Frau Detmers,' he continues, reapportioning his attentions. 'You'll be pleased to hear that that son of yours is an exemplary chap. One hundred per cent. Three kilos, as you know. There was a little concern to begin with, but he's come through with flying colours. Have you thought up a name for him yet?'

Petra shakes her head, abashed at the oversight. 'I've tried a few, but they don't seem right. Even "Leo". I mean, it's like turning him into a memorial, isn't it? Sharkey – what's your name?'

'Sharkey.'

'How'd you get a name like that? It doesn't even sound Austrian.'

'It was a nickname the English teacher at the Gymnasium gave me. It just kind of stuck.'

'Sharkey like the fish, huh? Did you go round eating your schoolpals for breakfast, or what?'

'Actually, I reckon the prof was thinking of the basking shark. It eats nothing bigger than plankton. A harmless layabout of the high seas.'

'But your real name, Sharkey – your real name! What your mother christened you . . .'

'Actually, it's Oskar.'

'Osss-kah! Oh-skar! Orrr-sker!' she says, varying the pitch and pronunciation comically and trying it out for size. She watches for our reactions. 'Oskar,' she repeats with normal inflection, looking down at the kid. He gives the semblance of a grin. He shadow-boxes with his prune-size fists and bubbles at the lips. 'Oskar I think it is,' she says decisively, glancing up at us and then back to the baby. 'You seem to answer to it, don't you my little man? Would you like me to take you home?'

I wince involuntarily at the question. In my mind's eye I see the black blood-spattered shell that's 'home', and I notice that Büchner flinches too. As he does so, a little enamel pin in his jacket lapel catches the sunlight from the window.

'Perhaps not *right* now, eh, Frau Detmers?' he says in slow, dissuasive tones. 'Not straight away, I should think. You're tired and – well, we must still keep an eye on little Oskar, mustn't we? Make sure he comes to no harm. Just for two or three days. We don't want any relapses.'

'If you say so, doctor.'

'Meanwhile we'll treat you to some liposuction. Get rid of a little of that flab. Though you won't be quite back to normal for about six weeks, you know that? The time of the puerperium.'

'May I keep him with me now? Oskar, I mean.' She smiles self-consciously at the unfamiliarity of the name.

'Of course. Of course you may.' The doctor extends a forefinger and hooks it under Oskar's chin, tickling it up and down like a door-latch.

'We'll be back for him this afternoon. Not for long, mind. In the meantime, eat well. And above all, get some rest.'

With a last pinch of the chin, Büchner disengages himself from Oskar and backs off. He raises a hand in farewell. The hand comes down on the nurse's shoulder and steers her adroitly out of the room.

'You're a little tree! A little sapling! Aren't you?' says Petra to her baby. She hugs him close to her breast and holds his head to face the Nitinol tree. 'Look! A tree. Well, not a real one.' She turns apologetically to me and alludes with a glance to the orange square. 'But you get the idea.'

'Petra.'

'Yes? What is it, Sharkey?'

'Where are your clothes?'

'Over there. In that cupboard.'

'Well get up and put them on. We're leaving.'

'Why? What the hell are you talking about?' She's genuinely aghast. The pethidine euphoria has worn off completely.

'I've got the car down there in the car-park. I want you to walk out of this place very calmly, with Oskar in your arms. We'll wrap him up well against the cold. I'll be beside you. When we get to the car, I'll explain. Things have been going on while you've been in here. Things you ought to be told about. And then there's that guy, that Dr Büchner. I'm sorry, but I don't like him.'

'Why on earth not?'

'I don't like his taste in lapel-pins.'

I think back to a moment ago, the sunlight streaming through the window. I think back to the momentary flare of the coloured design from the tiny holographic pin. It was a simplified diagram of the uterus, the male arrow to one side, the female cross to the other – Mars and Venus, emblematically. And beneath each, for a reason I'm beginning to figure out now, was the number twenty-three.

hannah delbrück

'If you'd like to wait here, Frau Delbrück will be with you in a few minutes.'

The maid has shown me into a large, high-ceilinged library. The room shimmers with afternoon light from a big open window. There's a sliding ladder for the higher shelves, an upright Bechstein piano and an imposing table heaped with books in the centre of the room. A few Mundus bentwood chairs are angled around it as if pushed back carelessly after a late-night seminar. Then, beneath the window, a plush Danhausersche Möbelfabrik cherrywood sofa with glowing upholstery and, to one side, a low table with Chinese mother-of-pearl inlay and a patinaed leather armchair. 'Have a seat,' she says, indicating the sofa. She's a smart, angular woman with hair sheared abruptly just below the ear and thick ankles. She's dressed in sacerdotal black and lace-collared white, an outfit that implies a domestic code of stark simplicity, utterly lacking in gradations. 'Some tea, perhaps?' I shrug indecisively. 'Frau Delbrück will certainly be having some.'

'In that case . . .'

She leaves.

I stand up again and gaze out of the window. A long pair of net curtains billow up in the gentle breeze and twist and turn, dancing round each other like the skirts of a Dervish in slow motion. Their coiling, undulating movements are strangely meaningful to me and suddenly they usher in a memory from two decades back, as fresh as if it were yesterday. It's my childhood bedroom at Perchtoldsdorf, early morning, and the curtains are flapping merrily in the matinal wind. Tommy, our old grey donkey, trots across the meadow and puts his head in through the open window. He's eating a windfall apple and he brays in greeting. I must be nine, no more. I laugh, climb out of bed and fling my arms round his large, dusty head, then rub my hand on his velvet muzzle.

All at once, the net curtains sag and fall down around my head. They fold me further into their seductive white maelstrom, their curious tunnel into the past. I blink, catch my breath and push them aside. The view comes sharply into focus. Delbrück's flat overlooks Heldenplatz and the Neue Burg, a big curving block of imperial bombast with a terraced central bay. I can never see that bay without mentally superimposing the famous news footage of Hitler declaring the Anschluss there in 1938. And that was – let's think . . . over eighty-nine years ago, for it's now 2027. Today is Sunday 3 January. For a week, now, Petra has been living at Karl Marx-Hof in the spare room of Marta's flat. As for Oskar, the little boy-god has three handmaidens waiting on him, Petra, Marta and Svetlana. Like Petra and Leo before her, he may be wondering who his mother is, but at least he's spoilt for choice. Petra knows about the bomb-blast and Argos's demise, but to her it's like somebody else's bad dream – mine, to be precise. Maybe Uscinski's too, for his forensic investigation at the Hundertwasser Haus, aided by the check-list of guests, has turned up nothing. Petra can't believe any of this, and it's best that way. She has Oskar to live for now. For the moment, all the bad stuff's shrunk to an invisible little ball of intractable anti-matter in the lumber-room of her mind. It forms part of the unthinkable and, consequently, the unthought.

I look round.

This spacious room, the serried ranks of books and the soft light, twirled through the delicate mesh of the long net curtains, a light that pulses back warmly from the wood-panelling, the discreet, expensive furniture, are heralds of the person who lives here. They speak class, education, culture, money, intelligence. I wander over to the library table and pick up the first tome to catch my eye: Hannah Delbrück, *Genetic Engineering: Patent Protection and EEC Law* (Zurich, 2025). I flip the hard cover open and on the flyleaf is the author biography: Austrian-born; educated at Cornell, then Cold Spring Harbour, New York; a founder of modern bioethics through her agit-prop Web site in the 90s; Council of Europe; World Health Organisation; European Fertility Society's Ethics Committee; Austrian National Institute of Health; Recombinant DNA Advisory Committee; Biomedical Ethics Review Board; UNESCO's International Committee of Bioethics. The list goes on. She is, in short, one of the key players in the annual review of the European Bioethics Convention. No wonder both Reik and Beate at the *Tageszeitung* recommended her. Her connection with the BKA goes back a long way too. As Reik reminded me, Ulrick Leiter – who notoriously 'confessed' to serial homicide in 2013 – was got off his own hook thanks to Delbrück's ground-breaking DNA evidence. A case that sold a lot of papers.

I close the book and cast an eye across the spines of the other works lying around. I read off the authors' names from one pile: Mendel, Galton, Kuypers, Herder. Another reads: Pearson, Brand, Lynn, Rushton, Jensen, Murry & Hernstein. There's a document called *The Pioneer Fund Report*, a bound monograph entitled *Fire-bellied and Yellow-bellied Toads in the Danube Basin* and an English book, a copy of

Aldous Huxley's *After Many a Summer*.

'Guten Tag.'

My eyes jump up. Someone has spoken. A pinched, high-pitched voice. I'm confused. There's not a soul in sight.

'Guten Tag,' again.

Then I notice it. In the far shadowy corner of the library, half-draped with a cotton cover, is a large domed cage with five – no, six – budgerigars within. I cross over to the cage. Up to now they've been keeping quiet, but as one of them repeats its formal greeting the others ruffle their wings, cock their heads and burble sleepily.

'Aren't they beautiful?'

I didn't hear Hannah Delbrück enter, but she's behind me. I turn to shake her hand. I recognise her. I've seen her before, probably on a TV chat-show. She's in her sixties, a tallish, remarkably handsome woman with pale, powdered complexion and clear nimble-witted eyes under eloquent eyebrows. It's always in the neck that a woman's age shows, but hers has kept its slender femininity and suppleness. It's set off with a single pearl suspended from a fine gold chain. She has a way of holding her head forward and looking at you from one side, smiling, as if peering benevolently into the windows of your soul. The hair's streaked with grey and tied back, exposing a shrewd forehead. She's dressed in a fresh white Tyrolean blouse with engraved bone buttons and embroidered flowers and an ankle-length velvet dress that looks Indian in inspiration. It's to her credit that she carries off this vestimentary mismatch well, personalising it, making it expressive of her own idiosyncracy.

'What you have there is two families,' she explains quietly, approaching the cage. 'There – see? – you have a Lutino Light Green cock and over there, an Olive Green hen. The little bird over to the left is their son, Dark Green-Lutino. The other pair, at the back, are a Sky Blue cock and a Cinnamon Sky Blue hen. Their offspring is female and purely Sky Blue.'

I screw up my eyes and peer into the shadowy cage. I'm experiencing some difficulty making out the distinctions. Hannah Delbrück watches me with ill-concealed interest.

'There are dominant and recessive colours to bear in mind in budgerigar breeding, but one always gets what one wants in the end, Mr Sharkey. I've been keeping budgies since I was a child. Genes, of course – all genes. That's one thing I've never managed to get away from.'

'It was good of you to see me. Especially today, on a public holiday.'

'It's best, though, isn't it? I'm busy at the Institut für Genetik tomorrow, and no doubt you're at work. But, you know, I'm very pleased. I'm very pleased that you've come.'

She takes me gently by the wrist, a lost child in a department store, and draws me across the room to the rosewood sofa.

'Not just because you came through Walter, I must add. What you sent me – when was it?'

'On Thursday, I think.'

'Yes, on Thursday. What you sent me was so interesting. Their names, now . . .'

'Leo and Petra Detmers.'

'That's right. He died, you said, and she is still alive. Extraordinary. I've been looking at their eletrophoresis profiles, and I've run their ACGTs through my own computer diagnostics. I must be frank. I've never seen anything like it. Never.'

The maid comes in with the tea and the opening of the door levitates the tall net curtains again in a sudden current of air. They swirl in mad, rapturous transports above our heads.

'It's Orange Pekoe,' says Hannah Delbrück, 'and there are some ginger biscuits. There's something about Orange Pekoe that always seems to me just right for three o'clock in the afternoon. I don't know, maybe it's just the name! With ginger biscuits, always with ginger biscuits, or cake. And I love this sugar, the large crystal sugar. Listen!'

The tea-cups are Hungarian Herend porcelain, white with gold rims. She drops a few brown crystals into the rich, gold tea. There's an exquisite tinkling sound as they fissure in the heat.

She smiles, peering at me askance. 'It reminds me of Japanese wind chimes. There's something perfect, almost nostalgic, about the sound.'

I sugar my own tea. We listen again, then sip in silence.

'Detmers,' she muses, furrowing her brow. 'You told me something about this case in your covering letter, didn't you?'

'Yes, I did. If you remember, I didn't want to burden you with details so I boiled things down to two questions. Questions that required your expertise. The first was: are they brother and sister?'

'Absolutely. There's no doubt about that. They each share fifty per cent of their genes. Cousins share 1 in 8 genes, second cousins 1 in 32. Third cousins are scarcely more related than any two human beings chosen entirely at random. Your couple were definitely dizygotic siblings.'

'Meaning?'

'Brother and sister – not twins – but the same father and the same mother. Different sperm and eggs. But they were also *married*, you told me?'

'Yes. They were conceived through IVF, from the same embryo culture and through the same maternity clinic. In Leo's case, his parents opted for IVF, but the mother was unaware that another egg – not her own – had been used, in addition to donor sperm. In Petra's case, her parents were utterly unaware that IVF had been performed. It sounds astonishing, but that's the fact of the matter.'

She brings a hand up to the pearl at her throat and fixes me with her eyes. 'The name of the clinic?'

'Hofburg. The Primogen chain. The mother ship is Reprotech.'

'Diessl,' she whispers, bringing the free hand round to the back of her neck with an anxious, spasmodic motion.

'That's right. Peter Diessl. You knew him at Cornell. You knew him at Cold Spring Harbour. Of course it was Biomass then, not Reprotech.'

'If there were two people responsible for turning me into a lobbyist, it was Diessl and Lubitsch.'

'He moved back to Austria in the mid-90s. As you did, yourself.'

She has slumped into a profound contemplation, but pulls herself up. She straightens her back and shoulders and returns my gaze directly.

'I know. You've done your homework, haven't you? I haven't seen him in twenty years. We keep Reprotech under review, naturally, as we do all bio-tech companies. But Diessl's kept his nose clean since the Biomass days.'

'It wasn't so clean back then?'

She shakes her head grimly. 'There were a lot of obvious abuses in those days. Blood and body parts came in through the back door from patients in Argentinian mental hospitals, for example. Biomass didn't get mixed up in any of that, but they had their own brushes with the law.'

'Such as?'

'Chiefly concerning the misuse of foetal tissue. Foetal tissue is good transplant material, because it doesn't reject. When Biomass first moved into reproduction technology, they used to induce abortion for foetal tissue – though not without the mother's consent, of course. In one case, for example, a teenage girl had bone-cancer. Her mother deliberately got pregnant and aborted the foetus to save the daughter. Then later Biomass were accused of taking embryos without permission. But they always escaped prosecution.'

'How did you come up against them?'

'As you said, I knew Diessl and Elsa Lubitsch from Cornell and Cold Spring Harbour. I knew that she – in particular – was totally unscrupulous. She'd cottoned on to the fact that bio-tech was way ahead of bio-ethics. There were no end of metaphysical loopholes through which fast science and quick profits could be made. And she didn't miss a trick. I fell out with her when we set up the May '87 group to stop the patenting of animals. In fact, that's a good example of one of their winning bets. Biomass-USA now makes much of its money through patents on transgenic animals. The farmers pay royalties on them.'

'Elsa Lubitsch,' I say, thinking back to what Beate told me. 'She died, didn't she? A car accident in Orange County, I think?'

'That's right. In '97. She was Peter Diessl's lover, you see. She had a certain power over him, in those days. When she died, he was heartbroken, but at least he brought the whole Reprotech operation – in Europe and the States – back on the right side of the law. However, what you've shown me changes the complexion of things, doesn't it?' In a little gesture of alarm she brings both hands up, prayerfully, to her lips. 'The parents of your Leo and Petra were the victims of deception. And the deceptions occurred in 1998 – here in Austria, after Elsa's death.'

I nod and take the liberty of replenishing the porcelain. 'The question is,' I begin slowly, 'why? Why were they deceived, and what kind of deception was it? Then, if Leo and Petra met in childhood and ended up getting married, was that accident or design? Just now – you said you'd never seen anything like this case. What did you mean?'

the complexion of things

Delbrück stands up and smoothes her long dress down where it has rumpled over her knees. She goes over to a neat stack of papers on the

Bechstein. She gathers together the ACGT data-clips I gave her and a few sheets of handwritten notes then returns to her chair.

'Have you shown these to anyone else?' she asks.

'No, but I shall do. If you can't throw any light on the matter, that is.'

'That won't be necessary, Mr Sharkey. Here,' she says, holding up one of the small grey data-clips, 'you have the genome of your friend Petra. It's the book of her life. There are three billion letters in the book, the equivalent of about seven thousand printed paperback books. The Creator, if there is one, may not always turn out best-sellers, but he or she is a little prolix. It never fails to remind me of what Emperor Josef II said about Mozart's *Die Entführung aus dem Serail* after hearing it for the first time. Do you remember?'

' "An awful lot of notes." Isn't that what he said?'

'Precisely. And Mozart replied, "No more notes than necessary, Your Majesty." Any more notes, or any fewer, and it wouldn't have been *Die Entführung*. Agreed? Similarly, if there were one note less in this data-clip it wouldn't be Petra Detmers. However, the human genome-book is complex and simple at the same time. It may be incredibly long, but the whole book's written using only four letters: A, C, G and T. That's what you get inside the DNA molecule. The DNA's made up of 46 chromosomes in 23 pairs. In each pair, one's inherited from the father and the other from the mother. The chromosomes themselves contain nearly 100,000 genes in 300 billion base pairs. And the whole DNA molecule uses only four letters. Adenine, cytosine, guanine and thymine – A, C, G and T. That's our Rosetta Stone. Our lexicon for deciphering the creation. With those four letters you can spell out every living thing on this planet, from *you* – Mr Sharkey – to the ladybird that's climbing the sleeve of your jacket.'

I look down, surprised, and sure enough there's a little unseasonal yellow ladybird with black speckles climbing my sleeve. When it reaches the cuff it raises the glossy twin cups of its shell and flies off dizzily on minute black wings.

'And don't assume your genome's bigger than that ladybird's. A salamander, for example, has a genome that's forty times longer than the human genome.' She raises her head and smiles sleepily, following – with one part of her mind – the white curtain in its fluid spirallings.

'It's the most complex thing in existence, and the simplest. When you have illnesses or disorders, these are often due to misprints among the genetic letters. There are about 2,000 single-gene defects and each of us contains about five. If they're inherited in a double dose – one defective gene from the father, and the same deleterious allele from the mother – they lead to disease. Many of the medical applications of genetic engineering are based on this simple fact.'

'Forgive me, but we're in 2027. I thought the Human Genome Project was completed in 2005. That's what my researcher at the *Tageszeitung* told me. Haven't we got tabs on the whole thing now, so to speak?'

She shakes her head slowly, the smile fading a little, then raises a finger in earnest concession. 'We understand a lot. A lot of headway's been made. We've sequenced and tabulated the entire genome through machinegun-sequencing and flow cytogenetic analysis. But there's a world of difference between that and understanding what the genes do. Many genes are pleiotropic, affecting more than one characteristic in complex ways. Others switch on and off at particular times. There's one, for example, which gives foetal haemoglobin a higher affinity for oxygen than adult haemoglobin, enabling the foetus to capture oxygen from the maternal blood. And of course this switches off automatically when it's no longer necessary. Then there are genes that belong to our past. We still have ape genes in us, which are switched off. I'm sorry – is something amusing you?'

'I was just thinking, I've always been rather fond of bananas.'

'Me too. Perhaps you're right. Perhaps that particular gene hasn't been switched off entirely.' She pauses, then laughs with brief indulgence. 'In fact that's the case with the genes we have for tails, an ancient vertebrate feature. Human embryos have tails but they lose them before birth. And while we're on the subject, embryos have gill pouches too, which they also lose, a genetic vestige of the fact that 400 million years ago we were fish. Of course, some of our ancient history stays with us. Our inner ear bones, for example, come from bones that once articulated the jaws of ancient fish. Similarly, whales have vestigial pelvises. But the truly odd thing is that most genes have no function at all. They're the ones that particularly interest me, though a lot of people dismiss them. Their detractors call them "pseudogenes" or "junk genes" – padding – functional sequences that are no longer operational because they're no longer necessary for survival. You see, 3% of the human genome makes proteins. The 97% which remains contains gene regulators – control switches, if you prefer. 10% of that 97% is made up of telomeres and centromeres – capping the ends of chromosomes and forming attachment sites for the cellular cables that separate chromosomes – plus introns, or intragenic spacers. But 85% of DNA's just junk. In a way, those who dismiss it are right enough. It serves no function. Like cars in a breaker's yard. They were useful once, but not any more. They're wrecked vehicles on the Autobahn of evolution.'

'What exactly's the interest of this junk?'

'All genetic material – functional, malfunctional and non-functional – falls into distinct, individual patterns. The patterns that allow us to carry out genetic fingerprinting of this kind.' Again she holds up the clip, the four-letter transcript of Petra's inner workings, between her forefinger and thumb. 'There are discrete stretches of nucleotides which we call minisatellites within a core sequence of DNA which enable geneticists to pinpoint individuals. Then there is mitochondrial DNA, which is a quite separate collection of DNA residing in the mitochondria. It forms a record of maternal descent. These stretches give us incontrovertible information about the person they come from. Similarly, the Y chromosome tells us about paternal descent and reveals relationships among and between different populations of the same species. From this kind of research we know that all humanity is descended from the Khoisan bushmen. They live in South Africa now, but they probably emigrated from the Rift Valley of East Africa.'

'We're also talking about the techniques used by forensic scientists for identifying killers and rapists. Or by lawyers in paternity suits. Is that right?'

'Right. Or insurance companies to detect susceptibility to future diseases. Blood, semen, saliva, hair – all will provide enough DNA to reveal genetic relationships. But these techniques also take us way back into the family history of the animal in question. They can tell us if pandas are bears or racoons. Or if cheetahs are really cats.'

'Or if humans were fish.'

'For example. As far as humans are concerned, there are particular stretches that can be put to very specific use. You remember the case of Ulrick Leiter?'

'I do indeed. You saved his skin.'

'And do you remember how I did it?'

I try to think back to this case in my teens, but my memory fails me. Delbrück registers my difficulty.

'Ulrick Leiter confessed to serial murder. You remember that much? He was an Austrian whose maternal grandmother came from Hungary and whose paternal grandfather was a Croat. By analysing samples of the killer's hair and blood found at the murder scenes, I established to the satisfaction of the court that the DNA was not Leiter's, but also – and this is the point – that the killer was indeed Austrian but in no way could he have had Hungarian and Croat blood two generations back. The real killer, in all probability, had a Turkish grandparent on one side. Leiter was freed, or at least put into psychiatric care. And the real killer, regrettably, was never found.'

There's silence between us. From the corner of the room, the budgerigars twitter softly and flutter their wings. I'm trying and failing to see the relevance of this to Leo and Petra.

'You're telling me that DNA fingerprinting can identify race?'

'In a way, yes. But the word "race" belongs to an outdated concept. We talk in terms of "population groups" these days. It's curious, but this takes us right back into the history of real fingerprinting. Not the DNA variety. Dermatoglyphic fingerprinting, the thumb-on-the-inkpad variety, came into being in Bengal under the British Raj. The English army officers wanted a way of differentiating between their colonial subjects. Then at the end of the nineteenth century, Galton, the eugenicist, tried to find a way of identifying race from fingerprints. He didn't succeed. But DNA testing's another matter. In criminal cases, it can be used to predict the population group of the culprit and so the skin colour, facial features and so on. The Leiter case was a breakthrough here, you see.'

'What you're saying,' I begin, groping my way forward, 'is that until Leiter, DNA tests were used to confirm the guilt or innocence of a particular suspect. In the Leiter case, though, what you did was to predict the origins of an unknown party. The origins, and also the physical appearance of the party in question. Not an arrested suspect, but someone out there, at liberty in society.'

She gives a professorial nod. 'The kinds of probabilistic tests necessary had been under development since 1993, but it was only at the time of the Leiter case that they became viable and legally binding. You see, there are genes that influence the colour of hair, eyes, skin. Others that indicate build, facial features and height. Skin colour's a good example. Generally speaking, it's 80% determined by genes – four gene pairs, in fact, that cooperate incrementally – and 20% by environmental factors.'

'Sunlight, for example.'

'Right. Same for eyes and hair, in fact. But there are other DNA sequences and signatures which come into play too. What interested me in these signatures was their frequency, which varied considerably between population groups. Blood-protein analysis confirmed these shifts in frequency, and there are thirty different systems in the blood for genetic analysis. So, as I said, the notion of fixed racial types is old hat. It reflects how we talk and think about each other, and if you've seen the Rassensaal, the Race Hall in Vienna's Naturhistorisches Museum, you'll know that these old ideas die hard. But they're fundamentally flawed biologically, that's the thing. Population groups *do* exist, though, but not as closed systems. Obviously enough, with the movement of individuals between countries and regions, with intermarriage, the differences between these groups are not cut and dried. They're more like sliding positions on a gradated scale. Except, to a certain extent, in totally closed systems. Small undisturbed island populations, for example. These days, we think in terms of between 4,000 and 8,000 approximately distinct population groups. The police have been using CODIS, the Combined DNA Identification System, for over twenty years. That's how I know Walter. We go back a long way. But it was when the Human Genome Diversity Project came to fruition that we really had the necessary database to make these subtle predictions.'

'That was part of HUGO, wasn't it? DNA samples were collected from hundreds of isolated ethnic groups around the planet. Their cell-lines were stored in laboratories and analysed.'

'That's it. Active genetic material has its story to tell here. The HLA genes of the immune system, for example. Human Leucocytes Antigens. They're the little demons that reject organ transplants. And there's tremendous frequency variation amongst them. From 0.2%, for example, amongst Japanese, to 19% in white French people. A_2B_{12} suggests an Irish migration, A_3B_7 is Nordic, and so on. Now, remember I told you about the junk genes, the non-coding sequences?'

'Yes.'

'Well it's there, in the non-protein-producing DNA – the rubbish – that we find an enormous number of neutral differences between different individuals. And by analysing those differences across population groups we arrive at "racial" categories.' She winces and wrinkles her nose. 'I'm sorry. I don't like that word, but we just seem to have to live with it. VNTRs – variable number of tandem repeats – for example, are very rich, very population-specific. And there are many other stretches. We're discovering more and more, as time goes by. In the past, we could distinguish crudely between caucasoids, mongoloids and negroids from DNA testing. Now, as the Leiter case proved, the distinctions are much more fine-grained. We can predict the epicanthic fold of skin at the corner of an Asiatic's eye, or nose-shape, or body-weight.'

'We've been talking about criminal applications, but I guess there are other uses for this science.'

'Certainly. For example, there's an allele known as Fy. This gene is part of the Duffy blood group system and, because it simply doesn't exist in peoples who migrated to Europe before the Middle Ages, it's a good marker of European stock. In the States, they've been using it for a long time to determine the degree of white admixture in African-Americans. Of course, non-DNA tests also point up differences. Blacks, for example, have higher intracellular sodium concentrations than whites, and there are about six other metabolic systems that can be looked into. Cardio-respiratory functioning, for example, or bone dimensions. But it's the DNA that really pins us down. Through a better understanding of population differences, medical databases can tissue-type organs for transplant more efficiently. And genetic disorders can be isolated very precisely. It all comes down to one thing: differences in particular variable base sequences of DNA. I'm sorry. I'm talking shop, I'm afraid. But I hope what I'm saying makes some kind of sense.'

'It makes sense, yes. Some kind of sense,' I say, crossing my arms, 'but where are you taking me exactly? I came here to ask you about Leo and Petra. Where do they fit in?'

Delbrück stands up. She places her hands on her midriff and stretches her back. Her compact bosom strains forwards as she draws her shoulders behind. Against the sunlit white of her blouse, the chunky Tyrolean embroidery – daisies, marigolds, flowery heart shapes – glows vividly. She walks over to the Bechstein again and brings her right forefinger down on the keys, playing eight notes in slow succession. Then she stops abruptly and glances over at me. 'What's that?'

'Beethoven. The Ninth. Everyone knows that.'

'Quite. You got it from eight notes. If I'd only played four you'd have probably got it too. Reading base sequences works the same way. From a few notes, we hear the ethnic folk-song. But here, and here –' she holds up first Petra's ACGT data-clip, then Leo's, to her ears, 'I hear nothing.'

'Nothing?'

'Perfect silence. A deathly hush.'

A silence intervenes between us, a metaphor listening to itself. It is not, however, quite perfect. There's a weird after-resonance of the struck piano, like the barely discernible vibrato of insect wings.

'Are you telling me that specific genes have been removed?' Before she has time to answer, another thought comes to me with alacrity. 'You know, this rings a bell. Before he was killed, Leo was finger-printed by an insurance company. According to Walter Reik, they told him that Leo may have been transwitched at embryonic stage. That parts of the HLA system had been switched off. They couldn't take it further than that. Anyway, it didn't affect their check-list of genetic defects, so his application was passed.'

'They were on the right track, I reckon. The HLA system is affected, but also VNTRs and other population-specific sequences. And it was certainly a case of germlining. Genetic engineering through somatic cells is confined to particular organs. Whatever changes have been made here affect the whole organism. But I'm not so sure about tran-switching. It's possible. Using antisense genes, certain stretches of DNA can be nullified. But that might, in the case of active sequences, have metabolic consequences on the person in question. Apart from a few little problems, your Petra is more or less a normal human being, is she not? And Leo too, before he died?'

'Uh-huh. As far as the eye can tell. But if it's not transwitching, what could it be?'

'I'm guessing now,' she says hesitantly, 'but it could be that those DNA sequences in their germlines that reveal ethnic origins have been chemically masked. It's been done in very specific fields. Sequences of nucleotides are chemically protected by additional methyl groups. The effect would be that, if active, those sequences would continue their jobs, but on an ACGT read-out they simply wouldn't appear. They're not picked up, or they're chemically scrambled in some way. That's what we have here.' She slides the data-clips slowly around on the table-top with her fingertip like counters in a mind-game. 'It's extraordinary. As I said to you earlier, I've never seen anything like it.'

'Yet however this was performed, it was done in the late 90s.'

'I know.' She widens her eyes and runs her tongue across her thin upper lip. 'And that's not all.'

I throw her a questioning look.

'Your Petra and Leo are unusual people. They both have plenty of antibodies for Hepatitis B.'

'Walter mentioned that. It came out when Leo died. He had a Harvest Contract card.'

'I see. Anyway, the antibodies, if you like, are a little gift of nature. But there's something else they share which isn't so natural. I told you earlier that each person is calculated to carry about five single-gene defects on average. Well, your Petra and Leo only have one. A little one at that. G6PD deficiency. It's a pretty harmless defect, except in particular circumstances. It leads to a tendency to anaemia in people who're exposed to antimalarial drugs. What's more, it can be carried by women but it only affects men. But what's surprising is that there was only this one. It's statistically improbable. It suggests they were indeed germlined and whoever did the germlining, in addition to masking the sequences we mentioned earlier, was trying to ensure that they and their offspring would be free of any disorders caused by single-gene defects.'

I bring my hands together at my lips and tap each finger against its opposite number, one after the other. 'Two things, then,' I say, drawing the strands apart. 'Masking ethnic sequences and producing beings with only one inherited disorder. Let's take the first. Why should anyone do that?'

'You tell me.'

She's either testing me or admitting her own ignorance, I'm not sure which.

'Well, in the light of what we were saying earlier about the forensic use of this evidence, I can only think of one thing. If Petra or Leo had committed a crime and escaped detection, the DNA evidence could not have been traced to them.' My heart skips a beat. It's suddenly occurred to me that Leo was indeed a criminal, and fairly big-league at that. He was not, however, the variety that leaves blood and hair around the place – except of course in the Prater park, by the Lusthaus pavilion. But that was the scene of somebody else's crime. That was victim-blood. Delbrück quickly pulls me up.

'You're wrong. If they were hauled in as suspects, the DNA evidence would be quite substantial enough to inculpate them.'

'In that case, if they were *not* hauled in as suspects – if, that is, there were *no* suspects – there's no way in which the police could put together a workable racial and individual profile of the person they were looking for. No DNA Photofit.'

'You've got it.'

'But that's absurd.'

'I agree,' she says, shrugging her shoulders lightly.

'I can't envisage any circumstances in which this would present advantages. Furthermore, whatever advantages there might be were clearly planned for by someone else. They were planned even before the birth of the two people who would, we suppose, reap the benefits of the genetic changes that'd been made. Their germlines, we were saying, were altered while they were still no more than embryos.'

She nods and shrugs again. 'It's preposterous!' She throws her hands in the air. And as she does she cracks into fulsome laughter. It's lovely, girlish laughter – civilised laughter too, set off by a joke conundrum – and I find myself joining in.

'You have no theories at all?' I ask, still smiling at our joint impasse.

'None whatsoever!'

'Then that leaves us – where? *Nowhere*, unless I'm much mistaken.'

'You're forgetting the second thing. The apparent elimination of all but one single-gene defects.'

'Oh yes. Tell me about that, then. What does it mean?'

'No, *you* tell *me*!' she says again, still smiling. Now I know she's indulging in the Socratic method, eliciting answers rather than dishing them up.

'Give me a clue. Why should someone do that? To create healthy, happy individuals, I suppose.'

'I would suppose so too.'

'And if one defect remained, the G6PD deficiency, maybe they overlooked it. Or maybe in the 90s it was something they couldn't correct. Anyway, you said it was harmless enough, under normal circumstances.'

'Yes. Unless they travelled to the tropics. Unless they were treated with antimalarial drugs.'

'I don't think Leo or Petra ever left Vienna. Except once, if I remember. To go to New York.'

'No problem there, in that case.'

Delbrück brings a hand to her mouth and wipes the humour from her lips. It's as if it had never been there. There's a long thought-laden intellectual moratorium during which she narrows her eyes and stares directly at me, or *through* me, I now realise, fixing a precise juncture in conceptual space. For a split-second I have the uncanny sensation that her thoughts have pierced me like a laser, inscribing their invisible trajectories upon my own.

'They were brother and sister,' I say, thinking aloud. 'This must have something to do with it.'

'What, in your opinion?'

'Let's suppose their marriage was no accident. Suppose that someone at Reprotech wanted them to get married and, presumably, to have babies. Now *why*? Why should that be? I'd always assumed that inbreeding was bad for the genetic stock. Hence the incest taboo, no? But I'm suddenly reminded of something my uncle told me. He's a cattle breeder in Steyr. Obviously enough, livestock breeders don't want to have sick herds. They want genetically strong animals. But according to Uncle Kurtz, they also want uniformity. They want Guernseys that all produce lots of milk, or heifers that are all high in muscle and low in fat. They want a standardised product. So breeders actually tolerate inbreeding. Isn't that so?'

'It is, yes. Racing stables work to a similar agenda. So do wheat farmers. And you get a parallel phenomenon in certain societies. The pharaohs intermarried, as aristocratic families continue to do. "Birds of a feather," Mr Sharkey. Arranged marriages also function within limited gene pools in other communities. There's a persistent prejudicial belief that hybrids are inferior. We use words like "mongrel", "bastard", "half-breed", "half-caste" . . . This is largely cultural and tribal pseudospeciation. Social groups assert their separateness. They consider others outside the group to be less than human. But remember what I told you earlier. When two defective genes coincide, disease follows. In any of these inbred communities or herds or crops there is, on the face of things, an appreciably greater risk of inherited disease. Here in Austria, for example, legally one can marry a second cousin, but not a sibling or a first cousin. The incest taboo isn't the vestige of senseless primitive prohibitions. It serves a very real biological function. It's a precautionary measure to protect against disease.'

A thought crosses my mind and I snap my fingers. 'Of course! It protects against disease, but the threat of inherited disease only exists where there are deleterious alleles in the pool. Uncle Kurtz used to say as much. Inbreeding's okay, provided there are no bad genes. And what did we say about Petra and Leo? No bad genes! Except – what was it?'

'G6PD deficiency.'

'Right. You said it wasn't so serious. So apparently they fit the bill. Prize human breeding stock. Uniformity of offspring guaranteed. Tell me, am I on the right track?'

'You're not doing badly,' she concedes, settling back in her chair and meshing her fingers. 'The terms we need here are "homozygous" and "heterozygous". An inbred individual has two identical alleles of a particular gene and is homozygous for that gene. An outbred individual has different alleles and is heterozygous. Geneticists tend to agree that a species gains if it is fairly heterozygous. It's what we call "hybrid vigour". Of course, a homozygous population can be very varied too, if each homozygous individual carries a different pair of alleles to its neighbour. The point is that allele variation equals biodiversity. In most societies you get a balance between inbreeding and outbreeding, a degree of protective gene-shuffling. Pure inbreeders, as you deduced, are at a disadvantage unless their gene pool is cleansed, or almost cleansed, of deleterious alleles. Smart cattle and horse breeders sometimes manage this.'

'So it's quite possible, outside the tiny hermetic island populations you mentioned earlier and without resort to illegal cloning, to create a family or community that's totally self-contained and uncontaminated. First overcome the incest taboo. How? By making sure that brother and sister are unaware of their sibling relationship. IVF is the route. Leo and Petra the result. Would there be any biological disadvantages in such a scheme?'

Delbrück's staring through me again, a beachcomber staring out across the ocean. 'In a stable eco-system,' she says at length, 'the answer is "no". But we live in a world where viruses mutate with frightening adaptability. In a sense, like cloning, sibling marriage combined with natural selection leads to genetic uniformity and, hence, increased susceptibility to infection. The gene-shuffling that's necessary to adapt to new viral threats would have diminished, you see. Any such couple, or community of sibling couples, would always have that vulnerability. The same applies to uniform cattle herds, or the uniform use of one strain of wheat-grain. If one potent virus emerges and wipes out the herd or crop, then you're stuck. You're in big trouble.'

'Unless, of course, the kind of genetic variation that outbreeding produces could be created artificially, by genetic engineering.'

Delbrück stands up abruptly and raises her head with an oddly impetuous gesture. It's as if she's suddenly lost patience. Recollecting herself, she flashes an uneasy smile at me and walks over to the bird-cage where she pushes a little finger gently against the grille. She has her back to me and when she speaks she speaks into the corner of the room. Her voice is softened, muted. 'You have a good mind, Mr Sharkey. A very good mind. It's very stimulating to discuss these matters with you. I only wish,' she adds, turning to face me with renewed self-assurance, 'I only wish that all of my students at the Institut could pick things up as . . . as *intuitively* as you do. Tell me, did your Leo and Petra have children?'

not to mention love

'No,' I reply. 'Or rather, yes. *She* did. It would seem that about a year before he died, Leo discovered that he and Petra were brother and sister. He stopped conjugal relations dead. She had an affair and a child was born, a little boy. It was born just a couple of days ago.'

'So much for somebody's master-plan.'

'Exactly. It was odd. We did our best to keep her away from the Mariahilf – the maternity hospital where she was booked in for the birth. It's part of Reprotech. I got her into the Allgemeines Krankenhaus. But the obstetrician turned out to be from Mariahilf. Büchner was his name. I found out later that he works in private and state sectors. He happened to be on standby at the Allgemeines when Petra came in. Perhaps it wasn't such a coincidence after all. I certainly have my doubts. I overheard him bipping someone. It was strange, the conversation. I'm sure he was talking about Petra and Oskar.'

'Oskar?'

'The child. I got the two of them out of hospital as fast as possible. They're staying with friends, my neighbours. But it's clear to me that Büchner had time to DNA the baby, something the Mariahilf hadn't done in ante-natal. He had time to discover it wasn't Leo's son.'

Delbrück returns to the open window and stands there staring down at me. Her hands are clasped behind her back and, against the white rectangle of light, against the billowing curtain, she's a two-dimensional silhouette. Whatever expression her face bears, it's a mystery to me. Her face is a black plasticine egg. When she speaks, her voice lacks vigour. It's sabotaged by sorrow and disquiet.

'We've talked our way around this subject, Mr Sharkey. We've turned up matters that someone would prefer to remain undisturbed. But where precisely are we? What conclusions do you draw?'

'My conclusion is that we've stumbled on a clandestine programme of involuntary surrogate motherhood. The purpose of the programme seems to be to create germlined individuals who can elude DNA detection in criminal investigations. It's impossible to be more specific for the moment. The programme began in the 90s. Perhaps it's still continuing. I think I'm right in saying that surrogate mothers, even when they know what they're doing, have no rights. Isn't that so?'

'Yes. We're talking about the US and the Third World now. Surrogacy's officially illegal in Europe. In those countries where it's permitted, the surrogate mothers certainly have no parental rights. That was a decision based on law of tort, intellectual property and commercial contract law. Of course, laws can change, which may be one reason for the deception in this affair. On the other hand, there's the obvious advantage that surrogate mothers are expensive. When the parents don't know it's not their child they're conned out of payment and – much more important – they're conned into rearing the children for free. When you look at child-bearing and rearing together, you're looking at a massive investment of time and money.'

'Not to mention love.'

She bows her head. The curve of her shoulder and neck has a sudden tragic elegance against the white swell of tulle.

'We know this happened to the parents of Leo and Petra,' I resume. 'But we don't know how many others were involved. But let's suppose for just a moment that there were more, that through Reprotech a deliberate criminal reproduction programme was put into operation. The question remains: why? What were, or are, the objectives? Are there any precedents here?'

She turns and holds back the curtain, gazing over the Heldenplatz. 'There have been previous eugenics programmes, yes. Overt policies of race-improvement. Before the First World War, Churchill tried to introduce a eugenic programme to improve the genetic stock of the British people. He considered that the weak-minded were outbreeding the intelligent. Then, of course, there were the Nazis. Their Law for Preventing Hereditarily Ill Progeny was based on Harry H. Laughlin's Model Eugenic Sterilization Law, an American scheme. The Nazi doctors, as we know, exterminated some 120,000 mentally handicapped people. But on the other side of the Atlantic, sterilisation was the remedy for mental retardation. Up to 1973, 100,000 feeble-minded women were sterilised in the US. The Indians had a sterilisation programme in the 70s, not to mention the unofficial programme of murdering female offspring because male children are preferred. And various African states have practised enforced sterilisation since the JAG7 virus broke out in Kenya eight years ago. Eugenic choices are everywhere. In the US, for example, one sperm bank is called the Repository of Germinal Choice. Women study the looks, IQ, race and so on of the donor before choosing the most appropriate sperm for artificial insemination. Where do you want me to stop? As you yourself pointed out, it all goes back to selective breeding in the farmyard and the stable. The same principles and techniques are easily adapted to human communities. Previous eugenics programmes have tended to be of the weeding variety. Weeding out bad material. With genetic engineering, the emphasis is more positive. It falls on correction of defects and the nurturing of strong characteristics.'

'Lubitsch is dead,' I say, recapping on our earlier discussion. 'But Diessl is alive. I know it's a long time since you've heard of him, but did he ever espouse beliefs that – in your opinion – could evolve into something like this?'

She turns, half-profile, into the light, and at last I can see her downcast eyes, the neat, straight nose. She speaks, and there is depth and soul-searching in the timbre of that voice. Suddenly, I trust her to the core.

'Not Diessl, no. He's not a bad man. Not fundamentally. But Lubitsch. She was a woman who lacked feeling at a certain level, Mr Sharkey. As I told you, she was young and moral subtleties were an inconvenience to her. She influenced Diessl. She pushed him into things.'

'But she died. In 1997. Apparently that was before the events we're talking about took place.'

'I'm aware of that. I have no real answer to your objection. I can only suggest that in certain cases the dead can perpetuate their influence. Plans they initiated while alive survive them. Their aura presses on, towards whatever objectives it has set itself.'

I can barely hear what she says. Her voice is that of someone speaking in their sleep.

'They killed Leo,' I murmur.

'Maybe,' she qualifies, turning and leaning her elbows on the back of the chair. I can see her full face now, and she smiles compassionately. 'Maybe they killed your friend Leo too.'

'And they tried to kill Petra.'

She looks ahead fixedly without a word for several seconds, then she stirs herself and speaks.

'You were right to come and see me, Mr Sharkey. Your words, your conversation with Leo before his death and these ACGTs are disturbing evidence. But they're not enough. If you want me to take action through the International Committee of Bioethics – and, indeed, the law – we will need something more substantial. I want to see how far you can get with this. I really do. How many other people know as much as you've told me?'

'Nobody. Only Petra.'

'The police?'

I shake my head. 'They know that I think Leo was murdered. Uscinski knows. But only Walter Reik knows I'm following the genetic lead. After all, he helped put me on to it.'

'Keep things this way. Don't involve anyone else for the time being. Assuming that the people responsible for these outrages are still operational, and still working through Reprotech and its outhouses, then they mustn't get wind of our suspicions. It may be that they already have you under observation, and Petra. From what you told me in your letter, Leo had made considerable progress in his own investigations. When he was killed, that is.'

'I think so, yes. He was a crack-hand at the computer. He got into Reprotech's system, don't ask me how. My own efforts to do the same came to nothing. And I don't know how far Leo got. He left very few records. There was a limit to what he could tell me, and a limit to what I remembered subsequently.'

'What exactly was he trying to find out?'

'That's easy. He was after the names of his father and mother. His genetic father and mother, I mean. He had codes, but no names. He was trying to find out who he was.'

Again, Delbrück brings a hand up to the back of her head, as if feeling for an errant hairpin. The gesture is half-conscious, an involuntary twinge.

'I believe,' I go on, 'that the details of egg and sperm donors must be kept by law.'

'Normally, that's right. To track down potential genetic disease, amongst other things.'

'Then *normally* Reprotech can answer Leo's question.'

'He made good progress, you were saying, until they homed in on him. Do you have any idea how?'

'Buczak. Nathan Buczak.'

I watch her closely, but she doesn't bat an eyelid. Her gaze is studiedly ingenuous.

'I've checked up on him. American. Expert in cryptographic algorithms. Freelancer. Employed by Reprotech sometime last year to firewall their computer system. Leo must've heard about him and deliberately made his acquaintance, unless they met coincidentally, which I doubt. It's my guess that Buczak was Leo's gateway into Reprotech. At least as far as that got him.'

'Have you met him?'

'No, but I'm planning to. I think he could tell me a thing or two.'

'I'm glad,' says Delbrück, leaning forward and grasping me earnestly by the hands. All at once, the distance has gone out of her eyes. 'I'm glad you've come to see me. Walter was right to give you my name. People make errors, whatever their motives might be. Sometimes other people have to set those errors to rights, even at risk to themselves. Mr Sharkey, I want you to promise me one thing.'

'What?'

'Promise me you'll take care.'

A car backfires on the Heldenplatz and a flock of pigeons scatters noisily into the sky. Within the cage, the budgerigars pick up on the commotion and gabble agitatedly amongst themselves like a shocked crowd at a traffic accident.

'I promise,' I say, compelled by the warm pressure of her hands.

On my way out, I spot a naïve but bright little oil-painting in a bamboo frame in the hallway. It's no more than a tourist souvenir, really. A lake. A forest. A shore-side village and an onion-domed church. Snow-capped mountains in the background.

'Nice, isn't it?' she says. 'I like it too. A little lake in Upper Austria, near Braunau am Inn and the Bavarian settlement of Simbach. I used to go there often.'

The picture intrigues me.

'I had a dream,' I begin. She looks interested but I suddenly feel foolish, embarking on a futile narration on the point of leaving. I smile and shake her hand again. 'It was nothing,' I conclude briskly, 'nothing but a dream.'

chapter eight

my life, my home, my doom

The sky's one blue-grey glare, up there where I'm heading. Beneath my feet, the 4th and 5th Bezirke swoon gently away. Parcelled out into their latticeworks of streets, their farrago of rooftops, an occasional smoking chimney, they fall back into chequered focus in my all-seeing eye. The cars are carapaced beetles, scurrying down narrow gulleys. What were mannikins on the sidewalks are now little more than random atoms, amusingly endowed with life. North-east, the Theresianum school for diplomats and civil servants, Radio House, the Sudbahnhof and Belvederegarten. Then rearing up in the distance on either side of the Donaukanal, the Riesenrad giant Ferris wheel, Hellevator and Möbius-strip rollercoaster of the Volksprater and the bland high-rises of UNO-City and cathedral-like pollution convection towers beyond Kagran. I could reach out and wrap Vienna up with both hands, that old blood-stained souvenir tablecloth of a town. Yet it feels like dying, this celestial ascent. For Vienna is me – my life, my home, my doom. As the *Tageszeitung* elevator rises in its transparent external tube, I'm possessed by the big timebound sadness of it all. My soul, it seems, is waving goodbye as it pulls out from the soot-grey terminus of the world.

On the 25th floor, the curved brushed-steel doors behind me glide apart and Dehmel enters. He glances at me, stiff-necked, and makes a guttural noise that approximates to a greeting. The doors shut and the elevator continues its ascent. There's something gauche about sharing an elevator that resembles the brief, shoulder-to-shoulder intimacy of the public urinal. In one case the duration of intimacy's dictated by the floor-indicator, in the other by the bladder's volume of contents and questions of flow mechanics. We opt, wisely, for silence. Yet when we arrive at the 29th and I squeeze past him, Dehmel calls after me with that lazy, educated drawl.

'Oh Sharkey, Beate Kaminer spoke to me. She said you may be

limbering up for an investigative piece.'

I'm about to damn Beate in my mind for letting on about Reprotech when, noticing my teeth-grinding, Dehmel sets things to right.

'She said you pinned down a neo.'

'Oh yes. Moos was his name. I know where to find him, anyway.'

'Good. Rudolf Dreiser's looking into where Neues Östmark gets its financing. Anyway, there's been an attack against a synagogue in the Seitenstettengasse, opposite the Kaktus bar. And a Jewish cemetery's been kicked over in Burgenland. If you could get an exclusive with the boot-boy – see what he knows – we could pair it with Dreiser's piece on the News-Web page. What d'you think?'

'The big time.'

'A one-off,' he says, with caution. 'But you never know. To tell you the truth, I'm pissed off with Sharkey's Day. Reckon we could relocate your talents.'

While we've been talking, the elevator doors have been opening and closing their robotic bite on Dehmel's shoulders. Now, as he steps back into the lift, they can finally engage, though not before the wry blip of a 'Happy New Year?' – a question rather than a courtesy – disturbs that linear mouth, inscrutable oscillograph of his emotions.

I have to cross the whole open-plan office to get to my hidey-hole, and it's a short trip from Heaven to Hell without passing Purgatory. I've yet to grasp why everybody else's workspace looks like it's been designed in Platonic cyberspace for maximum cognitive and ergonomic efficiency, with everything down to the last pencil-sharpener clicked into place with a mouse. Mine, by contrast, is a pigpen. There are tottering towers of books and papers shunted against the walls and the big cork-tile noticeboard is trophied with business cards and my favourite hate-mail.

Some years back I elaborated a brilliant variation on the Dewey System for filing but it proved so complicated that I switched my trust to Chaos theory, order arising from randomness. And I'm still waiting for those fleeting fractals of periodic order to emerge. I've been studying Mandelbrot's Cantor set, Koch and Peano curves and Sierpinski's gasket, but I reckon I'm closer to Scholz's Humpty-Dumpty Effect here: there may have been oneness in the past, but if all the king's horses and all the king's men can't put it together again, what chance has little old me?

I slump down and switch on the wallscreen, trash seventy per cent of the e-mail unread and forage around in my flyblown text-dumps for carrion to throw to the masses. Beate sidles up and runs her middle finger up the table touch-pad to one neglected mail-flag, then taps.

'It's from me,' she says. 'You could look at these things once in a while. Results of the New Year resolution competition, remember? I picked the best ones, for what they're worth.'

She sits on the desk beside me, her habitual parking spot. She's got a Lurex black tunic on and has cropped her blonde hair short, like Jean Seberg in *Breathless*. I turn my attention to the screen and do my best to concentrate on our readers' whimsies:

Dear Sharkey: I believe every citizen should do his bit. My New Year's Resolution is to think up solutions to Third World debt, overpopulation and global energy resources. But not before I've fixed that leaky washer under the sink!

Sehr geehrter Herr, it is my ambition this year to minimise wastage of energy and material resources at the domestic level. Readers who share this concern may like to try one or both of the following techniques. Wear-and-tear reduction on door hinges can be reduced by only partially opening doors and squeezing through the gap. In addition, why waste money on personal address books when you can take an old telephone book and simply cross out the names and addresses of people you don't know?

My resolution for the New Year. I get two weeks' holiday a year, but I can't afford to take my family away for that long. So this year I'm going to take them on a one-week holiday, but we won't go to bed. Smart, huh?

Hi Sharkey! This year I've made up my mind to keep the tube of haemorrhoid cream and the Deep Heat rub well apart in the bathroom cabinet. And in case you're wondering: yes, this resolution is born of bitter experience!

'It's pathetic, I know,' she says, 'but we promised to run it. What do I do about the champers?'

'Send them a bottle each. Who cares? We'll bung this tripe into Sharkey's Day and I've got a couple of gossip pieces to add. Prince of

Monaco spotted at the Bora Bora club with trousers unzipped. Flying saucer sighted over Graz. The UFO season's come round again.'

'And how about the other thing?'

'The neos?'

'No, stupid. The maternity clinics. Where did you get with that?'

'Don't ask. It's serious. I'm up to my neck in it.'

'So I hear.'

'What did you hear, exactly?' I ask, suddenly recalling the Holy Family awaiting the Star of Bethlehem.

'The blast. We heard about the blast.'

'Christ, yes. This should teach me to stick to trivia. By the way, you haven't blown my cover, have you?'

'Translation?'

'You haven't mentioned the research you did?'

'Course not.' She smiles wanly and stares me out with those Schiele eyes. 'I think you should take care of yourself, though.'

'You're the second person to say that this week.'

'Still getting your nose dirty?'

'Have to. Gone too far already. No turning back.'

'Well if you want any more help, you know who to turn to.'

'I thought you were hacked off with me. Everyone else seems to be.'

She shakes her head. For a moment I think I see tears coming, but it's only a stye in the corner of the eye, a watery patch of inflammation.

'I thought it over. I'm glad you're going with it. It's about time you got your act together.'

'If you really mean it – about helping, that is – there is something you could do.' I scribble Nathan Buczak's name on a Post-it. 'Get me an address. He was on the list of Reprotech personnel. Employed till quite recently. Anything else you can dig up on him too. Oh, and Beate –'

'Yes, Sharkey?'

'Lunch?'

She frowns and bites her thumbnail when the wallscreen livens up. It's the new receptionist downstairs. The woman looks harassed, burdened with the stress of unfamiliar tasks. She can't make up her mind whether to look at the videocam or my face on her screen. 'Shar- – Oskar Sharkey? Sorry – is that you?'

'Oskar,' Beate mumbles, running her chipped nail along her lower lip.

'Just Sharkey – Sharkey will do. What d'you want?'

'Someone to see you.'

She shifts aside and there's Petra, peering determinedly down the wire. She's got her hair in a plait and Persol shades pushed up on to her high forehead under the brown thistledown fur of a Russian chapka. She's made up with heavy-handed overcompensation, like a dispossessed movie-queen. The foxpelt collar of her leather coat is pulled up high around her neck. On second thoughts, she could be a gorgeous Soviet spy in a Cold War thriller, Venus in Furs. 'Sharkey?' she says snappily, and immediately I can sense it – something rattled in her manner, courting folly. But if Petra ever went mad she'd do it with style, like Ludwig II. She's a *poule de luxe* – a moneyed, big-time girl, with the will and the way that goes with it. Even on-screen, she knocks the little receptionist into a cocked hat. Beate's still perched on the desk. She crosses her arms and stares out of the window, her frown deepening.

'I'll be right down.'

nevsiedler see

This is Leo's place, at the pigskin-sheathed Rally wheel of his white Alfa Zentrum. It's self-drive, with no navigational aids save a plastic Saint Christopher statuette hanging remorsefully from a weak suction cup on the windscreen, its promise of corporal protection long since discredited. This is Leo's last place, to be painfully precise – the seat he left in the Prater Park, by the Lusthaus Pavilion, on November 20. The last resting place of his ample arse this side of eternity. I feel like his locum tenens. There's a built-in Networker but no sign of Argos's collar and pager. Perhaps Forensic trousered them. And Petra's beside me. I scarcely need look at her to sense her distraction. From behind her Persol shades, she glares dead ahead down Landstrasse 10 as we sweep out of the last suburbs of Vienna and past the squat blue-glass terminals and golf-tee flight towers of Schwechat Airport where it all began. She's either lost in thought or devoid of thought altogether – all or nothing, it's impossible to tell. Under the chapka, the impassive beauty of her features has the tender translucence of uncooked chicken breast, catching, at the extremities, the lavender tint of the winter sky.

We're heading south and Petra stirs once more out of her lethargy. She's none too pleased.

'This is not the way to Hofburg,' she complains. It's the third time she's made the comment since we left the 5th Bezirk. I pull the vehicle sharply into a rest station and turn to her.

'If you're not going to think straight, I have to think for you. Leo's dead, killed. You've got a child to care for. Who's looking after Oskar, by the way?'

'Marta,' she responds quickly, glancing off my concern, 'I expressed some milk with the Kitetmatic.'

'Okay. But on top of all that, someone booby-trapped your apartment. We'll talk about *who* later. The fact is, they wanted you out of the picture too. I mean, what *is* the problem with you? Are you and reality filing for divorce? Think about it. What happens if you go to Hofburg?'

'I ask to see the records. I have a legal right to look into the circumstances of my own birth. Leo didn't. Remember? He was IVF. A donor father. On paper, at any rate. Okay, we may both be secretly double-donored, according to you, but that doesn't change the legalities. On paper, I'm a regular baby. I have free access to my file.'

There's a moment's silence as we gaze out at a frost-rimed picnic area, enclosed by a low unkempt hedge. A starling levers at a refuse bin with its beak then suddenly capitulates and flits up into the sombre concealment of a Scots pine.

'Hofburg, Mariahilf, Donaufeld. It's the same show,' I recap wearily. 'Primogen, Reprotech – whatever you want to call it. They'll do to you what they did to Leo. They've already tried once. Whatever they've got to hide is more important to them than your citizen's rights.'

Petra shivers with castanet teeth and turns her head haughtily, looking at me hard over the thick fur collar of her leather coat. 'I don't get it. You don't want to give up on this any more than I do.'

'No, I don't.'

'There's a story in it for you,' she snipes gratuitously, a raised eyebrow of provisional reprehension.

'If by "story" you mean the truth, then yes. I don't know whether the truth is worth more, ultimately, than physical safety, or even life itself. I can't answer that one. But I *do* know there comes a point when not to continue to seek the truth constitutes an act of cowardice. If you take the wrong turn at that juncture then I imagine it becomes hard to live with yourself. And remember, you wanted me on board. So far my neck's been sticking out further than yours.'

I hate my pontifical stiltedness but the precisely weighed duration of her silence concedes the point. She drops her momentary guardedness.

'Then where to now?'

'By indirection, find direction out. I forget who said that.'

'Nice theory. Are you going to tell me where we're going?'

'It's time for an overview. Do you know the Neusiedler See?'

'The lake in Burgenland? Haven't been there since I was a kid.'

'Me neither. That's where we're going.'

She wants to know more, wired and curious, but senses stalemate and surrenders a sigh. She relaxes against the suede headrest and gazes vapidly out of the side window at the hypnotic parallax displacements of power-lines, oil refineries and cement works, followed by little but snow-encrusted fields and the clustered rooftops of isolated farms. We drive on in silence, slowing down only at the electronic behest of the fine beams of laser speed-regulators that twinkle like tripwires a finger's breadth above the road surface.

At Bruck an der Leitha we turn into the Leithagebirge range of hills, then up a track between vineyards and an almond grove to a vantage point at 300 metres. I park the Alfa at the summit and we clamber up on to a raised concrete knoll with a bench and a coin-op telescope. There's a whistly easterly wind, damp and garbed in miry, aquatic odours. At our feet, the land shelves away in terraces of vineyards, copses and fallow fields, sparsely dotted with high-tech domiciles on flood-stilts and bottoming out into marshy pasture and the great flat pan of the Neusiedler See. Exhaling a low tubercular mist, the lake is a drear smudge of reed-clogged wateriness on which only one lone yachtsman appears to have ventured today. Beyond the southern basin, the faint outlines of watchtowers on the Hungarian border stencil the uninviting January sky. They're dim reminders of the eternal vigilance of sovereign states.

Petra's truculence has worn away. Unconsciously, she's shed so many layers of bourgeois self-assurance that she has a child's face now. There's a vulnerable fleshiness to her cheeks, her chin, even her ears – flushing at the lobes now in the icy air – that the brown coney chapka only accentuates. Despite perineal re-education she still has pelvic pains from the birth, so she grabs my arm as we make our way to the bench, her stiff coat creaking at each step. For ten minutes we sit without a word passing between us in total immobility, her forgetful arm still tightly interlocked with mine. We let the landscape suck us into its substance, just as it is sucked into ours. We are turning our backs on Vienna here. And that other, humanless world – a quailing aspen, three herons stationary amongst the reeds, the cat's-paw breeze that corrugates the cloud-strewn lake – suffers our intrusion with a sad composure.

'There's a resort, at Neusiedl am See,' she says. 'Even a beach, I think. We used to rent out a paddle-boat for the afternoon. I remember it so differently. Of course it was summer, then.'

'It's unique, you know, in Central Europe. A steppe lake. Salty. No deeper than two metres at any point. You can paddle across, from Austria to Hungary. Or vice versa.'

'Hence the conning-towers.'

'Right.'

'I thought Schengen did away with frontiers.'

'With systematic frontier controls, sure. But Schengen's always been shaky because it only takes one weak link in the chain to screw the whole thing up. Drugs and illegal immigration being the main dangers. Neusiedler's a weak link because it's situated on a critical border and even a cripple could just about walk it. In fact, it's so shallow that when the wind's up it can actually blow all the water away from under a boat.'

'No shit.'

'Its biggest mystery, though, is that it breaks all the rules of hydrography. There's only one tributary, the Wulka – look, over there. It's just a rivulet, in fact. And the lake loses through evaporation four times what flows into it from the Wulka.'

'So where does the rest of the water come from?'

'No one knows. Underground, presumably.'

'I don't remember those houses, either. They look pretty neat. Not exactly fishermen's crofts, I mean.'

'Technotribes. It began as ecotourism through the hikeway systems then they recommunitised the area round 2010, homesteading tracts of land. The Slow Glass Company set up here. Remember them?'

She shakes her head.

'They patented a special glass. It's transparent and normal weight, but with a crystalline structure that slows light up dramatically. It can take photons five years to get through a single pane. So what they did was set up pane fields facing the lake. After five years, the view from the lake starts coming out the other side of the glass. At that point, the glaziers step in and put the glass into the windows of urban flats. You get a scenic view of the Neusiedler See.'

'And when it runs out, after five years, you swap it for the Zugspitze or the Stuben Falls.'

'Or wherever. They could drop an A-bomb on the city but you'd still go on getting the picture postcard. Slow Glass weren't the only people to come here,' I add. From my parka pocket I pull out some folded aerial photographs of the area.

'Fuck,' groans Petra, shaking her head. 'Who are you with, the CIA?'

'Declassified MARS satellite pics. The EEC keeps the whole of Europe under surveillance to counter fraud in common market agriculture. Anyone can download the old ones.'

I orient one aerial shot on my lap so it matches our viewpoint and our heads bob up and down, making topographic connections.

'Look here.' With a pen, I circle a small distinct area in the top right-hand corner. 'Across Strasse 304, just beyond Donnerskirchen. Where the Wulka feeds into the Neusielder See.'

'Buildings,' says Petra. 'Two central blocks. One quadrangular, with an inner courtyard. What looks like a parkade to the back of it. The other one's a large rectangle. Plus a few peripherals. Doesn't look like private homes to me.' She glances across to the real thing at two o'clock in the middle distance then forms an uncertain smile. 'Reprotech, right?'

'Right. Their admin offices, an R&D boutique housing Primogen HQ – that's the nerve-centre for Mariahilf, Hofburg and Donaufeld. Then somewhere in there you've got a Biowares outhouse. That's the affiliated distributor of US Biomass products. Remember? We went through this before.'

'Yeah, sure. I didn't take it all in, though,' she confesses.

a voice

I hand her the surveillance picture and move over to the coin-op telescope but some obliging citizen has rammed gum into the slot. Leo's car catches my eye and I help Petra back into the front passenger seat. I start it up and edge the vehicle to the brink of the hill, the front wheels bumped up on to the raised kerb of the concrete knoll. I swivel round the rearview video-cam on the roof so it's facing forward and angled down towards the Wulka's outlet. A brushed finger on the dashboard sensor pad and a high-res colour image appears on the panoptic strip above the inside windscreen. 'Is this the zoom?' Petra nods, and the Reprotech plant hoves into view.

'It's grown,' she says, comparing with the aerial photo. 'One new rectangle. South-east of the quadrangular block.'

'Built in the last eight years, then. That's the declassification period for EC sat-pics.' Again I peer at the icons on the sensor pad. 'Where's thermal? Here?'

The strip turns black and the buildings' inner tubes are picked out in scraperboard white. The whiter the white, the greater the emission. Heating and computer systems shine up fiercely like the finely etched circuitry on a silicon chip, while minute mobile dots are personnel or cars with still-warm motors. In the most recent block, two large rectangular inner structures can be discerned clearly. We observe this oddly nocturnal thermoluminescence with an exciting sense of trespass, as if the gift of divine vision has been mistakenly bestowed upon us for a few priceless seconds. Our concentration, indeed, is only broken when a great rent appears in the pale violet cloudmass above the Leithagebirge and silvery fingers of sunshine poke through, smoky as lamplight in a basement pool-room. The fine dew of condensation on the inside windscreen sparkles coquettishly in response.

'I don't know how far Leo got,' I say, 'but I reckon he was good. Good enough to go too far. It wasn't just the Hofburg he cracked. It was Primogen and Reprotech. Now, did he do it by remote system-infraction or did he get a foot in the door down there? I don't have the answer to that. But if we take things in order, this is what we've got. First, his dying mother tells him he had an anonymous donor father. The man he calls father knew about the IVF but had been led to believe he was the sperm donor. Next, when Leo uses his felonious skills to hack into the Hofburg system he discovers the egg's been donated too, something his so-called mother hadn't been aware of. He finds out, at the same time, that – unwittingly – you are the product of the same egg donor and the same sperm donor. His wife is therefore his sister. Now was this accident or was there some design behind it? Since my conversation with Hannah Delbrück, I'm inclined to assume the latter. It's when he realises you're his sister that he breaks off conjugal relations and little Oskar is conceived with the help of the U-bahn ticket vendor.

'Leo seems to know his life's in danger. He takes out life assurance and carries a Harvest Contract card, for both of which you are the sole beneficiary. But he's not letting things rest. His blood's up and he's pushing on one step further all the time, and this isn't good for his health. Someone somewhere decides it's time to rub out the meddling son of a bitch. The killer familiarises himself with Leo's dog-walking routines and on November 20 he's duly liquidated.

'The rest we know. You contact me. We blunder into Hofburg and give away your coordinates, so the next person on the hit-list is you. The plastic explosive's set up for your return from the maternity, but Argos is topped instead. Me too, nearly, into the bargain. So why? What's it all about? Well, we've made just a little progress down that road.

'Delbrück's analysis of your ACGT from the electrophoresis profiles confirms what ZKD, the insurers, had chanced upon but more or less dismissed because it wasn't their line of country. In the human DNA there are certain patterns that indicate ethnic origin. The HLA system, VNTRs. I think that's what she called them. When you and Leo were IVF embryos, at the start of the millennium, you appear to have been germlined. Your genetic code was tampered with so as to achieve two objectives. One: apart from a minor genetic defect in Leo, you're free of any genetically transmitted ailments or negative predispositions. Two: in both your cases, it's impossible to determine your racial origins from DNA samples. Why? When I discussed the matter with Delbrück we played with the theory of a programme of involuntary surrogate parenthood. A programme that was set up in the 90s. Leo's stings may be a clue. Was the programme designed to create some kind of criminal class which could evade ethnically-based DNA detection? I don't know, Petra, but it's too cops and robbers. It seems unsatisfactory. There would have to be others, apart from Leo, to merit the "programme" tag. But who knows? Maybe there are. The other outstanding question is whether you and he were intended to marry. Again, I don't know.'

Petra removes her Persols and puts a finger in her mouth, catching the nail against the edge of a front tooth on the lower jaw and clicking it nervously to and fro.

'It seems to me,' I persist, 'we have two avenues open to us. One's to piece together the pre-history of Reprotech, the other's to go on retracing Leo's virtual footsteps.

'On the first count, we know that Reprotech began in 1989 as Biomass in the States, with two second-generation Austrians, Peter Diessl as CEO and Elsa Lubitsch as R&D chief. Lubitsch died in a car accident in Orange County in 1997. In 1998 Primogen was set up in Europe. Primogen fronts the consortium of maternity clinics and genetic engineering labs, while Biowares is the Austrian façade to Biomass-US products – chiefly agricultural and livestock products. Both persist under the Reprotech umbrella. Diessl is CEO in Austria. A guy called Purkiss in the States. They don't have a completely clean bill of health. I'm getting my *Tageszeitung* researcher to delve deeper there.

'On the second count, the question of retracing Leo's steps, we also have a lead there. Nathan Buczak. The "Zak" in Leo's diary. They met several times in the year before Leo died. You knew nothing about him, but Uscinski's grilled him and says he claims to have been major buddies with Leo. Now Zak worked for Reprotech. He's the skeleton key here. I'm going to follow that trail just as soon as I can get a fix on him.'

Petra's reclined the carseat and gazes, as she listens, at the tiny kinetic microdots on the thermal strip above our heads. It's hard to think of them as human. They are bacteria under an electron microscope. They are motes on a sun-dazzled eye.

'You asked me for the guest-list from my party.' Her voice is quiet, her enunciation slow. I'm encouraged. There's method in her now. The reckless panic is over. 'You asked for names and stats. What was that about?'

'I figured the person who set up the blast was there. I've had to match up my memorial reconstruction with yours, and there's one guy you didn't mention. The pig. Remember? Rubber pig mask. Top hat.'

'Crimson hunting jacket. I remember.'

'You didn't identify him.'

'No, I didn't. It's true. Shit. I haven't got a clue, Sharkey. There was something familiar about him. His voice, I guess. Yes, I think it was the voice. I just assumed from that that I knew him.'

'Well try to think back. Think back to where you heard that voice.'

'On the phone, perhaps. That would explain why I can't put a face to it. Did you speak to him?'

'Once or twice. Not enough. I wouldn't recognise him again on that basis.'

'I think I would. If I heard him again, I think that'd be enough. But there's no face, Sharkey. Just a kind of intonation. A particularity. I can't make it come clear.'

The white isosceles triangle of the yacht has meandered South as we speak, South towards Mörbish. Its prow lifts and falls gently on the running crimp of the waters. Its sail leans taut into the breeze.

'What time is it?' I ask.

She glances at her LCD subcutaneous implant: 'Gone four.'

'What d'you think? Shall we take a closer look?'

By way of an answer, Petra shuts her eyes.

gone fishing

We drive down to Purbach am Neusiedlersee, along open road to Donnerskirchen, then due East on a broad asphalt track signposted 'Naturschutzgebiet'. It's a landscape of reeds, feathery grasses, sea-starwort and salt-water tarns that glint like metal under the sifting sky. At a given point, the track forks off into a concrete causeway, under-bored with culverts. 'Piano, pianissimo,' she breathes, and I take the car down to a crawl. There's a gentle upward ramp to the causeway that lifts it on to a broad artificial eminence, pulling clear of the salt marsh. The displayed Burgenland eagle, surmounted by two patté crosses, passes us, the federal arms posted on a rustic wooden shield. Then the track disappears from view ahead, turning coyly into a close-packed landscaped wood of massed evergreens. Another signpost: 'Reprotech Gesellschaft mbH,' and, in smaller letters, 'Primogen. Biowares.' The words form an escutcheon around a central device that glitters like lightning in my memory. It's the uterine emblem from the key-ring: cervix, fallopian tubes, ovaries. The number 23 on either side. For a shocking visionary moment I see Leo drunkenly scoring that selfsame image on to the paper napkin, back in Hamburg, back at the Paloma. Back in the days when he was flesh and blood.

Leo . . . unexpectedly I feel myself sharing the embers of his anger, perhaps even, to my shame, for the first time. To be lied to and swindled. To be robbed of the gift of consanguinity. To be grossly and unpardonably invaded, defiled, in every cell of your body, your deepest, most sacred human rights usurped at the very moment of conception and mangled to some obscure purpose. Oh, Leo. No wonder you were spitting fire. You saw yourself as they saw you. A thing. An item. A market commodity. Not even deserving of an identity. You drank, you stole, you fucked away your hate in whorehouses. You spat in the eye of their sunrise industry. But the bastards got you in the end. You were a thorn in their flesh, a miscreant of their own fabulation, so they made of you a votive offering on the altar of expedience. Death by misadventure. The mortuary. The rotary saw. Your body pulled apart and hawked like butcher's scraps.

And here's Petra, another victim, another cipher, another wild card in the game of life. God knows where compassion comes from, but, all of a sudden, that's what I feel, flowing without let or hindrance through my prematurely sclerotic veins.

At another bend, the trees bustle away to left and to right, freeing up a wide area of lawns, tennis courts, a football pitch. A white picket fence runs around the perimeter of the recreational compound. Then without warning, over a blind ridge in the terrain, a large preliminary building rears into sight. It's the quadrangular edifice with a central courtyard we'd observed from the Leithagebirge. A nineteenth-century Jägerhof, the groundplan of which has clearly evolved from an old farm of the Vierkant type that's common enough south of the Danube plain. Two storeys, an impressively long frontage, and a steep-pitched mansard roof, the latter being an unusual adjunct for this province. There isn't a soul in sight. I stop the car short of the main doorway, but Petra eggs me on. 'No security,' she murmurs.

'No *visible* security,' I correct, pulling the Alfa to a halt and pivoting round to face her. 'Look, I don't have a line up my sleeve. D'you want to make some kind of a play?'

'We'll think of something. It's worth a punt,' she replies with a reassuring tone. It's just a tone, though. Reassurance it isn't.

The door's open, and we enter a cavernous shadowy lobby, to the back of which a loggia gives on to the courtyard of the Vierkant. It's revamped into a contemporary mall-style atrium with pseudo-Renaissance fountain, hanging plants, paradisal floral odours and digital birdsong. It's one of those stress-antidote environments, scripted, colour-coded and soundtracked by committees of shrinks and New Age Zen Buddhists. The lobby, on the other hand, bears the trophies of its Jägerhof past. Antlers, a tusky boar's head, still paralysed in its moribund expression of cornered dismay, and taxidermed teals, bustards and egrets in wall-hung cabinets with fake plaster scenery. The centrepiece of the area is a reception desk and a big slab of hardware sputtering with pilot lights around a lifeless Plasma screen. Four doors lead off and I try them in turn. They're all locked.

'You could've warned them we were coming,' she says.

We exit on to the driveway and make our way round the side of the Jägerhof. The windows are small, silvered and uncommunicative, but a pathway arcs round to an unprepossessing megalith of a building with clam-grey cement walls. No windows. No doors, on this approach at least. Only a multi-flex truss of piping egressing some 50 centimetres up then vanishing underground through a concrete boring. Another block behind it looks more promising. Three storeys, administrative, half-open slat blinds, glimpses of steel equipment and human commotion behind. We're about to circuit the megalith when Petra elbows me in the ribs. 'Company,' she whispers.

It's an old flush-faced geezer in a zippered Polartec vest and Tyrol cap with a tuft of chamois beard in it approaching from behind. There are haywire white side-whiskers sprouting from his jowls. He seems to pop up out of nowhere. One moment nothing, then there he is, hard on our heels. We wheel round, our brains lagging behind our facial expressions in the sprint for confident explanations.

'Lost?' he enquires.

'Um – yes,' says Petra.

'You'll be looking for the fishing.'

'How did you guess?'

'That's the only reason anyone comes down this way. You're lucky I'm here. That lot are never around to help. Always holed up indoors. It's not healthy. Still, I guess it's good of them to open up their grounds to people like us.'

'I guess it is.'

'Ecology, isn't it? These modern industries like to stay clean. Not like the old days. When I was a kid, nobody fished around here. Pollution. It just about killed everything off. That's all changed. It's good fishing now. Been here before?'

'No,' I chip in. 'It's the first time.'

'Where's your tackle?'

'We didn't bring any today. Just wanted to take a look. We'll be back next weekend if the going's good.'

'Morning's the best time. There's not much biting now. Just discovered that to my cost. You can use jigs, spoons and plugs, but nothing beats live bait. That's my opinion, for what it's worth. A graphite composite rod for good casting. A cork grip, that's important. They kick like hell, the big 'uns. And a good old-fashioned internal spool spinning reel. Manual line pick-up. Coffee-grinder handle. Don't go for anything fancy. The fish'll just laugh in your face. Well follow me, then. It isn't far.'

We tramp across a bland stretch of close-cropped lawn then duck our heads as we push through a sloping branch-impeded thicket of shrubs and low trees. The underwood clears rapidly to reveal tall reeds, bullrushes, teasels, skirting the western bank of the lake where the chill-factor is noticeably higher. The old guy's stuff is here. Folding stool, Thermos, fixed line, box of tackle, tub of maggots, net. He draws in the line and refreshes the bait. 'There's an eel in there, if you want to take a look.' He indicates the half-submerged net with a forward thrust of his chin. We pull up the hooped cylinder and watch the quicksilver creature kick like a ringmaster's whip.

'What else do you catch?' I ask.

'Tench and carp, mostly. There are minnows and gudgeon. Some small salmon and rainbow trout. Very rarely you get a seafish. Flatfish, for instance. The birds carry the eggs here on their feet.'

'Sounds good.'

'Never been better. This place used to be crawling with pike and perch. Some people love 'em. They were the local speciality. Hechtgulasch mit Salzerdäpfel. But they're bloody predators. The perch takes minnows, gudgeon – any baby fish. And the pike goes for bigger prey. Personally, I'm glad to see the back of 'em.'

'What happened? Overfishing?'

'Nope. Just disappeared. One morning, they were all gone. About a year and a half ago.' He hunkers down over his gear and feeds a maggot on to the hook.

'Gone?'

'Dead. Pike and perch floating on the water.'

'I thought you said there was no pollution?'

'That's right. It wasn't pollution. I forget what they said in the papers. Just some kind of fish sickness. Maybe it was the heavy rain. It kicks up the silt and the fish don't get enough oxygen. Anyway, as I say, I'm not complaining. Good riddance to the buggers. They always got to the good fish first.' He produces a little half-smoked meerschaum pipe with a hinged tin lid, tamps down the nugget of tobacco and lights up, spitting a wet strand from the corner of his mouth.

'Well, listen, I think we'll be moving along now. Good luck. And thanks for the information.'

'That's all right. Remember, mornings are best. Night fishing from boats is forbidden. And you'll need a permit. You can get the Fischereikarte from the Rathaus in Rust. One-day only, or a full week.'

We stroll a little further along the lakeside. The stiff shanks of the reeds thin out and the cool sweep of water throws back a scrimmage of shadows from the light-starved sky. We raise our heads at the strangely melancholy call of wild ducks and watch the broad chevron of their flight. Dusk gathers in. Beneath our feet, the earth, in its diurnal death urge, seems palpably to accelerate towards the West, throwing us off balance, exchanging the defined proportions of day for the spatial deceptions of night.

'We should be making a move,' I say, stirring myself reluctantly.

'Let's not go back to Vienna,' she replies quietly, her head still raised with an air of abstraction. 'We can go to Rust. It's the stork village, isn't it? Storks' nests on the roofs. We can eat something and stay in a hotel. Just for one night. I'll call Marta. I'm sure she won't mind. I don't want to go back now.'

'I have to be at the office no later than ten.'

She turns to face my hesitation.

' It's a two-hour drive. We could make an early start.'

'True.'

'I was thinking, perhaps we could share a room. I'd like it, also, if we could share a bed. Not to make love. I was cut – the episiotomy. I'd just like us to be together, it's as simple as that. Unless you don't want to, of course.' She pauses, turns away and catches her breath with a slight spasm of the cheek muscles, as if in pain. A light wind rifles through the reeds. 'I think I need you, Sharkey.' She turns, smiles easily now and places a forefinger to my lips. 'I know what you're thinking. That's a stupid thing to say. You're right, of course. But I have this feeling, sometimes, that the world is full of lies, full of damned intelligent lies. And the truth – well the truth is just itself, isn't it? Kind of stupid. A stupid, uncomplicated thing.'

what you see

In the room at the Hotel Sifkovits, I face the wall and read a dog-eared poster for last August's attractions at the local Seebad beach: Kleingolfanlage, Funny Jumping, Volleyballplatz, Miss Wet-Shirt, Ruster Operettenkonzerte. A tap squeaks shut in the bathroom and Petra comes in, her hands fumbling behind her back. She unhasps her bra. We lit a candle she found in a drawer and stuck it with drips of its own hot wax to the glass top of an escritoire. The irresolute flame lends a semblance of life to the motif on the Jouy cretonne wallpaper, a cute line-abstract of a Watteau-esque *fête galante*. Now Petra's naked at a cheval glass, her back to me and drawing on a regular cigarette. Smoke discharges from her small upturned nose. She watches me without visible emotion in the reflection. I strip off and lie on top of the bed, my head propped on the furbelowed pillow returning her unblinking gaze. She has long, graceful limbs, a fine back and – emancipated of grips, elastics and the chapka – her massy black hair unplaits itself and falls with a kind of drowsy grandeur over her shoulders. On one omoplate, in a gap between two strands, there's a tiny tattoo of an anchor, an imperial pretension. Now and then the smoke drifts into her locks and is trapped there in little struggling wisps. When she turns, her breasts are veined and heavier than I'd sensed them to be and I recall that she's been feeding. There's a slight puerperal sag to her belly which she carries with unselfconscious aplomb. The delta of her pubic hair is narrower than nature intended and gives way to a pointillist shadow of growth since the last electrolysis. She is lovely. The sight of her fills me with an intense, focused calm.

She stubs out the cigarette and lies down beside me. The room's at a comfortable temperature for being naked in. We are flat on our backs staring at the dead light fitting on the ceiling. It's a four-branched rustic wooden affair with one bulb missing and its shadow flutters and jumps in the ochre flamelight. There's that warm soft-boiled egg smell to her body again, though over it lie traces of Virginia tobacco and a perfume – rosewater or jasmine, I'm not too sure. Something old-fashioned, at any rate. She raises her left hand, palm upwards, and I look at it for a moment before realising it's an invitation. When I place mine in hers, she closes her long fingers (it seems unoriginal to see them as pianist's fingers, but pianist's fingers they are) and our hands lower slowly on to the bedspread between us, clasped in some kind of unvoiced union. I notice for the first time that her hands are larger than mine. I find it strange that, in all her nakedness, it's part of her body that has been in evidence all along which so claims my attention.

'Sometimes,' she says lethargically, 'I couldn't give a shit. I just couldn't give a fuck if I was alive or dead. I don't expect you to know what I mean.'

Her fingers tighten then loosen around mine as if to press her point home. I feel the hard impact of her wedding ring against my knuckles for a second.

'My grandmother – I mean, the person I called "grandmother" – told me she went like that in 1988,' she continues, 'when Irmgard Seefried died. You know, the star of the Vienna Opera House. Then the next year Empress Zita kicked the bucket and not long after there was the fire at the Hofburg Palace. I used to tell her she was the Last of the Habsburgs. An anachronism on legs. She reminded me of Prince Francis Liechtenstein. You know that story. On 12 November 1918 he walked into his Vienna haberdashers to ask for his new gloves, and they said "Your Highness, please come back tomorrow, today is Revolution day." Granny was like that. She just had the stuffing knocked out of her. She felt the whole damn ship of her generation was capsizing. That's how I feel right now.'

'You're not old. You've just had a rough ride lately. It's bound to get to you.'

'Oh, I'm not unhappy. I'm neither happy nor unhappy. It's not even baby blues. Like I said, I just couldn't give a flying fuck.'

She sighs and runs the back of her free hand against the tip of her nose to alleviate an irritation. From somewhere the gargle of evacuating bath-water meets our ears. There are light footsteps in the room above then the sound of a heavy object being dropped.

'I mean I don't even know if I love Oskar. Really, I don't. I feel nothing – nothing. And that's a terrible thing to say. Of course I'll do what has to be done for him. Maybe the love thing will come. I was born old in the head, Sharkey. Old and done in. It's the Viennese sickness. You catch life like a disease in Vienna, but without the first symptom of childhood happiness. Still, maybe it's just me,' she checks herself lightly. 'Did you get one of those childhood things?'

'I did, yes. My parents have always run a Heurigen in Perchtoldsdorf. We came into Vienna from time to time. I guess my first memory is of winter, of snowballs and tobogganing on the Laurenzerkogel hill in the Prater. I just remember everyone yelling and yodelling. I remember my feet being frozen stiff, but I didn't care.'

'They sound like good times.' She releases my hand and props herself on an elbow. She looks at me askant. 'I envy you.'

'It's funny, we always put the good times in the past, don't we? If it's not your childhood, then it's some idealised version of the medieval world, the Renaissance, or a favourite decade – the 60s, the 90s – but always way back when. Either that, or a past of pure myth. The Hesperides, the Land of Cockaigne. Unless you go along with Pope Paul VI who said that Austria was an Island of the Blessed. No, it's always a progress into disillusion. There must be some psychological reason for that. Yet it's the future we're heading for, at the rate of sixty minutes an hour. Nobody's found a way of doing anything about that, so far at least.'

'Aren't they all myths for childhood? A time before the knowledge of evil, suffering and death. But you have to have had a childhood to get that. I just don't feel I ever had one. I was always so serious. Whereas you, you were lucky in that respect.'

'Maybe it was being in the country, too. Having seasons – you know – everything always on the move. No time to get bored. It's rich urban intellectuals like you who come down with the brainsickness. Künstlerleben, you know. The artistic temperament.'

'Fuck your mother, Sharkey,' she drawls back, slightly surprised at herself. Her pale eyes narrow and she smiles slyly.

'Fuck yours.'

'You with your stupid bastard newspaper column. You're as urban as the rest of us!'

We both laugh and her languid gaze travels the length of my body then back again.

'I guess Leo and I had our moments,' she begins again with renewed seriousness. 'He was a crazy little fat guy. Used to set fire to napkins in restaurants to get the waiter's attention, that sort of thing. Once he fell out with some little shit and he broke into his flat while he was on holiday. Sprayed the prize Persian carpet with water and scattered mustard and cress seeds. I miss having him around. I was wild about him, while it lasted.'

'What are you going to do with the money?'

'What money?'

'Leo's. The life assurance. The Harvest Card thing.'

'Jesus!' She rolls round on to her back and laughs mirthlessly, raking the hair off her high forehead with her nails. 'Are you after it, Sharkey? Do you want a share? Wow, I don't believe this. Money talks, huh?'

'In my experience, if money could talk it would say "goodbye".'

'Har-di, har-di, haa . . .'

'I'm serious, though. What are your plans?'

'I don't believe this! You want to know what I'm going to do with the money, right?'

'Yes.'

'I don't know. Blow it, I guess. I've been thinking of getting a place at Karl Marx-Hof. Anyway, at the moment I thought I was just supposed to be staying alive.'

'So you *could* give a shit, after all.'

'For Oskar, mein Herr, for Oskar . . .'

'You could clear out of Vienna. You could make a fresh start.'

'Sure, sure. Rio, Montevideo, Santiago. I might get chummy with the progeny of some of our exiled compatriots. Alternatively, I could just buy into the Roter Engel club, drink Manhattans till they come out my ears and get screwed to death by sex-starved bebop musicians on the latest designer hallucinogens.'

'It's a thought.'

'Possibilities, Sharkey, possibilities . . .' Her voice trails away on an ebb-tide of expiring humour. 'Or I could just lie here with you. Just lie here and forget everything. Pretend my life's happening to someone else and that this is my other dreamtime life, here on this bed with you. Forever this. It'd be like something from a movie. The kind of movie I gave up watching a long time ago. Too corny for words.'

She takes my hand again, this time in both of hers, and kisses the fingers one by one. This is not done with passion, but a kind of reverence, like a nun with a rosary. It's not even a kiss. It's a suggestion of contact, the merest palpation of the lips. Each time she finishes, she begins afresh. One of her feet lies loosely, bone-to-bone, across my shin. Her body's half-gilded by the candle, endowed for a moment with the vestal eroticism of a Klimt nude. Her pure broad-boned face, three-quarters on, is framed by the uncurtained plane of the window where the sky must have cleared, for the silver wheel of the Marriott Space Hotel floats down obliquely and extinguishes its festive light in the dark billows of her hair. It is our star, our eye of heaven, haunting the latent recesses of our lives.

'Do you like me, Sharkey? Just a little bit?'

'Just a little bit, Petra.'

'Enough to get that cyber-date out of your mind? The one you speak English to – in Providence, USA?'

'We're friends. It's no big deal.'

'I'm not pushing you, am I Sharkey? No, I'm not pushing you. You notice I didn't even ask you if you loved me. It's not a word we use any more. It went out. It's been out for quite a time. Nobody could work out what to do with it, because it didn't fit anywhere. It didn't fit into the new pattern. Like "soul" – the word "soul". Do you believe in the soul, Sharkey?'

'I'm like most people. I don't know what I believe in. Sorry to disappoint you. Perhaps if you told me what you meant by "soul" then I could tell you if I believe in it.'

'Oh, that's easy. I don't mean anything Baroque or wildly mystic – you know, the kind of stuff the mullahs and dogmatists quibble over. For me it's just a little place inside us all that nobody else can get to. Unless you want them to, of course, unless you open the door and invite them in. It doesn't even have to be eternal. My soul can die with my body, I don't care so much about that. But I need to believe it exists, this place they can't get into. Because they're so fucking arrogant, they think they can go where they like. Know what I mean? Perhaps in the past you could call your body your own, but you can't any more.

They've broken into that little temple, the trespassers. That's why I say "soul". It's my charm word. It makes me think I exist.'

'I guess I can go along with that.'

'You have one too.'

'Yes. I go there sometimes. It's barred and bolted. It's armour-plated. But I'm not so sure they can't get in. We live in a world where people won't take no for an answer. If something *can* be done, it *will* be done. It's called "evolution". It's called "progress". Who was it said "progress" is a comparative of which we haven't yet settled the superlative? Anyway, that's more or less it. Civilisation and its discontents. That's part of us too. You can't opt out of it.'

'But I want to. Just for a while.'

'You want to sit in your garden, come rain or come shine, and watch the garden peas growing.'

'That's one way of putting it.'

'You could try, but then one day you'd notice that some pea-plants are tall and others short, that the pods are different colours, that some seeds stay round when dried while others become wrinkled. You'd begin asking yourself why. You'd begin working it all out in your head, looking at inherited characteristics, because it's not called "genetics" yet. And your name would be Gregor Mendel.'

'If only we could leave things alone. Nature, I mean.'

'But it's our nature not to. Our curse, if you like, but also our nature. Nature's dynamic anyway, and we're just one of the dynamic factors that acts and is acted upon. That'll always go on. Our difference lies in applying the framework of a moral dimension.'

'Are you telling me there's a moral dimension in what they did to Leo and me?'

'I'm not telling you anything. Maybe the moral dimension's kaput. But if it is, then so are we. Because it's that process which protects the sanctity of your little room. It preserves your soul. It allows you to be who you are, a being capable of self-determination and privacy and individuality, and so on. Even love, perhaps. And there are people who want to break down the doors of your *sanctus sanctorum* and set up their market stalls. If no one stands in their way, they'll barge ahead and do it. They'll slap patents on every brick in your wall, as if the chapel of your body were their brainchild. Petra – what the fuck are you grinning at?'

'Forgive me, Sharkey, but you know, you're not all that bad. At the talk, I mean. Ever considered a career in journalism?'

'You're unfair. You're not taking me seriously.'

'I am, you know. I've taken in every word. So tell me: do you think they've set up their market stalls in me? Have I been usurped and demonised?'

'I don't know.'

'Sit up,' she says on impulse, grabbing me by the upper arm. We sit up Lotus-style on the bed, backs straight, facing each other, our legs crossed and hands resting on our knees. The cheap candle spits and flares chemically for a moment, filling the air with its igneous illusionism. 'They say the eyes are the windows of the soul.'

'So?'

'Look in my eyes – go on, Sharkey. Don't be afraid.' She raises those smart eyebrows and holds me with her cool pale gaze. 'Just go ahead. Look deep in my eyes and tell me what you see.'

I look and see my own face, lambent with fire: my eyes in her eyes, her eyes in mine. I look into her dilated pupils and after a while what I see is neither Petra nor Sharkey, nor even a room. It's something other, entirely, something almost mathematical, the geometry of the circle. It needs a word like 'Infinity' to describe it, but for the moment it hasn't got a name.

chapter nine

a.o.b.

'What've you got?'

'Plenty.'

We're hoofing it on the 39th floor of the *Tageszeitung*, a Dehmel board meeting one hour off.

'Dreiser's genned up on Neues Östmark funding,' says Beate. 'Some of the same sources as FE, but not all. It's big time. Remember hearing of Wilhelm Hoettl? This is going back thirty years. The spy master who was supposed to know where weapons caches were buried by the Americans to help Austria if it was under Soviet occupation. There's a rumour that the caches included gold, a lot of gold, and that they were placed around Salzburg which the Americans occupied for ten years after the Second World War. Dreiser's got hold of some of Hoettl's personal papers which suggest the weapons were unearthed in 1956 to help the anti-communist faction in Hungary's civil war. Others were used during Austria's border dispute with Italy in the 60s. But the gold never turned up. He thinks it went straight into financing the rise of the far-right Volkstreue Ausserparlamentarische Opposition and the Freiheitliche Partei Österreichs in the 90s. As you know, the Social Democrats and the Austrian People's Party only just held on by the skin of their teeth then. The FRÖ was the third biggest party in Austria and the second biggest in Vienna. They were the strongest ultra-nationalist party in Europe, with twenty-three per cent of the vote and 42 seats in parliament. The VAPO, on the other hand, screwed up. They tried to retrieve Hitler's NSDAP, and there was that letter bomb terror campaign, then some of their mercenaries fought as fascist units in Croatia. But the hard right of the FRÖ bifurcated into the new movements, FE and NÖ, and their funds came with them. NÖ's power-base is in Carinthia, as was the FRÖ's. They use the Thule Netz German info-highway to co-ordinate with the REP, NPD and DVU in

Germany, the FN in France, the BNP, Blood and Honour and Combat 18 in the UK and the Flemish Vlaams Blok. Dreiser thinks he's picked up substantial cash transfer operations on the Undernet shadow of Thule Netz which coincide with recruitment drives and armed flashpoints with police or foreigners.'

'Good work.'

We steer into Rudolf Dreiser's space and draw up hydraulic chairs. Dreiser's an old hand. He has very fine receding white hair and one of those scored and cross-hatched faces that looks like a rough preliminary sketch for an indefinitely postponed heroic masterwork.

'You forgot some,' he says.

'Did I?'

'Agir, the Parti des Forces Nouvelles, L'Assaut, Jeunesses Nationalistes Revolutionnaires, Centrumdemocraten, Centrumpartij 86, Deutsche Volksunion, the Republikaner Partei, Deutsche Liga für Volk und Heimat, Pamyat, the Polish National Party, Vatra Romanescu, Hungarian Truth, the Union of Ukranian Officers, Movimento Sociale Italiano, the Fronte della Gioventu and the ARN, Sweden's Sverige Demokraterna and Vitt Ariskt Motstand, Denmark's DNSB, Norway's NMI, Spain's Frente Nacional and the Circul Espanol de Amigos de Europa. Shall I go on? You've probably got fascist organisations exclusive to Andorra, Monaco and the Vatican too – well the Vatican's an openly totalitarian state, isn't it? – but we haven't turned over those stones yet. Give us time.'

Ernst Ashmeyer joins us with Lederer. The News-Web supplement is Ashmeyer's baby. We back-pat him on the first number and Lederer fetches coffees all round. 'Sharkey – black for you and Beate?'

'Two blacks, yes. Ernst, what's our angle? National, European or international?'

'All three. At the top of the pyramid, you've got the US-based NSDAP-AO, the New European Order, which is organised from Spain, and Euro-Ring and the World Union of National Socialists. The first two are the big guns. Festung Europa has European-wide aspirations but they've fallen short of the mark recently. If we look at the next level down, the Germanic hard right is directed by organisations like Gesinnungsgemeinschaft der Neuen Front, Direkte Aktion and the Freiheitliche Deutsche Arbeiterpartei. There are strong links up to the NSDAP-AO and the New European Order, which was founded by the Belgian former Waffen SS general Léon Degrelle. Obviously enough FE and NÖ are very closely implicated in the German networks. Anyway, we've got to slice up the cake for this issue. I'm going to take on the hierarchy I've just been talking about.'

'Finance,' bagsies Dreiser.

'Perhaps Markus and others could carve up the political agenda,' Ashmeyer continues. 'There's the issue of historical revisionism, holocaust denial et cetera. That's vital here. We shift the blame back, forgetting that the Anschluss wasn't an invasion. We've never had the same conscience-purging the Germans have gone through. Instead, we've had the illusion of victimisation at the hands of the Germans. Next there's ideology. Third position fascists and the various ideologues. Then there's parliamentary tactics. That's where we want to take a close look at NÖ's intentions.'

'Maybe you could suborn Janowitz from the *Neue Illustrierte Welt*. He's done some good stuff in that area,' Dreiser interjects.

'"Borrow", I think, rather than "suborn". Yeah, okay. Give him a bell, will you Rudi?'

'What's Lederer doing here?' I ask. 'Are we following up with a rock musical?' Lederer gives me one of his sick-sweet schmaltzy looks.

'The rock's just one angle, Sharkey. It's what gets the boneheads going. They may not read your column but they listen to ultra-national lyrics. MDA, the music distributors, report a big revival of interest in some of the old hard-right bands. Their names, Jons?'

'Dirlewanger, Storkraft, Radikahl, Skullhead, Skrewdriver, Vit Aggression . . .'

'They just roll off the tongue, don't they?'

'Hey, wotchit you!' blurts Lederer, projecting his jaw gormlessly. 'You fuck with Skrewdriver an' you have to fuck wid me!' He does a little grunting, head-butting routine that puts everyone in stitches. 'An' whaddabout dis guy?' he says, winding up his performance. He gives me the finger so close it's almost up my nose. 'What's de gimp doin' here? Hey don't cry, Haifisch! – did dey flush your street-cred down de toilet? You can tell Onkel Bonehead!'

Ashmeyer pushes Lederer back into a chair. 'Sharkey does the vox pop, okay? You've flushed out a skin, right Sharkey?'

'Yeah, if I can find him again. I ran into him at the Florisdorf torching. Name of Moos.'

'Chocolate Mousse?' asks Lederer.

'White Mousse, naturally. Don't blame me. I didn't baptise the little wanker.'

'You're going to give us the hard talk interview with this guy, right?' says Ashmeyer. 'Get it on digital. We'll wire you up discreetly with a Personal Area Network if necessary. I mean, he's not going to advance our political understanding very far, but he's the genuine article. Grass roots. See what he has to say about refugees, Roma, Sinti, handicapped, homeless, Jews, gays. You know the territory. Get the anger. Get the vigorous vernacular.'

'I was thinking,' I begin.

'Hmm?'

'He may be a worm, but it's the boot boys who're clued up on terror plans. They're at the operative end.'

'Good. Get that. And weaponry. See what kind of arsenal they have. I know you've all got regular *Tageszeitung* assignments on the agenda, but we'll need all copy in within three weeks from today. Okay? Has everyone got things clear for Dehmel?'

There are noises of assent as Lederer stacks up the coffee beakers.

'A.O.B.?'

'One thing,' I say, 'How did Möll take the first issue?'

'Our proprietor sent congrats. As you know, that's not where the mandate comes from. We're independent. But at the same time while he's happy our shareholders are happy. Remember that. We stick within the ground rules of honest journalism. Nobody plays it too close to the wire. Oh by the way, Sharkey – seeing you here reminds me . . .'

'Of?'

Ashmeyer fumbles with the catch on his briefcase and brings out a stapled document.

'Some of you may have heard of the DOEW. That's the Austrian Resistance Archives, the Dokumentationsarchiv des Österreichischen Widerstandes. They keep up-to-date on racist manifestations. As you may know, the neos publish anti-antifa lists. Names and addresses of anti-fascists who're appropriate cannon fodder. The DOEW have just passed on the new list to me and I note that Sharkey's name is on it. Welcome to the club.'

'Show me that!' I grab the paper from his hand. I'm praying that it's a joke. It isn't.

'They got your name, e-mail and direct phone. No address, lucky you. I wouldn't worry, though. I've been on the Austrian list for over a year and I've had nothing worse than hate-mail. If you go ex they won't harass you. It's just scare tactics.'

'You're forgetting Sharkey's brush at the Hundertwasser Haus,' Beate points out.

'That wasn't my set-up,' I murmur. 'It wasn't for me. Shit. What am I doing on this? You people read my column, don't you?' Silence. An exchange of glances. 'I've never offended a Nazi in my life! Godfuck. Nobody takes anything I write seriously!'

'Maybe it's time they did,' says Ashmeyer. 'And if you want to know why you're on the list –'

'Yes?'

'Ask Moos.'

minimum means, maximum effect

'Did you get the other stuff? The other stuff I asked for? I want to go through it at home.' The editorial's done and Beate and I are heading out of the War Office.

'Here.' She hands me a dataclip.

'A run-through. Background on Biomass in the US. Any dirt?'

'Nothing hair-raising. You'll see.'

'Profiling on Lubitsch and Diessl.'

'It's all there. Is there some tie-in?'

'With what?'

'The neo number.'

'Not that I know of. Why?'

'Just thought,' she replies. 'You'll have to forgive me but I botched together some of my own conclusions on this.'

'Okay. Now, what else –'

'Nathan Buczak. Impossible to get a realworld address on him.'

'Uscinski parleyed, so he can't be that ungetatable.'

'No, I was going to say. The US embassy in Boltmanngasse gave me a non-locational Web co-ordinate. It's in there with the clip. You can talk, but he keeps well out in the ether. Jackson, their Press man, was very curious to get an enquiry. Says he's a maverick. Cranky. A bit of an embarrassment to them, I'd say. Oh – you remind me. Uscinski wants a confab.'

'What about?'

'Didn't say. Was there anything else?'

'No. On second thoughts, yes – one thing. What's the name of that online paper in Burgenland?'

'The *Burgenländische Freiheit*?'

'That's it. They must have an anglers' column. Local ecology, that kind of thing. Go back about eighteen months and see what you can find on a fish problem in the Neusiedler See. Something to do with pike and perch.'

My request seems to affect her adversely. She wears that slightly dour look of someone weighing up the pros and cons of resignation, but her innate pragmatism wins the day. 'Call Uscinski,' she says sternly, tossing the instruction over her shoulder as she turns into the Ladies Room.

The Prater. The Lusthaus. The Aspernallee.

It feels like fate, being here again: a personal zero option.

This is where Uscinski wants to meet, and I'm ahead of time.

There's no snow today but the conditions still look like a trailer for the epic nuclear winter. It's minus ten and the light's hard as granite. A frost like finely-ground quartz lends a wild, painful brilliance to the scene. Beside the road, there's a seagull of all things, one of its feet awkwardly tangled in the strap of a lightweight plastic bag from the Generali Shopping Centre. An assertive but emphysemic breeze, the kind that goes straight for the sinuses, teases the distressed creature by inflating the bag like a wind-sock and yanking mercilessly. Eventually the gull pulls free and flies off, a flash of white and grey wings over the regimented frozen skeletons of the trees that skirt the golf course. There's a very thin trickle of traffic, diminished by roadworks on the Hauptallee, the great avenue lined with chestnut trees which bisects the park. From across the Stemmerallee I hear the R20 high-speed suburban train rattling out towards Mistelbach.

It is two months to the day since Leo's death.

The human mind can inject a place with its own emotional toxins or euphorics. There's no doubting the prettiness of the Lusthaus at the hub of the roundabout. A little eighteenth-century octagonal pavilion, two floors with a balcony, shutters and white pillars set out from the walls, the Altes Jägerhaus opposite. There's no denying that this is a tranquil spot, with its gardens, woods, lakes and lawns, away from the clamour and fusty reek of the city. But I realise now that this place invades me with horror and sadness. It is, in fact, no longer a place, no longer out there, but a precise metaphysical node in the inner topography of my being, a conjuncture where fallibility, mortification and unease meet to gloat and whisper their incoherent secrets. It will be with me always, this dark inoperable little part of me. I must learn to live with it, but love it I will not.

I put some music on in the car and get out to stretch. I touch my toes fifteen times then jog and skip on the spot. A pack of teenage jet-bladers fire past, then before long a Bundespolizei Ford with magnetic blue light clamped to the roof tucks in gently behind me and Uscinski gets out. He cuts a dash in uniform, sporting regalia shoulder patches, Chefinspektor FGr.6, a Glock 19 9mm pistol holstered at his love-handled hip. I note that the poor sod's succumbed to the elements, labouring under a stinking cold. He blasts long and loud into a paisley handkerchief which, I swear, has a BMK police shield embroidered on it. When he's through, his nose is a sight to behold, more swollen and rawer than ever. There's a black PVC folder under his arm. He strolls over and greets me affably enough, lending an ear to the music.

'You like Webern,' he says in his nasal, congested voice. 'So do I. It's Opus 6, isn't it? Six Pieces for Orchestra. There's something of Mahler, you know, but more succinct. I think it was Stravinsky who said that Webern could express in a sigh what others needed a whole book to say. He was right there. Brevity and total organisation. Minimum means, maximum effect.'

'A victim to foreign powers,' I add, still padding up and down on my toes. From a little corner of my attention I lie in wait for his reaction.

'I beg your pardon?'

'Shot, wasn't he? Accidentally, of course. By an American sergeant in September 1945. Webern had just stepped outside his own house in Mittersill to light a cigarette at nightfall. The sergeant was trigger-happy. On edge.'

'These things happen. Look at Alban Berg. Killed by an insect bite.' Uscinski taps a finger on the press-stud of his holster, and gazes out indifferently towards the Freudenau racetrack.

'It makes you think though, doesn't it?'

'About what?' he asks blandly.

'I dunno. The meaning of life.'

He lowers his chin and pokes his tongue into his cheek, eyeing me with mild concern. It's the expression of a prim old biddy observing a wasp circling her Sachertorte at the Café Central. I stop jogging and bend forward slightly, hands on haunches, breathing deeply. He takes this as a signal to relax and leans back against the car, propping both elbows on the roof and emitting a vaporous sigh. It occurs to me that he's probably glad to be out of the office.

'So have you found the dog killers?' I ask, panting slightly.

He shakes his head thoughtfully, now running the tongue through his other cheek as if probing for cavities. 'A proper enquiry's under way. Forensics have already done their stuff. Bangs like that leave chemical fingerprints. Our people in the Explosives Unit remove residue with a chemical solvent and pass it through a chromatograph to separate out the molecules according to certain characteristics. Boiling point, ability to mix with oil – that sort of thing. Then the basic molecules go into a Barringer Ion Mobility Spectrometer.'

'What did they find?'

'RDX. It's stuff you can combine with an explosive like PETN to make Semtex.'

'It *was* Semtex, then.'

'No. The RDX specimen could've come from the detonator, since most detonators use RDX as a charge. But they've also scraped up a plasticising compound that suggests it was C-4, not Semtex.'

'The difference?'

'Semtex is easy to get your hands on. The FE use it all the time. But C-4 is harder to come by. It's true you get it in the commercial sector for use in quarry operations, mining and building demolition. But distribution's closely controlled. Basically it's a high-grade military explosive. The person who wired up that apartment was not your regular knucklehead. Had any thoughts?'

I tell him about the pig. 'Chase it,' he says with an encouraging look. 'You never know. We're keeping the Stapo informed.'

I nod in appreciation. The Stapo are the Staatspolizei, the secret service branch of the Federal Police. At the merest whiff of terrorism, they are there. It's rumoured their tracker dogs get nuts of Semtex mixed in with their Pedigree Chum. It sharpens their nose for it but the handlers have learnt to stand well clear when they crap. I duck into the car to switch off the sound system then sit up on the bonnet where at least my buttocks can enjoy a little warmth. 'We're here,' I say, 'Ergo, you want to talk about Leo.'

the two times table

'Right,' he replies with a businesslike frown. The frown's directed at himself. He's not too focused today and I like him for this. He's one of those people you can never imagine on holiday, in bathing trunks by the sea. He's progressively become the living incarnation of his job. So this blurred edge to his presence of mind humanises him, shading off into complexity and finesse. It doesn't last long. He hurriedly shepherds his thoughts into Central Planning. He turns those official shoulders and fumbles with his big, ginger-haired hands, first in the folder, then in the brass-buttoned side-pocket of his stiff serge jacket. Results of search: one large photograph; one small tin of propellant. 'Follow me,' he orders, and we march up to the Lusthaus pavilion, to the corner between the Aspernallee and the Schwarzenstockallee. His finger on the nozzle of the tin, he sprays and a neat bead of white foam, like milliner's piping, describes a rectangle on the tarmac.

'The BMW,' he says, perfunctorily.

We march back to a position some twenty metres ahead of our own two cars on the Aspernallee and he draws another rectangle.

'Leo's Alfa,' I put in, sensing it's my turn to make a contribution.

'Now look,' he says.

He gets down lumpishly on his knees and opens up the photographic print. It's about ninety by fifty centimetres, an aerial view of the road though very different from the staccato movie afforded by the Lepers video.

'This was taken on the morning after the event. OVIS-VLA. It's a low altitude incident-scene photo-documentation system. For visualisation of scene geometry. What you get is high-resolution imaging of car débris and skidmarks. Ground-level photos distort. Not these. We've put together a virtual animation based on this. I'll show you in a minute. There are a number of factors to bear in mind. The job is to reconstruct the exact variables. Speed and angle of impact. Occupant kinematics. Visibility and conspicuity of victim. In this case, the computer collision reconstruction used an MVS database to take into account the BMW's operating specifications: wheelbase, front and rear tread, turning diameter, rear and front overhang, that class of thing. The most important factor was tyre-road friction in winter conditions. No snow, that night, but fucking cold all the same. Like now, in fact. And that's where the OVIS comes in. Look. The treadmarks couldn't be clearer.'

He's right. We take the aerial photo out with us into the road beside the white foam rectangle of Leo's absent Alfa. Uscinski hands me the aerosol.

'Show me what you think happens,' he says. 'Spray the line at the notional centre of the BMW's chassis. Halfway between the tyre-treads on the photo.'

I take my bearings and spray away, then step back to admire my handiwork. The line rides up to a point two metres in front of the Alfa, but another line forks out of it some twenty metres back, returning on a different, slightly parabolic, trajectory. Both lines stop dead on the photo with the deep ingrained black tread of hard braking. The second parabolic line then takes off with a lighter imprint.

'Good,' he says, blowing his nose with some gusto. 'Now interpret.'

I look again. I feel like Paul Klee, famously taking a line for a walk. I rub my chin and pronounce my verdict. 'I'd say they had two goes at him.'

'So would I.'

'They hit him once, but it didn't do the job. They backed up here. Then a racing start to come round and whack him a second time, finishing Leo off.'

'Exactly. Come over to the patrol car.'

We sit in his car and watch the VR animation on a flip-up screen. The BMW Z10 has that perfect, otherworldly sheen of VR cyber-reality, accelerating frictionlessly round the corner, the butterfly wing-grille, the fat torque curve. A virtual tribute to Bavarian automaking. As I'd inferred, the front nearside corner of the hood ploughs into Leo's cartoon proxy, throwing it to one side. The proxy crumples, bleeding theatrically, then rights itself and tries to head for cover. But it's out of time. The Z10 reverses and heads back. Exceeding 60 kph according to the screen gauge. And it's here that the computer reconstruction outdistances my projections. On its second thrust, the Z10's not quite on course. Uscinski taps a button and slows the animation down to a grind. The Leo proxy, moving like a cosmonaut, has made it to a narrow space between the Alfa and the BMW's trajectory. Even with the tightest of turning curves, the vehicle can't slew in and top him. But something else happens now, something I hadn't foreseen. The nearside door opens and slams him in the chest. The vehicle brakes hard, losing road-holding momentarily on the back wheels, and lands up squinting at the kerb. A stop-check pause. The deed is seen to be done. It takes off, open throttle.

Uscinski turns his milky eyes on me but refrains from speech. I like the quality of his silence. It has brains and direction. It's charmingly pedagogic. It's as silent, in fact, as the Niagara Falls.

'And then there were two,' I deduce slowly.

'Quite. At that velocity of acceleration the driver couldn't have leaned over to open the door himself.'

'Or *her*self,' I interject, keeping the gender options open.

'There must've been a passenger. Two people in the car. The door had to be held open with considerable strength to deliver the blow. Side-window glass in the road débris confirms the hypothesis as does the coroner's report from Donaufeld on the nature of the fatal injuries sustained by Detmers. Those treadmarks tell the same story too. They indicate even distribution of ballast up front in the BMW – ballast, here, being human bodyweight. We can also predict crush patterns and impact forces very precisely. Wherever that car is, it's badly fucked up on the right, front side.'

'Quite a turn up,' I admit, thinking out loud, 'but Argos was definitely wagging on the driver's side.'

'I'm sorry?'

'Oh, nothing.'

'I haven't finished. We also examined the Detmers Alfa very thoroughly. From body hairs and material carried on the soles of shoes we're pretty sure that Leo Detmers was not alone either. We're persuaded there was a second person in his car too.'

'Jesus. Are you sure? He was out with the dog, remember.'

For the first time Uscinski loses a little of his friable patience. He turns away, hiding either irascibility or amusement, it's hard to say which.

'Forensic science,' he says, turning back with a splendidly poised, deadpan expression, 'may not be one hundred per cent reliable, but I think it can distinguish with some confidence between homo sapiens and a Jack Russell.'

His Networker winks but he puts it on hold.

'Look at this,' he says once his stricture has sunk home. He passes a print-out from his document file. 'It's a list of BMW Z10 A-Series owners in the Vienna area.'

Some fifty names in all, grouped by Bezirk. I run down it quickly.

'Anything?'

'Büchner,' I exclaim, running my thumbnail under the name. 'Doctor Büchner. He delivered Frau Detmers' child. He's an obstetrician at the Mariahilf. On Christmas Day he was an ancillary at the Vienna General Hospital.' I consider mentioning the good doctor's overheard phone-call, but decide against it. In the husbandry of doubt, a quiet and uncluttered latitude is sometimes called for.

'I'll put a man on to him.'

'Yes. And thanks for keeping me up-to-date. I appreciate it. I've learnt something today.'

'You've learnt the two times table,' he adds with a grin. 'It doesn't always work that way. Sometimes the factor's one, sometimes it's three. This time round we're in the binary world. Investigations of this nature often have an element of pure mathematics to them. Vector calculus, fluxions, trigonometry, calculus of variations. Or simple multiplication.'

'An interesting subject.'

Uscinski's eye-lids flutter, troubled by the dust of reminiscence. 'We had a teacher when I was at school. I was very fond of him. He used to say there's no such thing on earth as an uninteresting subject, only an uninterested person.'

His remark astonishes me. 'Hermann Goldberg,' I manage.

'Good Lord!' Uscinski exclaims. 'The Akademisches Gymnasium in Mödling. You too. A couple of decades later than me, I imagine. What did he teach, now?'

'He taught physics. Goldberg was a Jew.'

'He was, yes. A splendid fellow. I wonder what became of him.'

'He went the way of all flesh, unfortunately. But I thought –'

'Yes?'

'When I met you last, after the bombing, the Vienna Boys Choir went by in a bus. Forgive me, but you made some comment about Herr Singers and Bronfmans. I took it as disparaging.'

'If you can't have a laugh at your own expense, what can you laugh at? That's what I always say.'

'So you – I see. I'm sorry, I'd never have guessed.'

'Galician, originally. I hope you're not going to ask me to prove it.'

'Certainly not.'

'Jews can be Austrians and Austrians Jews, you know. How many Austrians are "reindeutsch"? That's a question! Johann Strauss, you know, had Jewish great-grandparents, and Otto Weininger, who was anti-semitic, was a Jew. Both Nazism and Zionism had their origins in Austria, after all. You know, a lot of Jews were enthusiastic Wagnerites. Theodor Herzl, for example. He realised that the Jews needed a home-land while listening to *Tannhauser*. Wagner's hero, you see, he follows his heart to lead him to his spiritual homeland, his Judenstaat. But Herzl, he was an oddball. His first dream was to be a member of the Prussian nobility. Maybe there aren't as many of us now as in the days of Herzl, but more than you might think. The statistical information, of course, is only available on a confessional basis. And I don't wear my kipah on duty.'

'Naturally.'

'I'm surprised Major Reik has never alluded to the matter in the course of your numerous summit conferences.' This time it's he who is lying in wait for my reaction, his face calm, his eyes steady and serene. The quality of his confidence gradually dawns on me. I meet his gaze and shake him warmly by the hand. 'By the way, Mr Sharkey,' he appends with a comic stage-whisper as I make to leave, '*Quid pro quo*, and all that. Now that you know what I am, I really think you should tell me.'

'I'm sorry?'

'Just what the blazes are you?'

sunsets don't give a damn

Home. The Superbaublock of Ehn's Karl Marx-Hof. I park out back and walk through one of the distributor courtyards. A gang of children's playing with firecrackers strapped to sticky X-shaped rubber Übermensch toys which flip down walls and windows when thrown up against them before exploding into knobs of coloured gelatine. Just the noble offspring of the socially homogeneous embattled working-class tenantry, peaceably working off their frustrations. Behind them, the slogans 'Wir sind das Volk!' and 'Jetzt erst recht' adorn the brickwork. Thence through one of the six huge pylon-shaped portals, with giant iron gates, to the border of the orthogonal garden of domesticity, Karl Marx Court, that flourishes between the complex and the entrance to the U-Bahn station.

I spot Petra out on the lawn, glowing like radium in a bath of evening light. Rolling along beside her is a remote-controlled Steyr-Daimler-Puch 'Proud Mum' Cot-Bot. I catch up and look in on Oskar who's sucking his tiny thumb contentedly to a lullaby version of 'Sauerkraut und Bier' which emanates from the high-tech pram's integral speakers.

'Trying to make the neighbours jealous?' I say, turning to Petra. She looks odd, and I notice it's the yellow Smiley contacts.

'It's practical, Sharkey. It goes up the stairs when the lifts are out of order. And it doubles as a cot and rocker.'

'All the same, it must've set you back a fortune.'

'I want the best for Oskar. And I've got my own place now.' She points up to an awninged balcony that forms the top branch of one of the brick pylons. 'I'm moving in the day after tomorrow.'

'It's not 5th Avenue, you know that.'

'I like it here. And I don't want to be a burden on Marta and Svetlana any more. They've been good to me. Since that bomb, I don't know – I don't want to put them at risk. And with Marta being ill, too –'

'I didn't know. What's the trouble?'

'Just flu I think. She went to an Austro-Slovakian Friendship do at the Stanislaus-Kostka Chapel the other evening and the heating was off.'

'I'll drop in on her later. Will you be there?'

'Yes. We're staying in tonight.'

'He's looking well, is Oskar.' I peek in at the sleeping homunculus again. 'I guess childhood's got a lot going for it. First it's all sleep and breasts and milk. Then it's sheer fun and no holds barred. You can collect rainbows, take bubble baths, eat just the chocolate stripe in your Neapolitan ice-cream, invent magic words, fall down and get up again –'

'Talk to the animals and trust the universe,' adds Petra.

'Yeah. Then some time after that the whole game falls to pieces. You smile at the man in the moon and he doesn't smile back. Your imaginary friends stop talking to you. You start wising up. Cottoning on to what really matters.'

'Money, sex, food and drugs. Then the same again, in VR.'

'And having babies so you can perpetuate the lies your own parents fobbed you off with.'

'We're so blasted cynical, Sharkey, aren't we?' She lights a Juju and purses her lips, watching the sun's spectacular death-throes through a veil of exhaled smoke. The scene on the skyline is like a volcanic eruption of magma or the histrionics of creation myths, gaudily depicted in a child's colouring book. 'Wow,' she whispers, bringing a hand to her chest, 'Check that out. It always gets me here.'

'At least you still enjoy sunsets. That's generally a healthy sign.'

'Maybe, Sharkey. But it's not reciprocal. I mean, sunsets don't give a damn about us. That's the thing about man and nature. It's wrong. The emotion – it all goes one way.'

The trouble with social housing is that it's social. I'd be all in favour of gregariousness if it weren't for the people. In the lift I'm up against a notoriously brain-damaged neighbour for six slow floors.

'You know they're coming,' she confides. She's absurdly small, has eyes like ball-bearings and a nose you could open a tin with. Her breath smells of ravioli and she wrings her hands ceaselessly.

'Who would that be, Frau Stemmle?'

'The men on horses. I saw them last night.'

'There were four of them as usual, I suppose.'

'How do you know?' she hisses. 'Have you seen them too?'

'No, but I've had the pleasure of discussing your visions with you before. The Horsemen of the Apocalypse generally make up a foursome. I take it that they are the gentlemen you are referring to.'

'Behold, a pale horse. And his name that sat on him was Death.'

'Yes, that would be one of them. I shouldn't worry too much, though, if I were you. I doubt very much whether their hour has come yet – or yours, for that matter.'

'Oh, I'm not the one they're after,' she insists, glaring up at me. 'They want the men who have not the seal of God in their foreheads.'

'Well, let's wish them luck in their quest.'

'A great multitude, which no man could number, of all nations, and kindreds, and people, and tongues.'

'As many as that?'

'It's you – it's you people! They're going to take you off, once and for all!'

'Where to, I wonder.'

'A place called in the Hebrew tongue Armageddon.'

'Guten Abend, Frau Stemmle. My regards to your husband.'

I squeeze out of the barely-opened lift doors and make a dive for my apartment, locking and chaining the door behind me. However utilitarian, these few square metres are mine. No cats, no dogs, no hamsters or minah birds. An infrangible cell of personalism in the tribal hive. I lean heavily against the door and gaze around me. Birch floor, Ozbek cushions, Starck settee. A Droog Design carbon-fibre and epoxy stool, a Matthew Hilton ovoid Sputnik chair. The black rigour of the Serge Mouille industrial lighting overhanging and reflecting a hand-tufted Krickan rug, itself black but inset with a giant 'O'. The only artwork is the mad diabolic brainstorm of a reproduction Basquiat crayon sketch. There's nothing else, apart from a few books and gizmos, the wallscreen and an Ikea ironing machine, though the modest kitchen and bathroom are also bijous of stark conceptualism focalpointing on a Francis XI espresso machine, Kaledwei Centroform bath and Rapsel Nost glass sink with built-in pollutant and bleeding gum detector. Be it ever so humble, there's no place like home. I pour myself a Cinzano and slip Beate's dataclip into the Plasmavision slot.

no sorcerors' apprentices

Beate appears emblazoned on the wall, sorting notes and blinking into her cam. She's freeze-framed for a second and the screen self-optimises, configuring three ways for simultaneous video, text generation with underlined hyperlinks and document window. Parameters fixed, she thaws, glances up again and embarks:

'Um, okay, Sharkey, bear with me – I'll try to inject some order into all of this. Mini-recap, first of all. Biomass started in '89, right? In Orange County, USA. Five years later they were big, with a diversity of product-lines and services ranging from ag-bio to IVF. We've been over this before, but it's important to get the dates fixed. In 1997, there was the shift to Austria. Basically it was a question of nomenclature. Biomass-USA became Biowares Europe over here. Reproductive science fantailed into Reprotech and Primogen. So we're talking very rapid growth.

'So yeah, the first thing you asked me was to dig up the dirt. Not too tricky with bio-tech start-ups, I can tell you. They were kind of sparking off moral dilemmas as they went along. Biomass had Hannah Delbrück on their back from the start, first as a freelance lobbyist and then through the Biomedical Ethics Review Board. Remember she was at Cornell with Diessl and Lubitsch, before they went their different ways. I've tracked down some school photos of these guys, if you're interested. Delbrück was more or less a lone wolf, a rogue elephant – shit, talk about mixing metaphors! Transgenic metaphors, more like. Anyway, you know what I mean. She functioned from a private telematic office also in Orange County, a place called Huntington Beach. This is rich, south of LA, high per capita incomes, designer nursery and baby boutique country. Bio-tech heartland, in other words.

'Anyway, so here comes the muck. Well, scrapes really. Very few companies in this line of business came through with clean hands. Biomass's first problem came when they promoted human growth hormone – not for pituitary dwarfs, but for athletes. This was stuff that boosted performance, but it couldn't be detected by drug tests. It was a money-spinner. It sold big before governments got their acts together to regulate the practice. The Biomass proprietary brand was very popular with cyclists. Unfortunately, it also killed a number of them. The muscular growth put too great a strain on the heart. Biomass had payouts to make. The product was taken off the market. But the incident wasn't enough to put them out of business.

'With me so far?

'Well, next the problem of foetal tissue came along. Foetal brain cells were used quite early on for victims of Parkinson's Disease. Biomass was in favour of farming foetal tissue, primarily for athletes again. Apparently they can improve performance and wound-healing by injecting the stuff. There were rumours, also, that on occasions Diessl and company weren't averse to inducing abortion to harvest foetal tissue or taking embryos without permission. Nothing proved, there. But Delbrück's vigilance kept them in line. Then Clinton lifted the ban on the use of foetal tissue and a legislative structure of sorts fell into place.

'From what I've managed to figure out, the two big contentious areas for Biomass were patents and embryos. The patents problem has to be seen in the context of the Human Genome Project. Once a gene was located for the first time, it could be industrially reproduced and sold. It became a top dollar commodity, subject to licensing agreements and all that jazz. To begin with, the patents went to engineered genes, which were effectively bio-inventions. The first one was in 1980, to a man who created a micro-organism that could eat crude oil, to devour oil slicks. Then in 1988 a transgenic mouse, including chicken and human genes, was patented. Then in 1991, for the first time a part of the bone marrow, a natural part of the body, was granted a patent. Here no cellular alterations had been made. Biomass was in there with the rest of them, hustling for patents. For example, they applied for patents on the chemical tags of over a thousand brain genes and numerous transgenic animals, chiefly livestock. Delbrück was one of the main behind-the-scenes activists in the May '87 group which tried to stop the patenting of animals. Incidentally, remember I said transgenic life-forms were considered inventions? Well this didn't apply to humans, with the important exemption of embryos and foetuses again. Diessl and Lubitsch had set up a plant for the cryopreservation of embryos from the early days. Pre-embryos – that's what they call the frozen embryos. Basically that was part and parcel of their IVF business, the infrastructure. Okay, so there were big outcries in those days about what happened to frozen embryos if the parents divorced or died or whatever. Biomass just had to sit back and wait for the courts to pronounce on that one. But Lubitsch in particular was very vociferous on another matter, again relating to IVF. She was in favour of pre-implantation genetic screening of embryos. I mean this is something that's easy to do in IVF, but not in a natural pregnancy. Put simply, embryo biopsies can pin down the embryo that has preferred genetic traits. Designer babies, again. By screening, you can discard those which are the wrong sex or have a genetic predisposition to obesity or low IQ. Eugenics, right? Improving the human gene pool. She was also in favour of re-engineering defective embryos and patenting the results. If you fancy a soundbite from Lubitsch, I came across this from an article she wrote.'

Biology is destiny, the destiny of the individual and of the race. If, today, livestock breeding has become such an exact science, it is because two basic principles have been followed throughout history: negative eugenics, preventing the unfit, the cacogenic,

221

from surviving; and positive eugenics, encouraging the survival of the aristogenic. We live in dangerous times. Overbreeding in certain countries and sectors of our own communities is leading to a proliferation of deleterious genetic material which is undermining the health and sanity of mankind. The forementioned two basic principles of negative and positive eugenics, proven in their efficacy in the animal kingdom, are no less valid for the human community. New and ongoing developments in genetic engineering have supplied us with the ultimate tools to put theory into practice. Those at the cutting-edge of the new bio-tech industries are no sorcerers' apprentices. Nor are they a bunch of mad scientists indulging in megalomaniac plans to take over the world. This is a very real and imminent human issue. If steps are not taken within a generation or two, disease and mental deficiency could very well run like wildfire through the entire species.

'Fighting talk, right? And not necessarily politically correct, either. What's more, she was one of the main American proponents of the Swedish forcible sterilisation programme for non-desirables. Wasn't it Rudolf Hesse who said that Nazism is applied biology? Anyway, here comes the really meaty stuff. Ready? I don't know what to make of it myself, but that's not my job. I'm not the star investigative reporter. Not yet, anyway.

'The fact is, if Delbrück never made anything stick against Biomass it was also because they had a charmed life. Right from the outset, too. Whenever anything came to court, they had the best legal brains to defend them, with no expense spared. More legal clout, in fact, than any start-up bio-tech could properly afford. How come? I'm getting to that. Think back to HUGO again. The Human Genome Project. It seems the military always had a finger in that pie. For example, the US Department of Energy was involved because they were interested in the question of genetic mutation brought on by nuclear weapons programmes or civilian exploitation of nuclear energy. And these, remember, were the guys who were responsible for the design of weapons and producing safe nuclear reactors. The two main nuclear weapons labs in the early 80s were Los Alamos and Lawrence Livermore, and they both worked on a Gene Library Project. I reckon that Biomass came into their own in 1991, precisely 1991. This is Gulf

War time. Because of the war, the <u>US Department of Commerce</u> placed an embargo on access to a thing called the <u>Wisconsin Package</u>. This was the international genome database, held on computers in Baltimore. The embargo applied to non-US nationals. The fear was that it could come in handy to enemy powers. How? Well your guess is as good as mine. Now both Lubitsch and Diessl had dual nationality, Austro-American, yet not only did they have unquestioned access to the Wisconsin Package – they actually had privileged access to it, *very* privileged. Something was going on, Sharkey. No other bio-tech operation had that kind of free pass. What's more, there's no paper trail here. No contracts. No joint venture agreements. Just big fiscal input, all of a sudden, and allusions to an undercover project called "Winnow".

'So this is how it goes. Delbrück's effectively silenced, every time she squeaks up, as I said. And all at once everything's hunky-dory for Biomass. It's a six year honeymoon. From '91 to '97. It ends when Diessl starts packing his bags for Austria. The US government don't want him to go. They put major persuasive and even coercive pressure into getting him to stay, but it's no go. Then Lubitsch is killed in that car accident. Diessl's already in Austria at this point. The whole Biomass operation shifts over here.

'Okay, you know me, Sharkey. I'm sometimes too quick off the mark in making connections. But here's one to wrap your immense mind around. Lubitsch died in the wee hours of 10 November 1997. On the same day – within less than twenty-four hours – Delbrück was on a plane heading out of LA for Vienna. Coincidence? I may just be fantasising here, but we talked about the fact that Lubitsch and Diessl became romantically involved. And before that, all three – Lubitsch, Diessl and Delbrück – were once a happy threesome at Cornell. You don't suppose that behind all Delbrück's lobbying and so on there was something more, do you? I'm talking jealousy, malice, the eternal triangle, the fury of a woman scorned. Okay, I'm walking the little brain-dog here, but it's just so damned suspicious. I mean, the *same* day! It can't have been she was heartbroken at Lubitsch's death. But it could mean she was involved in it, couldn't it? Unless it was a CIA job, preventing the relocation to Europe. Well, as you can see, my head's been full of conspiracy theories all day. Anyway, shit. I've said enough. I'll leave you with – what? – yuh, <u>here</u> it is. Stuff from the local rag about Lubitsch's accident. *Hasta la vista*, Sharkey. Take care.'

Monday November 17 1997
Bay Area Traffic Report

Deputies are still investigating the incident in which Elsa
Lubitsch, age 35, died at 3.05 am on Monday November 10,
after losing control of her vehicle, a 1991 Chevrolet Caprice
Classic. The automobile left the road at SB 1405 JSO Seal
Beach Boulevard, a notorious accident blackspot, colliding
with a utility pole. The victim was alone at the wheel and
there were no witnesses. The body, which was in
unrecognizable condition due to an ensuing fire, was taken
to Fullerton Memorial Hospital where death was certified
and DNA was extracted from the victim's vertebrae. A
technique known as PCR and Short Tandem Repeat (STR)
Typing was employed. Results were compared with DNA
samples from Biomass Industries, 1200 W. Valencia Mesa
Drive, Orange (where the victim was head of R&D), and a
positive identification was made. Orange police chief
Robert Lowenberg said the Chevrolet was in an unroad-
worthy state. Examination of the brakes showed that there
were no pads left and that the rotors and drums were badly
scored. Vehicle maintenance history indicated that the
Caprice had recently been fitted out with a new water
pump. To replace the water pump, it was necessary to
remove the +12V battery lead to the alternator. When the
mechanic did this, he did not replace the rubber protective
boot. Fuel lines run behind the alternator and the unpro-
tected +12 post came into contact with the grounded fuel
line every time the car vibrated. The ensuing sparking
eventually ate through the fuel line and allowed gasoline to
flow into the engine compartment. Lowenberg maintains
that this almost certainly contributed to the violent com-
bustion of the vehicle on collision. The enquiry continues
and it is likely that charges will be pressed against the
garage in question. The funeral service will take place
tomorrow at Huntington Beach Cemetery.

I skim the article, frequently losing the thread and backtracking. I'm tired. And two collision reports in one day is a lot. The details start getting tangled up in my mind. To my inner eye, for some reason, there appears the sleek Gräf & Stift convertible car in which Archduke Franz Ferdinand and his wife were assassinated at Sarajevo. There was, however, something Beate said earlier at the office that's nagging at me and I have to clear it up. I bip through to her at home. She appears on-screen in the kitchen, doing something strenuously ethnic with a wok. She has company. There's movement visible through the serving hatch and background chat.

the tight spring

'Sorry, Beate. Listen: that was really good work. There was just one thing. You asked me if there was a tie-in with the supplement number on the neos. What made you think that?'

'Hey, Sharkey, you didn't follow through on all my links! It was nothing really important. To do with the background on the parents of Lubitsch and Diessl. In both cases they emigrated to the States prior to the Anschluss – hold on a sec! Sorry, Gisela, what was that? No, I won't overdo it with the Tabasco! Sharkey – where was I? Oh yes, they both had clean war records in the sense that they were well out of it. But Lubitsch's parents had a Nazi past. Her father joined the Hitler Jugend in 1929 and the Nazi SA storm troops a year later. He travelled to Munich with Adolf Eichmann and Alois Brunner in 1933 as a member of the Austrian legion. The mother was in the Nazi's League of German Girls. Both the Lubitsch and Diessl fathers emigrated independently as part of a US recruitment drive on scientists. Lubitsch senior was part of a team monitoring Japanese warfare, tactics and technology. So there you are. That was all. Scoop of the century. Austrian has Nazi past! It's no big deal, I know.'

'Okay, well thanks anyway. And *bon appetit*.'

'Before I forget, you asked me for the fish stuff. Hold on a second. Right, I've got it. And "Send". You should have it now. See you tomorrow, Sharkey.'

Beate shrinks into a pixel of light and I pull up a new document window.

Burgenländische Freiheit

Die Burgenland Woche. Die besten Seiten von daheim!
Tuesday 12 August 2025

Anglers in the Neusiedler See were startled, last month, to find numerous dead pike and perch floating on the lake's surface. The incident immediately brought back memories of industrial pollution at the turn of the millennium and eutrophication problems caused by tourism and agriculture. However, examination of the dead fish by the Ministry of Fisheries showed that they had hepatoma (cancer of the liver). One theory is that the fishermen themselves are to blame for using peanut meal, cottonseed meal and some other oilseed meals to encourage fish to congregate in certain areas of the lake. Some of the feed ingredients can contain the mould Aspergillus flavus which carries a toxic metabolite known as aflatoxin. The aflatoxin leads directly to hepatoma. The mystery remains, nevertheless, of why other species of fish in the lake were not contaminated. Albert Fehling, a local fish farmer, suggested that if coarse feed granules were responsible this might explain why only larger predators were affected.

I save the file and scroll back over Beate's speech-text to the link I want: 'I've tracked down some school photos of these guys, if you're interested.' The first photo is headed 'Cornell University, Ithaca, NY, USA 14853. Section of Genetics and Development. Progress on a Human Chromosome Database based on ACEDB. Workshop Participants, Fall 1986.' About a dozen fresh-faced graduates on a sunlit lawn link arms in comradeship, beaming cheerily for the camera. It looks as if someone has just made a mildly amusing witticism. I recognise Delbrück third along from the left across some forty years: the courtly photogenic smile, that dainty tendency to hold the head slightly to one side. I read across the list of names: Xiaoyen Yu, Peter Diessl, Elsa Lubitsch, Hannah Delbrück, Dave McGough . . . A fugitive sensation of coldness runs lightly over my body, closely followed by warmth, a hectic flush. I read the names again. I'm feeling decidedly uncomfortable. I shift in the Starck sofa to relieve what I take for cramp. I scan the photo and names again. It could be no more than an error in the order, a stupid misprint at the photograph studio.

I call up the second photo Beate has supplied. It's titled 'Bio GD Graduation, Summer 1984'. Here there are about fifty students in gowns, bands and mortar boards, clutching their scrolled diplomas. They're arranged in three seated tiers in front of a backdrop of fluted neo-classical columns, those man-made tree trunks in the Edenic groves of academe. The names beneath are also arranged in three tiers. This isn't an informal snap. The students have been lined up in alphabetical order. So Delbrück is right up there in the top rung alongside Diessl while Lubitsch sits apart from them in the middle. This time there's no doubt in the matter at all. The Delbrück sitting there is not the Delbrück I know. Not by any stretch of the imagination. This Delbrück is a rather ungainly young woman with large shoulders and auburn hair cut into a pudding-bowl fringe. She wears tweeds and a cameo brooch at the neck. She could be the wife of a moderately prosperous turkey farmer, or chaplain in a small presbyterian church. There's no vanity or sexuality in her shy, guileless camera manner. Only the chaste, homey seriousness of a good, if prematurely middle-aged, student.

And suddenly everything falls beautifully into place. I see the whole dead and buried story with extraordinary limpidity. This Delbrück – it strikes me – is a deceased Delbrück, killed on Seal Beach Boulevard, Orange County, 10 November 1997. A highway statistic. Victim of poor vehicle maintenance. The Delbrück I know from Vienna is old now, but back then – oh, then she was a prettier little thing altogether. I can almost feel the heat of that long-gone sun on my face, smell the distant magic of champagne and strawberries in the air. I'm standing with the photographer and admiring the bright young things, hearing the peals of laughter and murmur of conversation. Elsa's sitting over there now, her head daintily angled to one side, her fur-hooded gown neatly ironed. She's about halfway along the middle row, in the days when she was still Elsa Lubitsch. She looks sexy and intelligent, a creature of pure promise.

Up in the top left, Diessl's tall and dark, a handsome, quick-witted fellow who's understandably pleased with himself today, the day of his graduation. His hands are behind his back (no doubt gripped around his diploma). He holds himself fair and square, head high as befits an accredited member of his nation's intelligentsia, and he's looking down at a slight angle, perhaps stealing a glance at the back of Elsa's shapely head. I know what he sees in her, and I know what she sees in him. They simply can't wait for the photograph to be taken. They're going to run back to their rooms, put those red-ribboned scrolls on the bookshelf and change into jeans and T-shirts. They're going to celebrate. And perhaps tonight, energised with success, they'll dance in evening dress, fused into one spritely shadow under a grand marquee. There'll be a big cool swing band, playing 'Jeepers Creepers'. And when the music stops they'll walk out, his arm held gallantly round her waist, on to the lawns at Cornell. It will be midnight, on the dot, the start of something new, and the moon will linger like dew in her eyes.

I look again at Diessl, the plain self-effacing figure of Delbrück at his side. There's definitely something of his daughter in him, the dark, handsome features, the long torso, a slightly daft but impressive Austrian grandeur in the bearing. I look again at Lubitsch. And I see it all plain as daylight, the tight spring of their conjugated potential. For one forgettable and forgotten moment in their unsuspecting lives, the future is staring them full in the face.

I cross the landing and Petra lets me in. Svetlana's tinkering with a box of circuitry on the living-room table. And to my surprise the graduation photo's up on their wallscreen too: snowy and unstable, but there all the same.

'What *is* this?' I say in amazement. 'That picture! It's what I've been looking at in my apartment.'

'Oh damn, I'm sorry, Sharkey,' says Svetlana, looking up remorsefully. The blonde spitcurl drops across her blue, Slav eyes. 'It's my project for the Technische Universität. Van Eck Freaking. That's what it's called. Your wallscreen gives off electromagnetic radiation like radio waves, and I'm picking it up. I haven't got this tuned properly. I thought the pic was coming off the Stemmle's screen upstairs.'

'Where's Marta?'

'She's in bed,' says Petra. 'I told you she was ill. She's not in good shape. The doctor's been round. He told her to get some rest.'

'Can I have a word?' I whisper. 'Not here, but back in my apartment. It's about this picture.'

'I was about to make dinner. What is it exactly? Can it wait?'

'That's for you to decide. I don't quite know how to put this, Petra. I just thought you might like to meet your Mum and Dad.'

zak

Yes, Zak. Here he is at last.

Nathan Buczak.

Zak, zakky, zakko.

He was only a bip away in nowhere land. It's where we all live now, at infinitesimal reticles, silken intersections on Arachne's cosmic web, or the Indian Net of Indra, a net of gemstones, where at each point that a thread crosses another there's a gem in which the reflection of all the other reflective gemstones can be seen.

He's just a man in a room, as I am, yet this moment of bright reflection's very special for me. I've been looking forward to it. For this is Zak, my alter ego, Leo's other friend. We're both accessories to the fact. And Leo is the fact. He meted out his time to the two of us – in unequal rations, granted. But, all the same, Zak and I have this much in common. We have things to talk about. We have tender memories to trade.

'Yeah, wassup? Who wants me?'

A man and a room. I take them in with a snapshot look, retinally mapping the terrain, an internalised Mercator's projection. The man looks rattled, as if my call has put him off some intellectual stroke. He's late twenties, chunky and dark, with a scribbly beard and moustache, goatish black eyes and something intemperate around the lippy mouth. It's the ambivalent face of a kerb-crawler, on the look-out for easy pleasure and jittery of the law. It's the face of someone who's so behind with the bills that cosmetic surgery or suicide seem like realistic options, yet there's still one last-hope lottery ticket nestling in the wallet. He wears a cocky pork-pie canvas hat, the rim turned up to create an all-round gully, a Tommy Hilfiger co-ordinating outfit, a woollen neck-scarf and a Pacific Sunwear T-shirt with the slogan 'I am a pelican of the wilderness' slanting across it in a Looney Tunes popsicle font. He's tossing a sizeable coconut from hand to hand as he glares into the video-cam.

The room is chaos. Sheer mind-boggling chaos. The wall behind him's composed of uneven shingles on brick, with ancient wallpaper samples slapped on every which way and peeling pustulously. Shunted against it is a wrecked Pianola with what looks like a wartime Enigma machine on top alongside several Van Houten cocoa tins, empty pizza boxes, a crate of Ceptecol cough-mixture and a striding Johnny Walker statuette. On a metal chest with plastic drawers, overflowing with wires and electrical components, there's a black box with an eight-digit LED display that races through scrambled sequences of numbers. A gas boiler with grimy metallic duct snaking upwards. A Pirelli calendar depicting five cheerleaders, clean of limb, red of lip and in no need of silicon implants, embellished only with pom pom fluffballs like overblown mimosa. Postcards of Brooklyn Bridge, a kangaroo with boxing-gloves and a bi-plane looping the loop in a canyon. An African tribal mask. Suspended wind-chimes strung with blown birds' eggs of various sizes and hues. And one of those flashy but intriguing rear-lit Chinese images of a waterfall where the water really seems to glitter and cascade with ingenious fakery. Even this inventory merely scratches the two-dimensional surface of the visible, one plane of the tetrahedron. It is not even collectabilia. The room is a slag heap, a cataclysmic gallimaufry of irrelevant jumble, the bin ends and toe-clippings of western civilisation.

'Who wants me?' he repeats.

'My name's Sharkey.' I speak English, hoping to put him at his ease. 'I'm a friend of Leo's.'

The coconut lands in the cup of his left hand and stays there.

'I know who you are. Whadda ya want?'

'I'd like to meet up. I'd like to talk about Leo.'

'Jesus.' He shakes his head irritably, looks off-camera for an unconscionable time, then turns back with hard decisiveness. His voice has that flat seen-it-all drawl of the urban East Coast, the demotic of diners, Wal-marts and Budweiser bars. 'Leo's dead. Dead and gone. Okay, we were kickin' it together for a time, but those days are over now. It bites like that. He was an ephemeron. We all are, man.'

'I knew him too. Not as well as you. But I knew him. You know he was killed, don't you? Uscinski spoke to you. I need to talk to you because I want to find out who did it. And why.'

I'm chucking fuel on flame. He bangs the coconut down smartly, then quickly smiles and checks himself, rolling it around under the broad palm of his hand.

'Listen, Sharkey, whatever your name is. I appreciate your concern but I don't know how Leo coulda gotten killed. I'm out in the open, man. Leo was always strapped for cash. He was like tryin' to make money and stuff, so maybe someone went ballistic on him, right? I just don't know. What I'm saying is that I'm not the person to ask, see?'

He picks up the coconut and starts nonchalantly tossing it up and down again in one hand.

'I have to ask you,' I persist, 'You're the only person I can ask. You helped him get inside Reprotech.'

This time the coconut comes down with a crack. He looks aghast at his milk-splattered touchpad and explodes.

'Fuck Christ! This is really pissing the fuck outta me.' His brow knots in anguish and he stares back up, almost in surprise. 'I'm like really sorry, man, but it is. I mean, why do I have to barf this mental garbage? Why? What are you man, a vampire? Hasn't anyone told you? Vampires can't drink dead blood. I read it in an Anne Rice book so it must be true. An' if you're not a vampire, then you're either some crazy dumbass shit or else you're blur as a sotong. That's Singaporean, in case you didn't know. Blur as a sotong. A sotong's a squid, see? So let's get this straight, once and for all. I don't wanna diss Leo, but basically he was a dork and a sociopath. Okay? His second name was "Zero" an' that's my second name too. I liked the guy but I don't give two shits about him now he's dead, and neither should you. He's a memory, that's all. Just forget the whole thing, man. Let it slide.'

'I'm not going to do that.'

He does one of those sitcom-inspired reaction shots again, looking away then back, this time with tungsten-tipped eyes.

'Mr Sharkey, I'm just gonna try an' explain my position to you. I don't know where you got my number, but I was havin' a mellow day till you showed up. Now, I'm the kinda guy who tries to value simplicity and I try to think about simple things sometimes rather than always talkin' 'bout deep stuff that not all people can talk about. If you want information, you follow the nice police officer. Oink oink. Follow Uscinski. Or whatever. Whatever floats your boat. You understand?

Just leave me outta the picture. As far as I'm concerned, you can do or say what you like, but it's not gonna do shit for Leo.'

'I know that, but you can help me get to the truth. I'm not trying to bring Leo back to life. I'm trying to see that a little justice is done.'

I don't know how many pauses there are in the human repertoire but this one is not brimful of patience and human understanding.

'Okay,' he drawls, nodding his head slowly, 'I see I'm gonna have to make myself plain. Let me put it this way. There are people out there who're trying to fuck with our minds. You know that, don't you? An' you, Mr Sharkey, you're on their fuck-list. Take it from me. You're there in black and white. A marked man. Now I've got enough goddam chaos to handle as it is, so what would I want to be havin' extra shit to deal with with you? Huh? I don't. I can do without that, see? So, not meanin' to be rude or anything, I suggest you think about the living and forget about the dead. Do yourself a big favour an' get back to your nice little hicksville newspaper column. Fly away, sweet bird of prey. Forget Leo. And hope the fuck that the forces of darkness decide to forget about you too. No offence and all that.'

He shrugs apologetically, the screen flashes and the wall goes dead.

So that was Zak.

Zak, Zakkety, Zak.

He's gone, now. And that room with no address could have been anywhere: Vienna, Perth, Bogotá, Helsinki. It could have been anywhere, but it wasn't, and I know damn well it wasn't. Because I took the liberty, in the course of our unsatisfactory conversation, of casually zooming in on that Pirelli calendar with the five well-stacked cheerleaders. I took the liberty of zooming in, and my eye slipped from the handsome cleavages to today's date, Thursday 21 January 2027. Below the print, in the little white box, Buczak had scrawled the single word 'Tigers'. Two days ago that would have meant nothing to me, but I'm in luck. Yesterday, in a rare access of professional conscientiousness or insomnia, I read the *Wiener Tageszeitung*, my own paper, from cover to cover. The announcement was in a little corner of the back page. Thursday 21 January, 14.30, Midi Bowl. The High Bridge Tigers from New Jersey play the Klosterneuburg Mercenaries. Venue: Hanappi Superdrome, Hütteldorf. It may only be semi-pro, but it's not every day that American football comes to Vienna. And Buczak will be there, that's for sure, along with up to 20,000 other people, the capacity of

Vienna's second stadium after the Ernst Happl in the Prater. He'll be an American needle in an Austrian haystack, but that's just the way it is. It's a tiny crumb of chance that Providence has dropped on her mysterious way, and I'm going to have to pick it up. Let's face it, I'm tired of living in the subjunctive mode, a subjunctive of potentiality. And, frankly, Zak's annoyed me. Yes, I have to admit he's hurt my feelings. The least he can do is to tell me what I want to know. I haven't finished with old Zacko yet.

Superdrome

I get down to the Superdrome out West of the city at half-time, entering by the Kaisslergasse turnstile. The players are back in the locker rooms, but a loud intermission commentary re-runs the first half with holographic action replays on the field: 'Brecker completed 14-of-27 passes for 246 and has been playing virtually mistake-free football. He's put the Mercenaries ahead to stay at 17–14 with a really long play from scrimmage, an 81-yard touchdown pass to Heinz Fröhlich in the second minute of the second quarter. Czinner beat rookie safety Tieck at the line of scrimmage, and Tieck got no help from safety Oswald Leni as Czinner dashed down the right sideline for the Mercenaries longest TD pass of the season. The Mercenaries stretched their lead to 27–14 by half-time.'

It's a flat winter day, grey as a destroyer, and the floods are on. The bleachers are about seventy-five per cent full, some 15,000 spectators. I mentally grid out the stands opposite into A to H and proceed methodically, scanning left to right within each section with my Zeiss opera glasses, looking for that Zak face, the face I saw for only a few minutes this morning. It's cold now and he's bound to be wearing a coat, so I'm short on distinguishing particularities. There's just that pork-pie hat (which he may not be wearing) and the facial hair. Not a lot to go on. Occasionally a flag or banner swings in the way and my eyes tick back to check I haven't missed him.

The whistle goes.

The players trot out for the second half in their grilled helmets, their bulky body-armour. As time wears on, my arms tire and the view through the glasses gets less steady. It's the identity parade to beat all identity parades, and I'm working against the clock.

When I'm satisfied I've criss-crossed each square in the A to H matrix I exit the stand and circle round to the other side. It's time for I to P, the other half of the oblong where I'd previously been sitting myself. I concentrate on groups of Americans in the High Bridge colours, where I can find them, but they're few and far between. The vast majority of the spectators are Austrians. And everyone's in winter coats and hats, dark colours, an amorphous mass of uniformly clad humanity. The only niceties of variation are in the faces and from this distance, even with the aid of the glasses, they're so small, so huddled together, that the fixed mosaic of pale ovals rapidly transforms into a kaleidoscope of swarming dots. My eyes swim.

A dull headache bristles up into thorny cusps of pain, just behind the temples. I check my watch. Over an hour has passed. I've lingered on every unusual hat. I've scrutinised every bearded face. As I shift to the end of the last rows in my grid, there's little doubt about it. He's not here. I slip the opera glasses into my pocket and mentally curse myself. It was too much to hope for. And yet I'm still nagged by the possibility that he's here, that even in my scrupulousness I missed him – he ducked to tie a shoelace, he turned to look behind. Maybe I simply blinked.

I want to leave, but I can't. I even turn to leave, but my feet stay rooted to the spot. It's too late to start again, that's for sure. And it's now that someone up there in the celestial troposphere wipes a tear of sadistic mirth from his eye and decides to take pity on me. The guy next to me is listening to the match commentary on a radio. I'd been listening all along too with half my attention but suddenly I can't believe my luck or my ears: 'Well, the Tigers got back in the game when Brenton broke up the middle for an 18-yard touchdown, but New Jersey has had no time to gain momentum. Buczak returned the ensuing kickoff 99 yards for a touchdown. Ritter hit tight end John Hurst for the two-point conversion, giving the Mercenaries a 35–21 cushion. That makes Buczak the fourth guy to be up for Most Valuable Player honours in the Midi Bowl, the only American in the Klosterneuburg team. In addition to his touchdown, he's set up two other scores with long punt returns so far into the match. That's four kickoff returns for 154 yards and six punt returns for 90 yards. His 99-yard kickoff return was the longest in Austrian Midi Bowl history. He must be pretty chuffed with himself because nothing much is going to stop the Klosterneuburg Mercenaries at this stage in the game.'

I tap the man with the radio on the shoulder. 'Which one's Buczak?' He points out the number 8 in the Austrian team, and there he is, indistinguishable from the others in terms of physique: Nathan Buczak, this time in flesh and blood. He's obviously well pleased with his star performance. Another player slaps him on the helmet and there's a little swagger of vanity as he turns to acknowledge. He shrugs those prosthetic shoulders and clasps his hands above his head. He's a champ. I'm happy for him. And I stay put to the end, a 35–21 victory for the Mercenaries.

Lap of honour. National anthem. Interviews. Shower.

I wait at the players' exit, behind the crowd barrier at the end of a line of docile autograph hunters. It's an hour before he appears. He's got that pork-pie hat on again. It's such a self-conscious fashion accessory that it's evidently a kind of personal signature, a badge of individuality in a world of conveyor-belt consistency. He's prudent enough, though, to wrap up against the cold in a sweepingly long brown overcoat with astrakhan collar, the kind that rich black funk guitarists swanked around in back in the 70s.

I don't know what emotion I expected from him: surprise, anger, fear. He spots me early on, as he comes down the line, and it's none of these. In fact, it's indecipherable. He just looks, identifies, and looks away with a trace of coldness. He moves closer. He signs. He shakes hands. He modestly deflects accolades. Then all at once he's in front of me.

Plasmavision's not always an objective recorder of events. It's true some people come across as they are. The orchestral arrangement of voice, facial expression, gesture and appearance is infallibly thus and not otherwise. With others there's dislocation, fission. Perhaps it's a question of integrity, as if one's electronic presence reveals or conceals significant dimensions of personality. Buczak's not only a head taller than I'd thought but the leering, neurasthenic impression he left earlier in the day has gone. It might have been simply pre-match nerves, amplified and distorted. Now there's simple ebullience, an excess of animal energy. The man in front of me has papered over the cracks. He's cool, dressy and vigorous, basking in big-limbed American triumphalism, his moment of gridiron glory. When we're face to face, the bravura only decomposes slightly in the eyes and at the edges of the wire-haired mouth. His gaze is, paradoxically, too steady, and a tiny uncontrollable pulse in the lower lip rebels against the specious smile of self-assurance.

'You don't give up,' he says starchily.

'Neither do you. I watched the match.'

He scratches his beard and grins uncertainly. His performance was clearly a surprise to him as well. He turns and looks back down the gangway, clutching his sports bag and rubbing one trainer against the back of his trouser leg. He's irresolute. He takes one step forward. He takes one step back. It strikes me he's nervous of cameras, and there are several further down. They're presently trained on the emerging players from the defeated American team. Buczak's on his guard. His face speaks poise and control. His voice is tense, electric.

'I thought I told you to climb up your thumb, man,' he murmurs, glancing rapidly at me to make sure I can hear. 'You're bad news. I don't wanna be seen with you.'

'Damn, I forgot. If those cameras picked us up, there's sure to be people out there who know who I am and then they'll see you with me. Still, I'll try my hardest not to draw attention to us. My car's round the corner. It'd be so much simpler if we drove somewhere quiet and had a cosy little chat. Out of the limelight, so to speak.'

Suddenly his composure blows to pieces. 'You're a lousy douchebag man,' he hisses. 'I swear to God you are. Wassup? Did you get oxygen shortage in your mother's womb?'

'You accept my offer, then.'

'Yeah, let's go somewhere I can kick the crap out of you.' He all but spits the words out of the side of his mouth. 'The Krah Krah. Bermuda Triangle. It's as good a place as any.' Then he looks at me again, bites his lip thoughtfully, and all of a sudden he pats me on the arm, relenting into unexpected good humour. He even chuckles under his breath. 'Oh, fuck it, man! I'm sorry. Why don't I just be sweet to you? I'll tell you about Leo. I'll tell you anything, anything you want to know. After all, Sharkey baby, what the hell good's it gonna do you now?'

the bermuda triangle

We park on the Rabensteig in the Bermuda Triangle, the former Jewish district. It's a small square blocked in by the lumpy, asymmetrical façades of ancient buildings. In summer it's a delightful spot to linger outdoors and drink a beer. But on winter evenings such as this the place hovers in a dank and insalubrious mist of moist greyness, sluicing silently inland from the Danube. The fog is punctured only by the warm street-level glow emanating from the surrounding beisls and bars. The Krah Krah is one such. We head for a corner table, under a spluttering electric candle on a gargoyled wall-bracket, and Zak flings off his coat and orders fried chicken livers in red wine on a bed of lettuce. He eats ravenously, then flags down the waiter with a napkin.

'A shake. Pepsi and milk, mixed,' he calls.

'For the milk: cow, goat, human or soya?'

'Human. And you?'

I opt for a half-bottle of Styrian Chardonnay and turn the talk to Leo. He warms to the subject with surprising alacrity. Before very long, no subtle prompting is necessary. Zak opens out like a meadow daisy in the sweet sunbeam of reminiscence.

He and Leo had first met in May 2025 at a conference on steganoprophy, the art of hiding information in noise. They met again at a follow-on colloquium on generating random numbers from noise caused by leak-currents in diodes and transistors. Like most computer buffs, they'd begun as teenage hackers and the dangerous edge of info-piracy still held them in its thrall. It was a marginal zone of derring-do and shady inducements. They had this in common, but there was much much more. There was the Zwölf Apostel Keller, the Kaktus, Rasputin, the Loos Bar, the Bluebox, the Salzamt, the Europa, the Tunnel, without forgetting the Casino Wien and the Black Jack Café. They were soul mates, bosom pals, a latter-day David and Jonathan, the tall crack-brained yank and the stumpy stuttering Leo. And their natural habitat was this flipside Vienna, the potent, lunar shadow-world of lurid bars, clubs and cathouses. I think back to Leo at the Paloma to get the big picture. But Zak was Leo's secret, a secret Petra knew nothing of. He was the dark confederate, the fellow scam-monger.

Zak grins. He's finished his shake and orders a Maryland rye. He folds his arms on the table and edges forward. 'You know,' he breathes, still in a dream of recollection, 'I've theorised this before, but I guess he and I just hooked up well. We had these stupid goddam plans. We were gonna go white water rafting down the Congo. We were gonna open a diner called the Starla Café in the middle of the Arizona desert. It was chaotic, you know. When I was twelve, man, I did fifteen dollars worth of shoplifting from Casey's General Store on Main Street. That was like the extent of my entrepreneurial skills back in Solitude Village, NJ. But Leo – he saw things on a bigger scale. He was phat as hell, an' sometimes he scared the shit outta me. So, yeah. Hats off to Leo. He was barrels of laughs, and smart with it. I miss the fucking pothead.'

'Tell me about Reprotech.'

Zak wipes his mouth and pokes at the ice-cubes in his drink with a swizzle stick. 'How much do you know?' he asks warily.

'Some. Not all. Leo wanted to tell me more, but we ran out of time.'

'Then you know what he found out about his wife. You know what he found out about his parents. He went nuts, man. He flipped on me more than once. Especially when she got pregnant. He was withering in unlove, unlife and unhope. He just wanted to buzzkill everyone. I mean one day he's a family man, with parents an' a wife, and the next he's a coon cat like me – the stray kind you get from the pound. Shit. Who can blame him? It was his downfall, his crash. His life was in ashes.'

'He wanted to find out who his genetic parents were and why they weren't owning up to it.'

'Right.'

'And did he? Did he find out that their names were Elsa Lubitsch and Peter Diessl?'

Zak stops poking at the ice and looks me briskly in the eye. The tiny pulse of irritation returns to his lower lip. Some kind of quandary toggle-switch is tripping back and forth at quantum speeds in his mind. He allows his predatory eyes to drift off on the trail of a slender vamp in seersucker as she swings across the floor. It's a smart move. It draws my attention away from the external signs of his dilemma. As far as I'm concerned, I realise, his is a floating vote.

'I guess he found out the truth,' he prevaricates. 'He didn't tell me everything. He was killed before he got the chance.'

'Tell me how he got into Reprotech's system. He didn't do it through the Net. It's off limits. I had a go myself.'

'Sure, they're firewalled all right. You can go to the public end of the clinics and stuff, but no further. It used to be different. They used to have a multilayer kernel/proxy architecture. The security of an application proxy and the speed of a packet filter combined. They had real-time notification of unusual network activity and a suspicious activity monitor. Leo got through the first layers with no problem, but they also knew someone was out there tryin' to get in.'

'When are we talking about?'

'Lemme see, June '26? Yeah, that would be it, 'cos they put out the tender soon afterwards.'

'What tender?'

'A tender for complete security encryption. Registry-manipulation tools. Centralised control over user access to settings. Tailored user profiles. Plus system administrators had to have the final word on enabling. The usual routine in these cases, where infiltration's suspected. But they wanted one step further. You know they're based in Burgenland . . .'

'I've been there. I've seen the place, from the outside at least.'

'Well when they started gettin' paranoid, they put out this tender I mentioned. They wanted the best cryptographic architect in the business.'

'You.'

'Right, me! Shit!' His laughter's like the hiss of air-brakes. 'I got it. Leo's buddy got it. They wanted complete modular segregation of the Neusiedl site from all other peripherals.'

'Tight security?'

'Tight as a duckling's ass. Totally closed architecture, man. Maximum security with proprietary algorithm descriptors. The descriptors can be associated with dynamic passwords and digital log-ins for user authentication, even voice and biometric authentication. But no remote-access whatsoever to core information in restricted zones.'

'So only people within the Neusiedl site can log on, and even their access is customised.'

'Right. It's strictly cellular, like espionage networks. Nobody but the top dogs get the panoramic view. But within site the cryptosystem's the same as you'd get via the Net, using public key algorithms. Reprotech opted for Elliptic Curve Engine technology. The best. It uses a different key for encryption and decryption, but the trick is that the decryption key can't be derived from the encryption key. The algorithm's very fast. And it uses large integers that are difficult to factor.'

'You've lost me.'

'Okay, look, I'll try to eschew obfuscation. It's basically a piece of cake, man. Any cryptographic system needs strong random numbers that can't be guessed by an attacker. The numbers generate session keys. The generator's the weak point in the system so it has to be good, and the best source of randomness is just noise. Listen!'

We turn our attention to the acoustics of the bar. Voices, music, the creak of the door spring, the clatter of cutlery, the rippling arpeggio of an incoming call on a Networker.

'Put it together, and what've you got? Pure randomness. Reprotech didn't want freeloaders mooching off them, in-house or out. So they got the Alpha and the Omega of cryptosystems. It uses the ambient noise of the Neusiedl lake to generate randomness. Wind, water, reeds, birds. Awesome, huh? That was my inspiration. The best goddam job I ever did. The pure unsullied sounds of Mother Nature, man. Processed with a suitable hash function, 160 bits or more, and it's unbeatable.'

'Indirectly, then, the noise generates the decryption key.'

'Right, that's at the top level. Once you get through that, the bulk of the data's encrypted with symmetric ciphers. Here it's the same key for encryption and decryption. This is breakable with the right hardware, but frankly you'll never get that far.'

a little chink

His features crack up into that self-satisfied grin once more, he snaps his fingers and orders another rye. We make it two. The bar's filling up. He leans back and spreads his upper arms along the top of the banquette and lazily bites at a thumbnail as those unbridled satyr eyes flit about the latest additions to the feminine clientèle. It occurs to me that he's into kinetic-dye T-shirts. While we've been sitting here, the slogan's already changed from 'I am like an owl of the desert' to 'I watch, and am as a sparrow alone upon the house-top'.

There's something both foolish and scarey about Zak. It could be that sporty pork-pie hat, pulled down so hard over his head that his ears bend forward dopily under the rim. It could be the 25-cent signet ring or the Aztec bead watch-strap. Then again, it could be that doodled graffiti of a beard, which I now realise is trying to camouflage a receding chin. Or it could be all of these, plus the unpredictable marriage of juvenile hypothalamus, that primitive nerve centre of physical and emotional behaviour, and bulldozer brawn.

'I want to do what Leo did. I want to see what he saw.' I speak with deliberation so he gets the message loud and clear. I'm not giving voice to a spur-of-the-moment impulse.

'I know you do,' he says, turning to face me. The grin broadens into a wide ductile slit.

'I need your help.'

'You do,' he acknowledges smugly. 'You need a lot more than that. You need the wishbone, man. You need the devil's own luck.' He hunches forward again and scratches an insect bite on his forehead, pushing the hat so it sits on the back of his head. 'What happened to Leo can happen to you too. But you got on a roll, and you just can't stop. That's what it is, isn't it? It's a one-way street. Shit, I know that feeling. So listen, man, I'm gonna help you out, but only so far. It's like football. There's this saying that you never know if a guy can run with the ball unless you give him the ball in the first place. So the bottom line is this: I don't want you to go away thinking I'm not a sport. Not old Zak. I'm gonna give you the benefit of the doubt. A fighting chance, man. Do with it what you will. First, I want you to get out your Networker. Right. Now put it on the table.'

He places his own unit next to mine, linking the ports with a short retractable wire. He touch-types a key sequence and downloads.

'Leo got in 'cos I had the tender. I signed him in as my technical assistant. We had the run of Reprotech, with three-day multi-passes. Now that kind of luck dried up long ago. It was one-off. Remember, the only access to Reprotech's system comes from inside. You have to be physically inside the premises.'

'I went there with Petra, Leo's wife. We just walked in. Nobody stopped us.'

'That's what they'd like you to think, but don't kid yourself. You see nothing, but that place is alive. Video, guards, sonic trips, and all approaches – driveway and lawns – are dusted in this chemical shit you pick up on your shoes. Holy smoke, man, they don't leave anything to chance. If you've been there once, they'll have you tabbed already. But what I'm saying is, that's your problem, okay? What I'm gonna give you's something else. Now like I was saying, the Reprotech cryptosystem works on pure randomness. The randomness of noise from the Neusiedl lake. So the decryption key changes all the time. Fuck, man, we were installing the software and even *we* couldn't crack it. No precomputations are possible and there are no visible implementation bugs. The generator's constantly hashing an arbitrary length byte string into high bit values. So Leo and I decided to open a debug port. A little chink in the outwardly chinkless armour. Let's talk this thing through for a moment. That random noise, like I said, comes from the lake, but how d'you capture it and send it to the number generator?'

'A mike, I suppose.'

'That's the baby. A mike. An external mike's what it has to be. There's a big kind of bunker at Reprotech. You probably saw it. It's the closest outhouse to the lake, and that's where we rigged up the mike. It's about one metre up on the eastern facing, boxed into a little wire-grilled casing next to an overflow pipe. Now Reprotech's a strictly No Dogs camp, apart from the guard dogs, and the first day we showed up we had Argos, Leo's dog, in tow. Where were we supposed to put the crazy mutt? It was a problem. So we talked over our little spot of bother with the nice guard on duty there and got permission to hook the dog's lead up on that overflow pipe. Just the first day, that was all. We left him stuff to eat and shit. And the guard looked in on him on his rounds. But the point I'm gettin' at is that Leo had a system.'

'The pager. The pager on Argos's collar.'

'Hey, you're quick, man. Yeah. The pager. That's the thing. On that first day we set up the mike and the random number generator and when we were inside with a live terminal Leo bipped through to the pager. He couldn't do it for long, 'cos that goddam dog was goin' apeshit out there, strainin' at the leash. He thought walkies were over. He thought it was time to go back to the ranch. But Leo bipped for long enough.'

'The beep from the pager. It'd be anything but random.'

'Right. Anything but. It was so beat. I mean the idea was so gross, we knew from the outset it was gonna kick. In digital terms, the beep from the pager was a periodic data-flow. A little island of perfect order in a sea of acoustic chaos. The generator delivered like clockwork. A perfect decryption key, just for Leo.'

'That's amazing. But he must've needed Argos every time he hacked in.'

'No way. We simply recorded the whole encrypt-decrypt sequence on his Networker. The next time, all the smartass needed was to couple the Networker up to the audio port on the terminal, download the protocol and key in the invariable decryption key. I'm tellin' you, if it weren't illegal as shit there should be some kinda Nobel prize for stuff like that.'

'So my little present from you is that sequence.'

'You've already got it,' he says, unwiring my Networker. He shows me how to activate and a raft of code streaks across the small screen. 'If they've wised up to this, you'll be in trouble. A reject on the sequence sets up an nth-complexity infinite binary loop. The processor'll blow in your hand. I wouldn't worry, though. Leo was hot. He was in a class of his own. Reprotech's system operators were just a bunch of preppy college kids. That old bastard tore strips off of them.'

'You mentioned the bunker, where the overflow was. We saw it when we checked the place out. There were two giant tanks on the thermal imaging. Any idea what's in them?'

'Di-hydrogen oxide in one. In the other, a gaseous composition of nitrogen, oxygen, argon, carbon dioxide, neon, helium, krypton and xenon.'

'Water and air, I presume.'

'You said it. Water and air. They're used to test dispersal rates for crop-sprays and waterborne anti-pollutants.'

In a dark, angular niche to one side of the central zinc bar a hollow column of top-lit transparent plastic lowers from the ceiling like a nuclear reactor rod. A nimbus of dry ice refrigerant swells up from apertures in the base plinth and the slow drug of jazz seeps into the air. 'The show!' says Buczak, rounding his lips into an 'O'. He's rubbing his hands. Suddenly he's full of childish enthusiasm. He knocks back the ice-cube from his rye and swallows it whole.

'The next phase,' I insist. His attention's adrift and I sense that I'm losing him. 'There's a second key. Remember? Symmetric cipher, you said.'

'Don't ask me, brother.' He waves the question away like a bothersome valet. 'There's a six-digit fixed code. I never knew what it was. Leo had it. Hell, maybe it was an inspired guess. Maybe someone gave it him. It beats me.'

I try another tack.

'Does the name Büchner, Dr Büchner, mean anything to you?'

'No, man. Should it?'

'He's a Reprotech employee. Drives a red BMW Z10 A-series. That's the car that killed Leo.'

Zak shakes his head despairingly. 'I told you, didn't I? Blur as a sotong. Wise up, man. Just about everyone at Reprotech drives a BMW Z10 A-series. It's the old company fleet. When they upgraded, they sold off the vehicles to their own employees.'

'And Diessl. Where do I find Diessl?'

'Come on! Give me a break, will you? Nobody gets to see Diessl. Diessl leads a really quiet life out in Simmering, just off the Simmeringer Hauptstrasse. Quiet as hell. Very low profile. Under an assumed name. Nobody sees him and he don't answer the phone.'

The slow swing number rides up in volume. From the floor of the luminous cylinder, a woman with black spiked hair rises into the air like a Sci-Fi goddess on a steel piston. She's clad from top to toe in faux taffeta, an ebony Freshjive cyberpunk outfit. 'Hey babe!' shouts Zak, clapping his hands, 'That's my baby!' She starts into a dance, a slow, writhing Salome of a dance, and as she turns she winks at Zak. Not a big, public wink. Just a little you-and-me one, a connivance. Then all at once she's in the swing, writhing in that loping pantherine bring-me-the-head way and lip-syncing the words. The joint's full and all eyes are on her. Zak mucks in, singing with blithe abandon. It's 'Dream a Little Dream of Me', an old Kann and Schwandt number. A song that sings of night breezes murmuring words of love, starlight and the soft chirruping of birds in the sycamore trees. He turns on me with dewy eyes. 'Listen to that baby, will you? That's my little Porcelina, man. Look how she shakes her butt. My Porcelina of the Vast Oceans. Jesus, man, I love that little bitch.' The music's slowed down till it's dripping with sex. And as she dances her clothes disintegrate. The edges simply crumble away into floating ash, like burning tissue paper but without the flame. I've heard of thermo-chemical striptease, but it's the first time I've seen one. I watch in amazement. The dense black vestments curl up into decay at the edges and float off in a fuzz of atomic dust. The wig, the skirt, the blouse, the bra. Till all that's left is the white billow of her body and the rolling wave of the dance. It travels down her coiling limbs, from the Balinese play of the hands to the slightest spin on the tip of her toes, then it travels up again. And suddenly it's over. The pale vision of nakedness is suspended in darkness for one heart-stopping instant like a cave-drawing glimpsed by torchlight. The lamps are killed. A puff of sorcerer's brimstone, and she's gone.

As the house lights go up, my eyes meet Zak's. There's an aura of spiritual elation about him, and he's nodding his head slowly. I notice the slogan on his T-shirt's changed yet again: 'Whoso diggeth a pit shall fall therein.'

'She drowns me, brother,' he sighs softly, 'She just drowns me. My little Porcelina. My Porcelina of the Vast Oceans. How does she do that weird shit? I swear to God, I'll never know.' His eyes fly up to the dividing line between wall and ceiling. 'Now go,' he adds simply. His gaze is still elevated but he gently shuts those goatish eyes. 'Just take that ball and run. I dunno about your karma, Mr Sharkey. I dunno if it's good or bad and undefuckable. But you're out there on your own and lookin' down the barrel of mortality, my friend, the same way Leo did. Remember, then, that you don't know me. And this evening never was. I gave up playin' leapfrog with unicorns a long long time ago. When I open my eyes, I don't wanna see you no more, and you don't wanna see me. So go, man, just go. From here to eternity, we're strangers, you and I. Amen, brother. Go.'

I leave the Krah Krah and sit in my car, tucked back in the shadows of the Rabensteig. The night is very dark and a soft feathery snow begins to fall in loose, careless flurries. I find a few flattened cigarettes in the glove compartment and smoke them slowly, right down to the tip. I'm exhausted and the heating doesn't work, but I'm not budging now, even when that dead hand of winter numbness tightens its grip on my extremities. My mind is void of thought, my body of sensation.

I watch as a drunken skirmish starts and expires outside the Roter Engel. Then around one in the morning the Krah Krah begins to empty. The silhouettes of bodies emerge and vanish against the lamplit rectangle of the open door. And after a while I see the one I want. Buczak, clutching his sports bag, the woman on his arm. They're slightly the worse for wear and rely on each other for support as their feet slither on the fresh rink of snow.

Home, as it turns out, is a short walk away, in the vestiges of the old Bassena quarter. They're so wrapped up in each other, these two, that they don't notice me for an instant, though I walk a few paces behind.

I am nothing to them. I am the echo of a snowflake. I am the third shadow on the wall.

in a dark time

I sleep fitfully. My mind's alive. It shuttles between stark consciousness and the mad semiotics of troubled dreams in which Buczak and Leo figure prominently. At length they conflate into the same beast, a dragon, a serpent with the wings of an eagle and two human heads. Words spit out from the creature's mouth in matt black letters on square white placards like teeth: *EYE SEE TIME DARK BEGINS*. The placards grow legs and scurry around giggling, switching places, breaking up and recombining. It's like a parlour game in a mental hospital, played to occult and impenetrable rules. *A DARK EYE TIME BEGINS TIME TO SEE SEE IN THE DARK*. At last I recognise their source: 'In a Dark Time, the Eye Begins to See'. It's the title of a Roethke poem I downloaded the other day. The placards collapse like a house of cards and from the theatrical wings of my unconscious Leo appears again – hale, human and alone this time – sauntering on-stage in a grey Styrian Tracht with green facings and half-open black cape, clutching an alpenstock. He's greeted by an excited flourish of music from the orchestra pit. He bows and gazes around him benignly with the polished charm of the professional crowd-warmer. After a suitable pause he brings a clenched fist up to his mouth, clears his throat with poise and ceremony and declaims: 'Suffer the little children to come unto me, and forbid them not: for of such is the kingdom of G-God. Spare a thought, meine D-Damen und Herren, for the poor orphans of the Caribbean!' A spotlight picks out a revolving door in a sloping cobbled lane with '8 Schreyvogelgasse' inscribed above it. Leo winks slyly then, with a vampiric swish of that cape, he disappears into the spinning blur of the mechanism.

I breakfast early and call in on Marta and Svetlana.

Marta's sitting up in bed against an enormous cushion with a patchwork woollen shawl wrapped around her. Above her head, nailed to the wall, there's a crucifix and a framed photograph of a Lutheran church, a wooden articular structure with white walls and a steep black roof. This small, hardy woman, with the fortitude of her race, has been diminished by illness. She's a pale porcelain doll, now, abandoned on the bedspread. It seems to be bronchitis. She's got a high fever and a wheezing cough, and the room has that fetid smell of the sickchamber. The doctor has prescribed antibiotics and a bronchodilator to open the airways and ease her breathing, but the condition hasn't improved.

We chat aimlessly and I fetch the album she wants. It's a Matej Lunter recording of folk music from the Upper Hron Valley. On the cover sleeve, the artist appears in black cap, a Heligonky button accordion on his knees. Svetlana looks in, her arms crossed, leaning on the doorjamb. She exchanges a few words with her mother in a foreign tongue, I'm not sure which. It's either Slovak or the Rusyn language, a dialect of Ukrainian from the Preshov region of North-east Slovakia where Marta hails from. Marta puts on headphones to listen to her music and Svetlana and I go into the living-room for coffee.

While Svetlana heats the water, I look around. It's more than two decades since Marta left Slovakia but she carries her phylogeny with her like a protective shell. The flat is so Slovak that it would hardly be a surprise to find the skyline of Dubrovnic or Nitra lurking behind the block-print curtains. There are folk puppets and painted icons, one of St Cyril signed Mikulas Klimcak, and a large tourist poster of haycocks beside a lake in the Turiec countryside. There's a flaky, crystalline lump of antimony from the mine where Marta's father used to work. And everything seems to be draped with little embroidered bits of linen: antimacassars, tablecloths, cushion and armrest covers. Svetlana, with her blonde spitcurl, apple-pie cheeks and gentian eyes, is as much a part of the décor as the overdressed puppets, though she's half-Austrian and has lived in Vienna all her life.

On a table by the wallscreen there's the machinery she was toying with the previous evening. There are several units packed neatly into a suitcase, the sides of which unclip and open down for ease of use. A couple of books lie beside it: *Radio Frequency Interference: How to Fix It and Find It* and *Federal Communications Commission Interference Handbook*. Then some photostat papers by Wim van Eck and Erhard Moller. I bend down and investigate the contraption, turning a dial, pushing the odd button.

'What did you say this was?' I ask on her return.

'It's my project for the Technische Universität,' she says, handing me a mug. 'If it's accepted, I get credits towards my degree, the akademische Grad höherer Ordnung.'

'But what is it?'

'A van Eck freaking machine. A Tempest device, if you prefer.'

'Tempest?'

'Transient Electromagnetic Pulse Emanation Surveillance Technology. Quite a mouthful, huh? It's for monitoring. It picks up white noise, basically. Spurious emissions of electromagnetic radiation. The sort of stuff that TVs, CPUs and peripherals give off all the time.'

'Yes, I remember. You intercepted that American graduation photograph from my wallscreen.'

She runs a hand down the nape of her neck and tries a glum, shamefaced look on for size.

'It's pretty amazing, actually,' I say, mulling the matter over. 'Is it legal?'

'It's not illegal because emissions are public domain. It's like saying it's illegal to listen to a radio station. You can shield equipment against pulse emanation, but nobody bothers to do it effectively. The whole thing's paradoxical. I mean, there's NACIM 5100A. That's a government document that defines standards. The trouble is, it's classified, so nobody gets to see it. I reckon the truth is the authorities don't want people to shield equipment because it would screw up their own eavesdropping.'

'Very plausible, as conspiracy theories go. Totschweigetaktik: a conspiracy of silence. How exactly does it work?'

square waves and clock speeds

'Basically, your wallscreen or your computer's like a radio station. It transmits signals. Behind every screen, even Plasmavision, you've got an electron gun that fires a scanning beam from top to bottom, in lines. It flashes on and off and it makes the pixels fluoresce, which gives you your image. Voltage changes give off pulses which generate radio waves. Then various things around the computer act as antennae. Unshielded cables on power lines, for example, telephone wires, water pipes, sprinkler systems. They're all great at boosting signals. Look, I'll show you.'

248

She activates the wallscreen and the dedicated CPU, then fetches a little wriststrap Networker from her bedroom and turns it on. As she passes the communicator over the screen, the CPU and the wall cabling, a hiss of static phases in and out.

'That noise is a radio signal. Computers radiate square waves and clock speeds. PIN numbers have unique electromagnetic signatures. So do individual keystrokes. You type a 'K' and you get a radio-signal 'K' flying off into the ether. As I said, you can snap on EMI filters, ferrite core attenuators and toroids, or ferrite split beads on cables. You can stick your CPU in a wire-screen Faraday cage. But nobody bothers and anyway it doesn't always work. Besides which, industry standards are lax. Class A shielding, which is used on business computer systems, is not very stringent.'

'You astonish me, Svetlana. I thought girls were interested in needlework and collecting recipes, pressing flowers and domestic science. That kind of thing.'

'Not modern girls, Sharkey. You've got some catching up to do.'

'So tell me, how do you pick these signals up?'

She separates out the various units in the suitcase.

'This is the basic equipment. It's not particularly expensive. You need a good commercial wide-band radio receiver. The best are the ones designed for surveillance with a spectrum display. Next, we have a horizontal and vertical sync generator. I've had to fine-tune it to get it to do what I want. Then a multi-scan video monitor with shielded cables. An active directional antenna, with a phased antenna array. Shielded cables again. A Think radio telescope. A small keyboard. Lastly, some kind of video recording equipment so you can keep an archive of what you pick up to review later. I've gone for a miniature digital clip recorder here. Keeping it small was the main priority. I managed that with custom circuits using specialised Fast Fourier Transforms. They also work wonders for image clarity and range.'

'What is the range?'

'The signal diminishes as the inverse square of the distance between the Tempest device and the computer or whatever you happen to be monitoring. One kilometre max. For best results, you have to be within three hundred metres. What do you say? Shall we give it a spin?'

'Here? Right now?'

'A flat's ideal. You get compromising emissions from all directions.

Look. I'll point the antenna up at the ceiling. The Stemmles live above. A spot of frequency tuning – here goes. And – here, we've got something. The image is rolling but we can correct that with the sync generator, and – Wow!'

On the multi-scan monitor, a naked couple suddenly materialise on a water-bed. It's a particularly graphic and energetic sex scene, doggy-fashion.

'Well that's certainly a compromising emission,' I say, with the beginnings of sea-sickness, 'but it doesn't look like the Stemmles to me.'

'No, stupid! Frau Stemmle must've gone out shopping. He always does this when she's out. Filthy bugger. It's a subscription satellite channel.'

The full potential of Svetlana's device begins to take shape.

'Just what did you have in mind doing when you built this thing?' I ask incredulously.

'I hadn't really thought about it. It was more of a technical exercise. With Jürgen, my boyfriend, we thought we could snoop in on brokers to get prior warning of stock market deals. We could target ATM machines to get people's credit details. Anything. I could blackmail Herr Stemmle, come to think of it. But that's not what we told the profs. We told them we'd use it for the war on drugs.'

'I see what you mean. Let me get this clear, though. You can lock on to signals from any computer whatsoever?'

'Sure. It even discriminates between different devices in the same room. You can pick up text from an operating printer, for example.'

'I guess you wouldn't have to be there all the time, would you? You leave the recorder running for hours then scan through your intercepts at a later time. But it's purely passive. I mean, what you get depends on what an operator's viewing, doesn't it?'

'That's where my machine's different.' She's looking fresh and sassy. She's clearly pleased with herself. 'There've been passive Tempest machines before. If I just recycled someone else's design, I wouldn't get my credits. So I've pushed the specifications. I can do quite a lot more than intercept. Watch this.'

She fiddles with the spectrum display and flips a couple of buttons. The porn film suddenly switches to a cookery class. There's an audible curse from the flat above and the thud of feet as Herr Stemmle storms over to his CPU.

'Clever.'

'Yeah. I can sift out system operating signals from remote controls, keyboards or voice activation units. Then I loop back on the signal wave and put my hand to the tiller. Again – watch.'

She switches back to the porn film. Footsteps again. Stemmle returning to his comfy chair. Then Svetlana types a short text on to her monitor: 'You are under surveillance by the cyber-police. Your name has been added to our central directory of filthy buggers.' She sends and there's a loud smash as Stemmle drops or breaks something, possibly a vase. The screen goes dead.

'Brilliant, Svetlana! It's positively Faustian. But this isn't limited to policing the porn waves, is it? I mean, for example, you could operate a complex data retrieval system from three hundred metres away.'

'No problem. The target VDU doesn't even have to be on.'

I sit down and cross my arms. I'm lost in admiration. It's the smartest little toy to come my way since those toasters that burn morning messages on to the bread.

'Are you free? Now, I mean.'

'This morning, yes. My first seminar's at two. Why?'

'I want you to do me a favour. I want you to teach me. Show me how to work this thing. And lend it to me, just for a day.'

'Sure, so long as you take care of it. The operation's a cinch. There are four skills, basically. Frequency tuning. Antenna manoeuvring. Reintroducing sync. And finding a good spot to monitor from.'

'Fine. Let's go through them. Oh, and Svetlana –'

'Yes?'

'D'you know anything about fishing? Anything at all?'

chapter eleven

a state of mind

I'm sitting alone on the bank of the Neusiedl lake. I'm waiting for the church clock in Donnerskirchen to strike one. My brand-new fishing rod's beside me, resting on a metal prop. And the line feeds out to the little ogee of a fluorescent float that bobs gently on the turbid water. I've chosen an isolated but open spot, a kind of bay hemmed in by thick stands of littoral reeds. It's right where Petra and I had stood before, less than three hundred metres from the Reprotech plant.

I've never been fishing before. They say it's good for the soul, and I can believe that. I'm about to commit an act of industrial espionage, yet I feel surprisingly at ease with the world. In fact, I'm in a philosophical mood. To my back are the vineyards of Austria, while in front of me are 320 square kilometres of tectonic depression, the serene sky-mirror of the lake traversed – right now – by a handsome mare's tail of cloud and the darting shadow of a red-footed falcon. Here I am at home. This country, this Austria, is where I'm from. The land of Haydn, Mozart, Strauss, Klimt, Schiele, Zweig, Canetti, Schnitzler, Freud and Sharkey. Yes, this is my land. And hence the paradox: I'm in danger, yet I feel safe. On the southern bank is Hungary, a foreign land – foreign to me, that is. But what is home? A mere parcel of soil demarcated and fought over by the tribe or race? We have a word for that: Bodenständigkeit. Is it such a place, or is it a state of mind? A sense of familiarity, perhaps, of belonging. A sense that is disturbed when we are displaced, for we become 'homesick'. So home is family, tribe, language and nation. A settled encampment too. But it's more than these things, much more. It's a fixed co-ordinate on the map of the soul. It's the myth of the autochthon, the aborigine, the man who springs from the earth he inhabits, the 'son of the soil'. Yet the sons of the soil are not men of peace. It's there in the legend for all to see. For Cadmus slew the dragon that guarded the well of Ares and sowed some of its teeth, from which sprang up the men called Sparti, or the Sown-men, who all slaughtered each other – all but five.

A single bell rings out to the west. Lunchtime.

I glance cautiously behind at the thicket of scrub and trees. There's nobody around. I open Svetlana's case and set up the Tempest device. I align the directional antenna and miniature radio telescope as she instructed me. Almost immediately a signal's picked up on the receiver and relayed to the multi-scan screen. I lock in and adjust the hold on the sync generator. The image is crystal clear. It's a Reprotech CPU, no doubt about it, and I'm on a base directory page headed by an integral Boolean search engine. I watch the screen for five minutes. There's no activity. It's a fair bet the operator's at lunch. Svetlana's little black box analyses the signal emission to determine the control configuration and buzzes when it's ready. I fancy I hear something and look around again. There's nothing. Just the rustling swish of the wind in the bending reeds, the grating cry of a distant crake. I type the word 'Changeling' into the search box and send. A single hit registers. I follow through and a window opens up:

This document is in a restricted zone.
The zone is double-protected by an elliptic curve public key cryptosystem and a symmetric cipher.
Authorised users should first insert their decryption clip into Port A.

I download Zak's decrypt key from the Networker and wait. A second window flashes up:

Your first-level decryption key has been accepted.
To enter the database, now log in your six-figure symmetric cipher:

This is where Zak couldn't help me, but this is where Leo could. When Zak had mentioned the six-digit cipher at the Krah Krah, I knew at once what Leo had done. He must have planned it from the moment we met, from our first and only evening together at the Paloma in Hamburg.

For Leo had discreetly written down the number of my Iridium
Mastercard and made a donation to that orphanage in Port-au-Prince,
Haiti: a donation of 1,011.97 Euros. The sum had appeared on my
statement. Six digits. A sum of money, but also a date. 10 November
1997. The day a Chevrolet Caprice Classic mysteriously crashed on
Seal Beach Boulevard, Orange County, killing its driver. The day Elsa
Lubitsch became Hannah Delbrück. Perhaps Leo knew I'd find Zak,
but he also knew that there was one thing Zak couldn't tell me: those six
little numbers. So he told me himself. He reckoned I'd make the
connection. Zak was right on one score, and of that there can be no
doubt – no doubt at all. Leo was hot. Leo was in a class of his own.

I type the digits into the box:

101197

The Changeling document materialises before me. I record it, but
curiosity outvies my sense of danger. Nothing can stop me reading
from beginning to end.

changeling, safe and winnow

security clearance red
internal document
dual-key authorisation only

Programmes Changeling, Safe and Winnow
Wechselbalg/Sicher/Wannen

(last revised, 30 December 2026)

Important Note

Programmes Changeling (Wechselbalg) and Safe (Sicher) were
first developed as a response to the threat of Winnow (Wannen).
While Winnow was initiated in the United States, with privileged
access rights to the Wisconsin Package, all research was moved

to Austria in 1997. It is believed that American geneticists have continued on analogous lines, but Reprotech's Winnow is now a top-security non-commercial Austrian research module. It has high-level endorsement, but officially it does not exist. Changeling and Safe, on the other hand, are purely internal Reprotech trial programmes embarked upon when the fear emerged that Winnow technology could get into the hands of unfriendly nation states. As in the case of Winnow, Changeling and Safe do not officially exist.

Changeling & Safe: an Initial Outline

The Changeling and Safe programmes were begun by Elsa Lubitsch and Peter Diessl at Biomass, Orange County, in 1992. Lubitsch died in 1997. Diessl continues as CEO of all Reprotech facilities. The aim of the dual programme was to create a large trial group of individuals from the same gene pool who would not be susceptible to the negative effects of Winnow capability.

Between 1992 and 1997 a batch stock of human embryos (deep frozen for long preservation) was created by Lubitsch and Diessl. Lubitsch was superovulated during this period. Ripe oocytes were recovered from her ovaries and fertilised with sperm donored by Diessl. These embryos, from donor sperm and donor egg, are referred to as 'research embryos'. Superovulation allowed a yield of up to 7 to 8 eggs per monthly cycle so the total preserved embryos within this period was 354.

The embryos were genetically re-engineered, some at 2-cell stage, some at 4-cell stage, but the majority as morulas. In most cases this was undertaken prior to cryopreservation, though a sub-batch was reserved for engineering after thawing and before implantation in the host mother. The new technique employed was christened 'Safe'. The effect of germline re-engineering was twofold. First, Safe embryos were rigorously screened for genetic abnormalities: Safe individuals, therefore, are guaranteed free of congenital defects such as spina bifida, Down's syndrome, haemophilia, cystic fibrosis, Huntington's Chorea, et cetera (with the possible exception of G6PD deficiency, not a life-threatening condition). Second, using a unique patented technique, population-specific sequences in Human Leucocytes

Antigens, manifest variable numbers of tandem repeats and non-coding stretches of 'junk' genes are genetically masked. The effect of this action is to immunise the Safe individual against all potential future applications of Winnow technology.

Beginning in the late 1990s, Reprotech's IVF clinics initiated the Changeling programme. They used the Safe research embryos to provide children for couples who had been diagnosed as suffering from infertility and recommended for IVF. To date, 233 individuals have been born from this embryo batch (SS15698/ES27372). Hitherto, the largest number of children born to a single mother was 69, the mother being a Russian peasant. It will be noted that the Changeling programme vastly enhances this capability, as does the ability to perform IVF from frozen embryos, first accomplished in the Netherlands in 1983. (Prior to that, the first test-tube baby was born in the United Kingdom in 1978.) In effect, Changeling is a programme for embryo donation and is equivalent to adoption, since neither of the adoptive parents contributes to the genetic make-up of the child. The mother, then, is a surrogate gestational mother who nevertheless has the full rights and obligations of a mother whereas, under present legislation, the donor or donors have no legal rights or duties (see Appendix A).

A decision was taken at an early stage to conceal certain aspects of the Changeling programme from IVF parents to avoid emotive reactions and negative consequences. 'Infertility' is an overused and inadequate term. In most sexually active pre-menopausal couples there is at least some degree of fertility potential. In many cases, in fact, there may be no fertility problems whatsoever. Couples recommended for IVF under the Changeling/Safe programmes, therefore, went through the usual procedures of egg collection and sperm collection. They were informed that their own egg and sperm gametes had been used for fertilisation, or – at the very least – that no more than one gamete, egg or sperm, had been donored. It was felt that this was the most sympathetic line to take, since greater love and bonding are engendered in families where parents are convinced that they are the genetic progenitors. Moreover, the advantages of using rigorously germlined embryos from the controlled batch were considerable, especially when weighed against problems that would have been created by screening the IVF parents' own embryos in which genetic defects might well have abounded. Moreover, while Safe is an immense force for good – both at the trial group level and, ultimately, on a national scale – it is new science and therefore ethically controversial. The code of silence, therefore, had the dual benefit of being good eugenic practice and sparing new parents (suffering all the stresses and strains of IVF) from becoming embroiled in a moral dilemma which, given the complexity of the issues involved, lay beyond the scope of simplistic or rapid clarification. There is a slim possibility that DNA screening of Safe parents or children later in life might reveal genetic mismatches that would alert the families concerned to the existence of the Changeling programme. To avoid this, all genetic screening of family members must fall within the ambit of Reprotech/Primogen facilities.

Reprotech's assistance programme, then, does not end at the moment of conception. Safe individuals are monitored with vigilance throughout their lives, as are their progeny. For this reason, we ensure that, where possible, from birth they are registered for a Reprotech healthcare scheme at highly preferential rates. It's our job to make sure that Safe families are happy families.

The world is a dangerous place. New technologies, in the wrong hands, are open to abuse. We believe that it is important to respond to new threats quickly and expediently. The Changeling/Safe programme is the incarnation of this belief. Thanks to our pre-emptive action, by the time the ethical questions have been resolved, Austrian citizens will already have crossed the threshold and rendered their house secure. In this we may well have a two- to three-generation head-start on other sovereign states engaged in parallel research. In today's world, that can spell the difference between life and death.

Changeling/Safe
An Abstract of Operating Procedures

At the turn of the millennium, the dual programme functioned as follows:

1. Selection of couples. Generally speaking, couples recommended for IVF (and, by implication in many cases, the Changeling/Safe programmes) were already patients at Primogen clinics or came to us because of infertility or simply the unfounded fear of an infertility problem. Simple criteria for selection were applied. Both individuals had to be in good general health and Austrian citizens, with Austrian or German parents, grandparents and great-grandparents. Those who failed to meet these requirements were simply recommended for the standard IVF programme (without Changeling/Safe).

2. The selected couples were diagnosed, informed of an infertility problem and recommended for IVF. In the case of males, infertility was usually attributed to oligospermia (a sperm count in a haemocytometer of less than 20 million sperm per cm^3). In cases where female ovulation problems were reported, a treatment from the standard range of prescription hormonal drugs was applied: Clomphene, Human Chorionic Gonadotrophin, Urofollitrophin or Metrodin, Pergonal, or Gonadotrophin Releasing Hormone. Wherever there were reasons for avoiding a precise diagnosis (e.g. if a second, external, opinion was solicited), the general formula 'idiopathic infertility' was found to be useful. Note that the usual success rate for IVF at this time was 13.5%. At Reprotech, given the fact that healthy foster-parents were selected with minimal or no fertility problems, this rate was closer to 90%. The success rates of the clinics involved in the programmes were systematically played down in order to avoid drawing attention to the nature of Changeling and Safe.

3. Ovarian stimulation, egg collection and sperm collection. The recommended method for oocyte recovery was transvaginal ultrasound-guided follicle aspiration. The recommended method for sperm recovery was masturbation.

4. Eggs and sperm collected from the IVF parents were destroyed.

5. For implantation, cryopreserved embryos from the SS15698/ES27372 batch were employed. At the time of freezing, cryoprotective agents such as glycerol, dimethylsulphoxide, ethylene glycol and propanediol were used. The embryos were then stored in liquid nitrogen at a temperature of $-196°C$. Embryos cryopreserved in this manner can be stored indefinitely.

6. For embryos that had not been rendered Safe prior to freezing, Safe re-engineering was generally undertaken at four-cell stage after thawing. Embryos were placed in a normal medium, containing ions, nutrients, a macromolecule and a small amount of the foster-mother's serum. The medium was equilibrated with a gas mixture containing 5% CO_2 and at a pH of 7.5. Embryos with two pronuclei were cultured for about 48 hours until a four-cell embryo was formed.

7. Implantation. Preimplantation embryos were loaded into a fine plastic tube which was inserted into the uterus via the cervix. The embryos were then expelled. Implantation at 2-cell, 4-cell, 8-cell and morula stage have all been attempted with consistently high degrees of success. It is well known that success in implantation is considerably enhanced if more than one embryo is used: two or three are generally implanted. Given the finite nature of the SS15698/ES27372 batch, it was standard practice at Reprotech to use no more than two. From the beginning, the Changeling programme set out to create an approximately equal number of males and females. In general, however, the gender preferences of the prospective foster-parents were taken into consideration prior to implantation. Double donoring has no negative side effects. As Walter Heape, the English scientist, discovered at the end of the 19th century during experiments with rabbits, the uterus of the foster-mother does not in any way reject the offspring. In cases where multiple pregnancy followed implantation, standard options and procedures were followed.

8. Lastly, at birth children were genetically screened from blood or saliva samples and, where possible, registered with Reprotech for life-time support. To date, 233 individuals have been born under the Changeling/Safe programmes. 3 of these individuals have perished. The remainder are kept under close scrutiny. Given that these individuals will, in all likelihood, partner non-Safe individuals, it is desirable that their own offspring be germlined. As such, wherever possible, couples in which one partner is a product of the Changeling/Safe programmes should be diagnosed as suffering from infertility problems and recommended for IVF. In one known case, a Safe male individual partnered a Safe female individual, though no offspring were produced (see Appendix B : Leo Detmers & Petra Olbrich).

Appendix A : Legal Matters

It is of the nature of the Changeling programme that offspring are unaware of the fact that their foster-parents and their genetic parents are not one and the same. In effect, the child is illegitimate, but under European law, as in all cases of sperm and/or egg donation, the birth certificate is falsified, naming the foster-parent or parents rather than the donor or donors.

In cases where children are aware that one or both of their genetic parents were donors, European practice has been to provide only non-identifying information on the donor when the child has reached the age of 18. To date, two Safe individuals have succeeded in penetrating the Changeling/Safe programme. The first was Nathan Buczak, an American citizen resident in Austria. He has in no way compromised the scheme, having given it his whole-hearted approval, and has subsequently rendered many services to Reprotech. The second was Leo Detmers, who broke through the security cordon but was unfortunately killed in a highway incident on 20 November 2026. See Appendix B and File XIVF/S/S/W/26LD, # security clearance black*.

Please note that all IVF and research carried out by Reprotech (Primogen and Biowares) are subject to controls by the Austrian Medical Research Council's statutory licensing authority. Their chief officer, Hannah Delbrück, is regularly kept abreast of developments.

Appendix B : Leo Detmers and Petra Olbrich

The case of Leo Detmers is unique. Detmers was a Changeling/Safe individual and he married another Changeling/Safe individual, Petra Olbrich. This was, in effect, a consequence of Reprotech's monitoring of offspring. Because both Safe individuals were registered with the same clinic, the foster-parents made each other's acquaintance while availing themselves of kindergarten facilities and a family friendship ensued which led to the marriage. During the engagement period, two possible courses of action were discussed at Reprotech. [1] Use whatever means available to discourage the two individuals from marrying, on the grounds that there is a social taboo against sibling marriages and children born to such a couple would be 'inbred' and hence prone to genetic defects. Naturally these grounds would not be revealed to the parties concerned. [2] Allow the marriage to go ahead and monitor the couple and eventual offspring closely. Peter Diessl strongly advocated the second option, arguing that the child of two Safe individuals would be born Safe, without the necessity for further engineering. A Detmers offspring, therefore, would be a unique case study, representing, in fact, the whole future of the project, when it is hoped that the entire adult non-Changeling population of Austria will be rendered Safe. Diessl dismissed the argument against inbreeding on the grounds that this was a solitary case and, anyway, since both Safe parents had near-perfect germlines the risks were negligible. The second option was accepted. Prior to Leo Detmers' death, Petra Detmers did indeed become pregnant and was monitored by the Mariahilf clinic. What Reprotech failed to discern until after the birth of the male child was that Leo Detmers was not the father. The father was, in fact, a casual partner, a non-Safe individual. Dr Büchner registered his dismay that screening during pregnancy had not established this fact. Clearly the mother had no wish to draw attention to her infidelity, but foetal DNA tests would have alerted us. The result is that the child is either a non-Safe individual or a defectively Safe individual, representing a deterioration in the Changeling/Safe gene pool.

It is known that when Leo Detmers discovered that he was double-donored and that his wife was his genetic sister, the information caused him considerable distress. Despite Peter Diessl's initial recommendation, therefore, the management board now considers that sibling partnerships between Changeling individuals should be avoided in future except in exceptional circumstances. This does not, of course, exclude partnerships between future Safe individuals who are not Changelings and not, therefore, siblings. The premature death of Leo Detmers closed the case, though the child will continue to receive regular medical observation. The manner in which the Detmers case was dealt with by Reprotech is discussed in greater detail in File XIVF/S/S/W/26LD, # security clearance black*.

Appendix C: a Note on Cloning

The possibility of integrating cloning procedures into the Changeling/Safe programmes was aired in the early 1990s. This would have involved removing the nucleus from a fertilised egg and replacing it with a nucleus from a cell of the individual to be cloned. However, at this time human cloning had not yet been achieved. Human cloning remains illegal in Europe. The first open production of human clones began in Hong Kong in 2005, though various states are believed to have clandestine cloning programmes. A number of clones produced in Hong Kong are believed to be living in Austria today. There may well be a significant future for de-criminalised cloning within the framework of Changeling/Safe, but there are also strong scientific arguments against it. The main argument is that cloning militates against bio-diversity. A large cloned group, being identical in genetic make-up, would run a high risk of collectively falling victim to potential virus mutations in the future.

Appendix D: Winnow

The nature of Winnow itself, and the precise manner in which Changeling and Safe respond to it, is laid out in file XWIN/C/S/01/EL-PD, # security clearance black*.

Note. Security clearance black files are not committed to electronic data storage and retrieval systems. Knowledge of their location, and access to them, is restricted to CEOs, CFOs, selected department chiefs and authorised personnel.

The 233 Changeling/Safe Individuals

Click <u>here</u> for a complete list of the 233 Changeling/Safe individuals and links to bio-data and medical records.

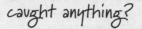

I click and download the list on to the dataclip. I'm about to read it when I hear a dry cough behind me. I look up startled. Flushed face, side-whiskers, Polartec vest, Tyrol cap, army satchel. It's the fisherman that Petra and I met on the last occasion. He's leaning against a tree, his arms folded, observing me.

'Guten Tag. You're back, then. Caught anything?'

'No, not yet. I haven't been here long.'

'That looks interesting. Never seen fishing tackle like that before.'

'What, this? Oh no – it's nothing to do with the fishing! Just some office work. It had to be done, so I brought it with me.'

He coughs again and comes closer, putting his hands in his pockets.

'Come to think of it, never seen a computer like that before either.'

'Well it's not just a computer, you see. It's really not very interesting. I won't bother you with explanations.'

'Well whatever it is, it must be interesting to you.'

'How do you mean?'

'You've got a bite.'

'I'm sorry?'

'A fish. It's been playing on that line for the last five minutes. You were too engrossed to notice.'

'Good Lord!'

I leap over to the fishing rod and release it from its clamp, pulling sharply back. The rod bends dramatically. I can feel the force of the fish, the vitality. Down there, under the surface of the lake, its body is flipping and kicking with might and main, fighting for survival. I try to turn the handle on the reel but nothing happens. It blocks.

'You've got the safety clip on. Like me to do that for you?'

'Oh, yes – please. If you wouldn't mind.'

He takes over the rod and reels the fish in expertly. It's a damn big fish now I look at it, and it's hanging just centimetres from my eyes.

'If you could just take it off the hook,' he says.

'Um, yes . . . I . . .'

I grab the struggling fish in one hand and peer into its open gullet. The fine barbed hook is stuck fast in the upper lip.

'You *do* know how to take a fish off a hook, don't you?'

'To tell you the truth, I'm a bit out of practice. Would you mind – ?'

He takes the fish and puts down the rod, then with a quick proficient gesture flips the hook out of the fish's mouth.

'It's a nice fat one, you've got there,' he says, smiling but watching me with discomforting interest. 'You know what it is, of course.'

'I suppose it's a tench.'

'No, it's a carp actually. Good specimen, as I said. What're you going to do with it?'

'Put it back, I should think.'

'Pity to do that. It's a good eater. I'll have it if you don't want it.'

'By all means. Be my guest.'

He takes the fish by the tail and walks over to a large stone embedded in the earth. With a swift whack he swings the head of the fish down on to the stone. There's a splatter of blood and the fish stops writhing. He takes a plastic bag out of his satchel and pops the fish into it, then transfers the bag to the satchel. He spits on his hands, rubs them together and returns to my side, looking again at the Tempest device.

'You don't know a lot about fishing, do you?'

'No, to be honest, I don't. I'm just an amateur. Only started recently.'

'But you got your permit all right, in Rust.'

'Yes. One-day. Picked it up this morning from the Rathaus.'

'I see.' He looks away and wipes some fish-scales that have stuck to his hand on to the side of his jacket. 'Well, good luck then. I'll be off. Hope the weather holds. And thanks for the fish.'

'You're welcome.'

He shuffles from view into the underwood behind. I stand with my hands on my hips and bite one side of my lower lip, looking out over the glint of the waters. My thoughts are vacillating. I don't know which way to jump. There's more documentation I'd like to access but time may not be on my side. What do I know about that fisherman? On the one hand, I've betrayed my utter philistinism with regard to the fine art of rod and line. On the other hand, so what? The world's full of dabblers and dilettantes. It's no cause for suspicion. However, the Tempest device obviously is, and it certainly intrigued him. He probably took it for a sophisticated and unsporting sounding radar, designed to detect large shoals of fish. But if that was his conclusion then it would sit unhappily with my patent lack of expertise. All at once, a blindingly obvious Leviathan of a gaffe rears up before me. The permit. Why did he look so hesitant, why did he excuse himself, when I mentioned the permit? 'A one-day permit', I said, and that's perfectly possible. 'Picked it up this morning from the Rathaus,' I said. And that's where he'd looked away to conceal his reaction. Because today, today is a public holiday. A relatively recent one, in fact, to commemorate the demise of Chancellor Helden. So today, the Rathaus in Rust is closed.

I pack up Svetlana's machine as quickly as possible, and it's not too soon. Out there, towards Reprotech, I can hear distant voices, a dry cough and the bark of a dog. The dry cough I know. As for the bark, it's the deep, thoracic bark of a large, spirited beast. I can picture him. He's feeling upbeat and go-getting because his muzzle's just been removed. Only the sprung clip on the leash is restraining him now. And, slowly but surely, that murmur of voices is getting closer.

There's no time for the fishing tackle. I leave it behind and head for the car, beating a retreat while there's still a retreat to be beaten. I mean, angling's all very fine and well. It's undoubtedly good for the soul, as I said before. But I've always maintained – and I'm speaking from personal experience here – that, for better or worse, the soul and the body make a great team. Let no man put them asunder.

When I arrived they removed the velcro-ed blindfold and withdrew behind me. I'm still here, sitting in this butterfly chair – not uncomfortable, I have to admit – and listening to what they're saying. I'm facing a curved concrete wall with what looks like a small deep-set square window, screened off to obscure the view. There's no electric light, but behind me a big fire coughs and sighs in a hearth and the vivid golden shimmer of its blaze throws our wandering shadows up on the wall like Javanese stick-puppets. There I am, in the middle, embedded in the low-slung seat, while they're on either side behind my back, Moos and the other man, talking to me in turn. Me and my shadows.

Moos sits sideways on in shadowplay, his hands under his thighs. I recognise his slight build and the compact shaved ball of his youthful skull, smooth as a phrenologist's china head, from the night at Residential Complex XI. The other man, the tall one, paces slowly up and down, his head lowered, his thumbs lightly interlocked behind his back. His long avian shadow swoops up theatrically in the firelight, bending round floor, wall and ceiling, and crosses the trophy of a Luftwaffe dress dagger that's nailed up beside an M42 single decal combat helmet, a photograph and a cheaply-printed flyer. The dagger has an elegant hilt and pumpkin-coloured handle, and the words 'Blut und Ehre' are engraved on the blade. The helmet sports a bullet dent above one of the grommet holes. The photograph shows four statues and is captioned 'Kriemhild, Siegfried, Gunter and Brunhild: full-scale plaster models for the "Nibelungen Way" bridge, the New Linz'. And the flyer reads: 'Anschluss II: the European Union Betrays Austria'. Below, stacked against the wall, are boxwood crates packed with small metal cannisters.

This started in the Bronxx Jugendklub.

I asked for Moos, a call was made, and I was driven here. They think I don't know where I am, but I do. This is a flak-tower, one of five or six such embarrassingly indestructible structures in Vienna. Concrete towers and bunkers, Flaktürme, built as the last Nazi bastion against allied attack to house up to 30,000 troops. Perhaps this one's in Gutenberggasse, or it could be another. I recognise it because there's one in the Esterházy Park, converted into a drear public aquarium, the

Haus des Meeres, which I visited as a teenager. I recognise the camber of the wall, the medieval slit of the window in four metres of concrete wall and above all the unmistakeable odour. It's the same stale odour I smelt once, much later, in the Maginot line near Sedan, locked for all eternity into those dripping underground tunnels and chambers. The odour of impotence and futility that lingers in these last ramparts of defence, the odour of dashed ideals and the imminence of death. It's the odour of history. A cold human odour, born of human pores. But here it is specifically the odour of Vienna for, as Hermann Broch once said of the Viennese, 'only despair gives us hope'.

I'm wearing a PAN shirt, with antennae woven into the fabric, and I've made no secret of it. Our every word is beamed back to the central digital receiver at the *Wiener Tageszeitung*.

'What would you say,' I ask, 'to those who put your anger down to being unemployed?'

Moos's shade raises its head. 'I'm not unemployed,' it says, 'I have a good job at the Imperial Hotel.' The pacing shade of the other stops and turns reproachfully towards the seated Moos. He's said too much. Moos makes a perplexed motion with his hand to the back of his head but goes on. 'Most of us in Neues Östmark are young and middle-class, these days. Either salaried employees or self-employed. We're ordinary, intelligent people who want change.'

'But you'd admit that the employment question's at the heart of the problem.'

'Sure. Jobs and housing. That's where excessive immigration hits hardest.'

'The Resident Alien Law,' says the tall shade, 'restricts the number of foreign workers from outside the EU and the EFTA to nine per cent of the workforce at the moment. If you include their families, they account for ten per cent of the population. Serbs, Turks, Germans, Poles, Czechs, Slovaks, Hungarians, Romanians . . .'

'. . . Croats, Roma, Sinti, Fidschis, Jews,' continues Moos. It's a litany of hate, but his tone is flat, uninflected.

'Certainly, Austria, with all its borders, has always been the theatre of immigration and east-west transit. Wasn't it Metternich who said that the Orient begins on the Landstrasse? This has been especially true since the Iron Curtain fell in 1989. But go back further than that and you'll realise that we were the most homogeneous of the successor states to be cut out of the old Austro-Hungarian Empire. We want a return to that homogeneity.

'Here in Vienna – would you believe? – a quarter of the children who're born are foreigners. There's a low birth-rate amongst the Austrian population, but not among the immigrants, that's the point. We're not fundamentally xenophobic. You've got to realise that. However, just as there's a limit to the number of friends you can put up in your house or flat, there's a limit to the hospitality a nation state can extend. There's a threshold. And the proper threshold's a lot lower than ten per cent.'

'And foreign workers,' interjects Moos, 'well, there are legal and illegal immigrants, aren't there? They don't all have residence visas and work permits. Some of them come in as tourists or seasonal labourers, but they simply stay put.'

'Which means more expense for the Bundesheer, which has to help customs and border authorities patrol the frontiers.'

'And then there's the crime. The Poles steal cars, the Serbs burgle houses, the Russians mug and blackmail our citizens, the Turks hawk heroin and the Gypsies organise theft and prostitution. As for the honest ones, if there are any, they can't even speak German.'

'Hence, higher social and educational costs,' intones the long shade. His voice is cultivated, slightly effeminate in its well-rounded vowels. I observe his slight stoop and realise what his shadow makes me think of. He's a heron, with the same improbable centre of anatomical gravity. 'They don't assimilate, they never will. Austria's a sovereign state, not a registered charity. And besides, the belief that multicultural societies work is a myth. They don't. On the other hand, Volkesgemeinschaft does. A closed ethnic community based on common cultures and values.'

'Doesn't a closed community depend somewhat on when you shut the door?' I ask. 'I mean, what is an Austrian? More than half the names in the Vienna directory are Czech.'

'A fair point,' says the heron. 'All nations are inventions at a certain level. Austria corresponds to a dynastic idea. François Bondy said that Austrianness is the smile of the Cheshire Cat left over from the old monarchy. All the same, the Austrian phenotype does exist. We can argue about degrees of purity and impurity, but it exists all the same.'

'Perhaps an Austrian is a German.'

'Perhaps at a racial level he is. But not culturally. Unlike Festung Europa, we in Neues Östmark are not interested in the impossible dream of a pan-German state. Nobody takes that as a serious possibility, and it's one reason why Festung are on the way out – that, and the violence. We, on the other hand, recognise Austria as culturally distinct. What we want is a Europe of fatherlands. Effectively, we want no more than any other European state lays claim to. Lebensraum, ethnic nationhood, integrity of descent, language, customs, history. We are a people, with a people's sense of their own destiny, practical and mystical.'

There's a slight twang of elastic and I notice that, as he speaks, he's watching his hand. The long fingers are moving rapidly and every few seconds that twang repeats itself. I've seen this trick before and it now dawns on me where. The night of Residential Complex XI. A tall, bony cop with a sardonic smile. He wore the insignia of the Bundesgrenzschutz, the border police, and he had that trick, that tic, with the rubber band, jumping from finger to finger. I recall his aristocratic allure. I'd taken him for Uscinski's man, but this now seems unlikely. The link's more probably with Reik, or Interior Minister Reinhardt.

'What makes you different from the Nazis?'

The heron laughs and Moos shift uncomfortably in his seat, silently deferring to his senior. 'I told you, we're opposed to the overcentralised bureaucracy of Brussels. We want a Europe of fatherlands. Not one, imperial fatherland, mind you. No conquest. No violence.'

'And Florisdorf? The Residential Complex?'

Moos visibly jumps. 'That wasn't supposed to happen,' he blurts.

'I was there, remember? It didn't look like an accident to me.'

The heron circles round and places a mollifying hand on Moos's shoulder. 'Florisdorf was unfortunate,' he says slowly. 'Some elements gave in to Festung tactics. It won't happen again. Those responsible have been reprimanded and may even be turned over to the law. What you must bear in mind is that our end is non-violent. We no longer live in an age of migrations. We live in an age of national consolidation. Strength comes from within, not without. The immigrant's a virus in the body politic. He must be persuaded to return to his own nation, however comparatively underdeveloped or unsatisfactory it may be. After all, countries that lose male workers through emigration suffer too. The workforce is enfeebled. If their economies are ever to get off the ground it's in their interests, too, to close borders and minimise seepage.'

'When it comes down to it, your ultra-nationalism is just tribalism. Tribalism with a face-lift.'

'Certainly it's tribalism,' says the heron, both hands now resting gently on the shoulders of the seated Moos. 'But why *just* tribalism? Tribalism's a fundamental human principle. Populations have to look after themselves and nurture their innate characteristics. A football supporter belongs to a tribe. A newspaper journalist belongs to a tribe. There are little tribes and big tribes, subtribes and supertribes. The nation's simply the family writ large. Let me put this to you. If you had a choice between saving the life of a cat or a member of your family, which would you choose? If your own son was left unemployed because an immigrant had ousted him from his job, whose case would you support? It's in the natural scheme of things that our first loyalty goes to our nearest and dearest, and to those who share our interests, fears and desires – ultimately the extended family of the ethnic nation state which protects the integrity of the individual family unit, the family of close blood-ties.'

'If you and I are family, why do you hide your face from me?'

'You'll be seeing my face soon enough. Mine and others. When the time comes. Neues Östmark commands a considerable following. Its operations will soon be far from covert.'

'Its terrorist operations, you mean?'

'Mr Sharkey, I know journalists are trained in provocation, but this is beginning to tire me. It's true that we're in the business of discouraging foreign elements from seeking permanent residence here, but not through terrorism. No longer. Where acts of violence occur, they're aberrations. Our means are principally dissuasive. We use reasonable deterrence. When immigrants find that life's not as amenable here as they had hoped, of their own free will they choose repatriation.'

'And what precisely would persuade them that life was not so pleasant here?'

The heron stalks back round the room, his hand held before him. I hear the taut flick of elastic – higher in pitch and more frequent now – as it hoops from finger to finger. He stands in front of the hearth and his shadow darts across the concrete floor, wall and ceiling, bristling and jittering with each fresh spit of flame. 'Each organism,' he begins, 'has its natural habitat. A parakeet in the New World. A penguin in the polar regions. A shark in the sea. Remove it to an alien habitat and it sickens. It contracts unfamiliar diseases. It goes into a decline. Human beings are no exception. Just as travellers can take the blight of disease with them into new lands, so they expose themselves to new and possibly life-threatening viral infections. Now Austria has a wet climate, and the winter has been unusually icy this year. It's hardly to be wondered at, then, if the foreigners who come here enjoy poor health. If your organism isn't up to it, you fall victim to colds and flu. Maybe worse. Ailments that are much less common in a warm, Mediterranean climate, for example.'

The heron's lost me. I stare blankly ahead, tongue-tied. His shadow moves aside and a warm flush of light falls across the boxwood crates with metal cannisters that are stacked against the wall. I narrow my eyes to sharpen the focus. The cans are grey and dumpy, like camping gas, with programmable spray nozzles of the kind you get in room deodorisers or insect bombs, but most of them are half-concealed behind the slats of the crates. Only a couple show their heads where the corner of a loose tarpaulin has failed to cover them. There's small print on the side of one and, above the block of text, the words 'Biomass. 1–5 micron particle periodic aerosolisation unit'. My back's hot from the fire, but my front is cold, and now it's colder still. It's a numb, petrifying cold that creeps inwards, a cold that chills the mind. The stale odour of the Flaktürme's no longer outside. It's entering my body with each breath, tainting my nose and lungs.

'The anti-antifa lists,' I murmur.

'What about them?' asks the heron.

'You must know about them. Where they come from.'

'I know your name is on the lists.'

'Who put it there?'

The heron's shadow suddenly sheers sideways and diminishes into a stunted, barrel-chested thing, only the distinctive stoop remaining from his previous incarnation. 'Someone high up, I imagine,' he answers casually after a while, then turns impatiently on the ball of his heel.

'And how do I get *off* the list?'

A door opens and others enter the room. There's a brief exchange. He tosses something into the fire – the rubber band, I presume – then retraces a couple of steps. 'These gentlemen will take you home. It's been a pleasure talking to you. I sense that, despite some understandable misgivings on your part, we see eye to eye on a lot of things. Fundamentally, I mean.'

'You haven't answered my question.'

'Goodbye,' he says. There's a note of sadness in his courtesy, as if the leavetaking has more than formal value. Moos eases himself out of his seat and walks over to the other man, dragging his feet lazily against the hard floor. As he reaches the door, the heron turns and hesitates once again. 'We'll look forward so much to reading your article,' he says quietly. 'Believe me. We shall.'

verfremdungseffekt

I'm passing through a changing world. Even blindfolded, even huddled on the floor of a closed van, I can sense transition, the imminent cosmic Zugzwang. After some prevarication, a hard winter has dug its heels in deep at last. We're certainly four in here, maybe more. There's the driver out front and a man on either side of me. When the van jolts and jars their arms and thighs press into mine. It's so intensely cold I'm almost grateful for the brief warmth of that accidental contact. Nobody speaks. When one man coughs his breath smells like damp hessian, like old oily sacks mouldering in a barn. At one road junction we hear men's voices, the low growl of a crawling truck and the loose, shingly sound of shovels spreading salt. A tram bell rings. A dog barks.

I have no fear of these people, nor of Moos, nor of the heron. I have no fear, though inwardly I know their knee-jerk violence. As yet, I'm not a threat to them but a means, a voice in waiting, a shut mouth at gunpoint. But here at least there's silence and stillness. Outside, the world grinds down invisibly into ever tighter cycles of change. The round of seasons chases its own frostbitten tail. What was familiar is now unfamiliar, passing out of recognition, beyond the pale. It's nature's stab at a Brechtian Verfremdungseffekt. Even the van advances diffidently, slithering on the treacherous soft crust of a new planet. I think of Maes Howe in Orkney, an ancient burial chamber. I read about it in the *National Geographic*. In the mid-twelfth century some Viking raiders sought refuge there from a winter storm, and one of them lost his mind. There are twenty-four runic inscriptions to tell the tale. The little nature of man, his delicate homeostasis, exterminated by the anger of the skies.

They drop me off, helping me unsteadily to my feet. Once the van has left I remove the blindfold. I'm at the exit of the Heiligenstadt U-bahn station, directly opposite Karl Marx-Hof. It's past eleven and a big startling moon bowls through the clouds. Thick, soft snow drives diagonally through the air, sealing the earth, by force of numbers, in a flimsy platinum film. An ambulance steers past out of the parkade. Its sequenced rooflights throw lashing colours into the naked boughs and branches of the trees. My nose is raw. My ears are burning with the cold. I grip my collar tightly round my neck and make for home, glancing up at the brazen façade. Marta and Svetlana are still up. A comforting little tetragon of light spills from their flat into the hostile night.

The lift's out of order.

I walk up to my floor. I'm about to let myself in when I notice that Marta's door is ajar. Through the crack, I see Svetlana sitting at the table. She's barefoot, in a white towel bathrobe. She stares dead ahead. Her hands are clutched together and she bites distractedly on her knuckles. I knock gently and push the door further open. She looks round, half aware of my presence, a slight distressed bunching of the muscles between the eyebrows. She has suddenly grown old. A gerontological page has been turned. Yesterday her face harked backwards to the child she once was. Today, it prophesies the careworn, middle-aged woman she'll eventually become. Her light has folded in. Even her hair has a lifeless, waxen sheen.

'What's up?'

'Mum. You must've seen the ambulance. She's been taken to hospital.'

'Her condition got worse?'

'She was short of breath. She complained of tightness in the chest. And then there was the fever. The doctor said she should be hospitalised.'

'Did he say what it was?'

'Not bronchitis, as he first thought. He calls it alveolitis. Inflammation of the lungs. Not pneumonia, but pneumonitis. I think that's what it was. I'm not sure what difference there is.'

I sit down opposite her, unzip my jacket and blow into my cupped hands, rubbing them together.

'You didn't go with her.'

'I'll go tomorrow. She's not in danger. I mean, she'll live. But it's not good. It's not good at all.'

'Remind me. How did she fall sick in the first place? Some kind of meeting, wasn't it?'

'The Austro-Slovakian Friendship Society. They met at the Stanislaus-Kostka Chapel. It was a cold evening and the heating system had broken down. Half the people there came down with what we took for colds and flus. That was the weird thing about it.'

'How do you mean?'

'Well it was precisely half. That's the point. We haven't phoned everybody, of course, but it seems a lot of Slovaks got sick. A lot of Slovaks, but not a single Austrian.'

On the sideboard, there's a pair of lamps with shades made of parchment squares stitched together with leather string. The low wattage emanating from them fluctuates uneasily. An irregularity in the current. A weak connection. A stook of overdressed folk puppets flumps between the lamps. Their lacquered faces, woolly hair and wooden limbs shudder in the fluttering light. The heron's words echo in my ears: 'Each organism has its natural habitat. Remove it to an alien habitat and it sickens.' My gaze alights on the large tourist office poster of haycocks beside a lake in the Turiec countryside.

'Pike and perch,' I whisper.

'Sorry?'

'The pike and perch get the hepatoma. Not the carp or tench.' The snow in my hair has melted and I wipe a droplet of water from my brow, glancing across at Svetlana. She has dark rings under her eyes. 'I'll explain later.' I draw myself up. 'Is Petra around?'

'She just went to fetch Oskar. She'll be back any second.'

'Ask her to look in on me, will you?'

There's the sweet smell of putrefaction in my flat. It's coming from the kitchen. I check the bin and find some rotting shrimps' heads, their black eyes buckled in above the sharp whiskers. They're scattered over a crumpled milk carton and a gluey mess of cracked egg-shells. I've been losing track. It must be two days since I last checked the garbage. I knot the bag and push it down the disposal chute, then go back to the living-room.

I dim the Serge Mouille lighting to the merest astral glimmer and place the Sputnik chair carefully off-centre on the black Krickan rug. Its base sits on the giant 'O' of the design. I sit down. Beside me, on the floor, is my latest electronic book download: the *Bhagavad Gita*. My body is at last *chambré*. A nice steady blood heat. And my mind's warming up too, the cogs and gears easing into action, teeth catching on teeth, engaging.

Petra appears at the doorway. She's carrying Oskar. The child's half asleep but clings dreamily to her naked breast. Without a word, she plants herself on the Starck settee and feeds the baby, stroking the down-haired dome of his head. After a few minutes, Oskar's grip loosens. His eyes roll up under half-closed lids and he falls away into sleep. One arm rests limply across his forehead. His lips are slightly parted. She swaddles him carefully and places him on the settee beside her, then she tucks away her breast.

'You did the interview, then,' she says, making conversation.

'I recorded it, yes. I'll write it up later. Once I've decided on an angle.'

'It's a pity about Marta. I'm going to drive Svetlana to the hospital tomorrow.'

I nod, and a silence intervenes. Petra sits back and stretches her torso and neck like a cat. She sighs the sigh of languid mothers. She's in a simple buttoned cotton nightgown and velvet Indian slippers, a grey alpaca coat over her shoulders for warmth. A large tortoiseshell grip restrains her hair from tumbling across her forehead. In the dim light, her pupils are exceptionally dilated and dark. She is beautiful. It strikes me forcibly that I've never met anyone like her before. For the first time this knowledge presents itself as established fact, incontrovertible. I realise too that everything I'm doing is for her. It has been from the very beginning. Without her, none of it would make sense. Without her, it would be a charade, devoid of value and meaning.

'An angel's passing,' she says, commenting on the silence.

'Yes, an angel's passing.'

She has a preoccupied air. The spell's about to break.

'You have something to tell me.'

'You know me too well.'

'What is it?'

'I was looking at the pictures. Of Diessl and Lubitsch. The graduation photo and the Cornell workshop photo. '84 and '86, I think. And the woman – Elsa Lubitsch – I suddenly realised where I'd seen her before. Or where I'd seen her *since*, if you want to look at it that way.'

'Where?'

'Remember my flat, at the Hundertwasser Haus? I had an Agent Program on the domotic system. The Agent Program had a face, the face of the butler-icon. A face and a personality. You may have seen it on-screen when you came round.'

'I think I did. The very first time we met.'

'It was her. It was Elsa Lubitsch. I'm certain of it. Much older, of course. A woman in her sixties. But it was definitely her. I know there's no way of checking on that. The whole Plasmavision unit was smashed out. You do believe me, don't you?'

'Yes, I do.'

'If, as you say, she was my mother, this means she found a way of putting herself into my life. Advising me on diet. Telling me my daily schedule. I relied on her a lot. Jesus! I thought those things were just software.'

'They are. But she may have modelled for the infographic artist and lent her speech patterns. We talked about this before. Soul catching. Some widows and widowers live with their deceased partners as Agent Programs. It's pure illusionism, of course. In Lubitsch's case it would have been a way of being there and not being there at the same time, if you see what I mean. The absentee mother. Did you fix the settings of the Agent? Did you feed in your likes and dislikes, your preferences – all of that?'

'Maybe. I can't remember. It was either me or Leo. But then she's his mother too, isn't she? I certainly kept it updated. You don't have an Agent Program yourself, do you?'

'No. Can't abide them. I can't stand being told what to do. Though I was offered one when I moved here, now you mention it.'

I think back to 28 November. I cast my mind back to our first meeting. I vaguely recollect the screen agent, Petra's semi-autonomous servant program. An elderly, kindly face, about the same age as Lubitsch – alias Delbrück – now. It reminded me of someone then, perhaps Leo himself in a sexagenarian, matriarchal incarnation. But I'd glimpsed it too briefly. Even meeting Lubitsch in the flesh hadn't stirred my memory of that benevolent piece of 3D modelling. The very thought of Lubitsch, however, quickens my pulse, goads me. I know more now than I knew then. I know, above all, what I *don't* know, and it has a name: Diessl.

'Were you ever frightened of anything?' I say. 'When you were a child.'

'Perhaps.' She glances down at Oskar. 'The dark. Loud noises. I don't recall too well.'

'In the village where I was brought up, there was a big house down a narrow side-lane. The house had a wall and a high iron gate. It wasn't a grille. It was made of solid sheet metal, painted black I seem to remember. Behind the gate there was an angry dog. The lane was gravelled over, so it was impossible to walk past without making a noise. And that sodding dog was always there, barking like fury behind the gate every time it heard someone passing. I had to walk past every day on my way to and from the Elementarschule. From the age of five or six, it must've been. It was bad in the morning, but the afternoon was even worse. All day long at school I'd dread that moment. It poisoned my days. I could think of nothing else. There was no alternative route. To get home, I was obliged to go past the high iron gate. It wasn't that I feared the dog would get out. I've always been okay with dogs, on the whole. It was the violence, the savagery of the barking – it was berserk. That, and the fact that I never saw the dog. It could've been a dachshund or a great Dane. There was no way of telling. It was the fact that I never saw the face of the enemy, as the enemy never saw mine. There was always the high black gate between us.'

Petra listens with unflinching eyes. At length, she raises her eyebrows and runs the back of a hand thoughtfully down her cheek. 'Shall I fix us a drink?'

'There's some Cinzano in the kitchen cupboard. Ice in the cooler.'

She stands up, straightens the alpaca on her shoulders and makes for the kitchen. As soon as she's out of sight, I switch on the wallscreen and call up Elsa Lubitsch. The maid answers. Lubitsch is away for the weekend. I switch my attention to Buczak, scrolling down the bookmark for his Web co-ordinate. In a couple of seconds, I'm through. Surreally, Buczak's hanging upside down by the legs from suspended exercise rings. His arms are folded across his chest and the pork-pie hat somehow sticks to his skull. His beard could be taken for head-hair and the hat for a collar. He looks like one of those cunning drawings that make a face whichever way up you turn them. I tip my head sideways and read the slogan on his T-shirt: 'Thus do I clothe my naked vileness'. When he speaks, it's in good but inflected German:

'Contrary to appearances, I'm not here at the moment. Leave a message after the tone and I'll get back to you, if the spirit moves me'. He grins, purses his lips and says 'beep'. A cartoon MC with Colgate smile and hair permed into the great tsunami wave of Kanagawa appears brandishing a hand-held mike. I kill the link.

The room's silent. Not even a clink of ice from the kitchen. I get up, curious, and walk over to the doorway. Petra's leaning heavily against the work surface, staring absently at the Francis XI espresso machine.

'Anything wrong?'

'That voice. The voice I just heard. That was him. Top hat. Hunting jacket. Leather crop. That was the pig. I knew there was something. An accent.' She turns round, expectantly. 'That was the guy who nearly blew you to kingdom come.'

I look her square in the eyes. 'How sure are you?'

'As sure as I am of anything. That was him. I'd swear to it.'

I open a bottom drawer in the kitchen and pull out a fat bundle, wrapped in an embroidered napkin. I place the bundle on the work surface and open it out. The pristine Five-seveN pistol in its gleaming shoulder-holster, a dozen 2-gramme bullets, their brassy percussion caps showing from the row of leather slots. I take the firearm in my hand to experience its weight.

'That was Leo's.' Her voice is rock-steady but her hands are shaking insecurely.

'Yes, I took it. I'm sorry. I should've asked.'

She fingers the leather girdle of the shoulder strap. 'Consider it a gift. It's not worth much in itself but – who knows? – perhaps it has magical properties. Perhaps it's a lifesaver. What are you going to do with it, anyway?'

'I'm thirty years old, and I'm planning on making it to thirty-one. I'm a simple soul, really. That's as far as my ambitions go for the moment.'

'That's further than Leo got.'

'Right. He was a great guy, I'm sure, but not much of a role model in the longevity department.'

'The world was a tougher place than he thought.'

'There's a lesson in there for us somewhere, Petra.'

'Yeah,' she agrees. 'If only we knew what it was . . .'

chapter twelve

where da wabbit go?

I motor down into the dark warren of Zak's Bassena district.

It's a grim working-class quarter of rundown houses turned inwards on to weed-encroached courtyards with cracked paving and forlorn standpipes. Architectural autism. I haven't been here since the night of the Krah Krah. Ivy and vines straggle in untamed profusion across frontages, shuttered windows, iron balconies and crotchety stairways.

Zak's dive is near an old pub called Zur Zukunft, the Future. It's at the back of a particularly dingy yard. There's a garage door grimed with the anatomical hyperbole of pornographic graffiti and a rusty spiral staircase to the upper level. The structure itself wouldn't be out of place in the gargantuan shantytowns of Calcutta or Mexico City. I park the Gringolet at some distance and enter the yard. No one's about. The snow falls richly, flossily, in the golden aura of light from a single ancient wall-lantern. I'm cloud-capped for a moment in my own breath. There's no sign of illumination in the surrounding dwellings. I check my watch. Past one in the morning, a Saturday night. Zak'll be out clubbing, at a guess. I climb the helical staircase with its triangular steps, slipping once on the buttery snow and making a grab for the railing just in time.

The door's solid steel. No keyhole, only a small rear-lit dactylo-scopic pad for thumbprint recognition. I check for CCTV but no cams are in evidence. The long iron balcony running round the first floor is rickety in the extreme. At several points the wall-bolts have worked themselves loose and it sways alarmingly. What's more, it's clear this mangled ambulatory is never used. A snarled curtain of creepers hangs darkly across the gangway, blocking the path. I feel lop-sided already, with the unfamiliar weight of the holstered pistol on my left side, and this creaking ledge doesn't help. Nevertheless, I push and bunch back the Gordian knot of climbers and twiners with my gloved hands. A small space opens up. I duck and squirm my way through across the buckled footplate.

On the other side is something I'd noticed from down below. A small window, top-hinged and angled open for ventilation with a salad fork as a prop. It's about 1.5 metres above the level of the balcony and in the wall's an old guttering bracket, a perfect toehold. I check once more round the courtyard. A muffled hubbub of voices and polka music debouches from the pub, but so far no late-night revellers are in sight. The slum opposite is clearly unoccupied. I push up the window, feel for the foothold and hoist myself in, landing hands first on a zinc draining board.

There's a blacklite in the kitchen, indiscernible from outside, but touching off the blacklite-responsive walls and fittings with a nebular phosphorescence. I roll down like a landing parachutist on to the board, twist and right myself. I jump on to the floor. A last recce outside, then back goes the salad fork. The kitchen's virtually bare, but for a microwave and a large Ariston fridge. I peek into the fridge. Cans of Bud, boxes of burritos, instant soups and bulk-buyer packs of Granola bars. Above this stock of all-American victuals, a large poster glimmers on the wall. It depicts the Ptolemaic planetary system, the Earth in the centre and each planet turning reverently on the large circle of its deferent and the small circle of its epicycle. A cosy, anthropocentric Weltanschauung. If only Copernicus and Kepler had held their peace . . .

I venture out into an exiguous corridor.

A door swings ajar with a finger's pressure and an acrid odour of stale sweat gasps from a darkened room. I open it further. I can just make out a rowing machine, dumb-bells, parallel bars. Further down the corridor is the crazy junk-tip I recognise as Zak's computer room. I shut myself in and flick on the light. The place is chaotic, a damn sight worse than I'd seen on-screen. I check out his wall-calendar and note that he's scrawled the words 'Wunder-Bar' in today's date box. It's a watering-hole I'm familiar with, near the Schwedenplatz U-bahn. If he stays put till closing-time, I've several hours to spare. However, there are no guarantees he'll be back.

I cast my eyes round the garbage tip once more. To my surprise, there's no computer to be seen. Only a table with a complex console of greasy touchpads under a translucent plastic dustcover. I raise the cover and brush a finger across the pads. Instantly, three walls buzz and light up. Zak's goatish face appears in triplicate against a VR decor of gently rippling stars and stripes. 'Hello me,' he says, 'Now where the fuck would I like to go today?' A second touch and the walls dim. An intelligent environment. No point looking round for a computer when you're standing in the bastard thing. I beat a rapid retreat. The place has ghoulish vibes. It's nothing less than intra-cranial cyberspace, the inside of Zak's crackpot skull.

A dribbling lavatory.

A bedroom, with a beat-up palliasse.

Then at the end of the corridor, a last shadowy room.

A loud crack of gunfire sings through the air. It's followed by a hullabaloo of frantic voices, a fulmination of cussing. I sneak towards the door and ease it open as gently as I can. My right hand's poised under my jacket, gripping the hilt of the Belgian pistol, one finger stroking the breech. Bang in the middle of the room there's a diminutive, bald guy in a hunting jacket and cap, about one metre high. He has a moonlike, simpleton face and stands on dumpy trotters. He's waving a massive double-barrelled smoking shotgun furiously from side to side. With one sharp swing he turns on me. The two deadly tunnels line up perfectly with my eyes.

'Where da wabbit go?' he squawks.

From off-stage right, Bugs Bunny skips in. He's dressed in a frilly frock, ribbons in his ears and a wicker basket over his arm. He flutters his lashes and pouts his lipsticky lips.

'Nah, what's up, Doc? Did you say *wabbit*??' he enquires sweetly.

'Yeah, wabbit! Dat's de varmint! Where da wabbit go??'

'A nice bunny wabbit wid long bwown ears?'

'Yeah!'

'He went dattaway!'

'Thankin' you kindly, miss. Ah sure am obliged.'

The hunter toddles off. Bugs takes a carrot out of the basket, snaps off the end with his teeth and turns to me: 'Why, the noive of those guys!! Of course you know this means war??' He produces a picture of the hunter with 'Elmer Season' written under it and nails the poster to a tree.

I push the door shut behind me and sidle into the room. The domotic's tuned into the Cartoon Network with laser holo-enhancers, one kind of TV I've never had the hots for. I like to keep things up there on the screen, not running between my legs. This is a living-room in more senses than one. It's a thoroughly smart-apart', alive and seething with cybercritters. I turn down the sound and poke around. Leather Club armchairs, leaking kapok. Books. Dead Bud cans, skittling the floor. Some Chicago Bears posters stabbed to death with darts. A series of three framed engravings from the *Ring of the Nibelungen*. In the far corner, Deputy Dawg is now brilliantly fleshed out in coherent light, snoozing in a rocking chair on the front porch of the sheriff's cabin. The newspaper over his head flaps up and down each time he snores. The sight of the hound brings me to my senses. From the inside pocket, I fish out my Networker and Leo's little black leather-bound notebook. His diary may have vanished into thin air, but this I managed to keep my mitts on. It's nothing but a book of numbers, mostly connected with his embezzlements, but one of those numbers sank in a long time ago. Beside it is the name of Argos. Now how many dogs that you know have phone numbers?

I squint in the Californian Toonlight from Deputy Dawg's porch and tap out the digits. There's a moment's silence, then a remote *ping-ping! ping-ping! ping-ping!* I cock my head and follow the faint noise, stumbling over the clinker and débris on the floor. On the far side of the room there's a gilt-framed text, the song of the archangels from the Prologue to *Faust*, transcribed in sanserif with illuminated drop-caps. The *ping* comes from behind. I lift the frame off its hook. A small wall-safe sits discreetly behind, the door unlocked. And inside the safe, sure as hell, is the pure legendary Rheingold I've been after all this time: Argos's collar, complete with pager, though the battery seems to be low. I turn the thing over in my hands, switching the device off. It's a simple leather collar with studs, a name-tag and a sprung clip for the lead and pager. There's nothing to it at all. Yet it fills me with infinite sadness, Christ knows why. It's almost a holy relic, a last material vestige of Leo himself – not to mention Argos – bearing silent witness to the events of the night of 20–21 November, 2026, 16 minutes and 10 seconds past the witching hour. I hold the devotional object up to my eyes. There are even a few Jack Russell hairs, white and black, clinging tenaciously to the soft anti-chafe fabric on the inside of the collar.

Hairs of the dog . . .

My pupils adapt to the gloom. A black rectangular gap materialises in the floor beside me. The hole's boxed in on two sides with a simple balustrade. It's a staircase, leading down. In the middle of the floor, beside a gaping Vesuvius pizza carton, there's a box of household matches. I pick it up and light one match, then another, as I feel my way cautiously down those steps. At their foot, another door looms forward. It creaks open with a nudge of my toe. I pull out a bunch of matches and strike them simultaneously. A large, tenebrous space, cold and fusty, flickers open. It's only the garage, the one I'd spotted from outside. There's a workbench and respray equipment and tools hung from bent nails on the walls, and that oddly endearing smell of garages, a mix of sump oil, gas, beeswax and grease-guns. But in this particular garage there's something that merits no endearments. A BMW Z10 roadster.

I look over the big, swanky Bavarian motor. It's a sleeping animal, bedded down in its lair. The A-range, naturally, with rhomboid wing mirrors. In the flare of the matches, I stare emotionlessly at the beast and shuffle forwards. The matches gutter down till the flames sit like little blue bubbles on the blackened wood and I strike another clump, leaning over to examine the bodywork. The vehicle's some years old now, but the front right wing and passenger door have a different sheen to them. Zak's tried his damnedest to get a good colour match, and I can't tell if he's succeeded, but in the garish matchlight the shade seems fractionally wrong, just a little on the dark side.

Something crunches drily under the sole of my shoe. I bend down further. A few stray powdery chips of safety glass. I could look further. With a bit of snooping around, I'm sure I'd come up with some RDX and a stash of C-4 plastic explosive, not to mention a rubber pig's mask and associated trappings. I could look further, but I won't. It's just that I feel tired. Tired and sick. Sick and tired. And all I want is Zak. It's his hide I'm after, ultimately. Vengeance, justice . . . call it what you will. I know one's supposed to be good and the other bad, but I'm fucked if I can see the difference.

Back upstairs, I slump down in a corner behind one of the bursting leather armchairs. I'm lurking for him here. And I'll lurk as long as it takes, as long as my body and mind hold out. Right now, time and patience are virtually my only resources. Time, patience and the hard metallic weight that still lies strapped to my left side, heavy against my heart. But Jesus, even Deputy Dawg's got one of them.

There's a loose, throaty laugh from the armchair and I wake up. Zak's sitting there, chilling out, his long legs crossed and propped on an empty Delmonte crate. He's got that hat on still. The long overcoat with the astrakhan collar's been tossed sprawling across the floor. 'I tawt I taw a puddy tat! I did, I did, I did!' Above Zak's head, Tweety Pie gawks out of his bell-cage as Sylvester scrambles for purchase on a window ledge, making vain grabs at the little bird. 'Sufferin' soccotash!' he moans. He loses his balance and falls backwards, in a cartoon spin, out of the window. The bird shakes his outsize head. 'Bad old puddy tat! Dat'll learn him!' Zak guffaws again and twists round to face me in my corner. 'Hot diggety! This stuff used to make me pee in my pants in first grade. The way things pop out at you, you know? I'm still bugged out by cartoons. They're so damn trippy. Want an Icebreaker?'

He holds out a stick of gum. I stare back, only half awake.

'I don't blame you, man. Chewing gum's tragic. Like life. You get that full flavour, which you'll never forget, but nothing can stop it thinning away to nothing. Fading and jading. The tragedy of chewing gum. Now Teaberry gum, that's crazy shit. Two thumbs up for Teaberry. It's pink, and it's got this awesome tea taste. Scrumdidalyumptious. I'd swap all the Jamaican Redhair in my dimebag for a stick of Teaberry right this instant.'

I shake myself, rub my eyes, gather my wits. There are no windows. I've no idea what time it is. I slide the pistol out and drop it into my lap. Zak spots the gesture. He chews thoughtfully then turns back to the cartoons.

'I guess you found the symmetric cipher, then. Those six little digits'.

'Sure. And Argos's collar. And a BMW Z10 A-series that's been in for repairs.'

'Negative perspectives,' he mumbles, still facing away from me. 'I don't like the f words man, exceptin' fuck. I don't like fake, fakery, false, falseness. They're not friends to my mouth. And I don't like firearms. Specially pointin' at me in my own goddam place. If you wanna act all tough and shit, do it elsewhere.'

'And *I* don't enjoy having plastic explosives blow up in my face.'

Zak eases himself to his feet and stands over me, one hand foppishly on his hip.

'That was meant for Leo's bitch. Hells, whoever. You too, if you like. For tryin' to crack Hofburg. Your intentions've been suspect from the dawn of time, man.'

'You helped me crack Reprotech. Later, of course. You gave me the means.'

'So? Change of policy. I changed my mind. And secundo, if you really want to know, that night – the night of the party – I saw you guys on the balcony. Smoochin', whatever you call it. I went nuts. That whore was gross with Leo. Screwin', partyin', sniffin', mainlinin'. She was bad. Way too bad. I saw through her fakery. I was longin' for the downfall, waitin' for the crash. If something smells, spray it with CKone. That's what I say.'

I'm still sitting, my knees cranked up, in the corner. I heft the pistol into both hands and angle it at him.

'You killed Leo.'

Zak laughs an empty laugh and scratches his beard. He shifts uneasily from foot to foot.

'You're putting me through a guilt trip, douchebag.' He grins and tries to change tack. 'Come on, put away that arm, man. Spare me the goosebumps. Let it slide. Drink your gin and tonika, smoke your marijuanika, and have a happy Hanukkah.'

Suddenly I hate him. The hate's so pure, as pure as virtue. It's a lance of white flame that cracks clean through my body. I want to control it but I can't. My finger slips, pulls. The gun detonates with a mulish kick. My head bangs hard against the wall. The room fogs and the reek of cordite shoots stingingly into my eyes and nose. Frankly, I'm shocked with myself. I gather my wits and review the consequences. The bullet took Zak's pork-pie hat clean of his head, holing it in one, and redrew his parting. He's standing there still, to his credit – upright and uncowed – but his lower lip's quivering uncontrollably. 'Amen,' he breathes. He picks up the canvas hat and turns it around in his hands. 'At last. I always wanted an Injun arrow hole. Street cred. I'd never have expected it of you.'

Daffy Duck waddles into the centre of the room and stares disapprovingly at Zak. 'You know what you are?' he splutters. 'You're *desss-piccc-able*!!'

'Take me there,' I say firmly. 'Take me to Lubitsch and Diessl.'

'I'll take you to Lubitsch. Where Diessl is, you don't want to go.'

'You told me before he was out in Simmering.'

'Sure. Simmering's Stiffsville – the Zentralfriedhof. Diessl's a little short on conversation these days.'

Our eyes meet.

An incipient shudder passes through me.

Zak's at the wheel of the BMW. I sit at the rear, my body melting like over-ripe Brie into the plush cowhide covers. I'm dog tired. I cradle the Five-seveN in one hand, adjust the heat ducts with the other. Outside it's still dark. The snow falls in luminous, weightless flakes. We quit the Bassena and steer out on to the Gürtel, then head on south, out of Vienna. Heading for Mödling, Baden, Mayerling, I'm not sure where. I'm not sure, and somewhere deep inside I hardly care. It's micro-sleep I'm experiencing, snap naps that suck you away from consciousness, then draw you back with a tingly start. I bring my legs up and lie out on the seat, my cheek flattened up against the frosty window. The cold and the vibration keep me on the *qui vive*. Now and then Zak's eyes tiptoe up on me in the rear-view.

After the last suburbs of Vienna, we veer round on to the A21. The clouds tease apart and a few tenacious stars wink like morse across the light years, from deep within the slow spiral rotation of the Galaxy. The snowploughs and gritters are in action and the road's clear, but on either side the drifts lie deep and unsullied in wind-sculpted dunes. Over their crests, the massed trees of the Wienerwald bristle the undulating hills, cowled in piecemeal white.

After half an hour or so, I've passed through the magnetic field of sleep and come awake. I watch Zak's composed features in profile, the straight nose, the risible beard. His eyes rest dreamily on the road ahead which is vignetted in the vaguely oblong compass of the head-lamps. 'One blast. One bullet.' That's what I'm thinking. In a strange way, we're quits and my flash of hate for him has gone. It's as if it were never there. It's been replaced by precisely nothing, a lack of sentiment so commodious that I could almost *like* him given half a chance, alone as we are, traversing this frozen latitude.

'Tell me about Delbrück, the real Delbrück. Back then, in 1997. Diessl and Lubitsch had her killed. Why?'

He smiles knowingly. 'Trichotomies, man. They bite. Division by three's most often inequal division. Take my word for it, I know a thing or two about numbers. Three-forked lightning. Three-headed dogs. Three Fates. Three Furies. The three enemies of man: the world, the flesh, the devil. Odd numbers are yang. They don't work out on the terrestrial world.'

'There was rivalry.'

'There was rivalry, oh yes. Over Diessl. At Cornell. At Cold Spring Harbour. Hell hath no fury – all that shit. But she was a threat too.'

'In what way?'

'She got a bead on Changeling. It'd already gotten under way in those days. She was all set to blow it apart. So they saw to her first. They had to. Plus, it was damn convenient. She was a Net hermit. No social life. No one missed old Hannah baby.'

'And no one knew it wasn't her who got on that plane on 10 November 1997, flashing her passport. A plane for Austria.'

'Nope. That was the day that Elsa Lubitsch died. She and Delbrück had the same background. It was no big deal for Elsa to take on her credentials.'

'Quite. A prime mover of modern bioethics. World Health Organisation. Recombinant DNA Advisory Committee. The UNESCO Bioethics Committee. They're nice credentials to have. They have a ring of confidence.'

'Something like that,' says Zak, amused. He changes down as we climb a densely wooded hill.

The LED says 7.

To the east, a soft, pale light rinses the lowest darkness from the sky and leaches gradually upwards. The last stars shimmy away and black shapes wing between the pine trees. An hour passes, perhaps more. My sense of time's adrift. Zak prods the radio buttons and hits on the Hofburg-Orchester. They're playing 'Vienna Blood'. I'm apprehensive. That damn music gets to me. It's nostalgic and oracular at the same time. It's music that infiltrates the veins. Zak glances at me in the rear-view, a brief instant of telepathic communion. 'I like it when it fills your ears and presses on the inside like that, completely inside of you,' he says. 'That's when you really feel music. Inside.'

Another dell. Another rise.

Then, as we clear the summit of a further elevation, a broad, snow-hushed landscape hoves into view. The road winds down through a plunging field of breathtaking whiteness, then rises again into a hilly landscape etched with vineyards which dilutes into a blue miasma of mountain headland on the horizon. In the middle distance, the rooftops of a large village clutter together companionably like well-fed burghers. A distinctive tower rises amidst them. For a moment, my heart's in my mouth. I sit up, shiver, and focus my gaze in disbelief.

The tower has a steep roof and, just visible, four ogee corner-towers. There's an old clock just below, set into the stone, and a sundial.

'Why are you doing this?' I gasp.

Zak fixes me in the rear-view, perplexed. 'Doing what?'

We drive past the town crest on a road-side sign, a turret with three small arched windows above a parapet.

'This is where I come from. This is Perchtoldsdorf.'

He whistles between his teeth, shakes his head. 'Boy oh boy. I didn't know, man. This is just the route. This is nowhere land. We all have to come from somewhere. At the moment we're tryin' to get someplace too.'

The car glides ineluctably closer and it all comes flooding in on me, familiarity washing in on each curling wave of the waltz. Plättenstrasse. The neat cobbled streets. Gemütlich, four-square bourgeois houses. Snow-steeped eaves, sabre-toothed with icicles. The Rathaus, with those curious frames painted round the windows, Saint Augustin church and the chapel. And then, as we crawl through the town centre, the Wehrturm, the great stone defence tower which is the emblem of the town. Before long, the Elementarschule sweeps past and, at the turn of a corner, a house with a black gate. The angry dog is long since in its grave.

A few citizens are out, buying bread or shovelling slush and snow off neat rectangles of pavement aligned with their houses. I search their faces for flickers of recognition, but they hardly notice our passage. Yes, this is Perchtoldsdorf. This is the past. And it is *my* past: not only out there, a past of bricks and mortar, but mapped indelibly on to the geometry of my heart. I want to reclaim it, to hold it to me. I don't want to let it go. I've forgotten and neglected it for all these years. Tears form in my eyes; incomprehension in my mind. A boy in a white Alpine jacket and blue cap stops moulding a snowball and stares horrified as we slip by. For a second, he's me. From across two decades, I'm peering back into the well of time, into the glimmering bottom of a child's soul. Then, with a nasty shock, I figure out why the kid was staring. I'm elbowed up against the seat, holding the pistol in full view. I shrink down, suddenly cold at heart. This is nothing, I try to remind myself. We're just two guys in a car. We're in transit. Two guys in a car, driving through a town. That stupid fact is the end of the matter. The rest is meaningless – meaningless and without occasion.

But as we pull through the far side of the town and the dazzling perspectives of snowbound fields open up once more, a Heurigen, slightly apart from the other buildings, draws closer. The Altes Presshaus. A Buschen, a bunch of evergreen boughs, hangs over the sign. It's an old, comfortable building arranged round a sheltered garden with a pergola and trelliswork for the vines. A single light burns at an upstairs window. I tell Zak to stop the car.

'Your home, right? You don't come here often, I guess.'

'No, not often. I'm not a good son.' I'm swamped with sadness as I gaze through the tinted glass at the place. It's the theatre of everything I was. In the upper window, a shadow passes across the light. 'It's like coming full circle, being back here,' I confess. 'I feel – I feel like death – as if my life's sifted through my fingers like sand. It was there, and now it's gone.'

'I know what you mean, man. When I'm back in New York, I smoke clove cigarettes while I look at the gold watches and other pretty things in the street. I eat broiled frog congee in those useless oriental cafés, or honey and mustard pretzel off the stands. It's another world. I miss it.'

'No, you don't know what I mean – it's not even another world. It's a dream, a tragic dream.'

'Dreams, strange dreams . . . They slip away like tadpoles darting for cover when you put a hand in the water.' He swivels round on his pelvis, lights an HB and shoves the hat on to the back of his head musingly. 'The place that gets me in the Wienerwald is the Bellevuehöhe. You've got that plaque there that says, "Here, on July 24, 1895, the secret of dreams revealed itself to Dr Sigmund Freud." That always kinda intrigues me. I figure if I sit there long enough I'll get the secret too. As if the place had anything to do with it . . . Listen, if you wanna drop in on the family, man, that's fine by me. I'll kick my heels here for a while.'

'They're not my family,' I whisper.

He grins and nods. 'I reckon those guys in New Jersey aren't my family either. That's crazy shit, when you come to think of it. You've seen the list, then.'

'There are 233 names on that list. Three of them have died.'

'And on that list there's Leo Detmers, Petra Olbrich, Nathan Buczak and Oskar Gewinnler. That last one's you, Sharkey boy, in case you've forgotten.'

'No, Zak, I haven't forgotten.'

'Oskar Gewinnler! Jeez. I'd stick with Sharkey, if I were you. Come on, brother. Let's go. It's not far now. Time to meet the bio-family, I reckon. We all come full circle in the end. It's the nitrogen cycle, man. We've all been put on this earth to fertilise the soil. Nobody gets out of that one alive.'

I slump back into the seat as he skid-starts and yahoos. Zak, the Bronco Kid. Pretty soon we're climbing upwards, through the low ranks of vineyards, upwards towards the Hochberg where a small neat crucifix stands out black and bleak against the break of day. Zak mutters something under his breath then slaps the steering wheel and sings out madly in a cracked voice, pushing his larynx to the limit: *'Sixty million snowflakes, falling from the sky. If the trees and ground can catch them, why the fuckin' hell can't I?'*

it had to come from you

'I knew you'd be here sooner or later,' she says, setting a cup and a tarnished silver spoon before me. 'It had to come from you. You had to be ready. I can't tell you how I've looked forward to this moment.'

Dug in on the north-east slope of the Hochberg, the farmstead is an ancient stone edifice on which the vineyards depend. We're in a long barrel-vaulted room with whitewashed walls, tin-shaded ceiling lights on ceramic pulleys and an old cast-iron wood-burning stove, the black pillar of its chimney disappearing into the roof. The furniture is sparse and rustic: an old Ottoman, a few oak chairs, a piano and a big worm-scribbled table. The warm morning sun pours in through a generous picture window which looks on to a patio and a swimming-pool enclosed in a convex all-weather bubble. In the distance, over fields of snow and the Wienerwald, the towers and domes of Vienna deckle the horizon. Vienna, waking to a new day . . .

I too have looked forward to this moment, I have to admit, but scarcely with pleasure. I've looked forward to it with deep misgiving ever since I read the list, the list of 233. Leo, Petra, Zak, me – there were other names I recognised. My thoughts flash back to Leo Detmers, drunk as a skunk in the Paloma, and later, the crazy scrawl on his office wall: SS15698–B/157 + ES27372–B/231 = ??????? Same sperm, same egg culture. Those question marks were us. Now I feel stupid. I'm sitting, unshaved and unkempt, at the old table and Elsa's serving breakfast. Tea, coffee, orange juice and thin slices of Guglhupf cake, with a pot of bilberry jam. It's served in simple white porcelain, achingly brilliant in the pure morning sunlight. She's wearing slippers and stands tall in a Chinese silk dressing-gown embroidered with bug-eyed carnival dragons, her hair done up in a neat, grey-streaked bun. She's charm itself, but I hardly know the woman. I have to keep reminding myself that this is my mother, that this is ES27372–B/231. So I sit here, drinking tea with mother, while brother Zak cat-naps on the Ottoman, and I'm clutching a 5.7mm Belgian bean-shooter in my hand. That's why I feel stupid. They're so damn polite that nobody's even mentioned my lack of table manners. Nobody's even asked me to put it away.

'I often saw you, you know, in the village,' she continues, 'I saw you when you were a child. The wine for the Altes Presshaus Heurigen comes from here. I used to take care of the deliveries personally, just to call on you. I still do, in fact, to see how Herr and Frau Gewinnler are doing.'

'And how are they doing?'

'Fine. You should see them more often, you really should.'

'You never had children – I mean, you never *bore* children yourself?'

'Peter and I tried. There were miscarriages. At the same time, we were working on Winnow in Orange County and Baltimore. It was early days. We saw an opportunity, that's all it was. An opportunity to create a pool of eugenically cleansed individuals. An extended family, if you prefer – Safe with a capital "S". Safe from Winnow.'

She's watching me in that characteristic way of hers, her head tilted to one side, scanning for reactions. Her sang-froid annoys me.

'Why didn't you tell me about this before?'

She looks away abruptly. 'I'm not in the business of imposing myself on the 233 individuals concerned. I don't hector for attention. It's always been my opinion that the finest knowledge has to be sought. It isn't delivered, gift-wrapped, on a platter. And the only people worthy of possessing it are those who embark on the quest.'

'But we met before. You knew that I was seeking. You didn't take me far.'

'I took you part of the way. So did Nathan. We sowed the seeds. However, for a long time your motives were in question,' she answers bluntly.

'And they're not in question now?'

'That's to be seen.'

I think of the fate of Leo and Argos. I sigh and give up on this particular line of questioning. 'Tell me something now,' I say. 'Tell me about Winnow.'

'It's the only part that's eluded you, isn't it? That doesn't surprise me, frankly. None of the archives are at the Neusiedl site. They're here, all here.' She sits down opposite me – those nimble eyes, that handsome head – and folds her arms. 'To understand Winnow, you've got to think back to the time of the Gulf War. The US knew that Iraq had production facilities for anthrax and the botulinum toxin, together with stockpiles. It was something of an embarrassment to them. Saddam Hussein, you see, originally bought the anthrax culture from a mail order store in the United States. He simply had it posted to Iraq. But the war, when it came, presented a risk and an opportunity. The risk was that Saddam would use those biological weapons against military and civilian populations, wreaking havoc that could well have extended beyond Desert Storm, beyond the theatre of war. The Americans quelled the risk by heavy sabre-rattling. The opportunity that presented itself to them was to blow out the production facilities and stockpiles with military strikes, but this opportunity was a problem in disguise. Biological weapons can be diffused by downwinds. A major strike on a plant could've resulted in thousands, even millions of deaths, including those of friendly forces if the wind had turned. In the end, they used the smart bombs to contain destruction within the concrete bunkers where facilities were suspected. And it worked. Saddam capitulated, but there were sanctions, remember. For years afterwards, the UN inspection teams had a hell of a time trying to work out if and where biological weapons were being produced.'

'They're easy to make, I imagine.'

'Easy and cheap. At all phases, biological weapons are damned difficult to pin down. Research, production, transit, employment – they all require minimum means. Tiny facilities can produce sizeable arsenals. That's why less developed countries see bio-weapons as a potential equaliser to counterbalance Western powers with conventional and nuclear muscle. But let's look at the Gulf War once again. One of the suspected plants bombed by the US led to an uproar. It was in Abu Gharyb. The Iraqis claimed it was a baby milk facility. The Americans said it was producing biological weapons. In the end, the matter was never cleared up. But the point is that the equipment used in producing biological weapons is dual-use. It can have legitimate commercial applications. So, you see, the camouflage is perfect. And bio-weapons win out over chemical weapons every time in convenience. Ten grammes of anthrax can kill as many people as a ton of Sarin, the nerve agent developed by the Nazis. You can produce enough bacteria, rickettsia, viruses or toxins to wipe out a city in a modest provincial plant. From the outside, it looks like a yoghurt factory, a brewery, or a milk bottlers.'

'Or a bio-tech company. Or a wine producer,' I add, gazing out over the vineyards. She ignores my remark, bringing a hand up anxiously to her hair.

'You may not have fully grasped what I'm saying.' She raises her expressive eyebrows and picks up a thin slice of Guglhupf, bending it carefully till it breaks in two. 'The kind of power we're talking about is terrible. It has military and terrorist uses. Economic too. Let me put it this way to you. Imagine a commercial airliner overflying Austria, or even an unmanned remotely piloted craft. There's no need for bombs or warheads. Undetected, using simple crop-dusting equipment, it sprays corn seed blight or grape louse over the countryside. The Austrian corn and wine crops are annihilated, forcing imports over several years. Livestock's equally at risk. But anti-personnel bio-weapons are devastating. There used to be at least sixty known agents: Brucellosis, Q Fever, Venezuelan Equine Encephalitis, Enterotoxin, and so on. Genetic engineering's multiplying that number to the nth degree. In many cases the proliferator of such agents can plausibly deny involvement. It's not as if there's a smoking gun. The attack looks like natural disease. Days, even weeks, may pass before symptoms show. Microbes and viruses need an incubation period, to find their way into the system, to replicate.'

'Killing people with disease. It must go back in history. In the Westerns, they put dead animals in rivers and streams.'

'That was one way, certainly. There were many others. In the fourteenth century, the Tartars broke the siege of Kaffa by catapulting the bodies of plague victims over the city walls. In the French and Indian war, the British suspected the Fort Carillon Indians of being loyal to the French and they gave them a poisoned gift – blankets infested with smallpox. Japan air-dropped flea-infested material over cities in China in the Second World War, causing bubonic plague. There are other cases where the truth will never be known. The use of chemical and nuclear weapons is easily documented, but that's not the case with germ warfare. Was "Yellow Rain" used in Indochina? What did the USSR do in Afghanistan? The point is, these weapons are deadly. Nature herself can do a lethal enough job with the plague, smallpox, Spanish flu, AIDS. But what do you think happens when men start creating these things? The island of Gruinard off Scotland where the British tested anthrax on sheep is still contaminated today.'

'Isn't there a treaty of some description?'

'The Biological and Toxin Weapons Convention was signed in 1972. It was signed with reservation by Austria. It was signed without reservation by Iraq and many other countries that continued and continue to produce bio-weapons clandestinely. Today a lot of countries are suspected of having active programmes: Iraq, Iran, Syria, Taiwan, Libya, North Korea, China, Israel, Pakistan, India. And others, doubtless others . . .'

'You were saying: about the Gulf War – you were in Orange County at the time.'

'We were, yes. The Gulf forced the US to look at bio-weapons seriously. The Department of Commerce placed an embargo on the Wisconsin Package, the international genome database in Baltimore. And they called the brains in.'

'Yourselves included.'

'We were a think tank, briefed to look into the future of germ warfare in the light of genetic engineering and to consider deterrents, refinements and protection. We knew that genetic engineering would multiply the nature of active agents available, and history's proved us right. Look at the Aum Shinri Kyo's Sarin attack on the Tokyo subway at the end of the last millennium. Sarin's old hat, granted, but police found the group had ordered molecular design software. They were looking into how to genetically re-engineer biological and chemical agents.

'Back in the 90s, we began by considering vaccines, but the tank was pessimistic. Gulf War Syndrome wasn't a reaction to bio-attack but a reaction to vaccination. However, prophylactic methods mean nothing unless you know what's out there to be protected against. There were doves and hawks in the think tank, as you might imagine, but – dove or hawk – we all knew that bio-tech would lead to one major refinement of potential weapons: targetability.'

'Meaning?'

'You take your biological agent and you re-engineer it to target specific genetic parameters. Basically, it quizzes the potential victim's DNA before attacking the host or passing him over. The scope here's enormous. You can target for gender, you can target for age. You can target for behaviour groups: alcoholics, gays, whatever.'

'You can target for race.'

She looks me in the eyes and does a slow hand-clap. 'Bravo. We got there in the end. Race. That word, again. You engineer your agent to search the HLA system and VNTRs for sequences specific to certain population groups. Seek and destroy. Discrimination. Containment. Damage limitation. Those are the mantras of modern warfare. You get your target without slaying innocent passers-by. In attacks on multi-ethnic communities you avoid, for example, killing members of your own population group who happen to be *in situ*. Winnow. That's Winnow.' She goes over to a bookshelf and pulls down a dictionary, flipping it open and thumbing the pages. ' "To expose (grain or other substances) to the wind or to a current of air so that the lighter particles (as chaff or other refuse matter) are separated or blown away. To subject to a process likened to the winnowing of grain, in order to separate the various parts or elements, especially the good from the bad; hence, to clear of worthless or inferior elements." '

'Does it exist?'

'Initially the think tank opposed its development. It ran counter to the terms of the Convention. But the hawks argued that the best deterrence is the threat of retaliation in kind. Since the sixteenth century, Machiavelli's *The Prince* has taught us that the effective use of power may call for unethical methods that are not in themselves desirable. And the germ warfare option becomes more attractive if you have some degree of invulnerability. In the end, it was decided that the development of the genetic targeting technology could go ahead quite independently of the production of outlawed biological agents. In fact, the development was positively encouraged. This technology was also dual-use. It had plentiful potential for medical and commercial – that is, non-military – exploitation. And it's now a patented process. Naturally, we hold the patents.'

'And the Safe programme developed in parallel.'

'Safe was our specific remit. We couldn't do it, though, without also developing the targeting system. It stands to reason. Historically, it's often the creators of toxins who're best placed to come up with an antidote.'

'And you needed a small Safe human population.'

'We did. Our own children. 233 of them, to date. Yourself included. It was totally in-house. Just Peter and I and a few core collaborators. I like to think that, whatever may one day be said against us, we've given you a unique privilege in life, one that you'll pass on to your children, and your children's children. It's now 2027 and it's a fair guess that all the bio-weapon proliferators and terrorist cells currently have Winnow development projects up and running. Water systems, subways, air-conditioning – urban populations are sitting ducks. Rural populations live under other threats. The risks don't bear thinking about. But they'll *never* be able to touch you. The population-specific indicators in your germline are chemically masked. To Winnow, you don't exist. You're a genetic impossibility, a man without race. You don't compute.'

'Does Winnow exist, here in Austria?'

'Officially, no.'

'But perch and pike die in the Neusiedl See. And Slovaks fall sick on cold winter nights.'

'There have been tests, I know. I'm not aware of the details. Tests with non-banned substances, I hasten to add. Flu viruses, for example, are not outlawed particles. They're simply a fact of life. Nor is it a criminal offence to pass flu on to another person.'

'Flu, or pneumonitis,' I specify. 'I grant you, passing the flu on with a sneeze or a handshake may not be a criminal offence. But spraying it into ventilation ducts with patent periodic aerosol deodorisers may well be.'

'You know of a particular case?'

'My next-door neighbour, Marta. A Slovak. She happens to be a friend of mine.'

Elsa shakes her head in commiseration. 'I'm sorry. Our continued freedom of operation in Austria depends on certain political arrangements.'

'That's what I gathered.'

'With a marginal shift in public opinion towards the right before the next elections, Safe could shortly become official practice – on a nationwide level, in the interests of national security.'

'Not to mention Winnow.'

an abandoned chapel

A robin lands on the patio outside and hops tentatively in the snow, stopping to peer with poppy-seed eyes through the picture window. I drop the gun in my lap and run both hands back through my stiff, unwashed hair. I feel tired, terribly tired, and the pain in my bruised hip has been aggravated by the wintry humidity. And still the situation sits a little off-centre, intellectually readable but in other respects a puzzle of sphinxian obscurity. I'm emotionally inert, incapable of engaging affectively. This life of mine is happening to someone else – a masque, a dumb show, rich in the polysemy of another culture, another time, but eluding some vital sentient part of me. It's as if I've missed the point. I spell things out to myself yet again. My mother. This tall, attentive, articulate woman. My brother. The goofy, misfit American on the Ottoman, now lightly snoring. And Leo, and Petra . . .

Elsa clears the breakfast things to one side and wipes down the table. As she passes near me, I grab her by the upper arm. She pulls herself free, surprised and offended.

'I could destroy it all. You know that. All of your well-laid plans.'

'But you wouldn't, would you? You're part of those plans. You'd be destroying the basis of your own well-being. Your past, your present and your future.'

I point the pistol at her rhetorically. 'Mother.' The word doesn't fit my mouth: I nearly gag on it. She remains standing, unmoved. She tightens the belt on her gown and clasps her hands in front of her. When she speaks, her voice is stiff with constraint.

'That fact – the fact that I'm your genetic mother – shouldn't be a burden to you. It might even, one day, be a pleasure. However, as I said before, I've no intention of making a nuisance of myself. Your life is yours to do with as you will. It always has been, for that matter.'

'You wanted me to get this far. You wanted me to gain possession of the facts.'

She drops limply into a chair and glances behind her. 'Nathan did the same. That's the nature of all human enquiry. Gaining possession of the facts. The truth empowers, but it only empowers those who ride with the hounds.'

'And Leo?'

There's silence. Our eyes meet.

'How is it that you want me to behave?' I ask quietly. 'What is it that you want?'

'Your happiness.' She smiles in sad earnest. 'No more, nor less, than any mother would ask under the circumstances. You have nothing to fear from me.'

'And him?' I nod towards Zak.

'Nathan's not someone who thinks things through. He acts hastily. I knew nothing of the bomb in Petra Detmers' flat until after the event. Initially, he trusted neither you nor her. I've taken him to task for this since. You may have noticed that his attitude towards you has grown more accommodating.'

A grandfather clock chimes the half hour behind her and she gets to her feet briskly, as if remembering something she had to do. 'Come with me, Oskar,' she says with newfound warmth. 'We'll go to the utility room. It's very cold outside. You'll need some boots, and what else? A hat, maybe – yes, and a scarf.'

We go out on to the patio, overlooking the vines. 'It's noble soil,' she says, scuffing through to the earth with the side of her shoe. 'We'll be pruning and cutting vine canes this winter to extend the growth. You'll notice that there are no trellises or wires for support. The vines are gobelet-trained, free-standing. They're easier to maintain. You're looking at Weissburgunder. It's fermented in oak casks, in our own vaults. We'll drink some at lunchtime. We've had good *vendanges* over the last three years.'

From somewhere far off, the sound of chopping.

We tramp through the fresh snow, past a small stable – hot with the aroma of hay and fodder – and a corrugated iron hangar for tractors and viticultural equipment. A tethered donkey snorts and nods his head in a small meadow, his soft grey ears flicking forward at our approach. We stop and Elsa places the flat of her hand on my back. The track we've been following continues up a slight rise to a mossy, dark-timbered barn with a steep roof topped by what looks like a belfry but is in fact an overhanging turret housing a winch. From a distance, the place could be mistaken for a Kapelle, an abandoned chapel to an abandoned god. The regular hacking of the axe is louder now, though no one's in sight. Elsa's hand rises to my shoulder. 'Go on,' she says. 'I must go back and prepare lunch. He's up there. He'll be pleased to see you.'

She heads back and I look up the incline. Hack, hack – a pause, then the softer tapping sound as the axe, wedged into the log, cleaves the timber open. The process repeats itself. I look down at the Five-seveN pistol that still sits, redundant, in my clasp, then unzip my jacket and slip it back into its holster. The chopping seems to be coming from one side of the barn. I depart from the track and cut out into the snowfield, labouring up through the uneven drifts. Hack, hack – then tap, tap, tap ... A couple of times I slip, fall to my knees and right myself. And, as I draw round past the corner of the strange barn, I see him. His portly form is portlier still in a lambswool flying jacket, striped scarf, corduroy trousers and woollen bobble-hat, crowning his premature baldness. He takes another log, stands it on end on an old anvil, then brings down the chopper somewhat inexpertly, sheering a sliver of bark off the side of the log. He stops, wipes the back of his hand over his forehead and turns round. On seeing me, he squints slightly, then drops the axe and raises a hand in greeting.

'Sh-Sharkey!' he calls. The eyebrows, like ropy sisal, rear in mild surprise over pale, baby-frank eyes.

I clamber up the last stretch to the summit of the knoll till I'm standing in front of him, slightly out of breath, and we're face to face. It's not surprise I feel, but something else. Karma, the Inevitable – a diaphanous abstract sentiment along those lines.

'Hello Leo.'

'It's b-been a f-fuck of a long time. We were sure you'd m-make it in the end.'

We shake hands politely.

'You're looking well,' I say.

'It's the exertion. Country l-life. Been going easy on the booze, too. I've l-lost a few kilos, I can tell you.'

'I was under the impression that you'd lost a lot more.'

He grins and rubs his hands together. 'P-pushing up the daisies, you mean? No, not me.'

'There's a grave in the Zentralfriedhof that says you are.'

'Diessl,' he says, suddenly serious. 'We had to p-put him somewhere. I regret what happened, Sharkey, but things had g-gone too far.'

'Your own father, Leo.'

'Yours too, old boy. But it was him or me, you understand. This all c-came to a head after you and I met in Hamburg. Didn't even realise you were on the list at that time. And as you know, I was doing what you've been doing. Z-zak too. Getting the hard news. Finding things out for myself.'

'Finding out who your father was, in order to kill him.'

Leo shakes his head mournfully. 'He didn't g-g-give us the choice. Elsa was in favour of Zak and me getting to the bottom of this. D-diessl wasn't. He had regrets, misgivings. He was also opposed to Neues Östmark. He and Elsa had been at loggerheads for ages over the b-b-bloody business. The love had gone out of it. Of course, now she blames herself for everything. But we can't bring him b-back. He wouldn't give any slack.'

'Your scams with the banks. They weren't just for your own enrichment.'

'Fund-raising, old boy. P-politics. The cash is laundered through a d-dead-letter box, an orphanage in Haiti.'

'Yes, I got a postcard, thanking me for my donation.'

Maybe it's just hale spirits and the wintry air, but Leo looks flushed. He glances away with a wince of embarrassment. 'Elsa and I saw the g-good sense of hitching the wagon on to the right p-political horses. Diessl was standing in the way.'

'Elsa grew to hate him, but you hated him too, didn't you?'

He raises his eyebrows and looks hurt and querulous, awaiting explanations.

'He had the power to stop you marrying Petra, but he didn't do it. He allowed it to happen on experimental grounds.'

He concedes the point glumly. 'It's d-damn well immoral, Sharkey, that's what it is. L-letting a chap go ahead and marry his own sister. I mean, I loved Petra, but I couldn't . . . when I found out, I was disgusted – with myself, with him, with her, with everybody. My whole life was f-f-fucked up. Buggered. It's the taboo, isn't it? It wasn't just social, it was in me – put yourself in my shoes. I felt cursed, nauseated. They say in Polynesia that if you b-breach a taboo you get sick and die. That's what I had to do. I had to die. To extricate myself, b-body and soul, from the situation.'

'So Peter Diessl ends up in Leo Detmers' grave, just as Hannah Delbrück ended up in Elsa Lubitsch's. Nice symmetry, Leo. How does it feel to be Peter Diessl? How does it feel to be king of the castle?'

'There are no k-kings here, Sharkey. Just family. The family circle.' He frowns a little and stamps his feet. 'It's damn cold, don't you think? Let's g-g-get inside the barn.'

The 'barn' is no more than a shack, Leo's shack, but it suits his simple needs. It's beautifully warm inside, with an antique Austrian oil stove burning on the dirt floor, Plasmavision and old, unravelling rattan armchairs. There's a pleasant hit of coal-tar from the treated timbers of the structure. The small casement windows are crazed and filigreed with frost.

'M-medicinal purposes?' he enquires, holding up a flask of Scotch.

'I thought you were laying off the stuff?'

'It's a special occasion, my dear. Return of the p-prodigal son.'

I sit back in the creaking wicker and shut my eyes, listening with half an ear as Leo stammers on. The man's a bore. I thought it then, and I think it now. I'll never doubt first impressions again. *Then* he was a doleful, maudlin bore. *Now* he's a cheery, roguish bore. *Then* we were simply getting acquainted. *Now* there's a bogus gloss of comradeship. *Plus ça change* . . . We're faking it – he is, or I am, or we are. It's as if we'd always known each other, long lost brothers separated by circumstance, the wily wiles of the world. And brothers we may be, but so were Cain and Abel. I regret wholeheartedly the compassion I've lavished on his departed soul.

'Tell me about the night you died,' I say.

He seizes the occasion, tripping and traipsing over his tongue as he launches into his account. In my mind, in the dark dream-zone behind my closed eyelids, his jabbered words pull together into taut, hard images.

I'm in the Prater, beside the Lusthaus Pavilion. It's just past midnight, the morning of Saturday November 21, 2026. To one side of the roundabout is a red BMW Z10 roadster, the A-range. An Alfa circles the pavilion and pulls in along the Aspernallee. The door opens and a Jack Russell jumps out, scarpering away under the trees. There are two men in the Alfa, one much older than the other, and they're arguing heatedly. The argument continues for some time, Leo waving his arms and stammering uncontrollably, Diessl listening frigidly – when he manages to get a word in edgeways his replies are polite and firm. After a while, Leo looks anxiously out of the window. 'Where's that d-damn dog got to now?' he says. 'B-bear with me. I'll just go and fetch him.' He clambers out of the car across the street, under the cover of the trees. He calls Argos up on his Bip-Bip. The dog appears and is intercepted by Leo. The beeper's jammed so he takes off the collar. Without a word, Zak shifts over to the passenger seat to make room for Leo, while Argos lingers at the driver's door, wagging his tail. Leo hands Zak the dog collar. This is goodbye. This is where Leo and Argos part.

The car starts and edges forward, till they fix their sights on the Alfa. They know it's just a question of time. The night's cold and Diessl won't wait forever. Nor will he drive away in another man's car. They sit in silence. At length, the Alfa door swings open and Diessl steps out. He wanders into the deserted road, looking around for Leo. Leo waits till he has his back to them then hits the gas. The car skids forward, out from its cover, and bears down on Diessl. He spins round and lurches aside. The car tips him, knocks him over, screeches to a halt. It backs up violently, as he staggers to his feet, and bears down again – only this time Zak's bracing the passenger door hard open. Diessl is struck flat on, with a thud of metal and a smash of safety glass. Leo and Zak jump out and rifle the dead man's pockets, replacing his papers with Leo's and slipping in Leo's medicard and Harvest Contract. As they drive off, Zak puts in a call to the Donaufeld general clinic – maybe to Büchner himself – and in next to no time the Reprotech ambulance is on the scene, beating even the police.

Uscinski had got most of it right, except for one thing. His precious two times table. It wasn't four men, but three – three into four. A three-four time signature, the beat of the waltz. Trichotomies, man. They bite. Odd numbers are yang. They don't work out on the terrestrial world. And Zak should know. He was there, making himself useful.

I open my eyes and Leo's observing me in silence.

'Just one thing,' I say. 'Petra told me she saw your corpse. I remember distinctly. "Eine schöne Leiche," she said, "a beautiful corpse".'

Leo raises those sisal eyebrows and smiles asymmetrically. 'There's no such thing as a b-beautiful corpse after a Harvest Contract. They take everything, like vultures and jackals. That m-m-might've occurred to you.'

'Then how?'

'She didn't exactly *see* the corpse, Sh-sharkey. It was a v-visualisation. At the Donaufeld mortuary visitors view the deceased through a g-glass window. They're told it's for purposes of hygiene. The window's – well, it's not precisely a window. Or not *just* a window, I should say. It's Cosmeti-glass. There's a layer of morphing membrane down the middle. The morticians can b-beautify and make the skin colouring more natural without actually interfering with the b-body. The idea is to minimise distress, the shock of seeing what death can do to people. Petra was looking at our father's body, certainly, but what she saw was m-mine.'

He stands up and swigs the last of the whisky out of the flask.

'We should be getting back,' he says. 'I just need to finish one or two logs, then we'll light up the stove b-back at the house. What d'you say?'

We find a wheelbarrow and roll it round to the side of the barn. I wrap my scarf tight round my neck and watch as Leo chips and chops clumsily on the giant anvil. We come to the last log and he tries in vain to stand it on its end, but it's sawn at an angle and refuses to oblige. With some reluctance, I hold it upright as he hovers fatly above, the axe gripped in two hands above his head, shuffling his feet in the snow to get his balance. The hatchet comes down with force. Astonishingly, it strikes the log dead centre, splitting the perfect rings of its years, and slices halfway down into the long, aromatic grain. The edge of the blade just brushes my hand, nicking the web of skin between thumb and forefinger. I hold my hand up to inspect the damage. A fine trickle of blood beads across my palm. Leo drops the axe and grabs my wrist contritely.

'Damn! I'm terribly sorry, old boy. I should've b-been more careful.'

'It's nothing.'

'Nevertheless, there's always a risk of infection. Wait there. I've got a First Aid k-k-kit in the barn.'

When he returns, he sits me on the anvil and wipes the tiny wound with disinfectant.

'Tell me,' he says with unexpected curiosity, 'what colour would you s-say that is?' He points with his fat forefinger into the pit of my palm.

'Red, of course. It's blood. I don't have aristocratic pretensions, if that's what you're thinking.'

Leo laughs in a bird-witted manner. Country life appears to have got to him. 'You only s-say it's red because you *know* that blood is red. Not because you *see* red.'

'What the hell are you talking about, Leo?'

'Try this,' he goes on, pointing at his bobble-hat. 'What c-colour's this?'

'I don't know precisely. Brownish, I'd say.'

'Green!' he laughs. 'It's g-green! To tell you the truth, I wouldn't have known myself if Elsa hadn't told me. Don't you s-see?'

'I haven't a clue what you're talking about.'

'G6PD deficiency. You've g-g-got it. I've got it. The only genetic defect they couldn't eliminate when they germlined us. When an egg's fertilised, gene-shuffling goes on. Genes that are neighbours on the chromosome have a tendency to c-cross over together, like cards sticking together in a shuffled pack. This is the case with the gene for colour vision and the gene for producing G6PD, a blood enzyme. They're both c-close together on the X chromosome. If there are mutant copies, they cross together. A tendency to anaemia and red-green colour blindness. Two-in-one. It only shows up in the men, you see. Women, being female, have two X chromosomes and don't exhibit the traits. It never occurred to you that you had this c-condition – not even at traffic lights?'

'Never. I've never had problems with my sight. I've never consulted an optician.'

'Yet *I'd* noticed, in the Paloma. You lent me your p-pen, remember? And neither of us could say what colour the ink was. Elsa noticed too. Apparently when you dropped in on her in Vienna you were having great difficulty distinguishing her b-b-budgies. The Lutino Light Greens and Dark Greens. She spotted it at once. Only red-green, mind you. The other colours are no problem. But you're lucky. It's never been a handicap to you. As for me, the b-bloody condition b-buggered up my chosen career. I wanted to be a pilot. If you're red-green colour blind, you're out on your arse.'

'Extraordinary. I never knew.'

'The condition's very common in male American blacks and Mediterranean J-jews. We're clearly not American blacks. As for Mediterranean J-jews – I'm looking back at the Lubitsch and Diessl ancestry at the moment. Genealogy, old b-boy. It's always been a hobby of mine.'

Leo stacks the logs into the wheelbarrow and we head back down the track, across the snowfield, for the farmhouse. He puffs and pants demonstratively with his load but I don't offer to help. The rotten sod's still far too fat as it is. It'll take more than a barrowful of logs to pare him down to eugenically desirable proportions.

As we approach the outhouses, I glance down at the nick in my skin and stop him. He's all too grateful for a break.

'Leo, before we get back – there's one thing I wanted to ask you. A favour, as a matter of fact.'

'Yes?'

'You weren't planning on coming back from the dead, were you?'

'Certainly not, old boy. Never been f-fucking happier. People say "He'd be better off dead". It's a figure of speech. In my case, it happens to be t-true. I've crossed the Styx to the other side, and the other side's where I'm d-damn well going to stay. What was the favour?'

'Just that. Don't.'

'Don't what?'

'Don't come back from the dead. Please.'

He clears his throat petulantly and looks a trifle miffed. 'I accept my demise with a certain m-magnanimity, Sharkey, but one likes to think one's p-passing is lamented. Sackcloth and ashes, you know. A decent period of m-mourning. It hasn't been that long, dammit.'

'Naturally, you're greatly missed.'

'Then w-w-what on earth are you talking about?'

'I'm merely saying that it's customary for the living and the dead not to communicate with each other, and I think the time-honoured tradition should be maintained. Not for my benefit, of course. Here I am, after all, conferring freely with you.'

'For whom, in that c-case?'

'For Petra.' I force a smile and hold him with my eyes. 'A widow's grief should be respected. And one never knows.'

'*What* does one n-never know?' he queries touchily, grasping the handles of the wheelbarrow and tensing himself to continue.

'Where there's life, there's hope.'

14.7 psi earth-normal

He laughs as he paddles his infant arms towards me, grabbing handfuls of emptiness. Shimmering ellipsoids of water float between us, wobbling with uneven surface tension, splitting and fusing into silvery marbles and double-pearls. Spilt mercury from a cracked thermometer, dancing water globules on the kitchen hotplate – they glitter madly in the filtered solar rays that shaft through the porthole. We're naked, he and I. Naked and weightless mermen, our hair swelling and subsiding like submarine weeds. I kick against the smooth wall of the module and my body drifts, gyrating slowly, towards him – my hand open, my arm outstretched. The droplets cling creepily to our skins or straggle uncertainly round our nostrils as we inhale. He's gasping, tasting the surprising wetness that trickles and tickles round his lips.

My hand reaches his, we grapple and lock, and I pull his floating form towards mine, hugging it close. I nudge a pedal with my toes and a fan kicks in to suck the moisture out of the air. The UV filter glides off the porthole and for a few seconds we roll as one in the direct, roasting heat – the searing whiteness – of the sun. Once dry, a system voice emanates from the wall: 'Ultraviolet non-ionising radiation skin dose: 0.003 roentgen equivalent man. Atmosphere: 14.7 psi earth-normal air. We hope you have enjoyed your shower. Please come again.' The UV filter glides back into place, an airlock hatch clunks open, and I grasp a handhold, pulling us through into the changing cubicle. For a few minutes the air is strewn with free-floating clothes as I struggle to dress Oskar and myself.

With grip shoes and bungee cords, near weightlessness is less spooky. We make our way out of the Marriott Space Hotel's Central Microgravity Amusement Zone then down a backbone utility unit to the crèche. I deliver Oskar to a stewardess. She makes admiring baby noises and asks his age.

'Nearly four months. He's a sweetie. I think he's ready for his bottle.'

The Hotel's a giant orbital centrifuge. By the time I reach the outer rim of the wheel, gravity has returned to normal. Petra's waiting for me at a table for two on the observation deck. It's too early for dinner and I'm glad to see that no other guests are about. She rests on her elbows, drawing lazily on a J. She's lost in contemplation. The deck's like the railed bow of a great ocean-going Cunard liner. Through a giant bay of hardened Plexiglas, the Earth takes the breath away. It's the stuff of visions, a fabulous ballooning of blue, crusted with continents, watered by the seven seas and feathered with the great white boas of cyclonic and anti-cyclonic systems. It is life itself, heartbreakingly beautiful, poised against the dark immensities.

In the magnificence stakes, however, Petra somehow contrives to go one better. Her black, wild hair has been styled into a spikey *coupe sauvage*, her skin has its own intimate troposphere and the oceans of her eyes twinkle dreamily through a cumulonimbus of Juju smoke. She's a planet in her own right, wallowing in a micro-climate of physical and mental euphoria. She's wearing a low-cut duchesse satin top – red or green, I neither know nor care – and a gold leather gladiator's skirt above the knee. How she does it I don't know. It must be Relativity. She dilates time and space. She bends starlight. She's a human event horizon, drawing all things to itself.

'I could stay here forever,' she glows as I sit down. 'Forever and a day. I've seen two sunrises since you've been gone. And cloudwatching. It's never been like this.'

'You're stoned.'

'You bet. Everything's going round. My head. The hotel. The Earth. If this is motion sickness, keep it coming.'

'The funny thing is that the Earth's core spins faster than the planet.'

'No shit.'

'You didn't read the bumph in the hotel brochure. The inner core's a sphere of solid nickel-iron, then there's a liquid metal layer, then a semi-solid rocky mantle, then a thin stony crust. The thin stony crust's the bit we drive around on.'

'Well I like it up here, Sharkey. I prefer looking down to looking up. At least it doesn't rain and snow upwards. Shit. I don't want to go back, home or no home.'

A waiter arrives with a bucketed bottle of Piper-Heidsieck and a serving of Petrossian sturgeon caviar. The roe nestles in a glass dish on a bed of crushed ice with two dinky spoons, a pile of neat squares of toasted bread and a Japanese fortune cookie in a cellophane sleeve. He uncages the cork, eases it out – flerrr-pop! – and pours two flutes. The glasses fog suddenly with condensation.

'Perfect!' she exclaims when he's gone. 'The 3 Cs. Champagne, caviar and cannabis. Perfect fucking bliss at last.'

There's a snatch of 'A Bicycle Built for Two' on the PA system, then the captain introduces himself: 'Those of you in Observation Bay G or any of the Earth-facing Condos might like to look out for a moment. A couple of sights worth seeing. We're crossing North America and if you line your noses up with Florida, you'll see the doomed Mir space station. It's just a billboard now. As you can see, it's covered in neon ads for the enlightenment of extraterrestrials such as yourselves. The other news is a special event. We've just heard from NASA that any second now there'll be a meteorite strike on earth's atmosphere. Look out into the Atlantic and you should see it coming up in about ten seconds.'

We sip the champagne and gaze out into the sapphire blue of the ocean. There's a streak of light then a sharp white flash.

'There we go. That little baby was about the size of a baseball. It hit the exosphere and exploded with the force of two Hiroshimas. No harm done down below. It's not a comforting thought, but a little bigger than that and the atmosphere wouldn't protect us. 500 metres wide, and it'd bite the dust at about 12,000 megatons. That's the force of all the nuclear weapons presently stockpiled on Earth. When that happens, the best place to be is up here. At least until the croissants run out. If you don't believe me, ask a dinosaur. Well, that's all from your captain for the moment. If you're at a loose end this afternoon, try the aerobics class in the Microgravity Amusement Zone or take a space-walk at End Unit B3. Over and out.'

'Oh, a couple of spacegrams came through on the SolNet link,' says Petra, producing the print-outs from her bag. 'More feedback on your article. Compliments from Reinhardt, the Interior Minister, and something from Heinrich Möll, press baron extraordinaire. Hints of promotion, if you ask me. Neues Östmark are riding high. Have you seen their drum major on the telly?'

'Yes, I have.'

'He's a smart son of a bitch. Looks like some kind of an animal to me.'

'A heron.'

'You're right. A heron. Lanky. A slight stoop. That's it exactly. But none of that seems to matter up here, does it?' she adds. 'Look.'

Below us, the Iberian peninsula edges into view. She stubs out the smouldering butt of the Cannaboid and sighs.

'It's hard to imagine, isn't it? Down there, that land. It's covered in people. Millions, billions, going about their business. Postmen posting letters. Bus-drivers driving buses. Housewives cleaning houses. Births. Deaths. Triumphs. Defeats. Jesus. All that activity! What's it all about, Sharkey? Why don't they all slow down and take it easy? Maybe some of them are looking up at us here, enviously, the way we used to.

'And the countries! All those frontiers. Who draws the lines on the maps, anyway? You can't see them from up here. Spaniards, Portuguese, French, German, English, Dutch, Italian. Languages. Races. Everyone thinking he's that little bit special, that little bit different. Well, I don't see what's so different, do you? In fact, I don't see anything at all. Sweet fuck-all, that's what I see. Not a single human being. Not a bus. Not a building, except maybe the Great Wall of China. It's crazy. All those things that seem so important down there – they're just footling and meaningless, ultimately. Good, Bad, Indifferent. One stray meteorite and they're gone. Boom! A lot of the first astronauts became Bible-bashers, didn't they? It was the bigness of the vision. They needed something like religion to cope. Just look. It's so pretty you can't believe how anything like evil can exist.'

'It's relativism, again,' I say. 'Creation's horrendous and magnificent at the same time. The truth, good and evil, are relative to the position in which you're standing. Take war. One man fights on one side, another on the other. They both believe they fight in the cause of good and against the cause of evil, and they kill each other. Yet in absolute terms they're interchangeable. The two men, and their causes. We can see that, because we're up here, in the transcendent sphere. But down there is the field of opposites, the field of time and decisions. Right and wrong, light and dark, life and death, man and woman, Eros and Thanatos, past and future. These opposites are aberrations. In the God's-eye view, the grandstand view, there's only oneness.'

She dips a little finger in the champagne and sucks it. 'So there's no right and wrong?'

'They mean something in temporal terms, in the field of decisions. Though the way they're often used, you might as well say "popular" and "unpopular" and be done with it.'

'And we have two perspectives, two judgements.'

'Right, judgement in the field of action and the judgement of the metaphysical observer. I've been reading Sanskrit literature. You get this in the *Upanishads* and the *Bhagavad Gita*.'

She smiles and plucks the *Bhagavad Gita* from my jacket pocket, and I prise it back from her.

'The point is that life's brutal and horrific. We live, we kill, we eat, we die. But it's beautiful too, and not to participate is to live in denial of life. Listen: *"He who withdraws himself from actions, but ponders on their pleasures in his heart, he is under a delusion and is a false follower of the Path."* And again: *"Action is greater than inaction: perform therefore thy task in life. Even the life of the body could not be if there were no action."* Action, Petra. Action and affirmation. Even if it means affirming that which you deplore. Keep the show on the road, that's the imperative. So long as we're alive, each individual's the expression of his or her entire ancestry. A point of diffusion, too, into the descendence of the species. That's the show, be it tragedy or farce. For the time being, anyway. At least until the next global cataclysm.'

We're crossing Central Europe and the snow-capped spine of the Alps crooks through France, Switzerland, Italy and Austria.

'Lake Balaton,' I say. 'So just northwest, where the Alps peter out, somewhere round there is Vienna.'

Petra stands up and props her folded arms on the railing. 'I know what you're saying. From here it all looks so perfect. But when you get up close you see the cracks. So which is the true perspective: long shot, or close up? You can't win. One way, nothing has any significance. The other way, everything's charged with so many layers of meaning that you end up getting life desperately out of proportion. That's my forte, isn't it? Look at me and Leo. But perhaps you don't want to talk about that.'

'I don't think there should be any taboos between us, Petra.'

'Well, there you and I were, cultivating our tentacular conspiracy theories, and what did it come to? Yes, Leo and I were double-donored and our parents weren't fully informed, but in those days the clinics kept quiet for humanitarian reasons. Yes, we were brother and sister, but these rare accidents happen in IVF clinics. Then Leo's death, and the bomb. Down there, in that imperfect world of ours, it's dog eat dog – and Christ knows, Leo had his enemies. It's life. It's death. Even Elsa Lubitsch, if she was my mother, has been dead these thirty years. It *was* the present, but now it's past. We've finally closed the door on it. It's been a long haul, though. I'm only sorry to have lumbered you with all my problems.'

'It's all in a day's work.'

She tucks the gold skirt in under her thighs and sits down, then lugs the Piper-Heidsieck out of the slushy ice, wipes it down with a napkin and refreshes our glasses. 'Oh! We haven't tried this!' she cries, falling on the Japanese fortune cookie. She slips it out of its packing, cracks it open and unrolls the tiny tube of paper within. '*What goes on four feet, on two feet, and three*,' she reads, '*But the more feet it goes on the weaker it be*?'

'Search me,' I shrug. 'I never was any good at those fucking things.'

She tosses the paper aside indifferently and it springs back into a roll. For a few seconds she stares blankly at the cluster of grey caviar eggs on the toast in front of her and, when next she speaks, a new quietism inhabits her words.

'Sharkey – when we get back, back to Vienna I mean, I want to go to the Zentralfriedhof. You won't mind, will you? I want to put some flowers on Leo's grave. I haven't been able to go there up to now. I couldn't bring myself. But things are different now. I think I've come to terms.'

'I'm glad, Petra. Time's a great healer. Nevertheless, we won't forget him. He was a great guy. The tops. In a class of his own.'

She turns away, lowers her head and sniffs. Her eyes mist up with the tender emotions. She mutters something in a small voice to herself.

'What was that?'

'I said "Poor old Leo".' She's ratty at having to repeat herself, but she forces a smile nonetheless.

'Yes, of course.' I raise my glass, she raises hers, and we chink on that. And all at once, the Earth, the universe, and all the rest of it, is nothing but a tired backcloth to her, only her. Our eyes meet: my eyes in her eyes, her eyes in mine. The charmed circle's complete. This is not just a pretty face. This is the Helen of Troy Effect, no less. She's a weapons-grade biological force in her own right – and nobody's Safe. In my mind, a thousand ships are launched, cities crumble and the topless towers of Ilium blaze to the ground. But then I *have* been overdoing things. It's the champagne, I tell myself, the champagne . . .

'You're absolutely right, Petra.' I take her compassionately by the hand. 'There's no doubt about it at all. Here's to Leo.'

'To Leo.'

'We miss the old prick, don't we?' I get a stiff dose of gravity into my voice, as befits the occasion, and for one last time our glasses sound his knell. 'Poor, *poor* old Leo . . .'

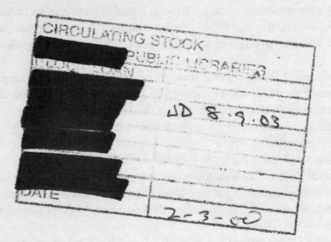